ST. MARTIN'S

MINOTAUR
MYSTERIES

Other titles from St. Martin's **Minotaur** Mysteries

EXTRAORDINARY ACCLAIM
FOR MARTHA C. LAWRENCE

AQUARIUS DESCENDING

"Fans of the independent, self-deprecating heroines of Marcia Muller and Karen Kijewski will enjoy Elizabeth Chase."
—*Booklist*

"A believable plot, well-developed characters, and a heroine with an interesting edge."
—*Library Journal*

"Readers will likely find it her most polished appearance yet."
—*Kirkus Reviews*

"By balancing Chase's psychic and deductive skills, Lawrence has done a decent job of making her acceptable and appealing to the somewhat or completely skeptical reader."
—*San Jose Mercury News*

"Elizabeth remains a fabulous and unique sleuth . . . A well-designed, very plausible, and extremely suspense-laden tale that shows that the dawning of the age of Martha C. Lawrence is upon us."
—*Harriet Klausner*

"A snappy blend of insight into cult psychology with smooth plotting."
—*The Poisoned Pen*

"AQUARIUS DESCENDING, Martha C. Lawrence's third Elizabeth Chase mystery, continues the intriguing exploits of what may be one of the most fascinating private detectives in fiction . . . [Elizabeth is a] strong, smart, and charming character . . . Fast-paced and suspenseful . . . AQUARIUS DESCENDING delivers a punch."
—*The Mystery Reader*

"Martha Lawrence has hit her stride and settled in for a long, successful run. The writing here flows with the deceptive ease of well-honed skill . . . The plot has a fascinating structure . . . The Elizabeth Chase mysteries . . . work so well largely because Elizabeth herself is an unusually attractive and believable protagonist . . . Her narrative voice rings true and never falters. She draws you along so surely that you will have trouble putting down this book. Tension is high and the pace is relentless. The final chapter will leave you gasping."
—Dianne Day, author of *Emperor Norton's Ghost*

THE COLD HEART OF CAPRICORN

"[THE COLD HEART OF CAPRICORN] offers a truly baffling mystery and a gutsy, intelligent heroine to solve it."
—*Denver Post*

"Just when you think you've seen everything, something new comes down the pike and astounds you. . . . Elizabeth Chase is one of the newest detectives on the scene, and she is certainly one of the most original."
—*Dallas Morning News*

"Run, do not walk, to your nearest bookstore, for THE COLD HEART OF CAPRICORN, Martha C. Lawrence's second book. . . . I loved every word."
—Judith Kreiner, *The Washington Times*

"Lawrence proves her initial success was no fluke, with her second—and even better—thriller."
—*San Diego Union-Tribune*

"Elizabeth proves to be a worthy protagonist: smart, mature, funny and sensible, as well as 'sensitive.' Looking into the future, I predict that we'll see this series continue for a long time as Lawrence's fans continue to grow steadily."
—*Minneapolis Star-Tribune*

MURDER IN SCORPIO

"Martha Lawrence's parapsychologist detective cast a spell on me: I couldn't put the book down, didn't want it to end. For a neatly plotted, fast-paced debut, try a little MURDER IN SCORPIO."
—Linda Barnes, author of *Cold Case*

"One of the most engaging mysteries I've ever read. There's no tougher critic than a Virgo and this Virgo says MURDER IN SCORPIO is flawless."
—Nancy Pickard, author of *Confession*

"Lawrence demonstrates the storytelling skill of a veteran and with this taut and suspenseful tale gets the Elizabeth Chase series off to a rousing start."
—*San Diego Union-Tribune*

"Fine prose, a matter-of-fact approach to some rather extraordinary perceptions, and a wry sense of humor characterize a remarkable first novel."
—*Library Journal*

"An innovative and exciting new mystery featuring a private eye with a difference . . . Peopled with fascinating characters and a well-crafted plot, this is a terrific read."
—Janet Dawson, author of *A Credible Threat*

"Elizabeth picks up clues using a believable blend of investigative technique and psychic information. In the end, she convinces readers as skeptical as McGowan that, while some phenomena can't be explained rationally, they can be enjoyed by readers."
—*Publishers Weekly*

ST. MARTIN'S PAPERBACKS TITLES
BY MARTHA C. LAWRENCE

Murder in Scorpio
The Cold Heart of Capricorn
Aquarius Descending

AQUARIUS
DESCENDING

MARTHA C. LAWRENCE

St. Martin's Paperbacks

To Kipp, always and ever

"Strawberry Fields Forever"
Words and music by John Lennon and Paul McCartney
Copyright © 1967 Sony/ATV Songs LLC (renewed). All rights administered by Sony/ATV Music Publishing, 8 Music Square West, Nashville, TN 37203. All rights reserved. Used by permission.

AQUARIUS DESCENDING

Library of Congress Catalog Card Number: 98-44604

ISBN: 0-312-97284-9

Printed in the United States of America

St. Martin's Press hardcover edition / January 1999
St. Martin's Paperbacks edition / January 2000

10 9 8 7 6 5 4 3 2 1

ACKNOWLEDGMENTS

For graciously sharing their expertise, thanks to Detective Howard LaBore of the San Diego Police Department, Kiara Andrich of the Los Angeles FBI, Harry Bonnell, M.D., of the San Diego Medical Examiner's Office, and Thomas A. Jones, M.D.

For intrepidly assisting me in my field research, thanks to Pat Muller, John Russell, Lauri Hart, and Beth Goodman.

For sharing their magic, thanks to writers Sparkle Hayter, Michael Peak, Janice Steinberg, Lillian Roberts, Ann Elwood, Mary Lou Locke, and Janet Kunert. Special thanks to Clark Lawrence for helping me brainstorm.

For their exacting standards and sharp insights, thanks to Hope Dellon, Carolyn Caughey, Kelley Ragland, and Regan Graves.

For being a literary and fiduciary angel, thanks to my agent, Gina Maccoby. Thanks also to Bill Hamilton, who takes such good care of things overseas.

Finally, thanks to the inimitable Scott C., whose wacky wit and wondrous wisdom have inspired me for decades.

The fault, dear Brutus, is not in our stars,
But in ourselves, that we are underlings.

—William Shakespeare, *Julius Caesar*

PROLOGUE

If the phrase "psychic investigator" makes you want to roll your eyes, you're not alone. I cringe just about every time I hear it. And I hear it a lot, because that's how I make my living. It says so right on my business cards: *Dr. Elizabeth Chase, Psychic Investigator.* Somehow I don't think this was the career my parents had in mind for me when they sent me packing to Stanford University years ago. At the time, I was planning to follow in my father's footsteps and become—I kid you not—a brain surgeon. Oh well, at least I nailed down the part about looking into people's heads.

My point is, I didn't set out to become a psychic. For years I didn't even believe in the existence of psi phenomena. My habit of dreaming things before they happened I passed off as coincidence. My ability to pull images and numbers from others' minds I chalked up as remarkably good guessing. As for my tendency to see translucent colors around people, I suspected an overactive optic nerve. Fact was, I'd inherited my father's aptitude for math and science. Calculus and lab procedure were precise and for that reason, comforting. The questions raised by my peculiar perceptions, on the other hand, were messy problems I couldn't solve. I avoided them.

No, I didn't seek out my psychic ability. I bumped into it face-to-face on an overcast morning during my sophomore year at college. I assumed she was a student walking a few feet ahead of me as we rounded the path near Hoover Tower. I remember admiring her cropped blonde hair and graceful, feminine gait. At the sound of my footsteps, she turned. Then, before I could so much as muster a hello, she vanished. One minute I was staring into her dark eyes, the next I was blinking and making a fool of myself, swiping at the air.

My ghost sighting caused me to drop my premed program and sign up for every psychology class I could find. I accepted that I was going crazy but I desperately wanted to understand why. I confided the unsettling experience to my favorite professor. He listened to my story with interest and the next day subjected me to a Rhine card experiment, a test designed to measure extrasensory perception. My results went over the top. At that point, I became a guinea pig in the parapsychology program at Stanford Research Institute. By the time I left campus, I had a Ph.D. in psychology, another in parapsychology, and a whole *lot* of messy problems I couldn't solve. Like where my psychic ability came from. And why it worked for me sometimes but at other times, failed me miserably.

A few years ago I got a private investigator's license and began focusing on problems I could solve. I seem to have a knack for finding stolen property. Sometimes this talent extends to finding people. The two occasions on which I delighted mothers by locating their missing children are highlights of my life. The thing that brings me special joy, though, is tracking down felons. Particularly, the bully variety.

Auras, precognitive dreams, apparitions, telepathy. What does it all mean? I've learned to live with not knowing. Some people can't take that. Some even barter away their freedom for the security of having answers. That can be dangerous. I had no idea just how dangerous until I encountered The Bliss Project, formerly known as The Church of the Risen Lord. I was hired to find a woman who had disappeared into the group. By the time the case was over, a lot of precious things were lost to that group, my life nearly being one of them. But I'm getting ahead of myself.

1

≋

I stood on the terrace of my childhood home looking out across a postcard-perfect landscape. Smoky-blue foothills rolled across the eastern horizon. A soft breeze carried the sweet perfume of a dozen acres of blossoming orange trees. Honeybees made a fuzzy murmuring in the purple bed of ice plant at my feet. Together with the warm, fragrant air, their buzzing lulled me into a hypnotic half-dream. A thoroughbred mare called to her colt, her whinny clear but faint across the valley.

It was picturesque all right. The spitting image of prosperity and tranquillity. So when the bulldozers resumed their ungodly grinding, it had the effect of a loud belch in the middle of a diva's tender aria. Quite rude. Still, I was fascinated. Once the mechanical beasts resumed their relentless annihilation, I couldn't tear my eyes away. Not that there was much to see at this point. The mansion had been destroyed last week. Today they were just leveling the earth.

Then I heard another sound. It came from behind me, the whistling of a familiar tune: *It's a beautiful day in the neighborhood. . . .*

I recognized the melody. It was the theme song of a television show from my childhood: *Mister Rogers' Neighborhood.* I turned around and recognized the whistler. Albert Chase, M.D. All cleaned up and ready for dinner. Silver hair slicked back, a teal-blue, V-necked sweater pulled over his clean white shirt. Slacks pressed. On his feet, a pair of Teva river sandals, very cool on a man in his sixties and the perfect rebellious touch to an otherwise conservative ensemble. Dad's eyes were gleaming as he joined me at the edge of the terrace. He continued to whistle the Mr. Rogers theme song, enlivening the tune with a couple of cheery eighth-note flourishes. Across the valley, the bulldozers roared.

"Dad!"

The whistling stopped.

"What?" His deep-set eyes were all innocence.

" 'A Beautiful Day in the Neighborhood'? Is that any way to honor the dead?"

His steady gaze held no apologies.

"I'll honor the dead when the last of the looky-loos are gone and I can enjoy the domestic paradise I've worked so hard for." He put his hands on his hips, looked across the valley and shook his head in disgust.

"Of all the places to catch a comet, they had to pick my neighborhood."

He was talking, of course, about the thirty-nine cult members who had offed themselves—shed their containers, if you will—in the neighboring mansion. It had been months now, but strange vehicles continued to poke around the nearby roads, heads bobbing out of car windows hoping to catch a glimpse of the planet's most bizarre launch site. In a final move of brilliant desperation, my father and a few of our neighbors had pooled some investment funds to buy the property, raze the place and restore the neighborhood to its former dignity.

The bulldozers surged and growled. Dad continued his merry whistling.

"Dad—"

But my complaint lost its steam. In truth, I wasn't exactly thrilled about Heaven's Gate either. It's hard enough to inspire confidence when you work as a psychic investigator. To hail from the site of the nation's largest mass suicide wasn't going to help. Maybe I'd just skip the part about growing up in Rancho Santa Fe. I could fabricate a whole new childhood entirely outside of California. Peoria, perhaps.

He stopped whistling and a thoughtful look crossed his face.

"Did you ever have a feeling about it?"

"Heaven's Gate, you mean?"

He nodded.

I was pleased that he'd asked. It showed open-mindedness. My dad's a medical doctor, and a fairly traditional one at that. He has a lot of reservations about the New Age. You get that right away when he pronounces the term—he rhymes it with "sewage." But he's seen enough instances of my ability to know that I can occasionally see into the future. He also knows that I can't turn my precognition on and off like a faucet, and that when my vision fails me, I don't lie about it.

I'd given his question some thought myself.

"No, I honestly didn't see Heaven's Gate coming. Thank God." I stared at the scar on the landscape where the cult's mansion once stood. "That would have been a cold shadow to grow up in."

Contrary to popular assumption, psychics aren't tuned in to every travesty happening on the globe. I think a few people might be, but for the most part, those folks live in mental hospitals.

We fell silent and watched the bulldozers. There were two of them, circling the property like waltzing machines. After a time, Dad spoke again.

"What do you think makes people go to such extremes?"

I'd given this question some thought as well.

"I don't know. Don't think I really want to know, either."

"No interest in seeing what causes fairly normal people to go that far-out?"

"None whatsoever. I wouldn't go near a cult for all the diamonds in Tiffany's."

Ever notice how when you say something untrue, you get this overwhelming sense about it? Almost as if an internal PA system starts announcing, "WRONG, WRONG, WRONG. . . ." No sooner had the words, "I wouldn't go near a cult," passed my lips than a weight in the pit of my stomach told me that time would make a liar out of me. I just had no idea how soon.

I turned away from what was left of Heaven's Gate and studied my father's face.

"Let's change the subject. Okay, Dad?"

"Okay. Looking forward to seeing old Tom McGowan tonight. It's been a while."

"Old" Tom McGowan was my thirty-something significant other, who for the most part lived out of state these days. I was looking forward to seeing him myself.

"You and he ever going to get married?"

That's one of the things I like about my dad. He gets right to the point. My mom, on the other hand, has been trying to ask me this question in a thousand different ways over the last three years. I gave Dad the same response I've always given my mom.

"I have no idea."

That statement must have been true. My internal PA system was quiet.

"Well, it'll be good to see him again."

The bulldozers erupted in a final frenzy, then fell silent. We watched the operators—tiny from this distance—get down from their seats and walk off the job site. Our conversation stopped and we stood perfectly still, as if listening for the sound of the shadows lengthening across the valley. Then we heard the humming of an engine, faint at first but growing louder. Next came the hissing of tires on pavement and the gunning of a motor as an approaching car accelerated up the steep incline of my parents' driveway.

Dad smiled. "That must be McGowan now."

2
≈

I left Dad to his whistling and went around front to greet the blue Buick Regal that came barreling up the driveway. I didn't recognize the car. Neither did Cinnamon, my parents' Irish setter, who burst into violent barking and nipped at the tires as the vehicle sped toward me. It was McGowan behind the tinted windshield, though. I knew by the way my heart rose up and that goofy grin crossed my face. As soon as the car door popped open, Cinnamon's tail began to swing. Her ears relaxed, her tongue hung out of her mouth and she put on a goofy grin, too.

"Hey there, Cinnamon Bun!" McGowan leaned out of the car, made a kissy-face and put his arms around the dog's wriggling shoulders. Cinnamon returned the affection with several slobbering licks to his eyes, nose, and lips.

After a few more seconds of this touching scene, I stepped forward and pulled the dog back by her collar.

"Okay, that's enough. It's my turn to lick your face."

McGowan pulled his six-and-a-half-foot frame out of the car and put his arms around me.

"Hey, stranger."

"I'm no stran—" I began, but his lips stopped mine, which was no loss. It would have been a lame joke anyway. When we stopped licking each other's face, he buried his head in my hair and gave me a bear hug.

"It is so good," he said, "to be here."

"Here" meant home, California. Three years ago Mc-Gowan had been an officer with the local police department. Then the FBI discovered his talent for hostage negotiation and recruited him for part-time assignments out of its San Diego office. His passion for the work led him deeper into the Bureau. The following year he became a full-time federal agent. Lately he'd been spending most of his time in Quantico, Virginia, but he still had ties to California: occasional fieldwork in San Diego, a house in nearby San Marcos, a gym membership. Me.

I stepped back to get a good look at him.

"So fine," I said.

"Oh, stop it."

"I was talking about your car. Is it new?"

"Actually, it's a rental. It wasn't making sense to keep paying expenses on cars in both states."

Another tie cut. The realization hit me and I felt a pang of regret. McGowan must have seen it in my face.

"Don't read anything into that—" he began, but at that moment the front door opened and my mom stepped out.

"Well, well, well. Look who's here. Handsome as ever."

She might have been talking about herself. My mother is one of those women whose looks the years seem to enhance, rather than fade. Maybe it's the way that time has emphasized her bone structure. Maybe it's the remarkable shade of silver her hair has become. Maybe it's because she's my mom and I love her. At least a foot shorter than McGowan, she stretched up on tiptoes and closed the gap to give him a hug.

"You're just in time. Dinner is served."

The spread was impressive. Shrimp quesadillas, chile rellenos, a variety of tapas, freshly chopped cilantro straight from the garden, and homemade salsa fresca. My parents love to cook. Mom has a way with rellenos and fish dishes. My dad performs magic with carbohydrates from around the world. He bakes European breads, makes genuine Italian pasta. He'd made the tortillas tonight from scratch, using a recipe he'd found at a taco shop in Ensenada. Family lore has it that he paid the shop owner *mucho dinero* to let him into the kitchen so he could watch over the cook's shoulder.

Dad swiped the edge of his beer glass with a lime. He tipped a bottle of Corona and poured carefully.

"What business brings you to California this time, Tom? Or is this just a pleasure trip?"

"Both," Tom answered. "In addition to the pleasure of seeing Elizabeth, I was also hoping I could persuade her to look into a case."

The compliment was nice, but the mention of work was music to my ears. Ordinarily I'm juggling at least three or four cases at a time, sometimes more. Things were a little slow at the moment. Let's be honest—things were dead. I'd be willing to serve subpoenas about now. I felt a surge of excitement as I helped myself to the salsa.

"Something interesting, I hope."

"Oh yeah. If there's one thing this case has going for it, it's interesting." His eyes met mine but I couldn't read them.

"I'm intrigued. Tell me more."

"Well, maybe we shouldn't discuss shop over this beautiful dinner your parents have prepared." He pointed to the sun-dried tomato pilaf across the table.

Mom picked up the bowl and passed it to Tom.

"Don't be silly. Your shoptalk is a lot more intriguing than life around here. Cult activity notwithstanding. And we're sick to death of that topic, aren't we, Albert?"

Dad's mouth was full. He nodded his head, chewing vigorously.

"This shoptalk may not be what you're looking to hear, then," Tom said.

"Nonsense," Mom fired back. "You can't bring up a thing like that without at least giving us a hint of what it's about."

"Well—" McGowan was hedging. He didn't want to talk about it. I love my mom's assertiveness and I probably get a good deal of my chutzpah from her, but at the moment I wished she'd quit pressing.

"Mom—" I began, but she cut me off.

"Just tell us what kind of case it is, generally."

McGowan dabbed at his lips with his napkin. "Missing persons."

One of my specialties. Now I was curious.

"Really?" Mom brightened. "Someone has disappeared. Oh, can we play 'Twenty Questions'? Is it a male or a female?"

"Mom—" I chided.

"Female," McGowan said.

"Okay, you said the case is interesting. A famous person?"

"No."

"An infamous person?"

A quick frown crossed McGowan's face. "Not exactly."

"But something interesting. . . . Oh come on, Albert, help me out here."

Dad swallowed some beer. "I'm staying out of this."

"Would I know who this person is?"

I was going to give Mom hell again, then decided McGowan could defend himself if he didn't want to play. I was actually starting to enjoy their little game.

"Let's put it this way," McGowan said. "You don't know her, but someone you know does."

Mom's eyes lit up. "Okay. Somebody has disappeared and someone *I* know knows this missing person. Someone I know—"

That's when I heard it. The voice. The one that speaks clearly, softly. The one that no one else can hear. The voice said, *Jen.*

"Is it someone Elizabeth knows?" Mom asked.

McGowan blinked thoughtfully. "Elizabeth knows of her."

Jen, the voice said again.

Mom gestured with her fork. "Elizabeth knows *of* her but someone I know actually knows this missing person?"

I didn't know a Jen. I racked my brains. I was sure I didn't know of anyone named Jen.

Mom's eyebrows knitted and she looked at my father. "Is it someone Albert knows?"

Jen, Jen.

"Who the heck is Jen?" I nearly shouted.

All heads turned to me. For several seconds, there was nothing but dead silence. Then McGowan sat back and smiled broadly. He chuckled and shook his head.

"You scare me, woman. I wish I knew how in the hell you do it."

Dad looked at me. "She guessed it?"

McGowan was staring at me like he was seeing me for the first time.

"I don't know if 'guess' is the right word. But Jen's the missing person all right."

"Well, who is she?" I asked.

Mom put her hand on my arm. "You don't know her, dear?"

"No, I don't know a Jen. Who is she?"

McGowan bit his lip. "Um, Jen Shaffer. You know. That woman I was, uh, going to marry."

Hold the phone. McGowan had an ex, and he wanted me to find her? My words came slowly.

"Of course. *That* Jen." But I was remembering now: a conversation we'd had early in our courtship, the one where we revealed past significant others and how and why they'd bombed out.

"Jen," I said. "Wasn't she the one who ran off with the religious cult?"

He nodded. "Yeah, that's the one."

"And you want me to . . . what? Find and deprogram her?" It came out a bit too snippily.

"Just find her. I wouldn't ask, but her father is going out

of his mind. He hasn't heard a word from Jen in nearly two years now. Apart from his son, Jen's the only family he has. His wife died years ago."

McGowan had never talked much about his former fiancée or her family. But he still cared about them. I could see it in his eyes.

He sighed. "Part of me hates to ask but a bigger part of me feels I should do what I can for them."

For once in their lives, my parents were speechless. Mom was actually looking a little horrified. Served her right for pushing the issue.

Something deep in my gut stirred uneasily. "I don't know if this is really a wise idea, Tom."

He drew lines in the water that had beaded on the outside of his beer glass. "I can understand your reservations. But I promised Vince I'd at least ask you."

"Vince is Jen's father?"

McGowan nodded.

I thought for a moment before speaking. "It's not like I'm the only private investigator in town, you know."

He shook his head. "He's tried others. Two of them came up empty-handed. A third PI flaked out and disappeared on him."

McGowan seemed to know an awful lot about the status of his ex's disappearance.

"You've been following her case, then?" I sawed off another bite of chile relleno and tried to look casual.

"No. I've done my best to forget about her. One of your fans at the police department recommended you to Vince. Told him about the amazing way you found those other kids. Told him he could reach you through me."

Mom found her voice. "This would be a miserable time to have a child disappear into a religious cult."

"I don't think Jen's a child, Mom."

"They're always your children."

In the silence that followed, I had the unmistakable sense of life-altering events looming just ahead. My appetite vanished. I did my best to ward off the premonition by feigning ignorance and smiling bravely at McGowan.

"Who's to say your former love is not off happily

marching to the rhythm of her own wacky drummer?"

He didn't smile back.

"A package arrived in Vince's mail last week. Based on the contents, he thinks Jen might be dead."

3
≈

Everything about it was ordinary—the size, the faded gold-enrod color, even the corners, which were scuffed and worn in the way that padded envelopes sent through the mail tend to become. I stared at it for several moments, asking silent questions. Where had it come from? Who had sent it? I reached for names, faces. Then caught myself. I was *trying* to have a psychic insight about the package. This never works. Intuitive knowledge can't be forced. It's like lightning: It comes when it comes, where it comes. I looked up from the table.

Vince Shaffer stared back at me, hope lighting his eyes. A partner in one of San Diego's top law firms, he'd taken time out on a Monday morning to meet me at his home. He made a good impression. It wasn't just the beautifully tailored suit or his well-cut hair. It was his air of utter self-respect. But for his daughter's disappearance into a religious cult, this man might have been McGowan's father-in-law by now. McGowan could have done worse.

"Tom was kind enough to do me the personal favor of having the package analyzed for fingerprints," he said. "I take it he's filled you in on the situation so far. About my daughter's abduction, I mean."

I'd understood from McGowan that Jen had gone willingly into the cult, at least initially. But I politely didn't take issue with Mr. Shaffer's opinion.

"He gave me a brief background on the case yesterday," I answered, turning the package by one corner. "So tell me again how and when this arrived."

"It was shoved into the box at the end of the driveway a week ago Saturday. I assume it came with the rest of that day's mail."

I looked again at the postmark. It was a priority-mail label originating from San Diego, California. No return address, naturally. I tipped the envelope so that the contents slid out. A dog-eared, brown-leather wallet rolled onto the glass tabletop, followed by a silver chain that landed with a soft swish. A Medic Alert bracelet.

"This was your daughter's?"

He nodded.

"Jen had a severe allergy to bees. An untreated sting could be fatal. She'd been wearing that bracelet since she was a little girl." His features were pinched with pain. "That's what tells me something's happened to her. She would never, ever, take that off willingly."

I picked it up. An eight-hundred number was engraved on the back of the bracelet, along with an ID number. My fingers closed around the metal. Again I felt myself straining to have some intuitive insight. I let the bracelet slide from my fingers back onto the table and looked over at Vince Shaffer. The only intuitive experience I was having at the moment was a worried father's agony leaking into me. I longed to put him at ease.

"I don't know much about this cult, but suppose your daughter's going through a phase—or is being pressured to believe—that her physical limitations can be healed by faith. Suppose some guru is telling her she has the power to overcome her bee allergy. Getting rid of possessions like this medical bracelet might be a symbolic way of expressing her faith."

It was an idea concocted solely by my rational left brain. When the words were out of my mouth they didn't jibe with my gut sense at all. Before I could modify the comment, Jen's father scowled at me. Up till now, he'd been giving me the benefit of the doubt. I could see by his frown that I was losing it quickly. He started to object but I interrupted him.

"Forget everything I just said. You're right. Your daughter's in trouble."

To my surprise, this statement seemed to comfort him.

"Thank you for saying that. The police have told me I have no case. The other investigators told me my daughter probably just doesn't want to be found. But I know my Jen. I know when something's wrong."

Wrong. The word hung heavily in the air between us and we looked again at the articles on the coffee table. They made a creepy still life. I picked up the wallet.

He watched me carefully.

"You came highly recommended. But is it true you've had success finding people before . . . psychically? I mean, how does it work, exactly?"

I held the wallet in my hand.

"It doesn't work exactly. It works *inexactly*. Unpredictably. Finding a child was actually how I started in this business. I was reading the paper one day, came across an article about a missing boy. An address literally flashed before my eyes. I reported it to the police and sure enough, it was a match."

The hope returned to his eyes.

"Like I say, it's an inexact skill," I cautioned. "The flashing-address incident had never happened to me before, and it hasn't happened since. Sometimes I come up completely empty-handed. That's why I have a private investigator's license. I can't guarantee psychic insight, but I can snoop around with the best of them." The wallet in my hand felt lifeless and inert, as if silently proving my point about not being able to guarantee psychic insight.

"The second investigator I hired gave me a ninety-nine-percent guarantee he'd find my daughter." He let out a disgusted snort. "The thief."

I have no illusions about my profession. Private investigators can be some of the scummiest people around. Don't even get me started on the majority of practicing psychics.

"I'm sorry to hear that," I said.

I opened the wallet. Inside was a driver's license, valid through the end of the year.

"This is your daughter, then?"

He nodded.

The stats said I was looking at a female, five foot seven, one hundred twenty pounds, red hair. I did some quick math and figured from the birth date that Jennifer Janine

Shaffer would now be thirty-three years old. Her picture was kind of goofy. Goofier, even, than most DMV portraiture. Her pale skin and tiny features were dwarfed by an oversized pair of black-framed eyeglasses. Either extremely trendy or extremely out, I wasn't sure which. The haircut was strange, a variety of haphazard lengths with very short bangs. It stunned me to think that this was the woman McGowan had almost married. I'd seen only one previous photo, a long-distance shot taken from way down the trail on a hiking trip. Close up, Jen wasn't what I'd expected.

"I take it no note came with the package."

He shook his head.

"And the address listed on her driver's license?"

"A house in La Jolla owned by the cult."

I searched the compartments of the wallet. No credit cards, no business cards, no cash. I flipped through the photo section and was relieved to find no picture of McGowan. I made eye contact with Mr. Shaffer.

"I have to tell you that I have some reservations about taking this case."

"Why?"

"Your daughter's former fiancé is my boyfriend now."

"Yes, Tom told me the two of you are dating. Would that be a conflict of interest for you?"

"That's one way to put it. But it's more than that. For some reason, the closer I am to a case emotionally, the less likely I am to get a clear psychic insight about it."

"I see." He looked at me with renewed interest. "Thanks for your honesty."

"I try."

He picked up his daughter's bracelet and stroked it gently with his thumb.

"Tom's got good people sense, that's one of the main reasons I want your help."

It occurred to me that McGowan's "good people sense" had allowed him to attach himself to a woman who'd run off with a religious cult. I kept that smart thought to myself.

He put the bracelet back on the table.

"I didn't get much of a chance to catch up with Tom over the phone. How is he these days?" he asked.

"Doing really well. Enjoying his police work."

He shook his head.

"I still have a hard time picturing that. Tom was an English teacher, you know, when he and Jen . . ."

Tom and Jen. He stumbled on that thought. I stepped in and gave him a hand.

"He has a gift for law enforcement. He did double duty for a while, with the local police department and the FBI. Last year he made the transition to become a full-time agent."

Jen's father had the look of someone who'd arrived in a brave new world and wasn't at all certain of the terrain. He shook his head.

"Life is full of surprises."

I felt for him. I would feel for any parent who hadn't heard from a child in two years. But the empathy factor was fogging my decision-making ability. I needed to get out of his orbit.

"Would you mind if I used your bathroom?" I asked.

"Not at all. Downstairs, end of the hall on the right."

Vince Shaffer lived in Encinitas, which at one time had been a casual beach town about thirty minutes north of San Diego. Like everywhere else along the North County coast, Encinitas had become more crowded and expensive. A few vestiges of the laid-back town remained in the taco stands and surf shops lining the beach and the funky houses decorating the city's older streets. The Shaffer house represented the new, yuppified Encinitas. It was a tri-level affair set on a hill about a quarter mile from the Pacific. An upstairs living room with a wall of west-facing windows took advantage of the ocean view, while the bathrooms and bedrooms occupied the lower two levels. I wandered out of the sun-soaked living room, stepped down the stairs and entered a dim hallway.

In the little light that was available, I scrutinized a gallery of family photographs along the wall. The first frame displayed a picture of a radiant bride wearing an ivory-colored satin dress. Her pale blonde hair had been teased and pouffed into a careful pageboy and was crowned by a veil of tulle. This must have been the now-deceased Mrs. Shaffer. In an adjacent matching frame was a youthful Vince Shaffer, hair still impeccably cut but honey-colored rather than gray. In a third photograph, the two of them stood together, gazing lovingly into each other's eyes.

I moved down the hall and glanced briefly at another series of photo subjects: a boy and a girl. First as toddlers, then as gangly legged kids, then as punked-out teens, and finally as respectable-looking young adults. I recognized Jen, sans glasses, far more lovely here than in her driver's-license photo. The young man, I surmised, must be her brother.

The last photograph on the wall was a portrait of Vince and his grown son, their faces somber and determined. Altogether, the photographs told the story of a California family broken by the absence of its women.

Inside the bathroom, I splashed cold water on my face. I was feeling disoriented. What did I intend to do?

Although McGowan and I had spent the better part of last night discussing the case, it wasn't his prodding that had compelled me to visit Jen's father today. Nor was it the challenge of overcoming my own petty jealousy. In the end, it boiled down to blatant self-interest. McGowan's former lover occupied a dark corner in the back of his brain; I'd seen that quite clearly. I knew that until this matter of her disappearance was resolved, he'd have no closure. A part of him would always wonder where Jen was and if she were alive. I didn't mind the idea of him carrying around fond memories of another woman. But there's a difference between a fond memory and a brain lurker. Part of me wanted to bring the Jen issue into the light. Still, I had no intention of being a masochist. I'd agreed last night that I would talk to Mr. Shaffer, but had also vowed that if anything about this case felt weird—anything at all—I'd bow out.

I looked at myself in the mirror. An uncomfortable Elizabeth looked back.

"What's it going to be?" I asked myself out loud.

My clear-blue eyes stared back, unblinking. No answer was immediately forthcoming. I turned the water from cold to hot, pumped some liquid soap into my palm and washed my hands. The bathroom walls seemed to close in on me and I felt the need for more air. Something *was* weird. But weird enough to decline this case? I would decide by the time I reached the top of the stairs.

When I returned to the living room, Vince Shaffer was standing at the west wall of windows, looking out. When he heard me come in, he turned and smiled hopefully.

My own smile was weak. "I've decided that I don't think I'm the person you need."

His face fell.

"But why?"

"If I were putting a financial deal together, I guess I'd say this doesn't feel like an arm's-length transaction. I'm too involved. Do you understand?"

He motioned to the sofa.

"Please, have a seat." It was more of a command than a request. "Before you make a decision, I want you to hear all the facts. Fair enough?"

What was I going to say? That I'd made up my mind and preferred to remain ignorant? I nodded my consent and sat down.

He removed his jacket and draped it over the back of his chair.

"Let's go back to nineteen eighty-seven, when my daughter first encountered The Bliss Project." He took his seat.

"Of course they called it The Church of the Risen Lord back then. Jen had recently graduated at the top of her class from the University of California in San Diego. At twenty-one years of age, she was on the board of the California Crime Victims' Association, working to get tougher drunk-driving laws through the legislature."

I could have asked what had sparked Jen's interest in politics, but at this point, I really didn't want to know. I was politely hearing him out, nothing more.

"Jen was young, but principled. She was just beginning to contribute to a society desperately in need of her kind of activism when they kidnapped her."

"Kidnapped her?"

"Kidnapped her." His eyes were fierce, daring me to disagree. "My daughter was not some drifter looking for an escape from the real world. She was manipulated into that group by a gang of sociopaths and I'm convinced that if she is alive, she's being held forcibly. They start out innocently enough. But I've talked to some of the lucky ones who've been able to get out. There aren't many of them."

He saw the dubious look on my face and raised his voice.

"This isn't just another one of California's offbeat spiritual communities, if that's what you're thinking. The Bliss Project is a hugely profitable, uncontrolled racket. They got that way by intimidating their members and using mafia-like tactics." His head shook with emotion.

"They're ruthless, terroristic, vicious . . . vipers." He spat the last word off his tongue.

Underneath the vitriol, I saw the fragile fear of a heartbroken dad.

He folded his hands together in a pleading gesture.

"Can I perhaps appeal to your sense of compassion? Justice?"

The persuasion was powerful. I could tell he was a lawyer, a cunning negotiator. Beware of charmers with law degrees.

"You wouldn't even be starting from scratch. The last investigator spent just three weeks on the case but he did quite a bit of worthwhile work." He reached around and fished in his suit pocket, coming up with a business card. "Says he'll be happy to turn over his file to you."

He held out the card. "Think of this not just as helping me, but helping my daughter as well."

I shook my head.

"If it were anyone else."

At that moment I realized how deeply I'd fallen in love with McGowan. Once again a premonition came over me: This case would threaten our bond.

He placed the business card on the table in front of me, then reached down and pulled a briefcase onto his lap. The locks made two sharp, popping sounds as he opened them. Without speaking, he retrieved a check and handed it to me. It was made out to Dr. Elizabeth Chase in the amount of twenty-five thousand dollars.

Like I said, he was a cunning negotiator.

"Elizabeth—may I call you Elizabeth?—my daughter means more to me than all the world. I've checked your references. They're impeccable. Of course I understand your hesitation, given my daughter's past association with Tom. I don't know you well, but from what I can see, you're a person who's big enough to put that aside." His face softened.

"I'll be fifty-five years old next month. It's a birthday I'd like to celebrate. Without my daughter, there can be no celebration."

I stared at the check in my hands and was appalled to see a brand-new Jeep Grand Cherokee flash before my eyes. I handed it back.

"This is obscene," I said.

His face tensed and I prepared for another verbal assault. To my surprise, his eyes welled with tears.

"This is my *daughter* we're talking about." His voice was an intense whisper. "Anything less would be obscene."

"But Mr. Shaffer, twenty-five thousand dollars?"

He composed himself and nodded curtly.

"I've concluded that the other investigators failed largely because they were insufficiently motivated to find my daughter. I don't want to make that mistake again."

I stared at the motivation in my hands. "If I were to take this on, it could take quite a while."

"Take all the time you need. Consider that check a three-month retainer. If the time comes when you need more, I'll see that you get the funds. If you find my daughter tomorrow, you keep the entire amount as a finder's fee."

A twenty-five-thousand-dollar finder's fee? I began to make compromises. I chalked up my low moment in the bathroom to petty insecurity. A personal weakness to be overcome, not indulged. I fabricated a bright future wherein my finding Jen worked out for everyone's highest good. Then—and here's what clinched it—my competitive instinct kicked in. I knew I could succeed where the others had failed. My next thought stopped me cold.

I handed the check back.

"I'm not convinced Jen didn't go willingly into that cult. Locating your daughter is one thing. Getting her to your birthday party is another thing altogether."

He handed the check right back. I'd never actually seen a check bounce this way.

"We can talk about that later. You'll accept the assignment to find her, then?"

I stared again at the twenty-five thousand dollars between my fingertips. *What the hell*, I thought.

4
≋

"The half-naked woman leaping onto me and dry-humping me, that's what finally did it." The investigator nodded and blinked thoughtfully.

I wondered if I'd heard him correctly.

"Come again?" Poor choice of words, but by the time I realized it, they were already past my lips. I hate when that happens.

Scott Chatfield, the mastermind of Chatfield's Value Added Investigations, fixed me with a scolding glare. I thought I saw mischief in the bright green eyes behind his glasses. One corner of his mouth looked like it might be trying to smile, but I couldn't be sure.

"That's when I dropped the Shaffer case. When that woman attacked me."

"So, Mr. Chatfield—" I chose my words carefully now "—tell me what led up to this, um, leaping thing."

"You want me to start from the beginning?"

"Sure, why not?"

He pushed off from his desk and rolled backward in his chair, bumping with a mild crash into the wall behind him. He turned to a scuff-marked beige file cabinet near the wall and opened the bottom drawer with a screech.

"Shaffer, Shaffer, Shaf—ah. Here 'tis." He grabbed the goods and rolled back to face me, plopping a bulging green Pendaflex file folder onto his desk. It was a half a foot high.

"Wow," I said. "All that's on the Shaffer case? Mr. Shaffer told me you spent only three weeks on your investigation."

"I'm very thorough." He pushed his glasses up on his pointed nose. That *was* a smile at the corner of his mouth. This time I was sure.

I did my best to mimic his half-grin. "Either you're very thorough or you're obnoxiously wordy."

He chuckled at that. "Naw, most of this crap is cult literature. *Fascinating* reading." He rolled his eyes. "Here, feed your head."

He handed me a white booklet. On the cover, an eerie green eye peered out from a gold pyramid. *Transformation Handbook* was the title. No author per se, but according to the byline, the contents had been "channeled by Abadanda." The book felt icky in my hands.

Chatfield laced his fingers together and rested his chin on them.

"Two months ago, Vince Shaffer hired me to find his daughter, whom he hadn't seen in over two years. He'd tried two previous investigators. Neither one delivered."

I'd heard this part. I nodded and as he talked, I opened the *Transformation Handbook*. My eyes fell on the following words:

> *To make the transformation to full awareness,*
> *one must be prepared to give up everything—*
> *every attachment, every trace of ego. . . .*

Chatfield pulled a couple of manila files from the large green folder on his desk.

"Shaffer gave me the names and numbers of the other PIs, much as he gave my name and number to you. At least you'll get a little more information from me than I did from the first two jokers."

He handed one of the files across to me and I slid the *Transformation Handbook* back onto his desk. He stared at the book.

"What's the matter? A little too rich for your taste?"

"A little too rank," I said. "Please, go on."

He smiled and leaned back in his chair.

"That file you're holding contains the sum total of the contribution made by the first investigator, Lisa Mann."

I looked through the folder. Inside was a splashy four-color brochure featuring Access Search Company, along with a promotion-heavy introductory letter signed by Lisa Mann, President. Copies of three invoices indicated that Ms. Mann had billed Vince Shaffer five hundred dollars each month for three consecutive months. The only other thing in the file was a printout of public records relating to Jennifer Janine Shaffer.

"No reports?" I asked.

"No, just the database search you see there." Chatfield blew out a disdainful breath. "Lisa Mann wasn't a detective—she was a computer operator."

He passed me the second file. "Now this next guy is really strange—" he began, but he stopped short when a barely audible knocking sounded at the door. "What," he called flatly, a touch of annoyance in his voice.

The door opened without a sound and a slender figure slipped into the room. He wore a tall black top hat, jet-black pants, and a matching black coat with long tails. On his hands were a pair of gleaming-white gloves. The visitor turned to me as he passed, showing me a face painted as white as his gloves. His oversized mouth had been drawn on in a loud shade of red, and his spiky eyelashes had been painted in black. The mime laid a sheaf of papers on Chatfield's desk, hunched his shoulders and hung his head.

"Oh, no." Chatfield sounded genuinely distressed. "Don't tell me."

The mime, of course, didn't tell him. Not in words. He conveyed the entire story in fluid gestures. From what I could make out, some terrible fate had befallen the papers he'd laid on the desk.

"You tried the second location?" Chatfield asked.

The mime nodded emphatically.

Chatfield lifted his glasses and rubbed his eyes wearily. "Damn it, I'm about at the end of my rope with this."

The mime slammed his fist on the desk so unexpectedly that I nearly jumped out of my chair. My knees jerked and some papers from the file in my lap fell out onto the floor.

"End of *your* rope!" he blurted. "You think I enjoy clowning around like this? Well, I don't. It's humiliating." He turned and fixed me with a baleful stare. His expression was made even more pitiful by his jolly makeup.

Chatfield suddenly seemed to remember that I was in the room.

"Greg, I'm in a meeting here. Can we talk about this later?"

The mime spun around to leave. On his way out, he picked up the papers that had fallen from my lap, handed them to me, then left without a word. The last thing I saw of him were his coattails going through the door.

"Sorry," he said. "We've got a client who's trying to serve divorce papers on her very reluctant spouse. He's eluded us every time."

"So you sent in a clown. Very creative."

"Yeah," he scoffed. "Chatfield's Value Added Investigations. But this is a very wary man. Suspicious of mimes—can you imagine?"

I shrugged.

He lowered his voice to sound like an evil villain.

"Now I must come up with an even more diabolical ploy!" He wriggled his eyebrows conspiratorially.

I had to laugh.

He resumed his normal speaking voice.

"Okay, where were we? Oh, yeah. Barry Bell. Very odd, this guy. As you'll see from the reports in there, Bell had a pretty good handle on the Shaffer case. He was asking all the right questions, following all the logical leads. Things seemed to be moving along. Then all of a sudden he just up and disappeared."

I leafed through the file contents. There were six narrative reports dated from June 1996 to January 1997. Then nothing. No summary comments, no letter of resignation. Most unusual of all: no final bill.

"After hearing nothing for several weeks, Shaffer finally reached the guy's partner, who told him Mr. Bell had cleaned out his desk two weeks earlier. Left the investigation business. The partner hadn't seen him since. He was nice enough to give Shaffer a copy of Bell's file on the case, which Shaffer then turned over to me."

I remembered what Jen's father had said about this investigator giving him "a ninety-nine-percent guarantee" he'd find his daughter. Mr. Shaffer had called him a thief.

The more I heard about Barry Bell, the more his disappearance sounded fishy—perhaps worthy of investigation itself.

Chatfield drummed the desk with his pencil.

"You with me so far?"

"Yeah, but I'm wondering when we get to the part about the woman . . . er, leaping on you."

Again he fixed me with his scolding stare. "You really seem to have an interest in that sort of thing, don't you?"

"You calling me a perv?"

He smiled wide. "See that little flyer?"

It was one of the things that had fallen to the floor when the mime startled me. A pale blue piece of parchment paper, folded in thirds. The front panel read simply: *The Bliss Project.*

I held it up. "This thing?"

"Yeah. Bell's report documented some interviews he did with Jen Shaffer's family and friends. According to them, Jen joined the cult in eighty-seven. The group was started by a minister named Malinda, who called it The Church of the Risen Lord. In ninety-two, Reverend Malinda became Master Malindi and her church became The Bliss Project. Guess Her Holiness didn't want her flock to be associated with the far-right fundamentalist movement."

I read the headline inside the flyer: "Intense Bliss Events." Four dates were listed. The following information was printed in very small italic type at the bottom of the flyer:

Financing is available.
For more information, or to register by phone,
call 800-222-4414.
Space is limited, so reserve early.

Apparently, transformation was a costly thing and required careful scheduling. Again I got a queasy feeling.

"So that's how you found these people?"

"Yeah. They hold these bliss events every once in a while to reel in the public. I went down there one night and started asking around for Jen Shaffer. Made up a sob story about how I recently found out I was adopted. Pretended I was having an identity crisis and was in dire need of getting in touch with my biological family. Told them I had reason to believe Jen and I may be related."

"Pretty good story."

"Chatfield's Value Added Investigations." He laced his voice with sarcasm. "Anyway, nobody knew anyone by the name Jen Shaffer. But they were very interested in my search for identity. Said that if I wanted to reconnect with my real family, I needn't look any farther."

"Because you'd found it, right? *They* were your real family. *They* could show you your true identity."

"Yeah, how'd you guess?"

"Forced intimacy. Classic. Sickening. Go on."

"I played along, but kept my focus on reconnecting with my 'sister.' Things heated up when I met Malindi. If you're going to take this case, brace yourself. She's a piece of work, a real piece of work."

I didn't doubt him. Just hearing her name put my hackles up.

"Malindi tells me not only is she going to reconnect me with my lost relative Jen, but she's also going to 'heal my aloneness.' " He drew quotation marks in the air around the last three words and rolled his eyes.

"This didn't appeal to you?"

Chatfield smiled wickedly. "I *like* my aloneness."

I chuckled. Fun as he was, I bet Chatfield was too popular to spend much time alone.

He sat back and continued his story.

"Malindi says she can see that my separation from Jen has 'wounded me' and that it's time to have a 'family reunion' to heal my wound. She asks me to meet her at one of the group's properties, a place in La Jolla. I'm thinkin' great, maybe Jen Shaffer will be there and I can wrap the case up.

"So I get to the place—this huge house off La Jolla Scenic Drive—but we're the only two people there. She says the 'reunion' is going to take place in an upstairs bedroom. She shows me to the master suite and has me lie down on this bed with a giant mandala bedspread on it. Says to just close my eyes until it's time. So I'm early? I ask. And she smiles in this real creepy way and says yeah, I should just relax. Then she lights candles, puts on some extremely annoying drum music—"

"Annoying?"

Chatfield attacked his desk with the palms of his hands, pounding a syncopated rhythm so loud that my teeth hurt.

"Okay, okay," I said, waving for quiet. "I got it."

He waited a beat before continuing. "Then she starts dancing. As the drums heat up, she starts to strip. She twirls around and around, spins like a top. I'm amazed she doesn't throw up. I begin to figure out there isn't going to be any family reunion. I start to get up off the bed. Suddenly she lets out this bloodcurdling scream, leaps on top of me and starts—"

"Doing that thing she did," I finished for him. "And that was enough to put you off the case?"

He widened his eyes in mock horror. "I should say so."

My bullshit detector went into red-alert mode. Behind Chatfield's charmingly eccentric humor, I saw a shrewd and determined investigator. I certainly didn't see a scaredy-cat prude.

"I don't buy it," I said.

"What do you mean?"

"I mean I don't buy it. You're no wuss. You wouldn't be scared off a case by a half-naked woman jumping on you."

"Thanks a lot, I guess."

"I'm not saying you'd like it, I'm not even saying you wouldn't be offended. I'm just saying you're not telling me the whole story."

He reached across the desk. "Hand me those files back, would you?"

I did as he asked and watched him return the files to the Pendaflex folder. He was buying time. After several seconds, he looked up.

"You're right. It was what she said, not what she did, that made me drop the case. After hearing this, you might think I'm a wuss after all."

"She threatened you?"

He nodded. "On my way out, she said something like,

'You can turn away from the family now, but you're going back to the same old troubles.' "

"What troubles?" I asked.

He pointed at me. "*Bingo*. I said to her, 'Wait a minute. You do a naked bonga-bonga dance with a near stranger, take a flying leap onto me, and you're telling me *I've* got troubles?' Okay, it was a little harsh, but she disgusted me, know what I'm sayin'?"

I nodded.

"She was pissed. Her eyes were like daggers. Then she stabs me with this: 'No troubles, brother *Chatfield*?' Just like that. I was a little alarmed, since I hadn't given these people my last name. Then she goes, 'What about—' " Chatfield stopped in midsentence. "Uh . . . then she went on to name a personal predicament I was involved in."

"What predicament was that?"

"The details aren't important. What's important is that she brought up business of mine that nobody else knew about. Business I didn't want anybody knowing about."

I wondered what business that might be.

"Nothing illegal, if that's what you're thinking. Just . . . very personal. But somehow this woman knew. It really gave me the creeps. *I* was the one who was supposed to be doing the hunting. I left that place feeling like I'd been had. I don't know about you, but I don't need that kind of complication in my life. I dropped the case the next day. Shaffer offered to double my fee to stay on, but I turned him down. No one can pay me enough to take on that kind of trouble."

This woman sounded like a worthy opponent.

"So the dancer—what did you say her name was?"

"Malindi. *Master* Malindi."

"Malindi." Again the name put me on guard. "Did you ever see her again?"

"No, and I hope to God I never do."

5

≋

I climbed into my aging Mustang and dumped Chatfield's bulging Pendaflex folder onto the passenger seat. He'd insisted that I take it. Said it gave him the creeps. His words that no one could pay him enough to take on "that kind of trouble" echoed in my mind. This morning I'd tucked Vince Shaffer's twenty-five-thousand-dollar check into a zippered compartment in my purse, rather than in my wallet. Now I wondered why. Did I think of it as some kind of fungus that might corrupt my legitimate money? I turned the ignition key and listened as the engine fired, then died. The motor ran fitfully after my second try.

I backed slowly out of the parking space in front of Chatfield's Value Added Investigations and reminded myself why I'd taken this case. In a word, cash. True, my parents live in Rancho Santa Fe and I come from a long line of folks who've been responsible with inherited money. But it's not like we hang out with Bill Gates or anything.

My parents got lucky when they purchased their Rancho Santa Fe acreage in the sixties. The rural township gradually became a ritzy enclave and by the nineties, real estate prices had gone through the ozone layer. Mom and Dad had gifted me with an excellent education and I hadn't asked for money since. I'd done very well with a clinical psychology practice I opened after leaving Stanford. The reserves from that venture were substantial enough to launch me into what I believed was my true calling: using my psychic talents as a private investigator. But over the past few months, pickings had been slim and expenses hefty. Lately I'd been wondering if, at the tender age of thirty-seven, I was going to have to mooch off my folks after all. Given that option, Mr. Shaffer's twenty-five-thousand-dollar check didn't look so terribly fungal.

My thoughts spun further rationalizations as I negotiated the freeway traffic home. I belonged on this case. Chatfield, I decided, was basically a good guy, but he had secrets to hide. I, on the other hand, lived an open-book life. All my affairs were aboveboard, perhaps tediously so. A Goody Two-shoes like me would make a poor blackmail target. I was not vulnerable. I would succeed where the others had failed. By the time I exited the freeway in Escondido, I was so convinced of my incorruptibility that I stopped by the bank and deposited the twenty-five grand.

I pulled into my driveway and looked with mixed emotions at the major reason for my current financial crunch. I live in a house that was built in eighteen eighty-eight, a stately old thing that eats more than ten times my grocery bill every month. It had been love at first sight, so I was completely incapable of reasoning when I signed the mortgage agreement. I hadn't thought about realities like ancient plumbing, wiring, and heating. Contending with such things cost money, too much of it. Selling, however, was not an option. I was still very much in love.

I tossed my shoes inside the front door and wandered into the kitchen, expecting Whitman to dart between my feet at any moment. The cat invariably sees me off and greets me upon arrival. His sense for my erratic comings and goings is uncanny. Then again, he probably just recognizes the sound of my sixty-five red Mustang convertible. The engine of my classic auto grinds louder with each passing month. But my precocious Himalayan wasn't around at the moment. I set my paperwork on the counter and imagined that he'd found an irresistible spot on my clean laundry upstairs.

I poured a tall glass of cranberry juice and stood at the kitchen window to drink it. The long rays of the setting sun cast an orangy glow over the yard, where the jacaranda tree was in full flower. Soon its blossoms would fall like big blue raindrops, my personal signal that summer was on its way to Southern California. For the next few weeks, I could enjoy its bright cloud of periwinkle blue.

Blue.

In a flash, the blue parchment flyer I'd seen in Chatfield's office appeared in my mind. As clearly as if I were reading it, The Bliss Project's phone number hovered before me. This was my subconscious, prodding me to get to work. I resisted the commonsense urge to double-check it before dialing. My gift with numbers rarely fails me.

To my surprise, the call was answered by an automated-voice system. A female voice droned in a perfunctory tone.

"Thank you for calling The Bliss Project. If you know the extension of the person you wish to reach, you may enter that number now. If you have a Touch-Tone phone, enter three. Otherwise, please stay on the line for personal assistance."

I waited for personal assistance. Meanwhile, I pulled the *Transformation Handbook* from the folder. I flipped to the inside back cover and was surprised to see an author photo. Pardon me—*channeler* photo. A one-sentence bio read, "Abadanda is a spiritual messenger sent to assist all who wish to get Free in this lifetime." This begged the question: Free from what? Presumably, Abadanda knew the answer. Staring out from hooded eyes, a smirk on his plump, liver-colored lips, he looked to me like a rather dissolute middle-aged man. Not exactly the guy I'd want ushering me up the stairway to heaven.

A man's voice came on the line.

"Thank you for calling The Bliss Project. How may I help you?"

"Oh, hi."

The blue parchment flyer was wedged into the *Transformation Handbook*. Once again my eye fell on the fine print that read, "Financing is available." I improvised from there.

"Um—" here I paused for a dramatic sigh "—I probably can't even afford it, but I'm calling to ask about your program."

"So, you feel called to the Process."

His pompousness rankled me. As far as conclusions go, he'd made a hell of a flying leap.

"Well," I hedged, "I just want to know more about it."

"You want to know more about the Process, then."

"Yes, the Process." Whatever that was.

"What's your name, dear?" Said the spider to the fly.

"Whitney." A quick alias in honor of my cat.

"Do you live in San Diego, Whitney?"

"Pretty close."

"Your timing is really a miracle, you know that? We're having a meditation this evening in our San Diego ashram. It starts at seven-thirty. If you think you can make it, I'll give you directions."

"Uh, great. Just a sec." I reached for a pen, knocking my faux leather personal phone directory off the kitchen counter. "Go ahead."

He gave me directions, which, lacking a notepad, I scribbled into the margins of the morning newspaper.

"We'll be looking forward to seeing you, Whitney."

"Yeah, thanks. See you later."

I hung up and bent down to pick up the directory off the floor. The pages had fallen open in the Fs, and Joanne Friedman's name popped out at me. I took this as an auspicious sign and dialed her number. Joanne happens to be a manager in a national finance company, a woman with access to untold electronic databases. Just my luck, she was in.

"Hi, Joanne. It's Elizabeth."

"Whose records do you want me to snoop into this time?"

Joanne rarely bothers with the niceties. She didn't get to a powerful perch on the high-finance totem pole by being passive and polite.

"Her name is Jennifer Janine Shaffer. Born February three, nineteen sixty-four."

"Okay, I'll run this one, but in exchange I want a psychic reading. Like now, right here on the phone."

I hoped that the serious tone in her voice was a put-on.

"Yeah, right. Like I'm one of those psychics who pulls answers out of thin air. You of all people know how I feel about psychic hotlines, for crying out loud."

I hated psychic hotlines and their ilk with a passion. I'd once counseled a victim of psychic hotline fraud. The young woman—recently divorced, between jobs, and clinically depressed—had run up twenty-thousand dollars in phone debt thanks to her so-called psychic friends. Joanne and my attorney friend, David, had helped me pull some strings to relieve her burden.

"You always say you can't, but just read for me this one time, okay? Please?"

Holy cow, she wasn't kidding.

"Tell me if you get any impressions about a guy named Brad Aiken." She drew out the vowels of his name and her voice got all sultry.

"Sounds like you've got the hots for him."

She gasped. "See! You can do this, Liz!"

"Don't be a ditz, Joanne. That was obvious, not psychic. Look, I can't talk now. By the time I call you back, I'll have figured out how to make it up to you, okay?"

"All right. Meantime, I'll see what I can find on this Jennifer Shaffer person."

"Thanks. You're a pal."

I hung up and searched the green folder for the file from Access Research. The computer-generated reports looked thorough but were now several months old. I didn't really expect Joanne to turn up any records on Jen Shaffer that this search company hadn't found. It wouldn't hurt to be sure, though.

I continued leafing through the folder. Chatfield had been right—most of it was Bliss Project literature, filled with strange jargon. The cult materials had a dead feeling, and I stacked them into their own little pyre. My fingers finally touched something that felt as if it had some life to it. Two pages, stapled together. The first sheet was a photocopy of a mailing envelope postmarked San Diego, California, July 15, 1995. The second sheet was a photocopy of a letter, written in a hasty, slanting hand:

Dear Jeremy,

Whatever happens now, don't blame yourself. I told you before and I'll tell you again. For the past eight years, every single step I've taken was where I wanted to go. My actions have been my responsibility, including what started it all. I believe this was meant to be. In a lot of ways, it was good. It led me to this special place where I had the freedom to live in a way that would have been impossible outside.

But things have changed. I don't see any other way out. I guess if I were to put it in Free terms (ha ha), I've learned all I can at Levels A and B. It's time to move on.

What this means is that you won't see me for a while. I don't know how long. Maybe not again in this lifetime. Please don't freak that I said that. Take things in stride, Jer.

You know I love you. That'll never change. Love is eternal. Don't be afraid. There's really never anything to be afraid of. We're all always Here, Now, Eternally, anyway.

Love,
Jen

So this was Jen. I presumed she had written the letter to her brother, Jeremy. I rechecked the envelope. It was addressed to Jeremy Shaffer, care of a San Diego post-office box.

Talk about strange jargon. I read her words over again, looking for clues behind the clichés. I paused at the words, "what started it all." I'd never asked McGowan his theories about what might have prompted his former fiancée to drop out of society. Her reference here to "what started it all" seemed concrete—a specific, fateful event. I made an entry in my notebook to talk with him about that.

"In Free terms." Huh? I made a note to get clarification on that one.

"Levels A and B." Another cryptic cult reference. Perhaps I should start a glossary. I speculated what it might mean. My best guess was that Levels A and B were planes of existence populated by lowly beings whose minds were filled with elementary things like work, family, and friends. I wondered which level I was slumming on.

"Until now, every step I've taken was where I wanted to go ... but things have changed ... you won't see me again for a while ... maybe not again in this lifetime."

Definite alarm bells here. Was this a suicide reference? I liked the way she told her brother not to get all upset by the fact that she might never see him again. Yeah, mellow out, bro.

As I held the letter in my hands, an anxious feeling came over me. I stared at the handwriting—dark, hurried, and intense—and sensed a state of alarm that the words sought to hide.

The grandfather clock in the hall chimed seven and I felt a twinge of panic. Time had slipped away. Even if I left immediately, I was going to be late to the meditation. I would have preferred to do more research on the cult before diving headfirst into The Bliss Project. Then again, going in without predisposed notions might actually help me. When it comes to creative problem-solving, few things are more valuable than a fresh perspective.

I hurried upstairs to get a jacket. As I dashed into my bedroom, I glanced over the clean laundry piled foot-high on my bed. I looked for a fuzzy ball of gray but didn't see one.

"Whitman!"

The house felt strangely empty.

Southern California is car and coyote country. Wanting my cat to live to a ripe old age, I've adopted a policy of never letting him outdoors. I went downstairs and searched in his favorite haunts. No cat. I jogged back upstairs and looked more carefully. As I was closing the window in the guest bedroom, I noticed a tear in the screen. It was possible that Whitman had squeezed himself out the space and onto the garage roof.

I left the house feeling unsettled. I was running late.

6
≈

It looked more like an industrial park than an ashram to me. The directions led me to the business district of central San Diego, down a black asphalt cul-de-sac to an outbreak of squatty cement buildings. I slowed under an amber-colored streetlight and checked the address again. The number on the building matched. This was The Bliss Project all right.

I parked my car out of sight a block away and walked back to the building. The June night was chilly and I was glad I'd remembered my jacket. My dress was short and my legs were bare. This probably hadn't been the smartest thing to wear to a cult event. I thought of the frumpy clothing worn by the pious Moonies who peddled flowers at the airport. Not to mention the asexual Heaven's Gaters, some of whom had gone so far as to castrate themselves rather than succumb to the weakness of the flesh. But I was posing as a worldly newcomer here. Surely my lost soul would be forgiven for flashing a little thigh. Then I remembered Chatfield's alarming tale of being guided to a mattress and accosted by a half-naked female cult member. The whole train of thought left me wishing I'd worn jeans.

Most of the buildings along the street were dark, businesses closed for the night. From the glass door of one of the buildings, a shaft of light spilled onto the sidewalk. As I approached, I could see that the door was slightly ajar. I pushed it open and walked into a nondescript anteroom, empty but for the sturdy gray carpet and a folding table and chair. The chair had the look of having been recently abandoned.

"Hello?"

No one answered my call. I glanced at my watch. I was fifteen minutes late. A guest book filled with signatures sat on the table, along with a pen and a box of adhesive name tags. A small stack of registration forms sat next to the guest book. The forms asked for name, address, phone number, and a tuition fee of $2,995. I whistled under my breath. Applicants were instructed to make their checks payable to The Bliss Project. Visa and MasterCard were also accepted.

Along the wall to my right were three closed doors. I tapped lightly on the first door. No answer. I turned the knob and the door glided open. I walked into a small office that had been converted into what looked like a gift shop. Books, crystals, scented oils, and other New Age paraphernalia were displayed on laminated shelves along the walls. A revolving card rack dominated the far corner.

I perused the card rack, curious as to what kind of greetings would be considered appropriate for this crowd. The cards, calligraphy on grainy recycled paper, appeared to be handmade. The messages were strange:

> *You must be aware of all that is.*
> *Not just the love and the light, but also*
> *the darkness.*

> *Thinking too much about what is happening to you*
> *as you grow spiritually can get in the way of*
> *your transformation.*

Some of the messages were downright creepy:

> *Those who are ready to leave this plane of*
> *existence will have the aid that they need.*

> *Come with Us.*

Not exactly Hallmark material. The other side of the card rack was weirder yet. Not cards, but a series of color photographs of a woman with a wild head of blonde hair, kohl-lined eyes, and bright red lipstick. Outwardly, the woman was stunning. But as I picked up the photo and looked intuitively, an ugly aggressiveness corrupted her beauty the way mildew might ruin a painting. A name was printed on the back of each four-by-six glossy: "Master Malindi."

"May I help you?"

The voice startled me and I stuffed the picture back into the card rack, feeling like I'd been caught shoplifting. I turned to see a slender woman standing at the door. She was wearing a fashionable shag haircut and a sleek lime-green dress.

"Oh, hi," I managed.

The woman's eyes glowed—a little too warmly. "She's beautiful, isn't she?"

She was talking, of course, about the woman in the photograph, Master Malindi. "Yes, um, very striking." Striking as in air raid, that is.

"And you are?"

"Whitney. I called earlier—"

The woman moved forward and rested her hand on my forearm. I got the fungus feeling again.

"I'm so glad you could come tonight, Whitney." The name tag adhering to her bosom read "Kami." Her eyes, close up, looked radioactive. "Master Malindi called to you on the inner planes, and you came. That's a big step."

Her hand didn't move and her pupils continued to bore into mine. I felt like a bug trapped in a beam of sunlight through a magnifying glass. A couple more seconds of Kami's intense focus and I might fry.

I turned away, faking a distressed sigh.

"I probably can't afford to take the course."

"We can talk about that later. You're here for a reason. Master Malindi welcomes you. Come." She walked back toward the door, her outstretched hand inviting me to come along.

Come with Us.

I followed her across the anteroom. She reached the third door and turned to me before opening it.

"We've just started our Let Go meditation," she said. "You came tonight with troubles weighing on your heart and mind. I can see the worry and fear when I look in your eyes. This is so great for you. You'll have the opportunity to totally let your fears go. Ready?" She smiled and turned the knob.

The door opened onto a large conference-sized room. What should have looked mundane appeared foreign and mysterious. The expanse was nearly black due to the absence of overhead lighting. The only dim illumination came from stage lighting—radiant dollops of purple, green, red, and blue along the walls and ceiling. There were no chairs or furniture of any kind. A gathering of perhaps two hundred people stood in a large circle around the perimeter of the room.

Just as my eyes became accustomed to the dark, a thunderous booming began. It seemed to come from everywhere and nowhere at once. I recognized the bass line from David Bowie's disco classic, "Jean Genie." As the music played, the colored lights along the walls began to dance and the human circle began to move.

Kami took my arm and tried to pull me into the sea of dancing bodies. Playing the part of the reluctant newcomer, I shook my head and pulled away. I leaned against the wall and watched as she gyrated away in her slinky lime-green dress, blending with the mass of writhing forms moving counterclockwise around the room.

It's a bit unnerving, being the only person standing dead still in a crowd of two hundred dancing bodies. Yet I might as well have been invisible. The others were lost in their frenzied ritual, paying little attention to what was happening outside of them.

Jean Genie, let yourself go!

As my eyes continued to adjust to the darkness, I took stock of the crowd. It was about equal parts male and female. The dress code for men and women alike seemed to be New Age Vamp. Several men lunged past wearing loose, flowing pants and no shirts. A few danced by in skintight jeans and tie-dye muscle shirts. They moved with a decidedly carnal rhythm. Judging from their pelvic action, I surmised that none of them had been castrated. The women were outfitted in everything from skimpy bra tops and gauzy skirts to sheer, form-fitting bodysuits. As one woman danced by, the scarf draped around her upper torso unraveled and floated to the ground. I watched as she twirled, bare-breasted, out of sight. I couldn't resist the urge to giggle. Chatfield hadn't been kidding, or even exaggerating. So much for my worldly short dress.

I looked overhead to see where the pounding rock 'n' roll was coming from. I counted fourteen enormous JBL speakers mounted around the room near the ceiling. Sensual Sensurround.

While I was on the subject of counting, I thought about the registration forms I'd seen on my way in. I did the math. If only half of these people had registered for the weeklong course at three thousand dollars a head, that was three hundred grand. How many courses were offered each month? It was safe to say at least two. That was six hundred grand a month. I subtracted handsomely for overhead and still came up with over seven million dollars a year. No wonder they called it The Bliss Project.

The music changed tempo. Bowie's pounding rhythm faded out and a familiar melody flooded the room. Violins swelled into the emotionally charged Beatles' song, "The Long and Winding Road." The colored lights around the room dimmed to black, and a single white spotlight shone down on the front stage where a woman stood in a long, flowing robe of pure white satin. The spotlight hit her platinum-blonde hair, creating a luminous white halo around her head. This was sheer theatrical lighting. I've seen plenty of real auras. A real aura is a living, undulating thing. Dramatic as the light around this woman was, it didn't move. It was static and inert. A stage illusion.

"I have come to take you Home," the woman said.

I looked around the room. The men and women who just moments ago had been supercharged with movement now stood still as stone. Every head was turned toward the spotlighted stage, every eye fixed on the woman with the fake aura.

"The Process leads Home, and when you reach Home, you'll be Free."

She held her lips close to the microphone and spoke slowly, in a breathy voice. Kind of a combination of Madonna, Marilyn Monroe, and the historical Madonna. In Hollywood parlance, she had It, the celebrity vibe.

"The energy that will transform the world has been

brought into this plane of existence. Each day, the energy is increasing in power all over this planet. *You* are a part of this transformation. *You* are a part of this power."

With that, the speakers overhead burst into a deafening rendition of the ubiquitous dance tune, "I've Got the Power." Fists shot into the air and the bodies once again began their mass writhing. I shrank back, weakened by an overwhelming wave of nausea. The sudden onset of my illness caught me off guard and I leaned against the wall, still as possible, waiting for the wooziness to pass. But the nausea pushed up forcibly. I ran out the door, desperate to find a bathroom.

Later, I stood at the sink, my face white and drawn in the mirror. My hands were still shaking as I washed them. I tried to think what I'd eaten that might have caused such a violent reaction. But I didn't really believe I was suffering from food poisoning. My body was talking to me. It often tells me things my brain is slow to hear. Something was going on it that room that my body wanted me to beware of. I wiped my hands and face with a paper towel and turned to go.

Kami stood at the door of the bathroom.

"Sometimes that happens," she said.

How long had she been there?

"What happens?"

"The part of you that resists the transformation fights against it. It's okay that's happening. Just notice it, but don't give it any power. It'll pass. Maybe we can sit outside and talk about it."

The thought of sharing my personal space with this woman brought on another tremor of nausea.

"I'm really just not feeling well," I said in all honesty. "I'll have to come back some other time."

She didn't make it easy for me to go. I had to push past her to get out of the bathroom.

"Whitney!" she shouted after me.

"Sorry," I called back over my shoulder. "Maybe to-morrow, okay?"

I walked briskly through the anteroom and out the door. The cool night air hit my face and I sucked it in as if I'd been drowning.

I'd just reached the curb when I heard footsteps behind me. As I turned, Kami grabbed my arm.

"I must tell you something," she said.

She was positioned perfectly for a swift rear kick to the kneecaps. It was all I could do to refrain.

"Not now."

"Part of your upsetness is because you've recently lost something very dear to you."

The classic fortune-teller bluff. I pulled my arm away.

She spoke faster. "A little one, specially dear to you."

My heart skipped a beat. I thought of the torn screen in my guest bedroom and my cat's disappearance, then chided myself for nearly falling for one of the oldest tricks in the book. Victims of groups like this one are often trying to fill a void left by a loss of some kind, be it job, relationship, or family. Kami knew that, and was banking on it.

I glared at her.

"The only thing I've lost recently is my cookies. I gotta get home."

I resumed walking and she followed alongside me, rubbing her arms against the chilly night air. I could feel her staring at my face, but didn't look at her.

She stopped following me halfway down the block.

"Good-bye for now, Whitney," she called after me. "But please remember that losses are simply reminders that you have not been transformed. Pain reminds you that you're not yet Free."

I waited at the corner until she turned and disappeared back into the building. I hurried into my car, slammed the door, and pulled out of there burning rubber.

7

≈

Four lanes of traffic turned into a sea of red taillights and I slammed on my brakes. A hundred feet later, I saw the problem. A Dodge van engulfed in flames sat burning on the median divider. A man in a white T-shirt waved the traffic on by. It was a troubling image, but not the one that haunted me the rest of the way home.

I kept seeing a human form appearing in the path of my headlights, then a nightmarish sequence of the body crumpling against the grille of my car. I couldn't connect this vision to any part of my life. Was this merely some flotsam and jetsam from the deluge of violent imagery the media exposed me to every day? I wasn't sure. I only knew how relieved I was to turn up Juniper Street and finally see my house coming into view.

As I pulled into the driveway, my headlights caught the shape of a real man huddled on the steps of my front porch. I noted a Buick Regal parked on the street and put it together, but wondered why McGowan hadn't simply used his key. What I saw as I came up the walk filled me with joy. My cat sat regally between McGowan's legs, enjoying an ear and neck massage.

"Welcome home. Looks like Whitman and I both forgot our keys. Isn't he supposed to be inside?"

"He certainly is."

I bent down to pet my little runaway, who calmly rubbed his whiskers against my hand, showing no signs of guilt or remorse.

"How long have you been here?" I asked.

"Just a couple minutes. I was about to call you on your car phone, but this old charmer here talked me into some petting first. I figured you'd be home any minute. You okay? You look pale."

"Let's talk about it inside. I need a bath."

I unlocked the door and the three of us piled inside. Whitman headed straight for his food bowl in the kitchen. McGowan started up the stairs, an overnight bag on his shoulder. When he reached the landing, he turned to me.

"Vince called me this afternoon. Told me you'd decided to take the case." His eyes held mine. "I really want to thank you for looking into this. You didn't have to. I know this can't be easy."

I passed him on my way upstairs and gave his arm a squeeze.

"Don't feel so guilty. Mr. Shaffer eased my suffering today with a handsome retainer." As retainers go, it was more like drop-dead gorgeous, but I didn't want to get into that just now. "Speaking of Mr. Shaffer, he said you'd had that package of Jen's things analyzed for prints. The Bureau's not taking an interest in her case, is it?"

"No. There aren't any grounds for that at this point. I got a freelance fingerprint guy to dust the stuff, as a favor to Vince."

I walked into the bedroom and turned on the light.

"You run the prints yet?"

"Yeah. Plenty of prints, no matches to anyone with a police record. But they might come in handy later."

"That's true. Thanks."

I took off my jacket and riffled the closet for an empty hanger.

"So I got a little taste of The Bliss Project tonight."

McGowan placed his overnight bag on the big wooden chest at the end of my bed.

"You're kidding. Already? What was it like?"

"Let's just say it wasn't what I was expecting. I guess I made some erroneous assumptions about Jen. Not that you've ever really talked much about her. I mean, apart from mentioning that perverted sex you and she used to have." I said it in my most serious voice.

His body froze and he looked at me sideways. I'd fooled him.

I smiled. "Just kidding."

He gave his forehead a dramatic swipe.

"Whew! You had me worried for a minute there.

Thought I might have let some of that stuff slip."

I felt my smile fade.

"What was she like?" I was serious this time.

He plumped some pillows against the headboard, then lowered himself onto the bed and sighed.

"Complicated."

"How do you mean, complicated?"

"Jen was extremely bright—almost as smart as you are."

His flippant tone annoyed me.

"Don't dance around this subject, Tom. Really. I need information here. Be straight with me."

His gaze was level.

"I am being straight with you." He got up and went to his bag, unzipped one of the compartments, pulled out a navy-blue photo album and began leafing through the pages.

"We met in college, when we were both finishing up teaching degrees. Jen sat in the front row of my Medieval Europe class. She was always the high scorer on tests. I used to tease her that she was ruining the curve for the rest of us morons. She started sitting next to me in the back after that. The rest, no pun intended, is history."

I closed the closet door.

"An era I know very little about. How'd you get from the Middle Ages nearly all the way to the altar? I mean, what attracted you to her, and vice versa?"

He sat down on the bed again and continued flipping through the album.

"I think the main bond we felt was a kind of mutual insecurity. We'd both lost parents at a young age. We were both about to be thrown out of the ivory tower and into the real world."

I'd known about the early death of McGowan's parents. His mother died of cancer when he was just seventeen. His father, who'd been considerably older than his mom, died two years later.

I sat next to him on the bed and looked over his shoulder at the photos.

"When did Jen lose her mother?" I'd wanted to put the question to Vince Shaffer, but hadn't had the heart to bring up the subject. Not when he was still so raw over the disappearance of his daughter.

"She and her brother were just little kids when it happened. I think Jen was like four and Jeremy was nine or ten. He became the ultimate overprotective big brother after that. They were real close."

He stopped turning the pages and pointed to a small photo.

"Here. This is a snapshot of Jen and me in front of her old car."

I picked up the album and squinted at the picture. The photo showed McGowan leaning against a VW bug painted an ugly seafoam green. His arm was cradled around a thin woman with long blonde hair. Were it not for the familiar shape of his broad shoulders and distinctive large stature, I might not have recognized McGowan. His features were blurred, partly by the out-of-focus camera, partly by youthful chubbiness. His hair, parted on the side, streamed past his shoulders.

"My oh my," I said, laughing softly. I looked closely at the girl. "This is Jen? I thought she had red hair."

"Not that year. She was always changing her look, even back then."

I flipped to the next page. In the center was an arresting close-up of Jen, now with red hair. No glasses. Her eyes, a beautiful shade of deep blue, looked slightly startled, as if the camera had come upon her unexpectedly. The next few pages were filled with landscape shots. The ocean at sunset. The Sierra Nevadas in snow. Pretty, but never as interesting as people pictures. Then the photos stopped. The last several pages were blank.

McGowan took the album from me and put it aside.

"Moving in together was a mistake, I can see that now. We really didn't know each other that well. The next two and a half years were difficult."

"In what way?"

"Too much work, not enough play. I got a job as an English teacher. Jen was really into politics and got a pretty demanding job as an activist. At the same time, she was working on her master's, so there was a lot of stress there. She had her hopes set on getting a teaching position at the university. She applied but didn't make it. That caused even more tension."

He sat back against the headboard. "But enough about that. Tell me what you saw at this cult thing tonight."

Just the mention of The Bliss Project brought back an unclean feeling.

"Not so fast. I have more questions about Jen. I need to get a better feeling for her. I want to understand what motivated her to drop a completely promising life in favor of . . . well, I'll get to that part later."

I walked into the bathroom and turned the big brass handles on my clawfoot bathtub. The water splashed loudly into the deep porcelain basin, the sound bouncing off the walls and tiled floor. I raised my voice to be heard above the noise.

"So about Jen's activist job. That was her stint with the California Crime Victims' Association?"

"Yeah." McGowan's voice was right behind me. He stood at the entrance to the bath, leaning on the doorjamb.

"What inspired her to do that? I mean, why a crime victims' association?" I walked across the room, lifted my hair and turned my back to McGowan. "Can you unzip me, please?"

As he pulled the zipper of my dress, I felt tiny kisses along my upper spine. I turned around.

"Was Jen a crime victim?"

"Not directly. Her mom had been killed by a drunk driver. Political activism was her way of working that out, I guess."

I thought of the image I'd seen on my way home tonight—a body crumpling against the front fender.

"Was her mom's body thrown from the car?" I asked.

McGowan made a face. "Kind of a morbid question, isn't it?"

"There's a reason I'm asking."

"No, the drunk ran a red. Her mom's car was broadsided."

"I see." So much for that connection.

I took a bottle of bubble bath and poured it into the water crashing from the spout. The room filled with the scent of

jasmine. I slipped out of my dress and underthings and into
the sudsy water.

"So when did you two get engaged? Was that when you
were teaching high-school English?"

"Yeah, we got engaged right before we moved in together. Then things got stressful for me too, when I was
teaching during the day and going to police academy at
night."

"Not a lot of time for the relationship, I'll bet."

"Not for that relationship, anyway."

I thought the rush of running water might have played
tricks on my hearing. I turned the water pressure down.

"What did you say?"

McGowan tried to dismiss it with a wave of his hand.

"Forget it."

"Tom, talk to me."

He put the toilet seat down and sat resting his head on
his hand, "Thinker" like. His troubled posture.

"I guess this is pertinent," he finally said.

I waited. My heart started to beat faster.

"After Jen got turned down for that university job she'd
wanted so bad, she started pulling away from me. She'd go
into silences that would sometimes last for days. Plus, she
was worried about her brother. He was a new prosecutor
in the DA's office and had just lost a really important
case—"

"Tom." I said it firmly and managed to get him to look
at me. "What happened?"

"I met someone at the academy. We had a thing."

In all the years I'd known McGowan, this had never
come up. The shock left me feeling like the floor had
dropped out from under the tub. The jasmine smelled sick-
eningly sweet and the bathwater felt too cold. My nakedness was suddenly uncomfortable.

"Why didn't you tell me this before?"

"I mentioned it once."

I had no recollection of such a conversation. My expression must have spoken for me, because McGowan went
on to explain.

"Remember? I told you about Lucy, from the police
academy."

I turned on more hot water.

"Yes, I do remember you talking about someone named Lucy. Guess I just never caught on to the part about you seeing her and Jen simultaneously."

McGowan bowed his head.

"I didn't go into detail because I was ashamed. I was ashamed about it then and I'm ashamed about it now."

Thoughts were crossing my mind in all directions. I decided to deal with most of them later.

"Well, I'm glad you're telling me about it now, anyway."

"Better late than never?"

I nodded slowly. "Yeah. Definitely."

The shock began to pass and my head started to clear. I tried to imagine this strange, straying Tom of ten years ago.

"Why'd you go behind her back? It seems so out of character."

"I know. Believe me, I've thought about this a lot. I'm not trying to justify my behavior, because I can't. I was immature and selfish. I punished Jen for all the attention she was diverting from me and putting into her politics. Not to mention all the energy she was giving to her father and brother. I had a lot of resentment about the amount of time she spent on them. It was ridiculous."

"How much is ridiculous?"

"She talked to them—I mean long conversations—literally every day." He sighed deeply. "I think that ultimately I was just looking for a way out of the relationship. It was hard to find a legitimate reason to break up with someone who was so smart and socially conscious and all that. I admired her like crazy but once that wore off, I wasn't really all that comfortable living with her. But rather than deal with it, I just screwed things up."

"Did she know about your affair?"

"Yeah, she found out."

I thought back to the letter I'd found in Chatfield's folder today and Jen's reference to "what started it all." Now I could see at least two reasons this young woman had dropped out. Her promising career hadn't taken off in the direction she'd wanted it to go and the man she thought she'd marry had been unfaithful.

"So when she found out about your affair, that's when she went into the cult?"

McGowan nodded. "Shortly afterward. It was all pretty sudden."

I reached for the long-handled brush and started to scrub my back but McGowan grabbed it out of my hands.

"Here, let me do that."

"So when was the last time you actually saw her?"

He moved the brush in a circular motion around my spine.

"A few weeks after she moved out. She came to tell me she'd be traveling out of the country with some friends from the church. She said she was sad about what had happened and wanted me to know that a part of her would always love me."

"Was she peaceful about it?"

The brush stopped moving on my back. When I looked up, McGowan was frowning.

"Hardly. She was even more upset than the day she moved out."

"Upset how? You mean angry?"

"No, she was crying." He dipped the brush in the water and resumed scrubbing.

"Do you think she was being coerced by the group in any way?"

"No. I'm sure about that. She was adamant that her old life was finished and she was turning over a new leaf. I remember she used those words."

"So let me get this straight. Even after she went into the cult, her dad and brother had contact with her—at least off and on—until two years ago, right?"

He nodded. "Very brief contact. You'll have to ask them about that."

"Then, after two years of silence, this package shows up."

"That's what I understand."

Again I wondered who might have sent the package, and why. I took the brush back from McGowan and hung it on the faucet, then stood and wrapped myself in a fluffy purple towel.

"I'm beat," I said. "What a night."

His voice brightened. "Tell me about this cult event. Lots of shaved heads and loose black clothing?"

Refrains from "Jean Genie" played in my head and I laughed under my breath.

"Not exactly."

"Well, what was it like?"

"If I had to put it in a nutshell, I guess I'd say it was sort of like a hedonistic New Age revival meeting."

"Hedonistic? In what way?"

I dropped the towel, unhooked the nightie hanging on the back of the bathroom door and slipped it over my head.

"Oh, you know," I said as I walked into the bedroom. "Half-naked bodies, loud rock and roll, that sort of stuff."

McGowan followed me and sat on the bed.

"The Church of the Risen Lord? Are you sure you got the right cult?"

"No, dear. This is the new, improved Bliss Project. Same founding messiah, new image."

"So did you see this messiah? Was he impressive?"

"Yes, as a matter of fact, I did see the messiah. *She* was a real showstopper."

McGowan's mouth was hanging open. "Wha—" He stopped mid-word and shook his head. "Forget it." He reached for my hand. "I don't want to talk about this anymore. I want to know if you're mad at me."

He gazed at me through his amazing brown eyes, large from a distance and enormous up close.

"It was cowardly not to tell you about what really happened with her."

I agreed completely, but didn't say so.

"What were you afraid I'd do if I knew the truth?"

He shrugged. "I don't know." A grin tugged at the corners of his mouth. "I guess I rationalized that you were psychic and probably knew about my past sins on some level anyway."

I lay back on the pillows.

"Tom, Tom, Tom. When are you going to believe me

when I tell you that once I'm invested emotionally, my psychic accuracy flies out the window?"

He rolled onto me and kissed my mouth long and tenderly. I did my best to put my doubts aside. When I opened my eyes, he was peering at me from three inches away. The color in his face had deepened.

"You're not the only one who's invested emotionally here."

We kissed again, and heard a loud thud—something had dropped off the bed onto the floor. We hung our heads over the side and saw that the photo album had fallen open to a picture of Jen, Tom, and a third man.

"Who's that?" I asked.

"Oh, that's Jeremy. Jen's brother. God, I resented that guy."

8
≈

I got my first real glimpse of Jen as I was brushing my teeth.

Or was it real? I was leaning on the bathroom sink, still groggy with sleep. Most mornings I'm coherent enough to remember that we have a chronic water shortage in Southern California and that I should turn off the tap as I brush. But the gremlins from last night's talk with McGowan had found their way into my sleep cycle. I'd lain awake listening to Whitman's and McGowan's measured breathing long after they'd checked out. What little rest I did get had been fitful. Which explains why I was staring, somewhat stupefied, into the water swirling down the drain.

Mesmerized by the spiraling liquid, I began to see images, as if I were remembering pieces of a dream. A cultivated green field. A red barn. A tower painted black. I thought nothing of these images at first. Literally, nothing. I was too groggy to think.

My mouth still felt stale. I reloaded my toothbrush and continued brushing, making an effort to prioritize the day's duties. I wanted to talk with Jen's brother, Jeremy Shaffer. I was just figuring out how I'd go about getting in touch with him when I realized I was still seeing the green field in my mind's eye. I decided to pay attention. I stopped brushing and turned off the water.

Visions, clairvoyance, remote viewing—call it what you will. It's like any of my other psi abilities. Gossamer stuff, easily blown away by too much effort. The minute I start to force a vision, it dissolves like a cube of sugar in a cup of hot tea. I had a memory of the green field, but was no longer seeing it in real time. I held tightly to the visual for a minute, bringing back the red barn and black tower as well. The images dutifully appeared in my mind but then just sat there, inert. I sighed and let them go.

I turned on the water again to rinse off my toothbrush. Jeremy worked in the DA's office and would undoubtedly be listed. Or I could get his direct number from his father. I realized I was seeing the barn again and tried not to get excited about it. *Yeah, I see you. So what?* I wondered if there would be any possibility that Jeremy could get free for lunch today. I had a number of questions about his sister and was curious to hear a prosecutor's perspective on what his father insisted was a kidnapping.

In my mind's eye, a woman was hurrying past the barn. She wore sloppy overalls and a knit cap, so it was practically impossible to identify her. Still, I knew this was Jen— the way you sometimes know in dreams who people are even though you don't have much visual information to go on.

The vision faded. I waited for a while, but no new images appeared and the old ones did not come to life. When I was convinced that this morning's psychic newsreel had ended, I put on my robe and slippers and schlepped into my office. I turned on my computer and opened the log I'd begun yesterday on the case. When the file came up, I wrote descriptions of the images I'd just seen, careful to include every detail.

"You're up and at it early this morning."

I turned to see McGowan headed my way with a steaming cup of coffee.

"Don't be fooled. Just because I'm sitting up doesn't mean I'm awake. Thanks."

I took the coffee gratefully and showed my appreciation with an air kiss. He'd be returning to Virginia tomorrow and I was going to miss him. I took a long draw of the steaming brew and noticed that he was completely dressed, shoes and all.

"So what's on your agenda today?" I asked.

"Wrapping up the hostage-negotiation conference. Should be done around four o'clock. After that, hopefully spending some quality time with you before heading back east. My place, like seven or so?"

"Sure. I'll call before I head over." I turned back to my case log.

"Elizabeth?"

"Yeah?"

He didn't answer until I faced him.

"Is there any part of your brain that thinks that because I cheated on Jen ten years ago, I might be capable of cheating on you today?"

I sat back in my chair and gave it some serious thought. Did any part of me seriously believe that? I shook my head.

"No. I just wish you'd told me sooner."

"Me, too. Sorry."

"It's okay. Nobody died."

My last words hung heavily. I'd said them in jest, but they begged the question: Did Jen run off and die?

Apparently, McGowan was thinking along the same lines.

"Least we hope not."

He sighed and left the room. I thought of the woman walking past the barn. With that in mind, I picked up the phone and dialed Jen's father.

I decided not to tell Vince Shaffer anything about the images I'd seen this morning. I've learned to keep my psychic insights close to the vest until I have corroborating data. For whatever reason, people expect miracles from psychics. I tell my clients up front that my gift is sporadic and occasionally unreliable. That it usually takes me some time to settle into a case before I can make sense of any extrasensory info I might get. I explain to them that I spent three years preparing to become a licensed, run-of-the-mill PI so that I could be making useful progress on an investigation when my psychic ability falls short. No matter how bluntly I convey this, people still carry a belief in magical, instant results. Not that I blame them. I do it myself from time to time.

I heard the hope of magical results in Vince Shaffer's voice on the phone now.

"Hello! I didn't expect to hear from you so soon. Surely you don't have news yet?"

His voice rang with an optimism I hadn't heard yesterday, a happiness he couldn't suppress. Although I'd barely had time to absorb the basics on his daughter's disappearance, Jen's father was wishing against odds that the answer to her whereabouts had come to me in an instantaneous psychic flash. It happened on TV, so why not to me?

I hated to bring him back to the real world.

"No news yet. I'm still just getting up to speed. I met with Scott Chatfield yesterday. I've got a few questions I need to ask, if you have a minute or two."

"Of course." His disappointment was palpable. "Go right ahead."

First I asked him to give me his son's number at the DA's office, which he rattled off from memory.

"Jeremy's in the middle of a trial," he added, "so I'm not sure he'll be able to talk with you right away. I guess you two can work that out."

"Thanks. Now, when I spoke with you yesterday, you mentioned talking with a person who'd left The Bliss Project. I've looked through Chatfield's file and I don't see any references to former cult members."

"No, there wouldn't be. That was a contact I made on my own."

"I see. I'd like to follow up where you left off. You still have the name and number of this person?"

He hesitated. "Ah . . . I gave this man my word that I would keep our communication utterly confidential. His name is Mike Hugo. But I can't pass out his number, not even to you."

"Could you call him maybe? See if he'd agree to talk to me?"

"I was just going to suggest that."

"Thanks. I'll be at my office number. Think you can get back to me this morning?"

"I'm not sure I'll be able to reach him that quickly, but I'll call you back this morning either way."

I thanked him and hung up. My call to Jeremy Shaffer was next. I was just reaching for the phone when it rang.

"Okay, Jennifer Janine Shaffer changed her voter registration in September of nineteen eighty-six, from Democrat to Independent." Joanne hadn't even bothered to say hello. She was all business this morning. "Other than that, no public transactions of any kind. No credit apps, no citations, no marriages, no nothin'. Now it's your turn."

Joanne's findings basically confirmed the first investigator's work. It had taken her a day to do what Access Research had dragged out for three months. That made me smile.

"Good morning, Joanne. How are you today?"

"Fine. Now tell me what you pick up about Brad Aiken. Come on."

Apparently Joanne was still enamored with her mystery man.

"Jo, we've been down this road. I'm not a phone psychic. What do you want me to do? Tell you that behind his suave, carefree exterior, Brad Aiken is a man running from the IRS?"

"He is?" She sounded incredulous.

"No, Joanne, I just made that up. I told you I don't do this kind of thing."

"But that would make total sense. And he is suave and carefree."

"I can't believe you're being so gullible right now. It's a coincidence, Jo."

"I thought you said there are no coincidences."

She was right. I often did say that.

"I'm telling you I made up the part about the IRS. Please believe me." I'd made up the part about Mr. Aiken being suave and carefree, too. Lucky guess, I suppose.

"Whatever," she said. "I'm going to check it out, though."

"Well, in my mind I still owe you for the info on Jennifer Shaffer. Thanks."

"No big. Talk to you later."

I was getting up to stretch my legs and refill my coffee when the phone rang again. I picked it up expecting to hear Vince Shaffer's voice.

"Is Elizabeth Chase there?" The voice was low, guarded.

"Yes. Speaking."

"Someone told me you were trying to reach me. You know who that was, right?"

I assumed this was the former cult member, Mike Hugo. For some reason, he didn't want to name names, which I thought was a touch paranoid.

"You must be talking about Vince Shaffer," I said.

"Yeah, that's right."

"And you are—"

"Please, I'd rather not say over the phone."

Definitely paranoid.

"Well, thanks for calling. Do you have a few minutes to talk?"

"Not on the phone."

I searched my mind for a crowded public place where we could meet.

"How about meeting for lunch at, say, The Fish Market in Del Mar?"

He made a strange sound, low and rasping. It took me a minute to figure out that he was laughing.

"I must have missed the joke," I said.

"It'll take a day to get here and back."

"Oh, I see." I cursed silently to myself. "Well, that changes things. I assumed you lived in the area."

"You want to talk to me."

"Well, that would have been helpful. But since you're not willing to talk on the phone—"

He made another rasping laugh.

"No. Again you don't get it. You *want* to talk to me."

His implication was clear. Either I talked to him or I was an idiot.

"And why do I want to talk to you?"

"Because what I have to say might save your life, that's why."

Inwardly, I felt myself protesting against his drama and hype. Protesting too much, perhaps.

"Okay," I said. "What's the next step?"

"Ask Jeremy Shaffer."

With that, the line went dead.

9

≋

"Jeremy?"

I recognized him in the sea of faces streaming through the courtroom door.

He turned at the sound of my voice, then pointed an index finger at my face.

"You're the PI?"

We were standing in the hallway of the San Diego Superior Court. It occurred to me that dozens of investigators roamed these halls on a daily basis.

"I'm *a* PI," I answered. "Whether or not I'm *the* PI, I don't know. I'm the one your father hired."

He looked over his shoulder as if he were concerned that somebody might be paying special attention to our exchange. When he was satisfied that the people hovering nearby were preoccupied with their own conversations, he extended his hand.

"Hi. I'm Jeremy. But then you knew that already. Dad said you were a psychic. Must be true." He pumped my hand, his eyes shining.

I pumped back.

"Not to destroy my mystique, but I recognized you from family photographs."

"Oh." The light went out of his eyes. "Well, sorry you had to wait so long for the court to recess. This morning's testimony rambled on like a boring joke."

"I'm just glad you could see me on such short notice."

"High priority." He lowered his voice. "This is my sister we're talking about. Come on, let's get out of here. Hope you don't mind if we put a little distance between ourselves and the courthouse. There's a decent Thai place up in Hillcrest. It's about a five-minute drive."

"Sounds great."

As we walked out the main entrance into the bright midday sun, Jeremy Shaffer replaced his pale-rimmed glasses with a pair of high-priced shades. He wasn't quite as tall as his father but he carried himself with the same authority and had the same impeccable taste in clothing. His thick, golden hair had been cut with razor precision in a style that struck a perfect balance between conservative and flashy. I tried to get a read on the man behind the image. I picked up tense shoulder muscles and lower back pain. Outwardly, he was in perfect shape; inwardly, he was carrying too much weight.

When we were halfway down the block, he pulled a sheet of paper, folded lengthwise, out of his inside coat pocket.

"This was faxed to you care of my machine about a half hour ago. It's from the Puma Man. He left a voice mail saying you'd know what to do with it."

I took the paper from him. The message had been handwritten, not typed. It was addressed to Elizabeth Chase from "MH" and consisted of highway directions in six haphazardly printed lines. A crude map had been drawn at the bottom of the page.

"Do you know this guy?" I asked.

"Mike Hugo. Former member of The Bliss Project. Besides Jen, he's the only contact Dad and I ever had with the cult. He got out a couple years ago, gave an interview to the *Union-Tribune*. We reached him through the paper. You know him?"

"Your father persuaded him to call me. He sounded a little strange."

Jeremy shook his head. "What can you say about a guy who calls himself Puma Man?"

"Good point."

Hugo/Puma Man had told me on the phone that my next

step was to inquire with Jeremy Shaffer. Now this. I read his directions over more carefully. The first line instructed me to drive north on Highway 101 for 432 miles. That was more than halfway to San Francisco. I wasn't sure I liked where this was going. I supposed it was better than no direction at all. At least I hoped so.

At the end of the block, Jeremy turned into an underground parking garage.

"I'm in the Beemer," he said, pointing to a black sports car one aisle over.

As I came up on the passenger-side door, I felt something was off. I was trying to ascertain just exactly what when I heard him yell out.

"Goddamn it!"

I turned to see Jeremy bending at the waist. At first, I thought he was hurt. Then he began circling the back of the car. I looked down and saw the source of his distress. All four tires had been slashed. That accounted for the oddness I'd sensed. With no air in the tires, the car sat lower than it should have.

Jeremy cursed again, then caught himself. "I'm sorry. I'm really sorry. These were brand-new tires. *Damn* it."

He walked around to the front of the car.

"Oh, Jesus."

The windshield had been pummeled into a mosaic of shattered glass.

I stared at the beat-up car. "Is this a random act of unkindness, or do you think it's personal?"

"What do you think, psychic detective?"

"I think that sometimes prosecutors are not very popular people."

"No, we're not, are we?" His face was turning red.

"We can take my car," I offered.

He shook his head. "Forget it. Let's walk. Do you mind? We can grab a sandwich in Horton Plaza."

If his muscles had been tight before, they were now hardening like cement. Physical exertion would do him good.

"Walking's a great idea," I said.

Jeremy's legs were long and he kept up a furious pace. I enjoyed the exercise and was glad I'd worn comfortable shoes. As we weaved through the lunch-hour crowd toward the plaza, I again tried to tune in on him. It felt to me as if a missing sister were just one of many complications in his life.

We stopped at an outdoor sandwich stand on the outskirts of the plaza. Jeremy bought a pastrami on rye and treated me to an avocado-and-sprout special.

"Mind if we sit on the bench here?" he asked.

"Not at all."

We unwrapped our sandwiches and popped open our drinks.

"There's so much I want to understand about your sister. I know you're the expert at asking questions, so maybe you can help me if I miss anything here." I reached for my purse. "Mind if I use a tape recorder?"

He held out a hand to stop me.

"Actually, I do. Sorry. If you need clarification on anything we discuss here, you can call me."

Bummer. This meant I had to pay attention to the content of his words, which left me less time and energy for paying attention to the context. Context—body language, the vibratory field around someone—was the place where my intuition came alive.

"This would be strictly confidential," I said.

He shook his head. "Sorry. I don't know you that well. The situation with my sister is a very sensitive issue. It could be used to undermine me professionally. I hope you understand."

I hadn't really expected him to give in. I pulled out a notebook and propped it on my knee.

"Okay, your dad thinks that Jen was kidnapped. That's quite a charge. You know as well as anyone how heavy-duty a crime kidnapping is. Do you think that's what happened?"

"Not at first. She definitely went in on her own volition. As for what happened two years ago—" He stopped eating and stared at the ground. "Put it this way, I hope it's only kidnapping. I'm afraid it's worse than that."

"Why? Because of the package that was sent to your dad this week?"

"Because I haven't heard from her since July of ninety-five. That's unheard-of between us. There's just no way she'd stop all communication unless she was being forcibly restrained. Or worse." A deep furrow appeared in his forehead.

"So tell me about the communication you had until two years ago. Did you have an address where you wrote to her? A phone number where you used to call her?"

"No. She always initiated the contact. Wouldn't give me a phone or address."

"I see. How about the package? Do you have any idea who might have sent it?"

He shook his head. "Not really. I mean, at first I thought Jen might have sent the stuff, but then why wouldn't she send a note with it? It didn't make sense. Doesn't make sense."

A pigeon waddled up on my left, looking hungry. I tossed a piece of my bread crust at its scaly little feet.

"There's something else I need to understand. You've worked for the DA how long?"

"About twelve years."

"Twelve years. Wow. So you undoubtedly have access to some of the best investigators in the state. People with powerful connections, important experience."

"Sure."

"So why hire me?"

In the bright sunlight, I could see his eyes squinting behind his sunglasses.

"That's a very good question. No offense, but I probably wouldn't have hired you. From the beginning, my father's insisted on handling this. I've helped where I can, and at this point, it's sort of a joint effort. In fact, I referred him to the last investigator on the case."

"Scott Chatfield?"

"Yeah. He's a real pro. Outstanding reputation, that guy. I was sorry to see him drop the case."

"Are you aware of why he dropped it?"

"Not his cup of tea, he said."

"He was threatened."

Jeremy frowned but said nothing.

"Your father has very strong feelings about The Bliss

Project. If I remember right, he accused them of organized crime. Think there's anything to that?"

The pigeon was now begging Jeremy for crumbs. He shooed the bird back in my direction.

"Look, I don't even want to go there, okay? I—we—just want to find Jen and get her out. The quieter, the better."

I nodded.

"You said Puma Man was your only contact with the cult. So during Jen's first eight years in the group, when you and she were still in touch, did you ever meet any of the people she was living with?"

"No. Most of the time we just talked on the phone. We got together a few times, but usually in public places—restaurants, parks, that kind of thing. She never came home, and I never visited her on any of the group's properties. What I gathered over the years was that the cult strongly discouraged family relationships. Jen said that family ties were viewed as obstacles to getting Free."

There was that word again.

"Tell me about this Free thing. That concept seems to be bandied about quite a bit in this crowd."

"Oh, it's just some crap about how a person's psychological hang-ups—old hurts and resentments and stuff—keep them bound to a lower level of existence. Supposedly, if you get rid of negative influences like family attachments, your consciousness rises to a higher level."

Nothing wrong with unloading resentments to grow spiritually, I thought. But eighty-sixing one's entire family? Kind of like cutting off your leg to lose weight.

"Did Jen ever mention any names you could give me as leads?"

"A few. I gave them to Chatfield. He should have them in his file. But you gotta be careful with names."

"Why's that?"

"No one in the cult goes by their real name. Changing your identity is part of the process of getting Free. Witness Puma Man."

"Did Jen get a new identity?"

"If she did, she never told me what it was."

Jeremy had finished his sandwich. He got up to throw

his wrapper into a nearby trash can. When he returned, I continued with my questions.

"Did you ever try to persuade her to leave the cult?"

"Of course. In the beginning there was a thin line, you know, between imposing my will and letting her make her own mistakes. I wasn't comfortable with her decision to join the group, but I respected her right to choose."

"So tell me about the last time you saw her, two years ago."

"It was at the beach. Torrey Pines. We met at the life-guard tower."

I flashed back to the black tower I'd seen in my mind's eye this morning. But that had been by a field, not the ocean. I jotted a quick note to myself as Jeremy continued his story.

"She told me she might not be able to talk to me for a while, told me not to worry. Something about an important phase in her spiritual growth that would require complete isolation for an extended period of time."

This didn't sound particularly alarming. Swamis were known to disappear for years into the Himalayas to meditate and reach enlightenment.

"What makes you think she's not still in isolation for spiritual reasons?"

He finished his drink and crumpled the can.

"I didn't buy it when she told me. I was worried about her. I had the feeling she was lying. I thought she was in trouble."

"What made you think that?"

"She was teary and shaky and preoccupied. I don't know, it was just a feeling I got." He frowned. "I have to admit, this is a little uncomfortable, being on the hot seat. As a prosecutor, I get irritated with witnesses all the time for being vague, and now I'm afraid I'm doing the same thing. Listen to me—'just a feeling I got.' "

"It's okay. Feelings go a long way in my book. So that meeting under the lifeguard tower at Torrey Pines—that was the last time you heard from her?"

"I got a follow-up letter from her about a week later. Nothing substantial. Basically just a repeat of what we'd talked about on the beach. That was the last communication

I had from her, nearly two summers ago now. That ought to be in Chatfield's file, too."

I didn't tell him I'd already read the letter.

He glanced at his watch. "I wish I had more time, but—"

"You can't be late to court. I understand."

I dropped my garbage into the trash can and tossed a last bite to the pigeon. Our conversation lapsed as we joined the foot traffic along Broadway. Jeremy paused at the courthouse entrance to say good-bye.

"Hey, I wish you luck. At this point, I'm almost afraid to get my hopes up. Let me know if there's anything else I can do." He looked at his watch again.

"Thanks," I said.

He pushed through the glass door.

"Nice meeting you," he called over his shoulder. The door swept closed behind him before he could hear my parting comment.

"Sorry about your car," I said.

10
≈

McGowan pointed to a location several hundred light-years away.

"What did you say that was?"

"Cepheus. But I like that pyramid constellation over there, near Cassiopeia. Such beautiful symmetry, don't you think?"

"Mm-hm."

We were swinging in his oversized backyard hammock, looking at the stars. Both of us were stuffed with too much barbecued corn and sea bass to do much else. I stared into endless space and a familiar awe came over me. I never tire of watching the night sky.

"The light we see from most of those stars left them

before our grandparents were born. Maybe even before re-corded history," I said.

McGowan pulled me closer.

"You really get into this stuff, don't you?"

"Yeah, it fascinates me."

"Before our grandparents were born," he echoed softly. "Makes the human life span seem pretty damn short."

We swung for several minutes in contemplative silence.

"Why do they twinkle?" he asked.

"By the time the light reaches us, it's been bent and scattered by Earth's atmosphere."

I thought about that for a minute. It seemed a good meta-phor. Heavenly light, bent and scattered by the muck down here on the earth plane. Sounded about right.

We fell into another silence and my thoughts turned to the case. After my meeting with Jeremy, I'd spent the re-mainder of the afternoon doing research. A call to the eight-hundred number on Jen's Medic Alert bracelet had confirmed her deadly allergy to bees but yielded no new information. A search at the library and on the Internet turned up plenty of controversial information on Scientol-ogy, the Moonies, The Children of God, Rajneesh's follow-ing, and, of course, Heaven's Gate. But as for The Bliss Project, there'd been only one reference, a small item in *The San Diego Union-Tribune* about the group's hosting of a fund-raiser for the homeless.

The only other written information was the cult litera-ture, which listed the San Diego ashram as the sole contact point. Chatfield's file contained a few cult aliases, but no traceable names or addresses. It was becoming increasingly clear to me that without a paper trail to follow, the only way to move forward would be to infiltrate the cult. Which meant I needed a fake car to go with my fake name.

I nudged Tom's ribs.

"Hey. I know you got rid of your police cruiser, but you still have the Charger, don't you?"

Tom's old muscle car, circa nineteen sixty-seven, was a special vehicle. The kind that for sentimental reasons in-spires such affection that its owner is unable to dump it, even as the decades pass. As long as I'd known McGowan, the Charger had been a permanent resident in his garage.

With its oxidized paint and gap-toothed grille, the car looked horrific. But it drove like a racehorse. And why wouldn't it? He'd always kept the engine in perfect condition.

His tone was reverent, almost shocked that I'd asked.

"Of course I still have it. I plan to be buried in that car. Why do you ask?"

"I need to borrow it. I'm assuming another identity in my dealings with these cult people and I don't want them to trace the real me through my Mustang."

"Sure you're not being paranoid?"

"No. But then it's hard to tell with so many people out to get me."

It was a lame joke. As was his habit, McGowan pretended not to hear it, one of the many reasons I loved him.

"The keys are in the top kitchen drawer," he said.

"Thanks."

"Promise you'll take good care of it."

"I promise."

In the black sky above us, a shooting star streaked toward earth, prompting memory of a childhood superstition: *Star's falling, someone's going to die.*

"Did you see that?" he asked.

"Yup. Big one, huh?"

"Yeah. Do they ever fall on people?"

"It's weird. Thousands of meteors fall to earth every day. Most of them are no bigger than pinheads so they vaporize before they land. But there're so many of them that they're increasing the planet's weight by like a thousand tons a day."

"Wow. You'd think we'd get zapped hard sometimes."

"I know. The only deadly incident I'm aware of was a huge meteorite that killed something like fifteen hundred reindeer in Siberia back in nineteen eight. For the most part, we earthlings have been pretty lucky, I guess."

McGowan shook his head. "I've got enough to think about without worrying that space rocks are going to fall on my head."

"No doubt," I agreed.

"So what do you think of Jen's father and brother?"

"Conservative, obviously. But complex. They seem like

easy people to admire but difficult people to know."

"That's the Shaffers. Jen was pretty much the same way." He sighed. "I have a hard time picturing her dancing with a bunch of New Age types. That really doesn't jibe."

"Maybe you didn't know her as well as you thought."

"That's been bothering me lately."

I felt him holding his breath. Something serious was on his mind.

"I've been thinking," he said.

"About?"

"Us. All the space between us."

This wasn't a new topic. Expressing frustration about the distance between us was a shopworn subject, like complaining about taxes or too little time. We'd spent hours of frank and sometimes painful conversation discussing the matter. We hated being apart, but so far neither one of us had been willing to release the attachments that kept us that way. In my case, a native Californian's love for her home and an intolerance of cold weather. In Tom's case, a passion for his work that made it more of a calling than a career. We loved and honored our interests no more—but no less—than we loved and honored each other. I braced myself for The Talk.

"The space between us sucks. I have nothing new to add on the subject."

"Well, I do," he said.

"Yeah?"

"Yeah. I'm moving to Los Angeles."

I tried to sit up and get a good look at his face to see if he was serious. The hammock rocked unsteadily.

"What are you talking about?"

"I'm talking about a promotion. FBI Los Angeles Bank Squad. The illustrious C-Three. Reporting to the assistant director, no less. It's a big step up. Not to mention a huge step closer to you."

"L.A. Bank Squad? Just like that, out of the blue?"

"I've been jockeying for this gig for months. I didn't want to say anything in case it fell through. I got the call yesterday and accepted on the spot."

"When does this happen?"

"I'm supposed to report to my new boss in three weeks. Don't ask me how I'm going to unload my Virginia condo that fast."

McGowan back in California. One of my most cherished daydreams was suddenly coming true. I could feel my nose starting to sting.

"You'd better not be kidding me."

He shifted his weight and stuffed his hand into his pants pocket. The hammock jerked abruptly toward his side and I had to put my foot to the ground to keep us from being dumped out. Moving cautiously, we settled back into the center. McGowan laughed at his own clumsiness.

"This isn't exactly how I'd envisioned this moment."

He pulled his hand out of his pocket and his laughing stopped. I felt him place a small velvet box in my hands.

"This is to let you know just how much I'm not kidding."

I opened the box. It was too dark to see much detail but a diamond ring is hard to miss. I honestly didn't know what to make of it.

"What—?"

"Don't feel pressured. This doesn't mean you have to sell your house and move to L.A. It's just a little token to show you where my heart is. Although I do hope we'll live in the same area code one day."

I grinned. "Maybe even the same zip code."

I took the gift from its box and slipped it onto my ring finger. Far too large, the band barely grazed my knuckle. I moved the diamond to my middle finger, where it rested snugly. When I raised my hand against the sky, the square gem glinted in the moonlight. The stone was exceptional.

"It was my mom's," he said.

I put my lips close to Tom's ear to thank him but words wouldn't come. I took his head in my hands and pressed my mouth to his, frightened by the intensity of my feeling for him.

When our lips finally parted, McGowan was leaning over me, his face three inches from mine against a backdrop of stars light-years away.

"I love you," he whispered.

Against the night sky, I could see a halo of energy surrounding his head, as clear and sparkling as the diamond he'd just given me.

"I love you, too," I whispered. "Always and ever."

11
≋

I placed two liters of bottled water on the floor of the Charger and filled the passenger-side seat with the rest of my stash—trail mix, apples, sugarless gum, my portable CD player, and a caddy of discs. I walked around and unlatched the hood to check the fluids. Radiator, transmission, windshield cleaner, and engine oil levels were all okay. Still, I had the sense I'd forgotten something. I went back into the house and packed my Glock nine-millimeter in my purse.

Now I felt ready.

I got in, turned the ignition, said a quick prayer to the god of aging engines, and headed north. According to Puma Man's directions, once I cleared Los Angeles, I'd still have nearly three hundred fifty miles to go. Now that Tom was moving to the City of Angels, I imagined I'd be making the southern leg of this trip often. I smiled, realizing that for the first time in years, our parting this morning had been free of angst. I ejected Muddy Waters from my CD player and replaced it with a sunny Mozart concerto.

Traffic slowed to a stop at the border checkpoint near San Clemente. Sixty-seven miles from the actual U.S.–Mexico border, the station gives U.S. agents a chance to apprehend illegals who might have slipped into the country via gulches and canyons. Many undocumented aliens on the run have been hit by cars along this stretch of Interstate 5, which is why signs are posted cautioning motorists to watch for humans fleeing across the freeway. With the San

Onofre nuclear power plant looming nearby, the area has always given me the willies.

As I waited for the green-uniformed agents to wave me through, my thoughts turned to Barry Bell, the investigator who'd closed up shop shortly after looking into Jen's disappearance and hadn't been heard from since. I'd followed up enough to know that neither a death certificate nor a missing-persons report had been filed on him. A long vacation, perhaps? Somehow, I didn't think so.

Three pit stops, five hours, and countless daydreams of Tom later, I turned east off 101 just past Los Alamos. The road dipped and curved past dark-green oak trees into the blond-colored foothills of the Sierra Madre. Puma Man's directions were clear and the road was well marked, but as the miles passed, I began to feel nervous. There were no houses out here, at least none visible from the road. I hoped to God I wasn't lost. I chalked up my anxiety to travel fatigue and kept plugging.

His directions instructed me to turn right on Sisquoc Lane and look for a copse of willow trees and a red barn. Was that a coincidence? I imagined so—many barns are red, after all. According to Puma Man, there would be a house next to the barn, with a white truck in the driveway. I was to pull in and wait. That's all the note said, ending with "See you there tomorrow." No meeting time, no street address.

I was bolstered that the landmarks I was supposed to be seeing were indeed coming into view. The copse of willow trees. The red barn. The white truck, a two-ton Chevy. More gray than white, actually, with an accumulation of dirt and plenty of dings. I pulled into the driveway and turned off the ignition. The engine stopped running, but my body felt like it was still humming. I sighed and sat back in my seat. My eyes felt scratchy and weary. I reached into my purse for some Visine, administered the eyedrops and closed my lids for a moment's relief.

My eyes were startled open by a tapping on the window. I turned to see the muzzle of a twelve-gauge shotgun pointing at my head. The man holding the weapon tapped the tip of the barrel lightly a couple more times against the glass. I took this to mean he wanted me to open the window. Slowly—very slowly—I lowered the glass. I craned my neck ever so slightly to have a look at him.

"Afternoon. Let's see your ID. Your PI license, too." He looked so normal in his Levis and short-sleeved plaid shirt.

"My ID's in my purse."

Of course my Glock was in there too, and I debated whether or not I should tell him. If he happened to see it, he might freak and send my brains all over the dashboard. My fingers found my wallet and I managed to pull it out without my purse flopping open. I handed it over to him, cash, cards, and all. Ordinarily, I wouldn't do this for a stranger. His gun was a definite factor.

He looked through the wallet and nodded.

"What's the plate number on your Charger?"

A strange question, since the plates were in plain view. Then I figured out he was doing everything possible to make sure I was really Elizabeth Chase. For a minute I panicked—this was McGowan's car, after all, and I didn't have the plates memorized. Fortunately, my memory didn't fail me. The license numbers flashed to mind as clearly as if someone were holding a sign in front of me. I rattled them off and couldn't resist adding my two cents.

"Don't worry. Nobody hijacked me on the way up here."

"Good. And if you're lucky, you'll make it back in one piece, too. Come on in."

I got out and wobbled on sea legs. I stomped my feet to get the blood flowing and followed him around his Chevy and into the house through the garage.

We walked into a kitchen, neat and plain as a Quaker's. He laid the shotgun on the counter.

"You can sit at the table there," he said. "I imagine you could use a drink after your long drive. Beer?"

"A drink would be great. Have any soda?"

In the context of this simple kitchen, he looked more normal than ever. A regular guy in his mid-thirties, starting to lose a little of his brown hair at the temples and getting a bit soft above his belt. The kind of guy you might see out mowing his lawn on Saturday.

"I've got root beer," he said.

"Perfect."

He pulled two cans from the fridge and placed one of them on the table in front of me.

"You want a glass with that?"

"No, this is fine, thanks."

"Sorry about the gun." He made a sad smile. "I just have to be careful. My life will probably never be totally normal again, but at least I'm safe now. I think. So how long have you been looking for Shaffer's daughter?"

"This is my third day on the case."

He lifted his eyebrows. "You sure you know what you're doing?"

I shrugged.

"Got family? Kids?"

"No," I said.

"That's good."

I saw where his comments were leading.

"Has it ever occurred to you that you might be paranoid, Mr. Hugo?"

He pulled out a chair and sat down.

"I'm sure it looks that way. You think I'm paranoid?"

I'd asked him a blunt question about his mental health to see how he handled it. His response sounded levelheaded enough.

"Don't know you well enough," I answered.

His face grew dark. "Are you recording our conversation?"

"No, but I'd like to."

"Sorry. Can't let you do that. But I'll tell you what I know. Listen up, because I won't be giving you my phone number and it's unlikely we'll meet again."

"Mind if I take notes? I use my own shorthand, which I assure you is completely illegible to anyone else. Even to me, sometimes."

He struggled with my request for a moment and finally nodded his okay. I pulled out my notebook and pen as Puma Man began his story.

"I was with The Bliss Project for three years. Deep enough that it really fucked with my head."

"What do you mean, deep?"

"Lot of levels to that organization, sister. Levels that go down all the way to hell."

By the intensity in his dark eyes, he meant every word. He popped open his beer and took a swig.

"Anyway, when I got out—when I started to straighten out and see what they'd done to me—I did an exposé-type interview with the San Diego paper. Didn't even mention The Bliss Project's name. Still, it was the biggest mistake of my life."

"Why?"

"They've been fucking with me ever since."

"They?"

"The people on Level X and all the little brainwashed automatons who are willing to carry out their power plays in the name of consciousness liberation."

"Level X. Let me guess. Master Malindi? Abadanda?"

He stared at me hard. There was a scar running through his right eyebrow and down his upper eyelid.

"You have done your homework, haven't you? Well, here's the Cliff Notes' version: Malindi and Abadanda are just figureheads. The real power is on another level altogether. Level X creates and destroys and fucks with Levels A and B for the sheer fun of it."

"Levels A and B?"

"Level A, rationals. The Joe Blows of the world who have no concept about consciousness, who are not aware that reality can be altered through the mind."

Ho, boy.

"So let me just take a stab at Level B," I said. "That must be more open-minded types. People who believe in the power of prayer, healing visualization, stuff like that."

He smiled. "Very good. The cult looks for recruits at Level B, because they're open enough to examine the Process but not sophisticated enough to protect themselves against it."

"The Process?"

"A training that gives recruits just enough power to feel high and just enough oblivion to get trapped. That's my definition, not theirs, obviously."

"When you say 'trapped,' do you mean they hold you against your will?"

"Yes. But they don't tie your body with rope or put you

in a cell. They tie up your thoughts, possess your mind. You might as well be locked up."

"Then why do they keep talking about 'Free'? I keep hearing that word. What do they mean by that?"

"They describe freedom as a level of consciousness beyond time and space, yin and yang, positive and negative. A Free has supposedly reached that level. But if you ask me, Frees are just people who've surrendered to the cult and stopped thinking for themselves. They've let go of the troublesome burden of conscience. No more right and wrong. Anything goes. You ever see *Silence of the Lambs*?"

"Yeah."

"Well, Hannibal Lecter could be the Free poster boy. Know what I'm sayin'?"

Somehow, Hannibal Lecter never struck me as the joiner type, but I think I got Puma Man's point.

"So how has Level X been fucking with you?" I asked.

"Every way possible."

"Name one."

"I got a job working in a mail house about three months after I got out. They vaporized it."

"How do you vaporize a job?"

"I'm not sure exactly how they did it. Any number of ways they could have gone about it. I just went in one day and the department manager let me go. Said he was sorry, but the position had been eliminated."

"What makes you think that wasn't the simple truth?"

"My car was disassembled at the same time and then what do you know? The IRS contacted me with some burning questions. I'm sure they were given false information about me."

"How does one's car get disassembled?"

"It disappears out of your garage overnight." He stood up and went to the window. "I know this sounds crazy. But if you're going after Shaffer's daughter, you need to know what you're up against."

"And why is it worth risking your safety to tell me these things?" I asked.

He turned around, his body silhouetted against the afternoon sun.

"When I got out of the cult, I picked up the burden of conscience again."

I saw the red barn through the window behind him and remembered the images I'd seen while I was brushing my teeth yesterday morning.

"Is there a black tower anywhere around here?"

His silhouette stood stock-still. After a beat, a voice emerged from his darkened form.

"Whoa. That came out of left field." He sounded afraid.

The insight had come out of right field, actually, but this was no time to discuss brain hemispheres.

"Is the black tower connected to The Bliss Project in some way?"

He came back to the table, pulled up his chair and peered into my face.

"Who gave you that information?"

"No one. I just stumbled across it."

"Like hell you did."

Inside my head a signal went off: *pay dirt, pay dirt.* Part of me wanted to jump out of my chair and do the old fist-pumping *Yes!* But I stayed cool.

He went to the window again.

"You're already in danger."

"Why?"

"Ask Zeus." He laughed darkly.

"Who's Zeus?"

"David Sandberg. He was in the Project when I was. For a while, anyway. There used to be a story that he committed suicide. Not anymore. It's all been uncreated."

"What does 'uncreated' mean?"

"Exactly what it sounds like. Not just David, but even the story of his suicide. The whole thing, uncreated. His existence, his death. Didn't happen, see?"

"All I want to do is go in and find Jen. I'll let someone else worry about David Sandberg."

"Just a cautionary tale, sister."

"Did you ever know Jen Shaffer, or see her when you were with The Bliss Project?"

"I don't think so. Hard to tell. People there don't go by their given names, you know. Her father, of course, wanted to know the same thing. I didn't recall anyone there that resembled the pictures he showed me."

I dug in my purse for an envelope and handed it to him. Inside were pictures of Jen from McGowan's photo album. Worth a try. Puma Man sorted through them, stopping at the close-up showing her red hair and arresting blue eyes. He studied it for a long time, then put the pictures back into the envelope and returned them to me.

"You know, maybe I do recognize her."

"Where did you last see her?"

"Not sure. She just looks kind of familiar."

That didn't help me much. "If you had to find her, where would you look first?"

"You'll have to go inside and be like them. Believe me, they know who outsiders are."

He snatched my empty can and carried it with his into the kitchen. The cans made a rattling noise as he tossed them into the trash can under the sink.

"If you're thinking of going into the cult undercover, don't be surprised when your personal records start getting illegally retrieved from an outfit called Light Works Education Services. Be prepared to talk to the IRS. Have an attorney available to handle the nuisance lawsuits that'll start cropping up. If you're framed for a serious crime, don't say I didn't warn you. Oh, and check your brakes often."

He looked up at the clock above the refrigerator.

"I've got to be out of here soon. This isn't my house, you realize."

"No, I didn't know that."

"I don't even live in this county. If you want to contact me again, you have to go through the Shaffers, just like before."

He went to the door and held it open for me, an invitation to go.

"Just two more questions," I said as I got to my feet.

"All right."

I started slowly toward the door.

"If The Bliss Project is as bad as all that, why didn't you go to the police?"

His eyes hardened.

"I don't want to be a dead hero. I got out. Sandberg didn't. That's as much as I'm going to say."

I stepped closer to him and noticed that the scar across his eyebrow was faintly red. The wound had been fairly recent.

"Last question. Why do they call you Puma Man?"

"The puma is a mountain lion. It'll kill if it has to, so people fear it. People hunt what they fear."

12
≈

I wouldn't go near a cult for all the diamonds in Tiffany's.

Hadn't those been my exact words to my father just earlier this week? Yet here I was, looking over a Bliss Project application form. I would have laughed at myself, but at the moment I was doing my best to act like cult bait—tough on the outside, insecure on the inside. I'd been researching the types of personalities that were most likely to get sucked into these things. Those most vulnerable tended to take themselves too seriously. So instead of laughing, I grimaced.

Kami looked up at me from behind the registration table. The slinky green dress had been replaced by black pants and a short-sleeved knit shirt. Both items clung tightly to her compact body.

"I knew you'd be back." She smiled—a bit smugly, I thought. If only she knew *why* I was back.

I tossed the application form back onto the table. "You were right the other night, about me losing a little one very dear to me."

A very good imitation of concern showed in her face. "I'm sorry to hear that." She waited for me to elaborate.

"I lost my cat." I narrowed my eyes.

She cocked her head sympathetically.

"It's tough, losing a pet. But everything happens for a reason. Do you want to talk about it?"

"He disappeared the afternoon I met you. Place feels pretty empty without him."

All true. Whitman *had* disappeared that afternoon, and right now my house *was* empty without him. This morning I'd dropped him off at my parents', anticipating an extended absence while I investigated the cult. I often board Whitman with Mom and Dad when I have to go away. The fact that they treat him like visiting royalty eases the pain of these separations. I'd once seen my father slip him some caviar. Mom lovingly refers to him as her "grandkitten."

For a moment there, Kami had actually looked human. But the glazed look came over her eyes again.

"The good thing about a crisis is that it provides an opportunity for us to grow. That emptiness you're feeling is calling you to make some changes in your life."

I braced myself for the sales pitch that I fully expected would come next. Prepared myself for heavy persuasion tactics and the high-pressure close. Was hoping for these things, actually, so that I could get a legitimate invitation into the cult. But I didn't get a sales pitch. Instead, Kami gave my hand a gentle pat.

"You're going to be okay. Here." She pulled a tape cassette from a box on the table and handed it to me. "Take this home and listen to it. Call me next week and we can talk more."

I took the cassette, feeling more than a little disappointed. Where were the brainwashing and mind control I'd heard so much about? More important, where was the abduction? I'd counted on being taken into custody today.

She scooped up some brochures from the table, secured them with a rubber band, and placed them in the box with the tapes.

"We're closing the ashram early this afternoon," she said. "Big bliss party this weekend." She got up from her chair and smiled, more to herself than to me.

"You're not having the party here?"

She looked at me like I'd proposed something ghastly.

"Yuck! We can do only so much with this place, you

know? No, we're talking *party*. What was your name again? Sorry, I forgot."

"Whitney. You're Kami, right?"

"Good memory. Yeah, they call me Kami Sutra." She winked at me, then picked up her purse and came around the table. "I think you'll find a lot of interesting stuff on that tape. Call me, okay? We'll talk."

She started to walk away.

"Hey, Kami," I called after her.

She turned to look at me but kept moving.

"Is it really true that there's a way to leave this plane of existence?"

That stopped her.

"What do you mean?"

"I read in one of your books that if a person really wants to leave this plane of existence, they can get help to do it. From Master Malindi."

She walked back to me.

"Which book are you talking about?"

"The *Transformation Handbook*."

"Where'd you get that?"

"I was browsing in your shop there—" I pointed to the room containing the books, cards, and guru photos. "I found that book and it really drew me in."

Her expression was cautious.

"And why do you ask about leaving this plane of existence?"

"Because I've been thinking about it."

She looked at her watch.

"Let's talk about this in private."

I followed her across the anteroom and through a door that opened to a small office. Brightly colored sofas and chairs lined the walls, and a plush black throw rug covered the floor. She closed the door behind us.

"Have a seat."

I made myself comfortable on a high-backed contemporary piece upholstered in bold yellow chintz. Kami sat in a neon-orange sofa to my left. Her eyes bored into mine and I got that bug-trapped-in-a-sunbeam feeling again.

"What did you mean by that, Whitney, when you said

you've been thinking about leaving this plane of existence?"

"I'm not sure, really. I just know that life is a struggle and I'm sick of the struggle."

She nodded, her eyes never leaving my face.

"You seemed pretty upset by the Let Go meditation the other night."

"I was. I got really sick. I don't know why." I shrugged. "Maybe I was scared."

She nodded with extreme assurance.

"That's right. Your ego was freaked. It takes a lot of strength to get past your ego and admit you were scared."

"Thanks, I guess." I kept my voice monotone.

"So you're thinking of going ahead with the Process?"

There it was again—the Process.

"I don't even really know what it is," I said in all honesty. "And I'm pretty sure I can't afford it."

"If you feel called by Master, don't worry about the money. The money will come. Listen, I have an idea. Why don't you be my guest at our party tonight? You can talk to some people, get a better idea of what we're all about. Does that sound like something you'd want to do?"

Inside, I was yee-hawing at the invitation. Outwardly, I was furrowing my brows.

"Well, I don't know. I mean, if it's a party . . . I don't really know anybody."

"You know me. You'll be my guest."

She picked up a pen and brochure from the table in front of us. I watched as she wrote directions on the back of the shiny paper.

"We're pretty much going to be partying all weekend, so come at whatever time feels right for you. If I'm not there, I won't be far off—probably in the pool or something." She handed me the brochure and got up to go.

As I followed her out, I glanced at her directions. They led to an address on La Jolla Scenic Drive. Nice real estate if you can get it. This must be the house Scott Chatfield had described, where he was accosted by the half-naked leaping woman.

"You're sure it's okay if I come?"

She nodded. "Trust me."

I felt a tingling on the back of my neck. This didn't surprise me. Those two words—*trust me*—always make me wary.

13
≈

By the time I arrived late Friday night, the party was in full swing. Given the La Jolla address, the place was about what I'd expected. A flagstone driveway curved in a graceful semicircle toward an impressive entryway. Outdoor uplights accented a row of majestic palm trees lining the drive. Beyond the palms, the house rose up into the clear California night, its smooth, sculpted walls painted a creamy shade of pale. The driveway looked like a luxury-car lot. Mercedes, Porsches, and late-model sport-utility vehicles dominated the parking spaces near the residence. I finally found a spot along the road about a hundred yards away.

The faint sounds of party music grew louder as I walked toward the entrance. A sign was taped to the front door: "Enter at Your Own Risk." Imagine that—a cult with a sense of humor. The decibel level went up dramatically as I opened the right half of the twelve-foot double door. The bodacious sound system was loud enough, but on top of that was the din of wall-to-wall people conversing in couples and small groups, raising their voices to be heard over the general fracas. The noise level was especially impressive given that the marble foyer opened onto a vast living room with cathedral ceilings at least twenty feet high. My ears grew accustomed to the chaotic sounds. I recognized the album playing in the background. Sade's *Love Deluxe*.

I moved through the bodies in search of Kami. It was impossible to squiggle past the crowd without jostling elbows and placing drinks in peril. I muttered apologies as I made my way to the other side of the room. Friendly, tolerant faces smiled and folks did their best to make way for me. There were a few tie-dye shirts, to be sure, but most of these people were dressed in casual yuppie attire, with nicely maintained yuppie hairstyles to match. The crowd appeared to be about equal parts Gen X and Baby Boom.

On the far side of the expansive living room, the party spilled into a lighted hallway. I made my way down the hall and stepped into one of the bedrooms, where the crowd thinned out. In the corner of the room, four men were standing around a state-of-the-art Mac, playing a game of "Jeopardy!" A man wearing a Yankees' baseball cap was reading out loud off the monitor.

"This Danish prince killed his uncle to avenge the murder of his royal father."

Sounded like the category was Famous Characters in English Literature. Not my best subject, but I knew this one. Nobody answered, and it was killing me. Hadn't they even seen the movie? I waited as long as I could. Finally, it just blurted out of me.

"Who is Hamlet!"

The men at the computer turned around. The guy in the Yankee cap smiled at me.

"You're hired. Come on in. I could use some brains on my team."

A lanky man in glasses standing to his right punched him playfully.

"Hey, no fair."

I backed away with a wave of my hand.

"No, that's okay. You guys go ahead."

"Nonsense. Get over here." Yankee Cap motioned me back in. "Hi, I'm Raj. Don't think we've met."

"Whitney."

They all said hello to me at once. The lanky, bespectacled guy looked at me eagerly.

"Are you a friend of Abby's?"

"A friend of Kami's," I answered. "Who's Abby?"

That must have been a faux pas, because they all exchanged knowing glances. Raj adjusted the visor on his baseball cap.

"Abby's the person who owns this house," he explained.

Oops.

"Oh. Well, Kami and I just met recently. Other than her, I don't know a soul here."

Lanky Guy extended his hand. "Well, now you know three souls—Kami, Raj, and me. Hi, I'm Lauren."

"Hi. Nice to meet you."

The man to Lauren's left chimed in. "Make that five souls. I'm Reuben, and this is Val."

I shook hands all around. A galactic screen-saver took over the abandoned monitor.

"So," said Raj, "how'd you and Kami meet?"

"I met her at the ashram in San Diego."

Lauren looked puzzled. "How'd you end up at the ashram?"

How indeed?

"Actually, I found a brochure that said something about 'intensive bliss.' That sounded good to me. There was a number on the back, so I called, and—"

Raj frowned. "You just . . . *found* the brochure?"

Yeah, in the file of an investigator who was researching your cult. Obviously, I couldn't say that. Which meant I had to lie. I thought back to that afternoon in Scott Chatfield's office and smiled.

"It was kind of weird. I was in San Diego and this mime picked the brochure up off the ground and handed it to me."

I was sticking as closely to the truth as I could. The closer you are to the truth, the less likely you are to trip off someone's bullshit detector.

"A mime gave you the brochure," Reuben said. "How incredibly freaking cosmic. That's a great story."

I shrugged. Tough, devil-may-care.

"I figured I'd check it out."

"What do you do, Whitney?" Raj asked.

Oh, man. I had to get out of here. There were only so many honest lies I could drum up in casual conversation.

"I'm a seeker," I said. Seeking a woman who's disappeared into your secret society, I refrained from adding.

"You earn a living . . . seeking?" Raj's question was impertinent, but his smile was charming.

"I've managed to make a buck here and there. For a

long time I didn't—I was one of those professional students."

Lauren pushed his glasses up on his nose with a long, elegant finger.

"Professional student, huh? Where'd you go to school? I'm a professor at UCSD."

Jen's alma mater. Perhaps Lauren had introduced her to the cult. I was relieved he'd turned the conversation toward himself. The last thing I wanted to do was go into detail about my phony identity.

"I went to college in the Bay Area," I said, which was true. "So you're a professor. What do you teach?"

"Biology."

"Biology." I said it with respect. "You must kick butt in those 'Jeopardy' science categories."

Raj cut in. "Yeah, but he bites on arts and humanities."

We all shared a laugh, and I sensed an opening to bow out.

"Hey, listen, I'd really like to connect with Kami. Have any of you guys seen her?"

"Last I saw, she was out on the patio," Lauren said. "If you get a chance, come back here and join us for a few rounds of 'Double Jeopardy.' "

"Will do. Thanks for the invite."

They returned their attention to the monitor and I watched as the game popped back up on the screen. Again, no heavy sales tactics. No discussion of gods or gurus. They certainly didn't look like the cult goons Puma Man had described. I had to admit it—I'd actually liked them.

Finding Jen Shaffer right here at this party would be like winning the lottery. A long shot, but I figured it couldn't hurt to look for her—or for anything else of interest. Maybe I could find the bedroom suite where Chatfield had experienced that leaping thing. Even now, it made me laugh.

I moved from room to room searching for clues about the owner of the house. Raj had said her name was Abby. The house was crowded with people but without all the bodies, it would have been practically empty. Furniture wasn't the only thing missing here. There was no clutter. No knickknacks, no family photos. I did notice a portrait over the fireplace in the living room. The subject was the same man I'd seen on the jacket photo of the *Transformation Handbook*. The artist had rendered a larger, more flattering version of the original photo. The guru's eyes were opened wider, his full lips now smiled faintly. What was his name again? Abadanda.

That's when it clicked for me. Abadanda—Abby. Duh. "Are you a friend of Abby's?" must be a code of sorts. *Are you one of us?*

I headed upstairs in search of the mandala bedspread Chatfield had described. This had to be the same house. After all, how many million-dollar La Jolla homes could one cult own? I ascended a plush, carpeted spiral staircase and paused for a moment to look down on the people below. An interesting crowd, and in some ways, appealing.

Watch out, the voice said.

I took note and continued climbing.

The party upstairs had an entirely different flavor than the scene on the first floor. Here people were gathered in intimate groups, talking and laughing quietly. It became more difficult to maintain my anonymity. I stepped into one of the rooms and a half-dozen faces looked up at me guardedly as if to say, *What are you doing here?*

As the fourth investigator on the case, I knew better than to tip anyone off by asking for Jen.

"You seen Kami?" My tone suggested that she was my closest friend. This seemed to put people at ease.

"Try the pool," someone said.

I left the room but remained just outside the door, eavesdropping. They resumed a conversation centered on popular music. No talk of messiahs or transformation, or even of astrology, for that matter. It was all so weirdly normal.

I continued down the hall, peeking into bedrooms. I did not find a mandala bedspread. In fact, were it not for the guru's portrait over the fireplace, I would have thought I'd crashed the wrong party. At the end of the hall, a door was slightly ajar. I pushed through and stepped onto the polished parquet of a small library. Two French doors on the other side of the room opened onto a balcony, where a prematurely gray-haired man wearing Armani spoke forcefully into a slim black cell phone.

"You better hope the fucking peso drops when the market opens Monday." He put his hand over the mouthpiece and scrutinized me with piercing eyes. "Who are you?"

Something about this man was different than the rest of the crowd. There was nothing ingratiating or New Age about him. He was pure street-smarts, dressed up in elegant clothes.

"I'm Whitney. I'm looking for Kami."

"Try the pool." He continued to hold his hand over the mouthpiece, signaling that his conversation wouldn't continue until I was gone.

"Sorry to interrupt, Mr.—"

"Lewis," he said flatly. He stepped back and shut the balcony door.

Party pooper. I shrugged and went back downstairs, pressing through the throng to the backyard. On my way, I passed a long table offering sparkling water, fruit juices, and even the demon alcohol. Quite a variety, too—tequila, vodka, gin, vermouth, imported beers, and an enormous ice bucket filled with California wines. No teetotaling in this sect, apparently. A rainbow array of plastic party glasses fanned out from the bottled spirits, surrounded by plates piled high with catered gourmet edibles. I loaded up a napkin with crab-stuffed mushrooms, pastry-puff canapés, and garlic olives and walked through the wide-open glass doors to the outside.

Screams filled the air. A furious game of volleyball was being played in the swimming pool that dominated the backyard. I could hear a wet pinging sound as the players hit the ball. A spotlight illuminated the white orb as it sailed back and forth over the net. Occasionally a play went wild and the wet volleyball sailed onto the patio, drenching nonplayers. Hence the screams.

I tried to find Kami in the shapes splashing on either side of the volleyball net. Everyone's hair was soaked, so I wasn't able to identify her by her trendy shag haircut. Finally, I approached one of the players near the edge of the pool and asked if she'd seen Kami.

"In the Jacuze," she said as she sprang dolphinlike from the water and arched toward the oncoming ball. Her attempt fell short and the other team scored a point.

A rolling lawn lined with burning torches extended be-

yond the swimming pool. The Jacuzzi sat in its own se-
cluded space up a small incline. I walked across the grass
toward the spa. The torches and spotlight didn't reach this
far. The only illumination came from underneath the steaming, bubbling Jacuzzi water. I squinted into the darkness.

"Anyone here seen Kami?"

"Seeing quite a bit of her," a man's voice said.

A chorus of groans rose up from the others. That was
when I noticed that beneath the bubbles, everyone in the
spa was naked.

"Oh, it's you! Hey, glad you made it." I recognized
Kami's voice. "Come on in."

I had about as much desire to disrobe in front of these
people as I'd had to dance with them at the ashram the
other night.

"No, thanks."

"Oh, come on," Kami said. "You can wear your under-
wear."

That didn't particularly appeal, either.

"No, really," I said again. "I'll just pull up a chair here
and eat my hors d'oeuvres, if that's okay." I grabbed a lawn
chair and pulled it over.

"This is Whitney, everybody," Kami said.

There were three people in the water with Kami—a
woman with jet-black hair and two men. They all said hello
at once.

"No wonder you want to leave this plane of existence,"
Kami chided. "You won't even get *into* it."

The black-haired woman piped up.

"Yeah, Whitney, the only way out is through." There
was the lilt of a British accent in her voice. Maybe South
African.

"Hey, don't let these guys bully you," one of the men
said. "Nice night, huh?"

"Very nice."

"You enjoying the party?"

"Matter of fact, I am."

This was another true statement. Their nakedness didn't
particularly offend me. All in all, the collective vibes from
the gathering were good. Friendly, but not overly so. Everyone in the spa smiled at me and then—to my surprise—

went back to their earlier conversation. I listened along to their discussion of the pros and cons of the death penalty. People were citing case law but tempers weren't flaring— unusual for this particular subject. I found myself enjoying the repartee. Then it hit me again: If this was a cult, where was the proselytizing? Where was the recruitment drive?

"I don't know—" the woman with the accent was saying. "That's one of the primary weaknesses of the American judicial process—"

I took that moment to make a blatant interruption.

"Speaking of process, what exactly is this thing I keep hearing about, the Process?"

The group turned its attention to me. One of the men answered.

"It's a path of study that leads to personal transformation. Is she going to do the Initiation, Kami?"

"Maybe," Kami answered.

"What's the Initiation?" I asked.

"It's an extraordinarily concentrated preliminary training," the black-haired woman explained in her eloquent voice. "But I'm not sure you're ready for that."

"Why not?"

"I don't know. Just a sense I get about you. Like you've got a withhold you're feeling about it. We don't want people to do the Process unless they're really enthusiastic. It takes a lot of energy and commitment."

Above the steaming water, heads nodded.

"What do you mean, I have a 'withhold' about it?"

The woman shrugged her bare shoulders.

"I get that you have some negative thoughts about our work that you're not verbalizing." Her bullshit detector wasn't half bad.

"You're right," I said. "There are some things that bother me."

"Like?"

Again I sought to stick closely to the truth.

"Okay, one of the big things that bugs me is what looks like hero worship of that woman, Malindi. All those photographs of her. The way people reacted to her when she came in the room during the Let Go meditation. Like you idolize her or something. That disturbs me."

"Understandable." In the undulating light of the spa, the face of the man who'd spoken looked rubbery. "You got right to the heart of it, didn't you? To answer your question, we don't worship Malindi. She's just a gateway out of the illusion. Just an enlightened being to focus on to get to the Beingness that we are. Does that help?"

"So you're focusing your energy on an allegedly enlightened being. If you'll allow me to be frank, that makes this seem like a cult."

With that, they all burst out laughing. The other man raised his voice.

"Ah yes, we've all been programmed! We're blindly allowing ourselves to be controlled by an evil force!"

Kami laughed along with them and then looked at me.

"We're not making fun of you. You're asking good questions. All that stuff is addressed during the Initiation. Think you really want to do it?"

I nodded. "Yeah. I need to do something. I'm in a rut in my life. I could use a new outlook."

"You'll have to get time off work," she said. "It's six full days and nights."

"Oh, my schedule's not a problem. I'm kind of between jobs right now. It's money I'm worried about. I mean, I can't cough up three thousand dollars just like that."

"You got a credit card?"

"Well, yeah, but—"

"No problem then. And·that kind of negative self-talk—saying stuff like 'I can't cough up three thousand dollars'—is one of the things the Process will help you get over."

"Get over three grand? That's an awful lot—"

"Of money? Whitney, once you go through the Process, you'll look back and laugh that you were so frightened about such a small issue. Promise."

Promise. A word that's right up there with "trust me" on my list of suspect phrases.

"Well—" I stammered.

The woman with the accent extended a soaking-wet hand to me.

"I'm Tiki, one of the trainers. It's kind of last-minute,

but our next Initiation starts Monday morning. Are you in?"

I kicked off my sandals and dangled my legs in the bubbles. The warm water did feel good.

"Yeah, I'm in."

14
≈

Six o'clock is not a time I welcome a ringing phone, particularly on a Saturday morning. If I hadn't known it was McGowan, I would have ignored it altogether.

"Only for you," I said, not bothering with the hello part.

"Hey."

His voice was soft and sweet. "Sorry to call so early but I couldn't reach you last night. I gave up around two A.M. Eastern. Having fun, I hope?"

"It doesn't get funner. Stayed up late partying with the cult. So what compels you to interrupt your morning schtick and wake me at this hour?"

"My morning schtick?"

"Yeah, you know. Reading the paper over a cup of Sumatra. You're probably halfway through the crossword about now."

I heard the riffling of newspaper pages.

"Creepy, the way you see things sometimes."

"Nothing psychic about that. Anyone close to you knows you're a creature of dependable habits. Now what's up?"

"Nothing. I just miss you is all."

"I miss you, too. But I know there's more to this call. Come on, out with it."

He laughed. "All right. I want you to move into my house in San Marcos while you're working on this case."

"What's the point? I'm going to be running off with the cult soon anyway."

"That's my point exactly. Suppose they find out where

you live and discover that a private investigator's business operates out of there?"

He was right. As sociable and mellow as The Bliss Project party-goers appeared to be, I had to remember that the group had somehow ferreted out confidential information about Scott Chatfield on the basis of his first name only. And in spite of his silly name, I also couldn't ignore Puma Man's rants about lawsuits and credit checks.

"Yeah, well suppose I move into your place and they discover it's owned by an FBI agent?"

"They won't. The title's held in trust. I took that precaution years ago. I hope you don't think I'm being over-protective. It's just that I'm the one who talked you into taking this case and I'd never forgive myself if some-thing—"

"I don't think you're being overprotective, Tom. If the ex-cult member I talked to is even half sane, this group doesn't hesitate to do a little background checking on its recruits."

"It's settled, then."

"I'll try not to wreck the place."

"Or the Charger," he added.

"Or the Charger," I repeated solemnly.

"You really running off with the cult soon?"

"I'll be taking their Initiation next week, but running off with them on a permanent basis may take some time. I'll have to see how it goes. Meanwhile, I'm working on a phony ID and brushing up on my bullshit skills."

"Need help on the ID?" he asked.

"No, thanks. I've got my resources."

" 'Cause I know you don't need help with those other skills."

"Very funny. Now, don't you have a crossword puzzle to finish?"

We hung up laughing.

I put in a call to Joanne, realizing as I dialed that the favors were stacking frighteningly in her favor. I scrambled to think of something to barter with as her line rang. When she heard it was me, her voice perked up.

"You were right-on with your hunch about Brad Aiken's IRS problems. Nothing too heavy—I mean, he's not actually running from the feds. No liens have been filed or anything. But he told me his tax problems are affecting his life. *Now* what do you think of psychic hotlines?"

"I think the potential for abuse far outweighs the occasional insight." I also thought I was amazingly lucky with my guess about her new heartthrob's IRS problems.

"Hey Joanne, since you're so grateful to me and all, can I borrow an identity?"

"What's the matter with yours? Apart from being a bit strange."

"I need to be someone else for a while. Didn't you tell me you turn down dozens of credit applications a year on the basis that the applicants don't exist? As I recall, some of those phony IDs were really quite inventive."

"You're not intending to defraud anyone with this info, are you?"

"No, I just want to use it as a front for some people who have no business looking into my background anyway. It's for a seminar I'm going to take next week."

"So you want me to custom design an ID for you?"

"That would be lovely."

"Okay, but you have to promise not to get me thrown in jail because of this."

"I promise. I need to be someone with little or no traceable credit history. Give me just one low-limit credit card or something. Make me a woman who's lived in San Diego for a while but not at the same address forever and ever. And do you think you can arrange to have me called Whitney? Whitney Brown?"

"You got it, Whitney."

"How long will this take?"

"I can fax you your birth date, Social Security, and driver's-license numbers later this afternoon. Can't give you actual documents, of course. Although there are people who do such things. I hear California drivers' licenses are going for a thousand bucks these days."

"One crooked step at a time. This'll be great for now. Thanks, Jo. And oh—one more favor. Then I promise I'll either quit asking or add you to my payroll."

"Yeah, yeah."

"Could you see if there's been any activity on a guy

named Barry Bell? He operated an investigation business until about six months ago. He seems to have disappeared."

"A crony of yours?" she asked.

"No. My client hired him to look for Jen Shaffer before I took the case."

"And he disappeared?"

"Seems so."

"I'll see what I can find. Be careful, Elizabeth, will ya?"

"Of course." The line buzzed in my ear. Joanne often doesn't bother with good-byes.

What next?

I'd be away for six full days and nights during the Initiation and had no way of knowing how long I'd be gone after that. Even with Whitman safely at my parents', I needed someone to watch my house. I said a prayer to the scheduling gods as I dialed the number of the high-school student across the street. Toby has helped me out with several miscellaneous jobs over the past couple of years. Like most teenagers, he has a constant demand for spending money. In the past, I've always been able to play the cool card: "Isn't it dope to work for a private eye?" Now that Toby had turned seventeen, though, I worried that he might have cooler things to do with his time than help the eccentric PI across the street.

His mom answered the phone. As soon as I identified myself, she started hollering.

"Toby! It's for you!"

She and I exchanged hellos and then I heard Toby's voice as he picked up the other phone.

"Hello?"

I waited for his mom to hang up.

"Hi, guy. I'm so glad you're home."

"Hi, Psi." His latest nickname for me.

"Please tell me you have an urgent need for cash and you're longing for menial freelance employment."

I heard him groan. Not a good sign.

"Sorry, Elizabeth, but I've started my own drug cartel at San Pasqual High. Don't need your stinkin' pocket change no mo'."

"Toby!"

He was laughing now.

"You're not going to make me sit on my ass for ten hours in front of a post-office box again, are you?"

"No, this is far more exciting than that. Your mission, should you decide to accept it, is to bring in the paper, water the yard, rotate the lights, and take over my job delivering books to the homebound on Saturday mornings. Oh, and keep an eye on my place."

"You leaving town or something?"

"I'll be staying over at my boyfriend's place for a while. Not sure how long. I'll pay you five bucks a day or a minimum of fifty, whichever's greater. Starting Monday. Do we have a deal?"

"If you're going to be gone for a while, why don't you have your newspapers donated to the library?"

Toby wasn't the geek this question seemed to imply. It's just that his mom worked for the library. He knew about such things.

"Good idea. Do you accept?"

"I'll come over and pick up the key in about an hour, if that's okay."

"Great. Hey, Toby?"

"Yeah?"

"Promise me you won't have any *Risky Business*-type parties while I'm gone?"

"Excellent idea! Wow, and you're gonna *pay* me for this?"

An hour and fifteen minutes later, I'd just finished scanning Jen's photo onto the Web site when I heard Toby ringing the doorbell. By that time I realized I had another task for him. I opened my office window and yelled outside.

"Door's open! Come on in!"

I looked up from my computer when I heard Toby's footsteps nearing my office. I'd seen him just a few weeks ago but as he walked in, I could have sworn he looked taller. His tan had deepened, too—Toby was a surfer on the junior circuit. He tossed his head, flipping a lock of sun-bleached hair out of his eyes.

"What's up?" he asked.

"I'm goofin' around on-line. Just a second." One more time I read over the message I'd typed:

REWARD

I am searching for information about my daughter, Jennifer Janine Shaffer, who joined a group called The Church of the Risen Lord in 1987. The group later changed its name to The Bliss Project. I have not seen my daughter in two years and am looking for any information that may help limit my search. There is a picture of her at: http://www.moosenet.com/jenshaf.gif.

Please send written information to:
Jen Shaffer Search, P.O. Box 2282,
Escondido, CA 92025.

Satisfied that the words said what I wanted them to say, I posted the message to *ex-cult.org*, a public bulletin board on the Internet.

"Wow, man, I didn't know you had a daughter." Toby was reading over my shoulder.

"I don't. My client does. Think you can swing by the post office a couple times a week and leave a message on my phone machine if any Jen Shaffer Search mail comes in?"

"Sure. Why don't you leave your e-mail address, too? People will be more likely to answer you on-line."

"No, I don't want this traceable to me. I also don't want to wade through a bunch of cyberjunk mail. If someone takes the trouble to hunt down an actual stamp, their tip is more likely to be legitimate." I signed off-line and shut down the computer.

When I swiveled my chair around, Toby was looking at me with suspicion.

"You're not really going to be staying at Tom's place, are you? You're going off to find this girl in the cult."

I grabbed his wrist firmly but gently.

"You don't know that, right?"

The swiftness of my movement startled him. For a moment the swaggering seventeen-year-old was replaced by a frightened boy. He quickly regained his cool.

"No, man, I don't know that."

"Good." I placed my extra keys in his palm and closed my hand around them. "You're cool, Tob."

His face softened and he even looked a little embarrassed. He started to say something but stopped himself. Guys Toby's age tend to have a hard time expressing sensitive emotions.

"Go ahead, say it," I urged.

He smiled sheepishly. "Uh—can I have that first fifty in advance?"

I spent the rest of the weekend packing my bags for the week-long, day-and-night Initiation and moving my essentials over to McGowan's. Sunday evening, I stayed at his place. As I got ready for bed that night, I was warmed to see that he still kept a picture of us on his bedside table. I removed his ring from my finger and stored it along with my driver's license in a small cedar box under his bed.

Everything was in order. I was now ready to begin my life as Whitney Brown.

15

"Two thousand, two thousand five hundred, and three."

The new guy at The Bliss Project registration table casually counted up my six crisp five-hundred-dollar bills. Joanne may have created a phony credit history for Whitney Brown but that didn't mean I could use it. No matter. The guy taking over Kami's usual post acted like he saw that kind of cash every day. He opened his money box and handed me a five.

"Okay, Whitney. You're all set."

His name was Brodie, according to the paper tag stuck on his colorful Guatemalan vest. He had a mop of curly silver hair and nice blue eyes, although the latter carried a touch of the cult members' distinctive glow. Friendly and energetic, Brodie handed me my receipt and a manila envelope.

"There's some paperwork in the envelope you'll need to

complete. First thing you want to do is check into your hotel room at the Traveler's Inn. Get back on Convoy and go about a half mile west. You can get settled in and fill out your paperwork there. Everybody gathers back at the ashram at noon. You have a car?"

I smiled, thinking of McGowan's Charger parked outside.

"Uh-huh."

"Be sure to give us the license-plate number when you sign in, so the hotel garage will know you're a Bliss Project guest."

"Okay, will do."

I gave him a nice fake smile. License-plate number. Nosy sons of bitches.

"See you back here at noon, Whitney."

I hoped that everyone in the cult repeated names in this smarmy way. It would help to remind me that I was no longer Elizabeth. Like a dutiful child, I followed Brodie's directions to the hotel down the street. I'd probably be taking a lot of directions over the next week. This could be a problem. As a kid in school, I was branded early-on with the disclaimer: "Doesn't take instruction well." A self-starter? Yes. Creative problem-solver? You bet. Original thinker? That, too. Cooperative? Not when I found the assigned project boring, insidious, pointless—or all of the above. Just thinking about sitting through a week's worth of lectures on spiritual gobbledygook made me squirm in my seat like a six-year-old. Uck.

The hotel was clean and corporate, the kind that would look identical no matter what city it was in. The clerk was on the phone when I stepped up to the registration desk. A slender man with perfect hair and spotless, wrinkle-free clothes, he held up his finger as if to freeze me in place while he finished his call. He hung up and sighed.

"Your name, please?"

"Whitney Brown. I'm here with The Bliss Project."

As soon as he heard that, his perfunctory attitude turned to butt-kissing.

"Welcome, Ms. Brown," he said brightly. "You'll be staying the whole week, then?"

"Yes."

"If there's anything we can do to enhance your stay, please don't hesitate to let us know."

For a moment I thought I saw the familiar glow in his eyes. Then doubted myself. Maybe I was seeing glowing eyes everywhere because I was hyperaware of them—the way people yearning for children see a world overrun by pregnant women and babies. He gave me a card to fill out and I used the phony Social Security number Joanne had created for me. When I handed the card back, he entered a few keystrokes into his computer.

"I hope you'll take cash for the room," I said.

"Oh no, no, no." He gave his head a quick shake. "Your room charge is included in the cost of the seminar."

That came as a pleasant surprise. Maybe this Initiation thing wasn't such a rip-off after all. A week's hotel stay was no small expense.

He handed me a small envelope containing a magnetic hotel key.

"I hope you'll take advantage of some of the hotel's amenities. We have a very nice spa and an Olympic-sized pool over by the tennis courts. The restaurant is quite decent, and a complimentary continental breakfast is available daily. Have a great week."

This really might not be so bad, I thought as I stepped out of the elevator on the fourth floor. However strange things got during the Process or Initiation or whatever it was, at least I'd be able to come back to the solitude of my hotel room and depressurize. I'm a loner by nature, and too much time in the company of strangers makes me insane. No brainwashing required. I found my room number, slipped the magnetic key into the lock and opened the door.

"Hi."

A naked woman was sitting on one of the two beds. Correction, she was wearing a towel. A glowing-white towel that set off her honey-blonde hair and contrasted starkly with her deeply suntanned skin.

"I'm sorry," I said, "there must be a mistake."

Flustered, I backed out of the room and shut the door behind me. Through the closed door, I could hear her voice calling.

"Whitney, hold it!"

Cautiously, I reopened the door a crack.

"I'm sorry, what did you say?"

"Come back in here. I'm your roommate."

Roommate. Oh, great. I opened the door to find her flicking on a gold lighter and igniting the end of a slender brown cigarette.

"My name's Tuesday. Tuesday Valentine. You're Whitney Brown, right?"

How did she know that already? She read the question in my face.

"The registration desk gave me your name when I checked in. We're paired up this week."

I stepped into the room and the door closed behind me.

"Well, how about that. Nice to meet you, Tuesday."

She puckered her pale, pillowy lips and blew out a long stream of smoke. I was about to tell her I'd requested a nonsmoking room when she spoke.

"Are you a cop?"

Cop. *Damn!* I tossed my suitcase onto the unoccupied bed and laughed.

"A cop? Only when I act out my fantasies. Handcuffs, big sticks, that kind of thing. Why? Do I look like a cop?"

"Yeah, kind of. You move like a cop. You're very uptight. I notice body language a lot because I'm a dancer."

I unlatched my suitcase and began hanging my things in the closet.

"Cool. Where do you dance?"

"Various places. For a while now, I've been working at Precious Metal." I recognized the name of the place. It was a skin show near the sports arena, featuring buxom babes doing an amped-out bump-and-grind to heavy-metal rock and roll.

"So what brings you to The Bliss Project?" I asked.

She lay on her side and swung her long, muscular legs onto the bed.

"I actually first came here to rescue one of my firm's clients. I thought this was a cult and that I was going to save him from it." She chuckled at the memory.

"Your firm?"

"William Morris. You know, the talent agency? I was the human resources manager there for a couple of years.

That was before I knew myself. It took a while, but I finally dropped the Hollywood-player act and started doing what I really love. Dancing." A dreamy smile crossed her face.

From human resources manager of one of the country's largest, most famous talent agencies to small-time erotic dancer. Interesting career move.

She stretched her arm over the bedside table and tapped her cigarette on the edge of an ashtray.

"But you don't need to hear about that. It's a long story and you've got things to do."

"No, please. Do go on. I'm fascinated. Who was this client you came to rescue?"

"Someone with heavy group-consciousness recognition. 'Famous' would be your word for him. I'll tell you about it later. It's already ten o'clock. Don't you have a questionnaire to fill out?"

"Yeah, I guess I do." I picked up the manila folder and pulled out the paperwork. The questionnaire was at least thirty pages long, bound by a heavy-duty staple in the upper left-hand corner. "Jeez, this is going to take some time, isn't it?"

"Yeah, it takes a while."

I sat down with a sigh and started hunting in my purse for a pen.

Leaving her cigarette smoldering in the ashtray, Tuesday Valentine got up off her bed and headed toward mine. The white towel loosened but managed to stay precariously perched on her ample chest. She plopped down beside me and began massaging my neck. My body froze.

"Oh God, you're worse than I thought." Her fingers pressed hard into my tense muscles, sending shooting arrows of pain into my shoulders.

I cleared my throat.

"Uh . . . not to be ungrateful, but to be honest, that's more painful than pleasurable."

"Of course it is. The way to bliss is often through pain. You'll learn more about that later." She gave my shoulders a final squeeze, got up off the bed and disappeared into the bathroom.

I exhaled, realizing I'd been holding my breath. The woman made me very nervous. When I heard the shower go on, I got up and put out her cigarette. It was going to be a long week.

Determined to get on with it, I sat back against the pillows and picked up the paperwork. In addition to the questionnaire, there was a release form, which I read word for word. It basically stated that I absolved The Bliss Project from all liability in the event of an accident, stress-related reaction, etc.

"It is likely that participants will feel resistance to some of the training procedures," read one of the clauses, *"and I authorize The Bliss Project to use gentle pressure while coaching me to explore new ways of thinking."*

I remembered what Puma Man had said about how the cult "tied up your thoughts." I signed the unfamiliar signature with a flourish, relieved that it was Whitney Brown and not Elizabeth Chase who was agreeing to these cockamamie statements.

Next, I tackled the questionnaire. I'm a licensed psychologist and have seen and even administered plenty of personality and learning tests. *WISC*, Woodcock Johnson, Rorschach. But never before had I seen a test like this. It was long enough, detailed enough, and cryptic enough for me to know that there would be no point in playing games with the tester. The questionnaire had been designed to ferret out inconsistencies. Any faking of answers would show, and even my fake answers would give insights about me. I decided to play it straight.

The test was set up as a series of statements. I was to respond by degrees: Agree, Agree Somewhat, Disagree. The first several statements were innocuous enough. Standard diagnostic fare:

I am a happy person.
I enjoy working with others.
I often feel anxious or afraid.

As the test went on, the statements hit some personal nerves:

I often remember my dreams.
I sometimes hear voices in my head.

I sometimes know the outcome of an event before it
actually happens.

At one point, Tuesday emerged from the bathroom. I
looked up to see her fully clothed body heading toward the
door. She grabbed her handbag off the dresser on her way
out.

"See you at the ashram."

I heard a heavy click as the door closed behind her.

I returned my attention to the test. As the completed
pages piled up, I forgot myself, forgot the role I was playing. The statements challenged me and told a story all their
own.

I would be willing to risk my life for an important
cause.

I would be willing to take another life for an
important cause.

It took me an hour and fifteen minutes to complete the
questionnaire. A paragraph at the top of the last page read:
*"To weight your responses accurately, we need to consider
the following information about your social and cultural
background."*

If you ask me, it was a thin excuse for invasion of privacy. The questions were blatantly nosy: Average annual
income. Highest level of education completed. Previous and
current church or religious associations. Previous and current group memberships or educational associations. Father's occupation. Mother's occupation. I was surprised
they didn't ask for favorite sexual positions.

Fortunately, I'd worked out a detailed profile of myself
as Whitney and had given her background a good deal of
thought. Both of Whitney's parents were deceased, which
would go a long way toward explaining her defensiveness
and insecurity. Her annual income was a bit less than average—as Dylan sings, when you ain't got nothin', you got
nothin' to lose. She was a college dropout, disillusioned
with the system. And much as I liked to think of myself as
a loner, Whitney was a true rolling stone, listing no group
memberships or affiliations.

Although Whitney's background was very different than mine, her personality mirrored my own dark side. It would be helpful to keep that in mind as I maintained my bogus identity. It wasn't going to be easy. I glanced at my watch. Eleven-fifty.

Ten minutes till show time.

16

≋

This was it. Zero hour. I stuck a name tag over my left breast, took a deep breath and shuffled through the door with the rest of the men and women embarking on the Process. No turning back now.

The entrance opened into a large auditorium. I knew this was where the Let Go meditation had been held last week, though it hardly looked like the same place. No half-naked revelers rock-'n'-rolling through the darkened room today. Instead, bright overhead bulbs cast a functional light on dozens of neat rows of chairs facing the stage. Sensibly dressed assistants stood at various points around the room, guiding people to their seats. I was surprised to see Tuesday Valentine assisting. Back in our hotel room, I'd assumed she was another hapless recruit. Wrong. Apparently Tuesday was on The Bliss Project staff.

I ducked into a middle row and settled into the first seat. My eyes wandered to a denim-clad couple sitting across the aisle. Not exactly a pair of young, wide-eyed innocents. The man's face was deeply lined and the woman's hair was streaked with gray. They spoke to each other with quiet intensity, their voices just beyond earshot. Nosy as I am, I strained to hear. Though I couldn't make out their hushed conversation, I noticed a humming sound. A very low pitch—barely audible—seemed to be coming from everywhere at once and nowhere in particular. Strange.

I surveyed the crowd. Who were these people? And why

were they willing to give up three grand plus a week of their time for this? The audience gathered here looked like a network television producer's dream—most of them fell into the twenty-five to forty-nine demographic. Apart from an occasional rebellious hairstyle—dreadlocks on a guy in the row behind me, a woman with a shaved head in the front—most of these people appeared to be upstanding Americans. That is to say, they wore lots of name-brand clothing and accessories.

"The Process will begin in five minutes. Please take your seats."

Like the humming, the voice seemed to come from nowhere and everywhere at once. I looked up and again noticed the bank of speakers mounted near the ceiling around the room. A hush followed the announcement and those who were standing hastened to their seats. Tuesday Valentine also took a seat. This made me wonder how many in the audience were already members of the cult. The room was nearly full. I scanned each row systematically, looking for any woman who could possibly be the object of my search.

Right at the five-minute mark, a man wearing jeans and a khaki-green military shirt slid into the empty chair on my left. He glanced at me sideways as he hooked a shank of his long, dark hair behind his ear. We nodded hello but before we could say another word, the room was pitched into darkness.

All crowd murmuring stopped. In the blackness around us, stars began to appear. Like a laserium, the walls and ceiling had become a three-hundred-sixty-degree movie screen, and a very real image of outer space—probably footage from NASA's *Voyager* expedition—surrounded us. I felt disoriented, as if I truly were drifting through outer space.

"Welcome, brothers and sisters."

The voice, like the image, was all around us. A feminine voice, breathy and low.

"Your presence here at this moment is very important. What you learn today and over the next week, and what you do with that knowledge, could have a profound impact on history. For we as a species are at a critical evolutionary juncture. With the millennium come problems that threaten the very existence of our planet."

Off to my right—seemingly in far outer space—a beautiful blue sphere came into view. The voice paused to let the image sink in, then went on.

"Never before has our world been so threatened. Rampant overpopulation. Deadly pollution. Shrinking natural resources. Virulent diseases that in another day would have been called plagues."

The planet Earth floated closer toward us—or we toward it, hard to tell. The view was so real it was breathtaking. I was sailing hundreds of miles above the surface, but still close enough to make out the characteristic landmasses going by: North Africa, Spain, the boot of Italy.

"There is an answer to our planetary crisis, but the answer does not lie in science or technology. The solution cannot be found in nuclear physics, or even in the exploration of outer space."

With that, the earth and stars disappeared. Again the room was pitched into blackness.

"Please, everyone, close your eyes."

The soothing female voice was all around us.

"That's it, just close your eyes. Close your eyes and you will begin to see where humankind will find the answer."

The humming I'd heard earlier now seemed to be coming from the center of my brain. I wondered how on earth they did that. It was a decidedly pleasant sensation.

"This year, right now, *today* . . . we as a species have an unprecedented opportunity to make a great evolutionary leap. The Bliss Project offers you the opportunity to take that leap."

The sensation created by the humming was so euphoric that I heard but didn't analyze her words. Knowing full well that I was sitting in a room with a hundred other people, I nevertheless felt as if I were alone and that the ubiquitous voice was speaking only to me.

"The evolutionary leap will occur in *inner* space," the voice intoned. "The answer to the planetary crisis lies in consciousness itself." The humming continued and I traveled on, a solitary explorer charting some new dimension. I didn't want the sensation to end.

The blissful feeling died abruptly when the humming stopped and the lights came up. I opened my eyes to see Master Malindi standing on the stage before us, wearing a smartly tailored white suit.

"Hi."

Though still amplified, her voice now came from the front of the room. I squinted my eyes and was able to make out the tiny mike clipped to the neckline of her jacket.

"I'm Malindi, and I'll be guiding you through the Process."

I couldn't take my eyes off her. Neither could anyone else. There was no doubt—Malindi had the kind of charisma that sucked attention from people whether they liked it or not. Movie tycoons have built empires by recognizing people with this quality, cultivating that lure, and feeding it like candy to the masses.

Malindi strolled along the edge of the stage, looking into faces in the audience.

"Is anyone out there wondering what the heck they're doing here?"

In one of the front rows, a hand shot up.

"Okay, we've found an honest woman. You're wondering what's going on, huh?"

The woman who'd raised her hand nodded.

"A friend talked you into signing up, and now you're worried that this is looking a little kooky, right?"

The woman smiled and nodded.

"Could you come up to the front of the room, please?"

The woman hesitated. A look of panic came over her face. She glanced from side to side and seeing no escape, awkwardly squeezed past the knees along her row and walked up the center aisle in front of the stage.

"Come on around and up the steps onto the stage," Malindi instructed.

The woman did as she was told, though her body language screamed resistance.

"So your name's Karen, is that right?"

Malindi was reading from the woman's name tag. Karen gave a little nod.

"You're feeling pretty uncomfortable up here, aren't you, Karen?"

Karen nodded emphatically.

"We're going to do something that I guarantee will transform that anxiety you're feeling into something a lot more pleasant. Would you like that?"

"I guess."

The doubt in Karen's voice carried across the room, even without a microphone. I sensed the audience pulling for her, empathizing with her discomfort. Malindi seemed to speak directly to the group conscience. She pointed at the audience.

"You're all going to do this, too. Turn to the person sitting beside you. Don't say anything to each other, just maintain eye contact."

The man in the khaki-green shirt turned to me and grinned. I returned a weak smile. Whatever this was, I was going to endure it, not enjoy it.

"Do not speak to one another," Malindi instructed. "Just continue to stare into each other's eyes."

I noticed all the outward things first. The name tag on his shirt. *Kyle.* How the green of the fabric complemented his smooth olive complexion. The way his dark brown hair fell in shining waves to just below his chin. How his neatly trimmed goatee accentuated a pair of full pink lips. How the strong angle of his nose made his face all the more interesting. The assignment was to look into each other's eyes, but I found myself resisting. I didn't like that weird glow in the cult members' eyes and for all I knew, this guy was one of them.

"As you do this exercise," Malindi continued, "notice your thoughts. Don't analyze your thoughts—just notice them. Perhaps you are judging what you see in your partner. Perhaps you are worrying about what your partner is seeing in you. Perhaps you are feeling embarrassed or afraid. Whatever thoughts or feelings you're having, just notice them."

I looked frankly at Kyle and wondered what thoughts were crossing his mind. Many people assume that because I'm a psychic, I can read minds at will. Hardly. As a child, I had an amazing knack for intuiting what number a person was holding in his or her mind. This became the basis for later research studies at Stanford. But reading random thoughts from an infinite source of possibilities? I wish. The idea made me smile.

Kyle smiled back. His eyes were the color of espresso. They didn't give off a weird glow—nor did they give anything away.

Without warning, the room turned black. Malindi's voice continued to guide us.

"Okay. Now look through the darkness at your partner as if you can still see him or her. Recall your partner's image. Place that image before you as if you're really seeing it. Can everyone do that?"

Around the room, affirmative murmurs.

"Here's where things get interesting. I want you to take turns telling your partner something you've been withholding about yourself. It can be a big thing or even a small thing, just something you've been holding back. Do this now."

It wasn't immediately obvious to me what making personal confessions to a stranger had to do with saving planet Earth. Perhaps this would become clear as the week went on.

At first all was quiet. Gradually from around the room, muffled voices could be heard confessing in hushed tones. Luckily, Kyle spoke first.

"I take dangerous risks with my life. Your turn."

"What kind of risks?" I couldn't help asking.

"Death-defying sports and stuff. Come on, your turn."

I was at a loss. What was I holding back? I resisted the obvious wisecrack. "I'm an undercover detective." What was *Whitney* holding back?

"I don't know myself very well," I said.

The lights came back up. Kyle was staring straight at me, a curious look on his face. I avoided his gaze by turning toward the front of the room. Malindi and Karen stood on the stage beaming at each other like long-lost friends. The audience appeared more relaxed and the room had a lighter feeling. This would have been just as easily accomplished by giving people in the audience time to introduce themselves and chat a bit, but Malindi was proving a point.

"How many of you feel less anxious than you did five minutes ago?"

The response was not unanimous, but most members of the audience put up their hands.

"Okay, we're going to do it again but raise the stakes. Here's a little secret, folks. The more courageous you are in here, the faster the Process will go for you. You'll have plenty of chances to see that as we go along. You guys paid a lot of money to be here this week. You came here looking for transformation. What you're going to get is a new way of being that'll not only transform your lives, but the whole world. The sooner you let go, the sooner you transcend."

Again the room was pitched into blackness and a three-sixty-degree backdrop of outer space surrounded us. I heard the humming again, and Malindi's voice from all around.

"The ohm tone you hear will get louder over the next three minutes. When it reaches full volume, no one will be able to hear you. That will be your opportunity to express out loud the thing in life that you most fear. Your darkest secret, your biggest worry. Don't miss this opportunity. It will transform you."

The humming steadily climbed in intensity. I climbed with it, riding another wave of euphoria. I felt a strong vibration in my body as the humming reached rock-concert decibels. The heavy volume didn't hurt my eardrums but strangely heightened the euphoric effect. I tested my voice with "The quick brown fox jumped over the lazy dog." I couldn't hear a thing.

The humming mounted, soared, widened into space. I saw swirling patterns of color against the blackness. At a point of unbelievable intensity, Malindi's words came back to me.

Your darkest secret. The thing in life that you most fear.
"I'm afraid of losing you, Tom!"

My shouting was completely absorbed by the din. My screams might as well have been silent.

Time was lost. It seemed like much more than three minutes had passed when the humming at last began to die down. As it did, another sound, far less pleasant, was filling the room.

The woman sitting across the aisle from me was screaming bloody murder.

17

≋

She was screaming louder than a starlet in a horror movie, but I have to admit she had good reason.

Her partner had slumped forward, his body crumpled awkwardly against the chairs in the row ahead of them. The woman's gray-streaked hair fell into her face as she struggled to lift his deadweight, all the while shouting frantically.

"Somebody, please help—we need a doctor!"

She was hoarse, as if she'd been hollering for some time. With the room pitched into blackness and all sound drowned out by the high-volume humming, no one had seen what happened or heard her cries for help.

A stout woman pressed forward from the back of the room.

"I'm a nurse. Step aside, I'm a nurse." The authority in her voice left no question.

Those of us sitting near the commotion stood and moved our chairs away, clearing a space for the nurse to begin administering CPR. But it was too late. The man's pale hands had already turned blue. I'd seen death several times before. There's a peculiar emptiness when a spirit vacates the body. I felt that emptiness now.

The reality of what had just occurred began to sink into the minds of the audience. Like electrical currents, fear and curiosity began traveling through the room. People popped out of their chairs and moved toward the clearing, trying to see what was happening. The air was buzzing with whispers. Voices began to rise. Just as the mood threatened to ignite into chaos, Malindi took control.

"An ambulance has been called," her amplified voice intoned. "Please take your seats and remain silent."

The group complied. People returned to their chairs. The

room quieted down until there was only a terrible hush and the lonely sound of the nurse thumping on the dead man's chest and filling her lungs, then his.

After what seemed an eternity, two white-uniformed paramedics hurried through the door. In a flash, the fallen man—now notably discolored—was loaded onto a stretcher and whisked from the room. His partner followed, her anguished face looking ten years older.

The audience was stunned. I was stunned. We'd been taken from an optimistic mood of infinite possibilities, raised into a state of uncanny euphoria, then suddenly cast back down—face-to-face with the terror of death—in just a matter of minutes. My mind scrambled for explanations. Perhaps it had all been staged, acted out like some macabre play to drive home a point. Not likely. I'd seen the deep purple-blue of the man's skin as he'd been carried out the door. That had been no act.

Malindi walked to the edge of the stage and sat, her legs dangling over the front. She inhaled deeply, her breath magnified by her microphone.

"The man who was just taken away is a dear friend of The Bliss Project. Ken Bastin has been with our group for a number of years. Those of us who know Kenny are aware that he has a heart condition. I'd like to take a moment right now and ask that we all send our highest thoughts and love to him."

The sympathy in the room was palpable. Heads bowed and lips moved in silent prayer. I thought back to the paperwork I'd signed just this morning. The release form had carefully exonerated The Bliss Project from any liability in cases of preexisting medical conditions.

"Thank you for your loving energy," Malindi said.

Near the back of the room, a hand went up. The questioner, a handsome, balding man in a yellow polo shirt, looked agitated. Malindi didn't call on him right away.

"Sometimes," she said, "experiences that feel bad move us further than experiences that feel good."

"Excuse me, I have a question." From the look on his face, the man with the raised hand was not about to be ignored.

Malindi pointed at him with her chin. "Go ahead."

"Is this Process dangerous?"

His question put words on the unspoken fear that was snaking through the audience.

"Because if this is dangerous, I want to know about it right now." He emphasized the last word with a pointing finger. "Not to mention that we should have been warned. I need to know if this is safe."

Again a buzz of whispers started up. Malindi crossed her legs at the ankles and stared at the man.

"Are you afraid?" she asked.

"I'm simply taking reasonable precautions to protect my health and well-being," he retorted.

"Are you afraid?" she asked again.

The man sat stone still. Even from twenty paces, I could tell he was beginning to fume. His voice, however, remained level.

"Are you going to answer my question?"

Malindi smiled. "What's your name?"

"Gary."

With the patience of a schoolteacher, Malindi asked the question again.

"Are you afraid, Gary?"

The man's mouth clamped shut. He stood up and said "Excuse me" several times as he edged past the people seated in his row. He strode from the room without another word.

If the man's abrupt departure bothered Malindi, she didn't show it. The door banged shut behind him and echoed in the hushed room.

"The path to bliss is not always blissful. Transformation is painful."

Not exactly the comforting words Malindi's audience wanted to hear, I suspected. How painful had Jen Shaffer's transformation been? I wondered cynically.

"As you go through the Process, you will experience fear. You will experience anxiety. You will experience confusion. Without these feelings, you would not recognize the illusion. And until you recognize the illusion, you cannot get beyond it."

There was an uncomfortable silence as the audience tried to make sense of her words. A fallen man had just been hauled out of the room. Was this really the time to be yammering about illusions and transformation?

"Now, to answer Gary's question. Yes, some of what we do here is stressful. But nothing we do during the Process is harmful or dangerous. The ohm exercise—that humming you experienced—is safe for your physical body, much in the way a roller coaster is safe. Someone with a heart condition obviously takes a risk when he gets on a roller coaster, does he not?"

She looked into the eyes of the audience. When a few heads dutifully nodded, she continued speaking.

"Kenny had a stroke two years ago. Whatever happened a few minutes ago might just as easily have occurred when he was gardening, or eating his breakfast."

The door at the back of the room opened again. Heads turned and watched as a young man walked directly to the front of the room and handed a note to Malindi. She read the paper, then folded it thoughtfully.

"We're going to take a short break. Your assignment during this time is to relax in the courtyard outside with your partner and talk about what thoughts and feelings came up for you during the ohm exercise, and how you're reacting to the incident with Kenny. We'll meet back here in fifteen minutes."

Though our seats had been separated when we'd stepped back to give the nurse room to work, Kyle appeared at my side as I stood to leave.

"Howdy, partner," he said.

People were exiting through a side door at the back of the auditorium. I noticed Tuesday Valentine ahead of us, accompanying a clean-cut man who looked more than pleased to have her company. Was it possible that a cult member was assigned like a watchdog to each newcomer? Was Kyle my watchdog?

Shuffling slowly behind the crowd, Kyle and I at last reached the exit, which opened onto a patio. A few scrawny pepper trees poked up through holes in the cement, but otherwise, the area was stark and unlandscaped. Harsh sunlight bounced in all directions off the white surface. I squinted and reached in my purse for my sunglasses.

Kyle followed my lead, pulling a pair of shades from his breast pocket.

"Much better," he said. He perched the sunglasses on his aquiline nose.

"So how long have you been with The Bliss Project?" I asked.

"A while. Boy, we must have made a really great impression on you today. That was awful. Poor Kenny."

"I was hoping it might be a hoax, staged to prove a point or something."

He pouted his lower lip and shook his head.

"I wish."

"Did you know Kenny well?"

Kyle rested his weight on one leg and crossed his arms over his chest. His shoulder muscles strained the seams of his long-sleeved shirt.

"Know him real well. We've done some motorcycle riding together. He's a good guy, all in all. Hope he pulls through."

Kyle seemed normal enough. His eyes probably didn't even glow, though it was hard to tell with his sunglasses on. Maybe some cult members were less fanatical than others.

"So," he asked, "what was your experience during the ohm exercise?"

Was I really going to have to play along with all these silly games? To refuse to cooperate would only call attention to myself. What had I experienced?

"Euphoria. It was wonderful."

Then it hit me. A man had suffered a heart attack and probably died not ten feet away from me. Sensitivity was supposed to be my forte. But had I even had a clue to what was happening? Not in the least. It was as if all my senses had been tuned out during the Process. Not just my sight and hearing, but my *inner* sight and hearing as well.

"You don't look like you feel all that euphoric about it."

I realized my eyebrows were knitted into a frown. "Actually, I was enjoying it thoroughly. It was just a drag to come back down."

He nodded. "No kidding. Particularly when someone's having a heart attack. Did it scare you?"

"No. Did it scare you?"

"No. I'm not afraid of death. Guess that's why I do all those death-defying sports."

In spite of the glaring sunlight, I couldn't see a wrinkle on Kyle's face.

"How old are you, if you don't mind my asking?"

"Pushing thirty."

"You have a lot of living yet to do."

"Maybe."

I wondered what was going on with him that he took his life so lightly. Perhaps it was the arrogance of youth, the denial of mortality that seems to invade the very cells of the young.

"So, what brought you to The Bliss Project?" I asked.

He put his hands in his pockets and scanned the crowd.

"I was looking for something I couldn't find outside."

That made two of us.

"And you?" He turned back to face me. "What brought you here?"

"Oddly enough, you took the words right out of my mouth. I'm also looking for something I can't seem to find anywhere else."

A deep gong sounded, summoning us to reconvene in the auditorium. The chairs that had been pushed aside for the paramedics were now realigned in neat rows. When everyone had taken their seats, it became obvious that the audience had thinned out.

Malindi appeared on the stage.

"Kenny is resting comfortably," she announced.

I was fairly certain that Ken Bastin was dead. Which meant that Malindi was lying. It was a big lie, and I wondered why she was telling it.

"His sudden illness sends us a message. While consciousness is infinite, our lives on this plane are not. We have an important mission and our time to accomplish it is limited."

I felt my stomach churn. The gun-to-your-head conversion technique: *Repent now, the end is near.* Same sermon, different lingo. If consciousness was infinite, I wondered, why the dire mission? Why the big rush?

Malindi walked over and sat on a tall stool that stood in the center of the stage.

"Those of you who witnessed Ken's collapse were not here by coincidence. You are a special group. It's significant that you were present to absorb this lesson."

I looked around the audience. Eyes, rapt with attention, were fixed on Malindi. From the empty chairs, it was apparent that many people had been sufficiently put off by the noontime creep show to bail out. But those who remained seemed to have been inspired by the trauma. However frightening, it had been a moment of rare intimacy, an event that pulled people together.

"Sickness drives home an important message: If you choose to stay on this plane of existence, suffering awaits you. Every type of suffering occurs on this plane, and always will. But you don't have to stay here. You can choose to let go of this illusion. You can become Free. But before you can do that, you must surrender your illusions. . . ."

I slumped in my chair as Malindi droned on. It was going to be a very long afternoon.

By the time I got back to my car—McGowan's car—I was mentally exhausted. I drove back to the hotel in a daze. I reminded myself that if I thought there were an easier, softer way to find Jen Shaffer, I'd take it. Unfortunately, the Initiation, like some dreaded exam, was an ordeal I had to endure if I wanted to gain entry into the world in which Jen had disappeared.

Back at the Traveler's Inn, a dank smell hung in the air as I made my way down the hall. Inside, the room felt cramped and dark, even with all the lights on. The smell of stale smoke seemed to ooze from the lackluster bedspreads and drapes. I slipped into a nightshirt and hoped I could forget the whole scene when I closed my eyes.

I had just rested my weary skull against the pillow when I heard the door opening. Tuesday dropped her things noisily on the dresser and bounced on her bed with an exuberance that hurt my already aching head.

"Well, what'd you think of your first day of the Process? Some day, huh?"

I was still curious to know who her famous client-turned-cult-member was, but the last thing I wanted to do was to embroil myself in a conversation with her.

"I'm not feeling well," I said.

She nodded all-knowingly. "Sometimes that happens—"

"—when your ego gets freaked," I finished for her. "The part of me that's resisting transformation is giving me a headache, right?"

She smiled sadly. "It's not enough to know it up here," she said, pointing to the place where she'd once had a brain. "You have to know it in here." She thumped a fist on her gravity-defying chest.

"Right. I'm working on it." I closed my eyes, hoping to end the conversation.

I felt her staring at me. Tried to ignore it. Held out five minutes and finally opened my eyes. She was looking at me as if I were her only child, lying in a casket.

"What's wrong?" I asked.

"I just feel so sad right now."

"Why?"

"Because I know you're lying to us. I don't know what makes you feel like you have to lie, but it makes me sad."

Uh-oh.

"Lying about what?" I asked.

"Why don't you tell me?"

I sat up and crossed my legs. Took a moment to center while I got into character. I began picking at the bedspread, the picture of anxiety.

"Look, I'm a mixed-up person, okay? I'm trying to change, that's why I'm here. You're right, I'm not being totally up-front with you guys. You people might find it easy to bare your souls, but I don't. I've taken a lot of abuse in my life, had a lot of people fuck with me. I don't trust people right off the bat. It takes a long time for me. That's just the way it is."

She was buying it. I could tell by the way her face softened.

"What would it take for you to stop being so defensive, Whitney?"

I shrugged my shoulders. "I dunno. I'd have to feel safe, I guess."

"Do you feel safe with me?"

Our eyes locked. I wanted to put her at ease, to tell her that I trusted her. But if I lied now, she'd know.

"No, not yet. But I'm trying, okay?"

"Okay." She smiled. "And Whitney, remember: If you can't trust me, trust God."

As if they were one and the same.

Later that night I stared at the ugly stucco ceiling long after Tuesday's breathing came in measured increments. What had she meant when she said she knew I was lying to them? Had they made me already? Was that even possible logistically? They'd had Whitney Brown's ID for just one day. Even if they had somehow figured out that it was a phony identity, so what? How much harm was really done? As long as they didn't know I was a PI, I would be all right.

The paranoia was making me restless. My legs twitched from having sat in a chair all day. As quietly as I could, I slid out from under the sheets. I slipped into the clothes at the end of my bed and quietly left the room.

I passed a clock in the lobby. One forty-five in the morning. The registration area had been abandoned and the glow of the computer monitor cast a lonely light. I stepped up to the desk. From this vantage point, I was able to see anyone who might come and go. I looked up, checking to see if any closed-circuit video cameras were watching me. All clear. Not only that, but a couple of monitors on the registration counter allowed me to watch the hotel exits and the elevator lobby. I would be able to see anyone coming.

The menu on the monitor read, "Enter guest name."

I reached down and typed in a name on the keyboard: Jen Shaffer. Then hit the Enter key.

The message came back: Not registered.

On a whim, I typed in: Bliss Project.

Score. A screen popped up, with line after line of guest names, apparently all registered under The Bliss Project. The names were numbered—eighty-four in all. Talk about your cash-cow corporate clients. No wonder the clerk had given me the butt-kissing treatment. I scanned the list, looking for Jen Shaffer. No luck, not that I'd expected any. The idea of printing the page was tempting, but I thought better of it. It was entirely possible that Tuesday or another cult member would go through my things with a fine-tooth comb. It simply wouldn't do to have confidential Bliss Project information among my personal belongings.

I started memorizing names, using clever mnemonic tricks.

Something moved at the edge of my peripheral vision. On one of the closed-circuit TVs, I saw the hotel clerk getting off the elevator. I hit the Escape button and the screen returned to its main menu. I scrambled out from behind the desk and ducked around the corner just as the clerk entered the lobby.

18
≈

I woke up punching. My opponent, Tuesday Valentine, was shaking my shoulder in an effort to rouse me. Luckily for her, my fists were caught under the blankets.

"Whoa! Easy there, Merry Sunshine! It's time to get up!" Her voice was nightmarishly chipper. "Sunrise meditation starts in fifteen minutes."

It seemed as if I'd just closed my eyes. "What time is it?" I slurred.

"Quarter after five."

I pulled the blankets over my head. "Get out."

"Whitney, you're going to have to work on that attitude of yours if you want to get Free. Don't be so quick to express those negative emotions! Notice them, but don't act on them, okay?"

It was *way* too early for this crap. The stinkin' Process. One day down, six to go. This rigmarole would drive anyone nuts. How was I going to maintain my sanity? By staying ornery. Hidden under the blankets, I stuck out my tongue at Tuesday. By the time I threw off the covers, I was all smiles.

"Sorry. I can be such a grouch in the morning."

"S'okay, I used to be the same way."

She was already dressed, sort of, in a lace bodysuit. She pulled a tunic-length top over her head, slipped into a pair of ballet shoes, and motioned me go get going.

"Come on. You'll have fun today. I promise."

I sighed and dragged my leaden bones out of bed. Shaky and myopic as a newborn kitten, I staggered to the closet and yanked on a pair of brown leggings and a matching cotton sweater. By the time I stumbled into the bathroom, my eyes were beginning to open. I brushed my teeth and washed my face but didn't bother with the froufrou stuff. Frankly, I was too sleepy to care. No jewelry, just my watch. I was fastening it to my wrist when Tuesday stopped me.

"No timepieces allowed during the Initiation," she said.

"What?"

"You're on Bliss Time now," she said with a smile. She took the watch from my hand and placed it back on the bathroom counter. "Come on, I'll give you a ride to the ashram."

The auditorium was quiet and dark, all fluorescent lights off. In their place, hundreds of candles glowed in glass cylinders along the walls. The spicy fragrance of incense filled the air. All the chairs had been removed and the floor had been filled with rows of padded mats. Several people were already sitting cross-legged on the mats, or simply lying down. I looked wistfully at those who were prone. Were they sleeping? If so, could I join them?

"What is this?" I whispered to Tuesday.

She pressed her index finger against her lips and scowled, then leaned so close I felt her breath on my ear. Still, I could barely hear her answer.

"Meditation," she whispered.

Tuesday settled onto a mat near the front. I found a mat near the back and assumed the lotus position, feigning contemplation. After a time I cracked my eyelids and peeked at the others. Around the room, eyes were closed and breathing was deep and regular. Careful not to make the slightest noise, I slipped out the auditorium door. Wristwatch or no wristwatch, I was still on Elizabeth Chase time.

I didn't get far. A young man met me in the hallway.

"Is there a problem?" he asked.

"Bathroom," I said, smiling sheepishly and pointing toward the women's head. The urgent look on my face kept him from asking any more questions.

As I walked to the restroom, I noticed another two men stationed near the building exit. This complicated my plan. I was determined to get to a telephone this morning. I dipped into the ladies' and brainstormed for a minute. Then walked right back out, straight for the exit.

The men came together and blocked the door as they saw me approaching. The bigger one spoke.

"Sorry, but you signed an agreement that no one comes and goes during the Initiation."

I smiled sweetly. "I know, but the ladies' room is out of . . . feminine supplies. I've got some in my car—"

Females have few birthrights in this society, but access to Kotex is one of them. The mention of feminine hygiene immediately disarmed the guards.

"Oh, sure. Go right ahead."

I made my calls from a public telephone in the empty office complex next to the ashram. First, I called Information for the number I needed. As I was dialing the number, I realized I'd gotten lucky. Most businesses wouldn't be open for at least another hour. Fortunately for me, ambulance service is a twenty-four-hour-a-day enterprise.

The female voice on the other end was polite and efficient.

"California Care Ambulance. How may I direct your call?"

"I'm not sure," I said. "I wanted to write a letter praising one of your employees. He was so wonderful yesterday, the way he helped my friend Kenny. In the commotion and everything, I didn't even get the paramedic's name. Could you help me?"

"Sure. Can you give me an idea of the time and place the ambulance arrived?"

"Convoy Street, yesterday around one or two in the afternoon."

"And what was the patient's last name? I can check our dispatch record to see who took that call."

"The patient's name is Bastin. Ken Bastin."

I could hear fingers on a keyboard. Then I sensed something on the other end of the line, a hesitation.

"I'm sorry we couldn't do more for Kenny," she said sympathetically. "There were two medics, actually, who tried to save your friend. Ed White and Don Gastwirth."

"Oh, I see. I suppose I should thank both of them, then."

"I'm sure they'll appreciate your thoughtfulness, especially under the circumstances. When a loved one dies, most people are too overwhelmed with grief to thank the health-care workers. That's really great of you."

"Kenny would have wanted it that way," I said.

I could question the medics if I needed details later, but I'd just gotten the information I was really after. Malindi *had* been lying—Ken Bastin was dead. I glanced at my wrist only to see that it was bare. I didn't need my watch to tell me I was pushing my time limit.

Eyes were still closed and breathing was still deep when I resumed my place on my mat in the auditorium. I had just settled into a comfortable position when I heard a loud bang behind me. The doors at the back of the room flew open.

"Hey, hey, hey!"

Heads turned to watch Master Malindi jogging up the center aisle between the mats. She streaked past in a white miniskirt and whiter-than-white tank top, her blonde hair waving wildly around her head. She stopped on the ball of her spotless white athletic shoe and spun around to the audience. Something on her bare arm caught my eye. A tattoo, blooming in rainbow colors just below her shoulder: *Have Faith.*

"How are you guys doing this morning?"

Her voice was amplified by a wireless mike. I could see the battery pack clipped to the waist of her miniskirt in back. A single spotlight followed her as she rounded the dim room, giving her a special glow.

"The energy in here is fantastic this morning!"

Malindi stretched her arms wide, puffed out her chest, and threw back her head, as if she were drinking in all that fantastic energy. The spotlight glow went up a notch, high-lighting her perfect body. I looked around to see the audience reaction. From the glassy eyes and dropped jaws, it appeared that several of the men had just experienced spontaneous conversions.

In the background, a dance beat started up. The ubiquitous JBL speakers again.

Malindi grabbed the hand of a woman in front and pulled her along as she moved around the perimeter of the room.

"The energy on the planet is changing now. Everything around you is moving faster."

They picked up another person, and another, forming a human chain. Malindi began rocking to the beat and her hangers-on rocked with her. The volume of the music went up and Malindi raised her voice.

"If you just tune into the energy and go with it, your transition will be easier. You'll find yourself dancing. Soon you'll be flying. Before you know it, you'll be Free."

It wasn't long before most of the room was moving to the beat. Tuesday joined in and beckoned me to do the same. Reluctantly I took the hand at the end of the chain. Instantly I noticed how much easier it was to dance with the crowd than to hold out on my own. Over the sound system, Malindi's throaty voice called out.

"If you're resisting, you're causing your own discomfort. You're the one standing in the way of your own bliss. When you feel that resistance, remember: Let Go!"

Malindi had It in the dance department, too. There was something decidedly seductive in the glamour of her fluid movements and the ecstasy on her face. I got into the rhythm but tried to maintain my autonomy by observing people. I looked around for Kyle but didn't see him. With a touch of envy, I wondered how he'd managed to wangle out of this morning's shenanigans.

I don't know how many hours we danced. The walls held no clocks and no one wore watches. By the time we broke for the late morning meal, I was ravenous. Sweaty and blissed out, the crowd poured into the anteroom, where the lights had been turned up. Tables along the walls were filled with platters of fresh strawberries and dozens of bowls of yogurt and cereal. I felt like grabbing two of each, maybe three.

Tuesday stuck close to my side. My guard dog.

"So," she said. "Feeling better now?"

"Um-hm." My mouth was already full. "These strawberries are divine."

"Aren't they? We get them fresh locally from a place in Leucadia. You're a good dancer, Whitney."

No small compliment, coming from a professional stripper. I swallowed my last bite and mumbled a reply.

"Thanks."

"Isn't Malindi an amazing dancer?"

"Yeah." And a shameless liar, I refrained from adding.

"She's the personal guru to a lot of people you know," Tuesday said.

"People *I* know?"

"People everybody knows." Tuesday named names. Journalists, artists, activists, and entrepreneurs—men and women whose work I respected. My eyebrows went up. I found it difficult to believe that these people would be taken in by a con like Malindi. Perhaps they'd written checks to worthy-sounding Bliss Project fund-raisers and Malindi had exaggerated her role in their lives.

"How did these people find out about the Bliss Project?" I asked.

"We have a very active ashram in the L.A. area. People come from all over the world for rest and meditation there. It attracts a lot of well-known people because they know it's a place where their privacy will be respected."

An ashram in the L.A. area? It didn't fit with my bucolic vision of Jen among green fields and barns, but for now, it was the only lead I had.

I waited until Tuesday was in the shower. When I heard the water go on, I went to the bedside table to use the phone. But there was no phone. There'd been no way to sneak away unnoticed from the Initiation again, so all day I'd been waiting for this chance to check the messages on my machine at home. Now I had no phone.

I stormed out of my room and down the musty hallway

to the registration desk. The skinny attendant sat calmly at his station, his clothes tidy as ever.

"Hello again. May I help you with anything this evening?"

"I sure hope so," I said with a strained smile. "There's no phone in my room."

"I'm sorry. Unfortunately, there's nothing I can do about that."

I stared at him, hoping he was joking. Apparently, he wasn't.

"I guess you'll have to move me into a room with a phone. Simple as that."

"I'm sorry, I can't do that."

"Look, it's the middle of the week. Surely you're not telling me that you have no other rooms available?"

"No, I didn't say that. It's just that our guest rooms don't come equipped with telephones."

"What?"

This was ludicrous. What kind of hotel had a spa and tennis courts but no phones in the rooms?

His smile was as wrinkle-free as his clothes.

"You're welcome to use the pay phone at the other end of the lobby."

I felt myself fuming. In my head I heard Master Malindi saying, *When you feel that resistance, remember: Let Go!* I answered her out loud.

"Shut up."

The clerk frowned. "Excuse me?"

"Never mind."

I was feeling trapped and needed to center myself. I visualized his white shirt smothered in chocolate cream pie. Then imagined actually throwing the pie. Made me feel better.

I walked across the lobby and picked up the pay phone, reaching into my pocket for a quarter. As I slipped the coin into the slot, a sudden instinct gripped me.

Don't touch that dial.

The cautious feeling lingered. I stood and thought about it for a minute. Then hung the phone back up.

Maybe The Bliss Project wasn't a cash-cow client for this hotel. Maybe The Bliss Project *owned* this hotel.

19

On my third morning in the cult, I stood under the showerhead and had a disturbing realization: I could not remember my dreams.

This may sound like no big deal. A lot of people tell me they don't remember their dreams. Some even say they don't dream at all—a scenario I find hard to believe. The dream-forgetters shrug their shoulders nonchalantly, as if a lost dream were of no more consequence than a cloud dispersing overhead.

I cannot imagine taking such a loss so lightly. For me, losing my dreams is tantamount to a pilot losing access to the sky. How am I supposed to know what's going on behind the scenes without my nightly flights into the unconscious? Stripped of this vital skill, I felt grounded. About as much good to my client as a plane without wings.

I rinsed the shampoo from my hair, cherishing these precious moments alone. Here at The Bliss Project the only time I ever had to myself was in the bathroom. Whenever I was with others, I was assaulted—not necessarily by a nonstop barrage of Bliss Project propaganda, though there was plenty of that, but more by the overwhelming one-way thinking of the group. Against an army of like minds, my dissenting voice sounded weak, even to myself.

"Might as well be in a cell," Puma Man had said. It was true. My sense of self was under siege.

My psychic senses were under siege as well. With each day I was feeling increasingly unintuitive. While I rarely can call up my psychic ability on command, I usually have at least one or two incidents a day that show me my intuitive faculty is up and running. *Knowing* where a couple entering a movie theater will sit, long before they reach the aisle. *Thinking* about a person I'm rarely in touch with and hearing from them that day. (Why I cannot extend this ability to knowing which line will move fastest in the grocery-store checkout is one of the great frustrations of my life.) The point is this: My daily insights are often small and inconsequential, but they come from the same realm as my more startling revelations. I count on them to remind me that I'm still in tune.

Was I in tune now? Hardly. For one thing, I hadn't had a decent night's sleep since I got here. The exhaustion dulled my senses. I was standing under streams of hot water and barely feeling it. I turned the water cold, hoping that might help. It only intensified my tired aching. I turned off the faucet and stepped out of the shower feeling like my batteries were dead.

I was bending at the waist toweling off my legs when Tuesday popped her honey-blonde head into the bathroom. Not cool. She spoke up before I could object.

"Want another ride this morning? We'd better get moving."

I straightened up, wrapping the towel around my torso.

"No, that's okay. I really want to take my car today. Can't let the engine sit on an antique like that, know what I mean?"

"If you say so. Mind if I ride with you, then?"

Of course I minded. I was determined to get to a telephone this morning and have some contact with the free world—the real one.

"Can you just go on ahead without me? I'm going to need a little more time in the bathroom here." Hint, hint.

But instead of graciously shutting the door, Tuesday opened it wider.

"Whitney, you just turned down an opportunity to help another person. You need to look at that. Is it really more important to follow your own agenda? One of the biggest stumbling blocks to getting Free is hanging on to your own self-centered little universe."

Somehow, my using the bathroom had been turned into a selfish and uncaring act. A retort was ready to fly off my tongue. Then I remembered I was playing the cooperative cult inductee. The sooner I gained the confidence of these people, the sooner I'd accomplish my goal of finding the elusive Jen Shaffer.

"Sorry, Tuesday. I just didn't want to hold you up. I'll be out in two secs."

She stepped into the bathroom and put her arms around me.

"I just love the way you can get off it so quickly," she said, squeezing me. "You're really catching on."

I squeezed back, but grimaced to myself in the mirror behind her.

Malindi sat on the edge of the stage again, her legs crossed at the knees.

"The world around you is just an illusion. But that illusory world is being transformed by the special energy coming to the planet at this time. That energy is here now, and is helping you break Free of the illusory plane. As you break Free, you will notice changes."

All this talk of freedom was making me long for the real thing. I squirmed in my seat. The lecture had started only fifteen minutes ago. To alleviate the boredom, I scanned the audience. My eyes stopped on a male specimen in the second row from the front. Kyle was back.

Malindi's sultry voice droned on.

"You will become aware of everything. Not just the love and light. The dark side also. Has anyone out there had their dark side come up this week?"

She looked to the audience expectantly but found no takers.

"Come on now, don't let fear stop you here. Who wants to share a piece of their dark side?"

I thought that it might do Malindi's soul good to share a piece of her own dark side. I nearly asked her to offer us an example, but a hand in one of the middle rows went up to save me from myself.

"Yes," Malindi said, pointing to the brave volunteer. "Just stand please and tell us your name, then state the darkness in yourself that you saw come up this week."

He rose from his chair. It was the man I'd noticed the first day, the one with the dreadlocks.

"My name's Toss. I stayed up all night doing cocaine."

"Great!" Malindi beamed. "Thanks, Toss. Now don't fight your dark side, just notice it. Just *be* with it."

Toss took his seat, looking befuddled. Malindi led the audience in applauding him.

"Being with your dark side," Malindi said as the clapping died down, "will raise your awareness."

I flashed on something I'd read in *Helter Skelter* years ago—a comment made by Manson family member Susan Atkins. She'd allegedly stated that stabbing Sharon Tate's pregnant belly over and over had raised her consciousness, exhilarated her, as if she were stabbing nothing more than a pillow. I frowned at the memory. So much for *being* with one's dark side.

Malindi stared straight at my frowning face.

"Are you confused?" she asked.

I nodded.

She raised her voice and directed her response to the whole group.

"As the Process continues, you *will* experience fear and confusion. It's important that you don't try to make sense of what's happening to you as you go through this. Your fearful thoughts, your confused thoughts, will make you want to bail out of here. When you have those thoughts, let them go. Remember: Let Go."

By now, I'd heard hours and hours of lectures along these lines. I stopped fighting the words so much. At first I'd torn apart their logic and sent back silent retorts. Now I began to let the sentences just roll off my back. Then Malindi made a statement that startled me.

"Every night we're working with you while you sleep. We're working with the part of you that's always listening."

Working with us while we slept? How? Was this why my dreams had stopped? I wanted to raise my hand, to ask her what she meant. But she made two loud claps and changed the subject.

"Okay, today we're going to focus on developing a part of the brain that's been slumbering in humans for far too long. We call this Level P."

Wait a minute. Level P. That was a few letters closer to the mysterious Level X I'd heard about from the former cult member, Puma Man. At this point, Malindi had my undivided attention.

"We're going to do an exercise to demonstrate Level P right now. You guys ready?"

Heads nodded around the room. Assistants came forward from the back and passed out index cards and pencils to each row. As the writing materials were being distributed, Malindi began her instructions.

"Think of someone you know who is not in this room today. On the card that's being passed out to you, write that person's name and city or town. Also list their sex, age, height, weight, and marital status."

The room was silent except for the sound of lead scribbling on paper.

"The cards will be used just for this exercise and will be destroyed after today," Malindi said.

I didn't believe that and had no intention of giving a real name. I blithely described one Penelope York, a single woman living in Los Angeles, California.

"Now list three adjectives describing this person," she instructed.

More scribbling. Penelope, I decided, was zany, smart, and ethical.

"After you're through with that, list three of this person's pet peeves."

More scribbling. Penelope hated mindless conformity, junk mail, and bad acting—with Brad Pitt in parentheses.

"Now list three more people that this person knows, and how this person feels about these people."

Level P, my elbow. This looked like a blatant marketing scheme to me, akin to buying an address list. Was that Level P as in Promotion? I racked my brain for three more names. Maybe I should give up the dirtbags who'd crossed me in my life. I smiled and penned with relish: Stan Ellis, Jeffrey Dietz, Pat Buchanan. No, better erase Pat Buchanan, lest they catch on to the fictitious nature of all my entries. I substituted with Gary Warren Niebuhr, then reviewed my list. A drug dealer, a rapist, and an embezzler. Not bad.

"Okay," Malindi said. "When you're done, pass your cards and pencils back down the aisle. Thank you."

The collected cards were handed to Malindi.

"Tiki, would you come forward, please?"

A pale woman with a black Cleopatra haircut stepped up from one of the middle rows.

"This is Tiki, everyone, one of our most outstanding Level P initiates."

Prompted by Malindi's example, the audience generated a polite smattering of applause. When the woman turned to us, I recognized her. We'd met at the Jacuzzi, at the party in La Jolla.

Malindi fanned out the cards in front of the woman and asked her to select one. Tiki pulled a card and read the name out loud.

"Penelope York."

Why me? This never happened with raffle tickets.

"Who wrote this card?" Malindi asked the audience.

I raised my hand.

"Would you please stand and tell us your name?"

I hauled myself out of my chair and gave a little wave to the audience.

"Hi. I'm Whitney."

"Just stay standing, Whitney," Malindi instructed. "We'll need you to verify Tiki's impressions."

Meanwhile, Tiki had closed her eyes and was holding the card flat between the palms of her hands. We waited several moments for something to happen. Finally, she spoke.

"I'm not getting a clear impression," she said in her lilting accent. "I'm seeing different faces. Is this person an actress?"

Without thinking, I answered.

"Yes, she is."

I was fascinated by Tiki's performance and getting the creeping feeling she was the real McCoy.

"Penelope isn't the woman's real name, then. This is her stage name, is that correct?"

Again I answered, "Yes, it is."

"I'm getting a strong impression of . . . how do I say this? . . . cops and robbers or espionage or something. Does she play the part of a detective?"

My blood was getting cold.

"Wow, you're really amazing," I said, with feeling.

The audience broke into applause and I sat back down, hoping to be exposed no further.

Another card was selected and again Tiki displayed her formidable intuitive power. Just as an experiment, I tried to play along with her. True, I couldn't hold the cards in my hands, but perhaps I could *see* information by listening to the names as they were called out.

Another name was read from the cards.

"Dennis Ferado."

I sat with my eyes closed, inviting images, words, feelings—anything. It was useless. I was about as psychic as a dead phone line.

I got a break at lunch, a real break.

Tuesday, who I now knew was more of a watchdog than a roommate, was summoned by Malindi to help serve the lunch that had been laid out on tables in the foyer: raw vegetables, brown rice, curried tofu. I smiled and said hello as I passed her in the lunch line. The servers kept our portions small. I wistfully remembered the tables of plenty at the party in La Jolla. Apparently the decadence around here was restricted to special occasions, or only accrued to the fully initiated. I wandered through the crowd, picking at my food and looking around for Kyle. He was nowhere in sight.

I finished my lunch, tossed my paper plate in a trash can and stood near the front door, waiting to make my getaway. After five minutes of scoping out the scene, I decided escape would be impossible. Several Bliss Project regulars stood near the entrance, ready to intercept anyone who might have the wayward idea of going out alone. After nearly being exposed by Tiki's reading this morning, the last thing I wanted was to call attention to myself.

The faces in the crowd were becoming familiar. I knew several people by name now. I sprinkled good-natured hellos to my acquaintances as I made my way back through the room. When no one was watching, I ducked into the empty auditorium. Once inside, I hurried past the empty chairs to the side exit that opened onto to the cement patio.

Outside, the heat rose in waves from the baking cement. I walked along the side of the building and stopped at the retaining wall separating the patio from the parking lot. It would be risky to climb over. How would I explain it if I were caught straddling the wall? But the decorative cement blocks had plenty of footholds and scaling the wall wouldn't take more than a few seconds.

I went for it.

The Charger was parked out of sight of the ashram entrance. That was good. I slid into the front seat and started the engine, wishing that V-8s weren't so awfully loud. Because the ashram was located in a cul-de-sac, I had no choice but to drive past the front of the building. I sped by and was relieved that no one was standing outside to see me.

At the end of the street, I turned right onto Convoy and into a deluge of lunch-hour traffic. It had been less than three full days, but already the outside world looked strange to me. The sun was shining harshly and the commercial buildings looked ugly.

Ah yes, the dismal illusory plane. Who wouldn't rather see it transformed into streets of pearl?

I pulled into a twenty-four-hour Mexican restaurant and went directly to the pay phone, ruing the fact that I didn't have a moment to spare for a chile relleno burrito. So far, The Bliss Project menu had been tediously healthy—no small criticism coming from me, a vegetarian. I dialed my mom and dad's phone number almost without thinking. They've had the same number since I was three years old. I knew it better than my own face.

When I heard my mom's voice, some of my numbness melted away.

"Hi, Ma."

"*Ma?*" Her voice was horrified. "Since when do you call me 'Ma'?"

"Forgive me, I'm feeling sentimental today. How's my baby?"

"Just fine. Sitting in my lap and purring louder than a broken motor."

I felt a twinge of jealousy. It was immediately supplanted by gratitude that I had such a slavishly devoted cat-sitter.

"How's *my* baby?" Her sarcasm was leavened by just the right amount of caring.

"Hanging onto her sanity by a thread. Keep the name of a good deprogrammer handy, will ya?"

"Elizabeth, don't joke about this. I read somewhere that the people most likely to be seduced by a cult are the people who don't believe they would ever be susceptible."

Mothers. Why do they worry so much?

"Only four more days and I'll be back at Tom's place. Tell Dad I love him, okay? I gotta get going."

"Okay. Be careful in there."

I next called my home phone. I heard my cheery greeting and after the beep, said hi to myself and recorded the names I'd memorized from the hotel registration computer. Then added an afterthought.

"While you're at it, look into the ownership of the Traveler's Inn on Convoy."

I redialed my number, this time to pick up my messages. The first message was from Toby.

"Hey, Psi, howzit goin'? Um, you got lots of bills and magazines and stuff but nothin' addressed to the Jen Shaffer Search. See ya."

Then Tom.

"Hey, you. I'm getting nervous. Haven't heard from you since Sunday. Just want to make sure you haven't eaten any phenobarbital-laced applesauce or anything. Call me when you can, okay? I love you."

McGowan's voice flooded me with a longing to connect with him. He'd left the message very late Tuesday night and his tone was soft and mellow.

By contrast, the last message was loud and urgent.

"This is Vince Shaffer. I need to talk to you as soon as possible. I've received another package. It looks bad. Very bad. Please call."

20

≋

"You can't possibly appreciate the horror of this until you see it firsthand."

Vince Shaffer's voice was barely audible over the chugging engines of the cars idling in line at the restaurant's drive-through window. I plugged up my free ear with a finger.

"I'm sorry, could you speak up, please?"

"You need to see this right away." This time I heard each exasperated word.

"If I could, believe me, I would. The work I'm doing now on your case requires me to be away until Monday. I simply can't see you until then. Can you just describe the package to me over the phone?"

"I prefer—no, I insist—that you see this personally." The voice of a man accustomed to getting his way.

"And I will, Mr. Shaffer, as soon as I've completed this part of my investigation. I'm laying important groundwork here. What you tell me now could make me more effective these next few days."

"Where are you?"

"It's better you don't know that."

An old Impala gunned its motor and I lost what Vince Shaffer said next. I turned my back to the noise and pushed the receiver tighter against my ear.

"I'm sorry, could you repeat that last?"

"It's a padded envelope, just like the last one. Inside was a lock of Jen's hair."

Even with the commotion all around, I could hear the tenderness in his voice.

"You're presuming it's Jen's hair, correct? I mean, she tends to dye it frequently, from what I've seen."

"That's true. But this looks a lot like her natural color, which is an unusual shade of red. There's also a poem that's—"

Either he didn't finish the sentence or I lost his voice in the background noise again.

"I'm sorry," I said. "I didn't hear that last part."

"It's splattered with blood."

A lock of hair and a blood-splattered poem. More work for Tom's forensics friend. I did my best to comfort him.

"I know you must be frightened, but let's not assume the worst until the blood and hair are tested, okay? Could you read the poem to me?"

His sigh was audible. "Just a minute."

I *saw* him reaching across his desk for his reading glasses. The impression was purely visual. Eyeglasses— stems open—sitting on papers, being scooped up by an arm wearing a white shirt with gold cuff links.

"Are you putting on a pair of reading glasses? Tortoise-shell frames, square? You're wearing gold cuff links?"

"My God. Yes, I am."

I sensed caution in his pause.

"Am I under surveillance?" he asked.

"No, I was just double-checking my second sight."

For the first time in days, a sincere smile crossed my face. My clairvoyance was back.

"Can you see Jenny?" he asked.

I didn't bother to explain again that my clairvoyance came when it came, beyond my control.

"No, I can't see her. Not yet. I don't have much time, Mr. Shaffer. The poem?"

He cleared his throat. His voice—tight, angry—spit the verses into the phone:

> *Pray for the woman whose hair is red,*
> *Love her now, she'll soon be dead.*
> *Each drop of blood is a reminder*
> *As sure as taxes, death will find her.*
>
> *She was breathing, now she's not.*
> *Executed on the spot—*

Somebody laid on their horn long and loud not twenty feet away from me and I lost the next several words.

"I'm sorry, Mr. Shaffer," I interrupted. "Could you repeat from that 'executed on the spot' part?"

He cleared his throat again and repeated in a raised voice:

> Executed on the spot,
> Hit-and-run, an ugly end.
> Enemies are now her friends.
>
> Look carefully and watch your backs,
> Pray to find all the facts.
> May this strand of hair remind you
> Every child has ties that bind you.

After an angry silence, Vince said, "Pretty awful poet, isn't he?"

"Why do you say 'he'?"

"I don't know. I assumed—"

"The handwriting is masculine, then?"

"It's typewritten."

After sitting for three days in the Process, I was finding it difficult to think clearly. I worked hard to focus.

"I'll have Tom get in touch with you about having the package sent to the forensics lab. Do you still have my card?"

"Yes."

"Send a copy of the poem to that address. I'll be back in touch as soon as I can. And Mr. Shaffer?"

"Yes?"

"I can't say for certain of course, but I get the sense your daughter is very much alive."

I used my calling card to contact Tom in Quantico. He was out of the office, so I left a voice mail updating him on the new package and asking him to get in touch with Vince Shaffer.

"Phones are scarce around here," I said. "This may be my last message until Sunday. Don't worry. I've sworn off all phenobarbital. Love you."

Without a watch, I couldn't be certain how much time

had passed. My internal clock told me that by now, the afternoon session at The Bliss Project was well underway. How was I going to explain my absence? On my ride back to the ashram, I tested out a variety of alibis. I hadn't felt so delinquent since cutting home economics class in ninth grade. My punishment then had been cafeteria detail. The stakes were a little higher now.

21
≈

"Whitney. We were worried about you."

Kami was again at the front table, guarding the entrance.

There'd been no point in scaling the cement wall to get back in. I knew that by now the auditorium was full— sneaking in through the side entrance without being seen would be impossible.

I shrugged like it was no big deal.

"Sorry I'm late."

"Do you remember the paperwork you signed at the beginning of the week?"

"Yeah."

"Do you remember the form you signed that said you agreed not to leave the premises while the Initiation was in session? Master Malindi went over those agreements the first day. You remember that, right?"

I crossed my arms over my chest and mumbled my reply.

"Yeah."

"The agreements are important, Whitney." She bugged her eyes for emphasis. "They're designed to give you the most out of your experience in the Initiation. A big part of your transformation is up to you."

"Sorry I screwed up." I headed for the auditorium.

"Hold it!" she called out. "You can't just walk in there during the middle of the Process. You've got to get clearance. Why don't you wait in the sitting room? I'll call you when it's okay to go back in."

So much for not calling attention to myself. Now I was going to have to be cleared for reentry, like some wayward jetliner from behind enemy lines.

I went into the small office off the anteroom and sat on the high-backed yellow sofa. The table held no magazines to read, not even cult literature. Nothing to do but sit.

After what seemed an interminable wait, the door opened. A woman wearing a long denim dress came in and took a seat. I recognized her from the distinctive gray streak running through her hair. She was the one whose partner, Kenny, had died in front of the audience. The man whom Malindi had implied was still alive. Surely this woman knew the truth.

"Hi, there," I said.

"Hello."

"How is your, um—"

"Lover," she finished for me. "He passed away."

"I'm so sorry."

"Don't be sorry. I'm sure he's in a better place now."

She said it nonchalantly, as if he'd hopped a plane to Maui for the week. I could feel my eyebrows coming together in puzzlement.

"What?" she said, seeing the question in my face.

"I don't know. I guess I'm a little shocked. Malindi told us your partner was resting comfortably."

"Lover," she corrected. "And I'm sure he is." She smiled eerily.

I didn't know quite what to say, so I remained silent.

"Why should Master upset the newcomers with details?" she went on. "It was a private matter."

She sounded like she was trying to convince herself.

"His name was Kenny?" I asked.

She nodded.

"Had you known each other long?"

"Nineteen years."

I tried to imagine how I'd feel at such a loss. Inconsolable, I thought.

"Adjusting to a change in a nineteen-year relationship is a great way to let go of attachment," she said.

Change. Not death, mind you, but a *change.*

"I've had some grief come up, of course, but there's so much love and support around me. Here at The Bliss Project, I have literally hundreds of friends to help me through this transition."

She looked at me proudly, as though I should envy her.

"We don't have to go through the transformation alone," she finished.

We sat together in silence for several long minutes. I began to wonder what she was doing in here. Had she been sent in to watch me? Before I could ask the question, she came up with one of her own.

"Why are you not in the Process this afternoon?"

"I was late. Got locked out."

She chuckled. "That happened to me in the beginning, too."

"Really?"

"Oh, yeah. It's an intense week. I actually dropped out." She smiled at the memory.

"But you came back."

"Yes, I came back. And stayed back." She put her feet up on the empty table and slouched comfortably into the sofa.

Why on earth would anyone willingly return to this tedious brainwashing? I wondered.

She seemed to read the question in my mind.

"I recognized my resistance for what it was—just my ego, battling against change. You get to this point where it's either let go or stay miserable, the way you've always been. I knew I didn't want that, so I let go. What's your name?"

"Whitney. And you're—?"

"Aura."

It seemed I'd been straining to hear all day.

"Laura?"

"Used to be Laura. I dropped the L. It's just Aura now."

Of course it was.

"Aura," I said. "That's a very, um—"

"Silly name?" she asked. The lines at the corners of her eyes deepened with her smile. "That's the whole point. I don't take myself so seriously anymore. What made you come back today?"

Her question caught me off guard.

"Come back?"

"You said you were locked out. Which means you left and came back. Why?"

"Oh. I didn't really mean to leave, exactly. I just . . . had to get away for a little while."

"To do what?" Her face was gentle. "I don't mean to interrogate you. There's a reason I'm asking."

I pulled out one of the alibis I'd concocted on my drive back. "This sounds disgusting, but I had to satisfy an ice-cream craving. Ben and Jerry's Chubby Hubby was calling to me so loudly I couldn't ignore it. No offense, but the food here is pretty damn spartan."

She laughed.

"I'll tell you a little secret about this place. If you hang around long enough, you get to have whatever you want. Seriously. We're not about deprivation. *Au contraire!* You want ice cream? You'll get all the ice cream you ever dreamed of. I'd always wanted a bedroom with an ocean view. Now I've got one."

"Where's that?"

"I live at the ashram in Malibu."

Malibu. The ashram near L.A. I'd heard about yesterday, most likely.

"You're welcome to come up and visit after you finish the Initiation. I'll show you my view."

"So you're just visiting San Diego this week?"

"Kenny and I came down to assist in the Process. You'll learn to assist too, in time. It's a great way to recharge the batteries and at the same time, help others in their trans-formation." She smiled. "We're all so guarded in the be-ginning. It takes a lot of love to help us open up."

I nodded, trying not to look guarded.

"The next few days here are easy, Whitney. Just quit fighting. Let go. Start dancing."

Kami knocked softly on the door.

"Whitney?" she called. "You can go in now."

I opened the auditorium door a crack, figuring I'd just sort of slither in without being noticed. As soon as I was through the door, I could see how mistaken I'd been.

The entire group was lined up against the stage, facing me. Eighty-something pairs of eyes zeroed in on my lone body. I felt like I'd just walked in front of the world's largest firing squad.

"Welcome back, Whitney!"

The sound was thunderous. Eighty-something voices, raised together as one.

Please, I said silently, *somebody shoot me*.

All the chairs were gone. In the center of the room, a makeshift platform towered perhaps fifteen feet high. Below the platform was a huge trampoline, nearly circus size. I was just beginning to take this all in when a trim figure in a white bodysuit sailed off the tower.

"Yaaaaaahooooooo!"

The body bounced, somersaulted, bounced again, then sprang from the trampoline and bounded toward me.

"Come on, Whitney, don't just stand there! Get in line!"

In a streak of white, Master Malindi reached my side, grabbed my arm, and pulled me into the line of initiates.

That's when I noticed that everyone had removed their footwear.

"Take off your shoes, girl!" she prodded.

I stared at her face, fascinated by the outward perfection of her chiseled nose and lips and her poreless, glowing skin. But where her hand held my arm, I felt unclean.

"Come on," she said as she tugged at me. "What are you waiting for?"

With a sigh, I leaned over to take off my shoes. Malindi let go of me and jogged down the line, slapping high fives as she went. The speakers around the ceiling piped out a bouncy Van Halen rock tune.

One by one, the initiates climbed the tower, walked across the platform, and sailed onto the trampoline. Expressions changed from rigid dread to open joy as each person overcame their initial fear. With every jump, high-voltage energy surged through the crowd. Spirits soared and the band played on.

Might as well jump . . . Go ahead and jump.

Gleeful, childlike screams filled the air. The playful mood was infectious. What would be the harm in having a little fun? After hours of sitting in a chair, the physical activity was a welcome release. When it was my turn at the tower, I rushed right up. The structure was made of hard plastic piping and I scaled it easily. I reached the high platform and hesitated, for a brief moment looking down. Suddenly I was four years old again, braving the high dive. The trampoline below did not appear so huge from this perspective. More like a saucer. I thought about the release I'd signed absolving The Bliss Project of any liability during the Initiation.

The initiates screamed wildly from below.

"Let Go!"

What the hell, I thought.

I sailed feet-first. Eddie Van Halen's guitar solo shredded in the background. In the fraction of a second before I hit the trampoline, I felt a delicious surrender akin to orgasm. When my feet touched the canvas, my knees buckled. I bounced back and landed on my butt. No harm done.

More than anything, I wanted to do it again. This was *fun*.

As I jogged back into line, fellow initiates slapped my back. Someone was passing out Dixie cups of water to thirsty jumpers as we passed the stage. I drank mine down in one swallow.

And so it went, over and over. I stopped counting the number of times I climbed and leaped. The pace of the jumps slowed but no one appeared any less enthusiastic. I certainly wasn't. At some point, I heard the laid-back rhythm of Tom Petty singing the praises of free falling.

There was no way to tell how many minutes or hours passed. My body felt heavier as I scaled the tower, but in a pleasurable way. My muscles didn't ache. I felt no fatigue. If anything, I felt exhilarated. Shapes began to swim a bit before my eyes and a new euphoria filled my veins. My leaps from the platform seemed to last minutes instead of seconds.

What a divine method of relaxation! I thought.

In the back of my mind I must have known that someone had put mood-altering chemicals into those Dixie cups. But anytime that idea came up, I let it go. I had no desire to dwell on negative thoughts.

I was Free.

22

≋

Perhaps you've heard the parable of the frog. You put it in a pan of cold water that you place on the stove over very low heat. The frog swims around happily, unaware of the danger it's in. Little by little, the water heats. The frog is too busy swimming to notice. Gradually the water gets hotter and hotter. By the time the frog notices, it's too late: It's cooked.

I wasn't quite cooked by the time the Initiation drew to a close on Sunday. But I wasn't entirely cool, either. Two voices were at war in my head as I packed my suitcase to leave.

Watch it, the first voice said. *You're getting soft.*

It cautioned me that I'd been subjected to a week of manipulation, mind control, and probably some subtle form of hallucinogenic drug. How else could I have let the rest of the week go by without paying much attention to my investigation?

Relax, the other voice said. *You know perfectly well what you're doing.*

After all, I was the one manipulating The Bliss Project for my own purposes. Wasn't I?

Four days had passed since Vince Shaffer had read the blood-splattered poem to me. In spite of his alarm, I'd decided not to risk leaving the ashram again to pursue that lead. Any more unexplained absences might have raised suspicion. My best bet for finding Jen was to pretend a bond with the group. To forge that bond, I'd quit fighting. I'd let go. And just as Malindi had promised, letting go had made my life much easier the rest of the week.

Exactly, the first voice said. *You're slipping into the cult. Watch it.*

Nonsense, the second voice argued. *Stop being para-*

noid. I'd freely agreed to take part in the lectures and programs. No one had pressured me to sign up and no one was pressuring me to stay. Yes, they called Malindi "Master"—but they didn't call her a messiah. That's probably why I hadn't found any reference to The Bliss Project in my research on cults. This simply wasn't a cult. Just another wacky consciousness-raising trip.

Then what about the blood-splattered poem? the first voice asked.

"Hey."

I looked up from my packing. Tuesday was standing at the door carrying a shiny gift bag stuffed with brightly colored tissue paper. She plunked it on the bed beside my suitcase.

"What's this?" I asked.

"A little something for the initiate."

I reached my hand into the tissue paper and pulled out a strange creation. Constructed of wood and about the size of a large hand, it had a head with a smiley face and five legs with wooden balls for feet. It resembled a giant bug made of Tonka toys. A paper tag attached to one of the legs said, "The Happy Massager."

"It's for those shoulder muscles of yours."

She took it from my hand and rubbed it along my upper back. The Happy Massager's little wooden feet did feel wonderful crawling across my muscles.

"Thanks, Tuesday."

A feeling akin to genuine warmth flooded me. What had happened to my aversion to this woman?

"Think of me when you see him." She flashed the Happy Massager's smiley face at me. "In case I don't see you again."

How could this be a cult if the good-byes were so low-key? I wondered.

She gave me a hug and then picked up her own suitcase.

" 'Bye, Whitney."

"Good-bye."

I watched her shuffle out the door and thought back to the beginning of the week. How put off I'd been by her touchy-feeliness, how trapped I'd felt. Where had those feelings gone? They were definitely gone, no question. At one point, I'd been counting the days—now I was in no particular hurry to leave. It scared me to realize that a part of me was glad my investigation would require me to continue with these people. In some insidious way, I'd grown attached to them.

That's what I mean, the voice warned. *Watch it.*

The fastidious clerk at the registration desk processed my checkout with seamless efficiency and made chitchat as the printer cranked out my receipt.

"Sorry about those phones, Ms. Brown. That's just how they like to run the seminar."

"It was actually kind of pleasant to live without them for a week."

That pleased him. A satisfied grin spread across his face as he handed me the receipt.

"There you go."

As I stepped away from the desk, he called out to me.

"Wait. I almost forgot."

I turned.

"You have a note here."

He handed me a small ivory envelope addressed to "Whitney Brown, Rm. 414." I opened it and read the note inside.

Dear Whitney,

Thank you for joining us this week. We hope you found your experience in the Process uplifting and worthwhile. A review of the questionnaire you filled out last Monday reveals that you possess some rather extraordinary aptitudes. If you have any interest in discussing our findings, please stop by Room 1505 before you leave.

Yours in the Light,
Malindi

I put the note back in the envelope and felt a thrill. I told myself that my excitement was because a one-on-one meeting with Malindi could help my investigation.

Bullshit, my cautionary voice warned. *You're thrilled to be getting personal attention from the so-called "Master."*

I hurried across the lobby to the elevator. If I played my cards right with Malindi, I might get some vital information here that would throw light on my search. How many members did The Bliss Project have, anyway? How many ashrams were there? Where were they?

I stepped into the elevator and rode up to the fifteenth floor. As I got off, I noticed the lens of the surveillance camera on the opposite wall. Room 1505 was all the way at the end of the hall. I lifted the weighty brass knocker on the door and rapped it gently four times.

The door swung open. Standing before me was a young man, barefoot, wearing shorts and a tank top.

"Kyle," I said in a surprised tone.

"Hello again." He stepped back and motioned me to come inside.

If the hotel had a Presidential suite, this was it. Though it was a good ten miles away, the ocean was visible through the plate-glass windows. The sun had already dipped below the horizon and a fading orange glow filled the sky. To the west, the urban sprawl of central San Diego stretched to the sea. To the southeast, the smog-shrouded hills stretched toward Mexico.

Malindi stood looking out at the view. Her caftan—bright white, the only color I'd ever seen her wear—glowed in the darkening room. Through the window behind her, the lights of the city were beginning to come on like stars in a new night sky. Dozens of votive candles were scattered on tabletops throughout the suite. They, too, twinkled like stars as the dusk outside faded to black.

"I love to just stand above the city like this and shower it with energy."

Her breathy voice filled the room.

"I love this time of day. As I watch each light go on, I like to think that another mind has been touched, another pair of eyes opened." She turned and smiled.

"Hello, Whitney."

One-on-one, the forcefulness of her presence caught me off guard. Every square inch of the room was hers, including the space I occupied. As I opened my mouth to speak, she stepped forward and took my hand.

"It really brought me joy to have you here this week."

In the dim room, her clear, light eyes reflected the flickering candles. They didn't look real.

"I'm . . . glad," I said lamely.

Talk about a bug trapped in a sunbeam. I felt as if my tongue had been fried off.

"Did you meet Kyle?" she asked, extending her arm. He stepped to her side and she squeezed him affectionately.

I looked at Kyle.

"Yeah, we met during the Initiation."

His eyes met mine and I regained my sense of self.

"I'll let you two talk," he said, stepping away.

I puzzled over their relationship as I watched him disappear into a sitting room off the central suite. He certainly didn't strike me as the boy-toy type.

Malindi led me to a table decorated with an opulent floral arrangement—hydrangeas, lilies, and summer roses in pastel colors. A chess set carved of black and travertine marble sat on the glass tabletop next to the flowers. She pulled out a chair.

"Please, have a seat."

Breathing in the heady aroma of roses and lilies, I lowered myself into the chair and studied the chessboard. A game was in progress.

Malindi sat across from me.

"Do you play?" she asked.

My father, an amateur champion, taught me the game when I was ten and we've been sparring ever since.

"Yeah, now and then."

"It's black's move. Go ahead."

I considered my options for a minute, then advanced the black knight.

"Check."

Malindi rested her cheek against her palm.

"Look at that," she said with a smile. "One move and you've got me on the run."

I saw a love of the game in her concentrated stare. This small gesture did more to win my respect than a week's worth of lectures.

She advanced her rook—the correct defense, in my opinion—and sat back.

"Do you mind if we finish some other time? I'd like to talk."

I shrugged.

"Sure."

"First, I want you to know that you're under no obligation to continue your studies with us. Please don't make a decision based on what you think I or anyone else in this organization wants. Any interest in further work must come from you—purely from your own desire. Do you understand?"

"What kind of further work?" I asked.

"I'll get to that. First I need your assurance that you are freely choosing to proceed."

"Proceed with what?"

She smiled warmly. "With this conversation, for starters."

"Okay. No problem."

"I know it sounds silly, but it's important to be sure each step of the way here. Now, do you remember the questionnaire you responded to earlier this week?"

"Yeah."

"You have some unusual aptitudes. Perhaps you're already aware of that."

I shrugged.

"Do you have any idea what I'm talking about?"

"Not really."

"Care to guess?"

Again I shrugged.

She cocked an eyebrow at me and grinned, as though I were being a naughty schoolgirl.

"That kind of fibbing might work out there—"she waved vaguely toward the glittering lights beyond the window "—in that world. But it won't cut it with us. We know better than that, Whitney."

Was there just a touch of sarcasm in the way she said "Whitney"? Or was I being paranoid?

"Now, once more. Do you know which aptitudes I'm talking about?"

"Chess?" I joked.

She didn't reply.

"In school I showed some talent for math and science."

Malindi took my hands and looked intently at me.

"Why are you lying?"

"I'm not lying," I objected. "At least three or four teachers told me that."

"You know perfectly well which aptitudes I'm talking about."

There was no escaping her naked stare.

"Are you talking about the intuition thing?"

Very gently, she squeezed my hands.

"Thank you," she whispered.

She stood and walked to a small kitchenette and snapped on an overhead light.

"That intuitive ability is a special gift."

She pulled a tall blue bottle from the refrigerator. Her fingernails were painted china-white and shone like tiles against the blue glass.

"Intuition shouldn't go undeveloped. Learning to harness your intuitive powers will really accelerate your transformation."

Here it was, the hard sell. I wondered if Malindi did a meeting with every newcomer, personalized according to each one's questionnaire results. It didn't seem feasible time-wise, but you never knew. Perhaps the recruits were divvied up between Malindi and other cult members.

"Would you like lemon with your mineral water?"

"Sure."

She filled two frosted blue goblets.

"And to answer your question, no. I don't ordinarily meet with new initiates. You're an exception."

"I didn't ask," I said.

"Not out loud." She handed me my glass.

She was guessing. Anyone in my position would have been wondering about all this personal attention. I *knew* she was guessing. But it scared me just the same. I had the feeling that whatever happened here, there'd be no turning back.

"So, are you interested in developing your psychic gifts further?"

I was interested in furthering my investigation. And for the first time on this case, afraid of what that might cost me.

"I have some concerns I'd need to be reassured about first."

"I'll be happy to answer any questions you might have. Go for it."

"I said this to Kami in the beginning and I have the same concern now: Why do I get the feeling this could be a cult?"

She smiled. "Answer your own question."

"Okay. The controlled environment, the repetitive phrases, the isolation from larger society—they're all hallmarks of a cult."

"True. They're also hallmarks of a lot of organizations that are good for society. Rehab programs, churches, temples, fraternities, sororities." She sounded so reasonable.

"Why were there no telephones in our hotel rooms? Why was a Bliss Project staff member watching me every minute of the day?"

"Focus. We told you in advance that the Process is a week of intense training. These practices are designed to keep initiates focused on the learning at hand. We don't want your attention and energies to be scattered."

"Why do I get the feeling I was under the influence of drugs during parts of the Process?"

Malindi laughed. "What feeling did you get?"

My bullshit detector glowed. It often goes off when someone answers a question with a question.

"I felt funny at times," I said. "Shaky vision, euphoria, stuff like that."

"Society programs us to numb life out. It's an established fact that we walk around using a fraction of our brains. Those wonderful feelings you describe were the result of letting go of old restrictive programming. It's ecstasy to get rid of that stuff. When you do, your body gets high."

She hadn't given me a straight answer.

"What was in those Dixie cups?"

She took a sip from her glass and then held it in front of my face.

"Water. And your questions are excellent. Definite proof that you're ready to take on the next level of training."

The next level.

"I'd like that."

"Are you able to travel out of town for further training, Whitney?"

There it was again, that funny inflection when she used my assumed name.

"That depends how far out of town, I guess."

"Only up the coast. We have a center in Malibu. Do we have a number where we can call you?"

I tried to remember if I'd given them a fake phone number.

"Let me give it to you, just in case."

I took a pen from my purse and scribbled McGowan's number on a piece of notepaper. If The Bliss Project had a good contact in the phone company, they'd be able to track down the address. I handed her the paper, making a mental note to remember that my actions at McGowan's could now be monitored.

As Malindi took the paper from my hand, one of her hard, white fingernails grazed my skin.

"We'll be in touch," she said.

23
≈

Soft amber light glowed through the window of the cottage. My heart rose. Linda was home. I hoped she wouldn't mind an unexpected visitor on a Sunday night.

I would have thought I'd be dying for some solitude after a week of nonstop *relating*. Scott Chatfield could have been speaking for me when he said, "I like my aloneness." But the prospect of driving straight back to McGowan's empty house didn't thrill me. After my exit interview with Malindi, I wasn't feeling quite myself. I needed to connect with someone who knew me and loved me, someone I trusted.

Linda is one of the few authentic psychics I know. She's a true friend, and my most unconventional, to say the least.

Even a little farther out there than I am. Okay, a lot farther out there than I am. She's taught me quite a bit about the psychic arts. While I don't understand some of the stuff she talks about, I've never seen evidence that she's been wrong about any of it.

The night was dark, so I stepped carefully along the rustic but uneven flagstones to her door. As a renter, Linda's got the ultimate sweetheart deal. Her two-bedroom cottage sits several yards away from the main house, a Mediterranean-style estate built in nineteen twenty-four on what used to be named Witherby Street, in San Diego's historic Mission Hills. Today the street is called Sunset. The property occupies the crest of a hill with a spectacular view of the San Diego Bay and Old Town. Linda supplements her token rent—two hundred bucks—by giving psychic readings to the owner each month. Like I said, a sweetheart deal.

Fuchsia blossoms, their hot pink color barely toned down by the darkness, spilled from hanging planters along the entry. The night was balmy and breezeless, unusual this close to the bay. The front window was open, so I called into the house.

"Land shark."

The door swung open and Linda positioned her considerable frame before me, like a football player guarding the last few inches of the goal line.

"Don't you dare come one step closer."

I wasn't ready for the jab and it bruised me.

"I've missed you too, darling."

She look pained, torn.

"I'm sorry, but you can't just drag that . . . that *stuff* in here. Where on earth did you collect all that garbage?"

I looked down at the purse slung over my shoulder. It does resemble a garbage heap, a rather daunting one at times. But really, to refuse me entry on account of a purse? Maybe she thought it concealed my handgun. It didn't.

"Linda, I'm clean."

"Clean, my patootie. Your energy field reeks of gunk." She screwed up her face, as if I smelled bad, too.

I felt ashamed, like I'd tracked dog poop onto her porch or something.

A troubled moan escaped her lips.

"I'll be right back. Wait there." She slammed the door in my face.

A couple minutes later the door swung open again and a waft of billowing smoke escaped into the night. Linda came out waving something that looked like a smoldering broomstick. A pungent aroma filled the air.

"Turn around, let me get the back of you."

"Linda what are you—"

"You know perfectly well what I'm doing."

I rolled my eyes.

"Isn't that sage-smudging business just a bunch of New Age hokum? A bastardization of an ancient American Indian ritual?"

The theory was that the burning sage cleared away negative energy. I could accept the Indian ritual. But I couldn't put faith in the hordes of white, middle-class suburbanites who were now using sage like the latest miracle product: Cosmic Comet for scouring away those unsightly aura stains.

"Depends on who's doing the saging. Turn around again." She leaned over and doused my feet, shaking her head. "What did you go and get yourself into this time?"

"Mind if I come in now? I'd love to sit down. It's been a long week."

She assessed me, hands on her hips.

"Let's sit on the back porch. It's a nice night. I'm sorry, I just don't want to have to deal with that energy in my house."

I followed her along the path that led through hibiscus shrubs to the back of the house. The porch wasn't such a bad deal after all. From this vantage point, the lights of metropolitan San Diego ringed the dark bay like a glittering galaxy. Ships' lights floated like tiny planets across the black water. A couple of Adirondack chairs leaned back and invited us to enjoy the view. I sat down and sighed.

"Can you please tell me what you're sensing that's disgusting you so?"

Linda pulled her chair a few inches away from mine before she settled in.

"It's as if you're not alone," she explained. "And I don't

like the company you're keeping. Oh, sweetie, I'm sorry. It's not you—it's *them*. I am glad to see you. I was very worried. I had a dream."

"A dream?"

Coming from Linda, a dream could be important. I looked to her for details, but she averted her eyes.

"Let's not worry about that now."

She sounded like she was talking to herself as much as to me. She got up and poked her head in the back door.

"Stanley! We've got company."

My heart rose. I hadn't seen Stan for ages.

"Hey, Stan!" I called. "Come on out and say hello."

He was grayer than I expected, but every bit as handsome as I'd remembered. When he first saw me, his ears came forward and his tail went up. He started to walk toward me but suddenly changed his mind and sat back on his haunches.

"Stan." I patted my thigh invitingly. "Come over here."

The cat didn't budge.

"Don't take it personally. It's not you he's avoiding. It's *them*."

Linda's comments were beginning to give me the creeps.

"Who is this 'them' already?"

"The entities who've taken up residence in your aura. They're feeding off you like flies on a carcass."

"What are you talking about, entities? Are you implying I'm possessed or something?"

"Not possessed. Just . . . visited upon. Your mind is filled with their thoughts. Wherever you've been and whoever you've been with, stay away."

"I can't stay away. The case I'm working on requires me to be with *them*."

"Then we'll have to give you some defense techniques."

By now, I knew she wasn't kidding around. I felt a quivering in my chest.

"Tell me about your dream first."

"No, defense techniques first, dream later. Now let me see who we're dealing with here."

She closed her eyes and began taking deep breaths.

"I see . . . oh dear, this is really something. Where do I begin? Let's take the dishy little devil first. Who is she?"

"Dishy?" My first thought was Kami Sutra. "What does she look like?"

"I'm seeing a woman with a black heart wearing a white gown."

"Malindi."

"Yes, Malindi the Malevolent. She's put a hook in you."

"Put a hook in?"

"It's not like the hook is real, not in the physical sense. It's a thought form, exists only on the mental plane. When you think of this woman Malindi, do any of her words come to mind?"

"Lots of them."

"Such as?"

"Let Go."

Linda made a hissing sound. "What else?"

"Transformation is painful."

At that one, Linda opened her eyes and glared at me.

"For her, it certainly will be. What else?"

The phrase popped to mind without my even having to think.

"Come with Us."

Linda sighed heavily. "I don't need to tell you how dangerous these people are, do I?"

"Probably not, but tell me anyway."

"Let me put it to you this way, Elizabeth. In some of the work you've done, you've risked physical danger and death. With this crowd, you're risking even more than that. There's a lot at stake here."

I got a sinking feeling. "Like what?"

For the second time, she wouldn't meet my gaze.

"Linda?" I prodded. "What's at stake?"

She let out a breath. "The well-being of your soul, for one thing. I certainly hope you feel it's worth it."

The picture of Jen—those startled blue eyes—flashed through my mind. Even with the advantages of age and forewarning, I'd already been affected by the spiritual mob tactics of The Bliss Project. When she'd first encountered Malindi, Jen had just bombed a job interview and suffered the unfaithfulness of her fiancé. She'd had no mother to turn to.

"It's worth it." I remembered my twenty-five-thousand-dollar fee and added, "I've fought for lesser causes. I'm all ears about those defense tactics, though."

"I've already taught you the first technique. Did you remember to surround yourself with white light?"

"Oops. How could I have forgotten that?"

"They're stealthy. You didn't think you needed it—but you need it now more than ever. Second technique: When you hear Malindi's voice, counter it with your own. If you hear her say, 'Let Go,' then you say, 'I let go of *you*, Malindi.' If you hear her say, 'Transformation is painful,' counter it with, 'I grow through wisdom, not pain.' If you hear her say, 'Come with us,' say—"

"—go to hell," I finished for her.

She gave me two thumbs-up.

"That's the idea. Actually, even just saying 'No' to any of their commands will do the trick. They've worked you over pretty good already. You'll need to do some counter-programming. What is that confounded humming I hear?"

"They have this audio system that emits that frequency at various times during the training."

She shuddered.

"I hear voices under that humming. Commands. Holy incense smoke, these people are scary. Whatever you do, don't go to sleep near them."

"I might have to. They live communally. The only way I can investigate this crowd is to make them think I'm joining them."

"And the only reason they're letting you investigate them is because they're confident the hunter will become the quarry." She shook her head. "I'm seeing flies on a carcass again."

Now she was really scaring me.

"I hope that's symbolic," I said.

"Me, too. Okay, defense technique number three: If you must lie down with these dogs, protect yourself. Do you have a pair of headphones and a tape player?"

I nodded.

"Put them on when you go to bed and counter-program yourself at night. Because believe me, they've been piping that propaganda to you while you sleep." She pursed her lips. "And don't forget to pray."

Linda's gaze was solemn, which wasn't like her. I hadn't heard her trademark giggle since I'd arrived.

"Hey, maybe you can save me a lot of time and effort by using your psychic gift to find Jen."

"That's the girl you've been hired to find?"

"Yup."

Linda shrugged. "No harm in trying."

She closed her eyes and started deep breathing again. After a few moments, she shook her head.

"It's no good." When she opened her eyes, they looked sad. "This challenge is your destiny, something you have to go through. There are some valuable lessons you have to learn here."

I hate when I hear the words "challenge" and "lesson." Out of nowhere, Malindi's voice kicked in: *Transformation is painful.*

"Go to hell," I said.

Linda looked crushed.

"I'm not talking to you. I'm talking to the black-hearted blonde."

She patted my arm approvingly.

"You're getting the idea."

The memory of my disturbing interview in Malindi's hotel suite was fresh in my mind.

"What about the dream you had?"

"I can tell you about that later. Right now you need to get in touch with a boy who's getting worried about you."

Toby.

"The neighbor kid across the street. He was expecting me back tonight."

I glanced at my wrist and saw that I hadn't put my watch back on yet.

Linda tapped my shoulder.

"Hey, before you run off, give me a hug." She opened her arms.

"Sure I'm clean enough?"

"You'll do."

She pressed me to her strong, solid body and I basked in her warmth. For the first time in days, I felt whole.

24

≋

I *felt* the car following me long before it came into view. I checked my rearview mirror. Nothing but blackness and an occasional streetlight. Yet for the last several miles I'd sensed the tail as an insistent pressure from behind, like a cold wind against my bare neck. I reached to turn on the heat but stopped when I realized I was perspiring. Again I checked my rearview. Nothing but the dark stretch of road leading to McGowan's house.

I flipped on the radio, a nervous habit of mine. FM 94.1 was playing Pink Floyd's "Dark Side of the Moon." Great song, wrong mood. Sometime during my search for an upbeat tune, my tail drew closer. When I looked up, I caught a glimpse of headlights about a quarter mile behind me. I rounded a bend and for a moment, my rear window was dark again.

It was possible the headlights belonged to another San Marcos resident, heading home late on a Sunday night. The chill at the back of my neck told me that was wishful thinking. I knew the road well and stepped on the gas. The engine of the Charger roared and I hit sixty in a matter of seconds.

So did the car behind me. The headlights reappeared, keeping pace.

I turned onto Sea Farm Terrace, a residents-only loop off the main road. The headlights followed. Perhaps these were locals on their way home, after all. When I completed the loop and turned back onto the main road, the headlights followed. Guess not.

My first instinct was to turn south on Twin Oaks and head toward the sheriff's station. A maneuver that would surely blow my cover. The headlights behind me weren't gaining, but they weren't losing ground, either. McGowan's place was less than two miles away.

I made the decision just seconds before reaching the base of the hill. At the last possible moment, I cut my lights and veered a hard left. The pile of mail I'd picked up at Toby's slid off the passenger seat and tumbled onto the floor. Without headlights, I rolled to a stop in pitch blackness. The high beams behind me blazed past along the main road, straight up the hill.

I watched the headlights grow smaller and disappear over the crest. My shoulders relaxed and I breathed for what felt like the first time in minutes. My no-headlights trick could have resulted in a fender bender, or worse. Thankfully, both the Charger and I were unscathed.

I circled back and took an alternate route to McGowan's. By the time I pulled into his driveway, I was feeling safe enough to begin thinking that it had all been in my head. It could easily have been a couple of hyper kids out for a joyride.

Still, the experience left me unsettled. On my way up the walk, I thought about Barry Bell, the investigator who'd dropped the Shaffer case and hadn't been heard from since. I wondered why Joanne hadn't gotten back to me on that yet. I'd ask her about it the next time we talked.

The house was quiet as a cemetery. In days gone by, Nero, McGowan's Rhodesian ridgeback, had filled this place with his reassuring, if somewhat slobbery, presence. Nero was now with McGowan in Virginia, which may have pleased the rabbit population around here, but it sure saddened me. This house without Tom was bad enough. This house without Nero was all but intolerable.

The clock over the stove showed twelve-thirty. The middle of the night, East Coast time—too late to call him. I put on some water for tea and realized my mail was still on the floor of the Charger.

I didn't sense any real danger but just in case, I looked behind the refrigerator, where McGowan always hid his twenty-two. The pistol was still there. I felt a lot better taking it along on my trip outside.

The dew had started to fall and the exterior floodlight created a vaporous, white glow over the driveway. As I approached the front of the car, I had an unexpected vision: A woman's form crumpling against the front fender. I knew this was happening only in my head, yet the image was so real that I felt the thump of the impact. Heard it, too. I paused to take it in for a moment, then quickly retrieved my mail from the floor of the car and hurried back inside.

I heaped the mail onto the kitchen table, thinking about what I'd just seen. This was the second time since taking this case that I'd had an image of a car hitting a body. In my childhood years, these visual intrusions had frightened me. My mother used to smile and insist that they were the product of my lively imagination. By the time I reached my teens, she'd seen enough instances of my clairvoyance to modify her standard response. To her credit, she learned to simply listen and calm my fears with motherly assurances that no matter what, everything would work out for the best.

I pulled out a chair and noticed that Tom had left the photo album from his college days on the table. Perhaps I'd leaf through it again. At the moment, I was eager to sift through my mail. I weeded out the catalogs, come-ons, and bills until I'd distilled the good stuff—three envelopes addressed to The Jen Shaffer Search, and one addressed to me from Vince Shaffer.

My excitement over the three letters generated by The Jen Shaffer Search Web site died quickly. One after the other, the writers expressed their condolences on my missing daughter. All three went on to describe their own experiences with runaway children. None of them offered a single piece of information about Jen Shaffer or The Bliss Project.

I was getting up to pour water for my tea when the phone rang. Who could it be but McGowan at this hour? Then again, I'd given Malindi this number, and days in The Bliss Project started early and ended in the wee hours. A dread came over me at the prospect of becoming Whitney again. I picked up the phone and answered with a tenuous voice.

"Hello?"

"You sound awake. Strange, but awake. Have you converted yet?"

I felt my grin spreading from ear to ear.

"I'm waiting for better incentives. So far, they've only offered eternal bliss. I'm holding out for stock options and a 401(K)."

McGowan laughed.

"Thank God your sarcasm is alive and well. I have to admit I was worried you might get woo-woo on me."

"Woo-woo?"

"You know, out there. Spacey. New Agey."

"Tom, I'm already a psychic. How much more woo-woo can I get?"

"Yeah, but you're not a woo-woo psychic. There's a difference."

"I'm so glad you called."

I could feel his warmth coming through the phone line.

"I was worried about you. Thought you'd be back earlier tonight."

"I stopped at Linda's, God love her. I needed to be with a friend. It was a rough week. You remember Linda?"

"Yes, of course. Speaking of woo-woo."

I was about to defend my friend but had a more pressing item.

"While we're on that subject, I'm having a recurring vision. Not to be gross, but are you sure that Jen's mom died in the car? Or was her body thrown from the car and then hit by the drunk?"

"According to the accident report, she died in the front seat. Why?"

"I keep seeing this image of someone hit by a car."

"Do you think that could be what happened to Jen?"

"I don't know yet. I don't think so. I haven't seen any sign of her so far, but I get the feeling she's alive."

Was it my feeling, or was it what I thought her loved ones wanted to hear? I hated it when I began second-guessing my instincts.

"Vince Shaffer sent me another package for analysis," he said.

"I know. Hope you don't mind. I told him to send it to you. Any word yet from the lab?"

"The lab's not sure there's enough to work with. The blood sample's old and contaminated. And the hair was cut,

not pulled out by the follicle, so that might be useless, too."
His voice went from businesslike to somber.

"Have you seen the poem?"

I picked up the unopened envelope from Vince Shaffer.

"Not yet, but Vince read it to me over the phone."

"What'd you think?"

"I think if I were Jen's father, I'd be sick."

There was a long pause. The line grew so silent that I
thought I might have lost the connection.

"Tom?"

"Yeah, I'm here. Hey, it's nice having you at the house,
looking over the place."

"I don't expect to be here long. I'm going on to advanced training at an ashram up in Malibu sometime soon.
I'm just waiting for the go-ahead."

"They have an ashram in Malibu?"

I put the envelope down and started flipping through the
photo album on the table.

"So I hear."

"Well, at least it's not Montana or something."

"I'll say."

"So how do you like deep cover?"

"Hate it. The lying, the constant deception. Gets on my
nerves."

"That's just it. Most undercover operators eventually
face the temptation to let down their guard to relieve the
stress. Or the loneliness. Or the boredom. That's where they
fail. It's not easy. You doing all right?"

"I'm doing okay. A little paranoid, maybe. Got freaked
out by some headlights following me on the way home
tonight. Probably just some kids joyriding, but I lost 'em
anyway."

"Never hurts to be careful," he said.

I'd opened the album to the picture of Tom and Jen
standing arm in arm by a VW bug.

"Hey, whatever happened to Jen's car, do you remember?"

"Her green Volkswagen?"

"Yeah."

I squinted at the picture but couldn't quite make out the
license-plate numbers.

"Weird you should ask that," he said.

"Why?"

"The way she got rid of that car was one of the things that made me understand how serious she was about joining the church."

"How's that?"

"She told me she and a friend were going to take her VW down to Mexico and just abandon it in the desert near Tecate. Leave it for some lucky Mexicans, she said. Told me she wouldn't be needing a car anymore."

That was odd behavior.

"When was this?" I asked.

"Last time I saw her, back in eighty-seven. Back when they still called it a church. What's all that racket?"

I'd gotten up to paw noisily through McGowan's half-empty kitchen drawers.

"Trying to find a magnifying glass," I said.

"Try the top desk drawer in my office. Do you think you'll be there when I stop by on my way to L.A. in a week or so?"

"I have no idea where I'll be in a week. I'll keep in touch, wherever I am."

The little magnifier did its job well and I was able to make out the first four letters on the VW license plate: 4KK2. Enough to start a DMV registration search, a lead the other investigators hadn't pursued. After Tom's story about Jen abandoning the car in Mexico, I didn't really hope to find anything. Yet in a case with so little to go on, it felt good to follow up on anything concrete.

I put the photo album aside and opened Vince Shaffer's envelope. Inside I discovered exactly what I'd expected to find—a copy of the poem he'd read to me over the phone. His photocopier had done an excellent job of reproducing the blood-splattered lines. Even in black and white, the droplets splashed across the words had a shocking effect. A phrase in the second verse caught my eye:

Hit and run, an ugly end.

How strange. Perhaps I'd been subconsciously remembering the poem tonight when I'd seen the image of a body hit by a car. But what about the first time, when I'd been driving home from my initial encounter with The Bliss Project? That vision had appeared to me before Vince had even received the thing.

I placed the poem on the table and stared at it with a soft focus, inviting intuitive insight.

> *Pray for the woman whose hair is red,*
> *Love her now, she'll soon be dead.*
> *Each drop of blood is a reminder*
> *As sure as taxes, death will find her.*
>
> *She was breathing, now she's not.*
> *Executed on the spot,*
> *Hit-and-run, an ugly end.*
> *Enemies are now her friends.*
>
> *Look carefully and watch your backs,*
> *Pray to find all the facts.*
> *May this strand of hair remind you*
> *Every child has ties that bind you.*

The insight was right there on the page. It was so spooky that I heard myself gasp.

25

≋

"The poem is a cry for help, Mr. Shaffer. The first letter of each line spells out 'PLEASE HELP ME.' "

Through the phone line, I could hear paper rustling.

"You're right, it does. I can't believe I didn't see that before."

His voice was faint and he sounded a little lost. It was nearly one in the morning—perhaps he was just tired.

I stared at the poem in my hands.

"You wouldn't see it unless you were looking for it."

"And you think this came from Jen?"

"Yes."

"Why doesn't she just tell us where she is if she needs our help?"

I put the poem back on the table.

"I don't know. Maybe she has good reasons for being so secretive. Look, I know it's late but I may not have time to see you again before I go back into the cult. I need you to tell me everything you remember about your last visit with her."

"Her last visit was two years ago, on the Fourth of July weekend."

That tracked with Jeremy's description of his last visit with Jen.

"Do you remember what she was driving?"

"I didn't see her drive up. When I heard her at the door, I looked out the window and saw an old Dodge van parked in front of the house. I presumed she came in that."

"What did you two talk about?"

"Nothing in particular. It was the usual strained conversation. I always had the sense that no matter what I said, she wouldn't open up."

I heard the same anguish in his voice I'd noticed at our first meeting.

"Did she tell you what she told Jeremy? That business about going away or into seclusion or something?"

"She told me she'd seen Jeremy but she didn't mention anything about going away, not to me. She was antsy and didn't stay long. Her mood was tense and distant but it had been that way for years by then, so I didn't think much of it at the time."

"What was the purpose of her visit, do you think?"

"I'm not sure. She didn't say. Of course I didn't realize at the time that it would be our last visit . . ." His voice trailed off.

"Was anyone else with her?"

"No, not that I could see. I suppose someone could have been in the back of that van."

"What color did you say it was?"

"White. An old white Dodge van with a rainbow painted on the side."

I hung up the phone and tried to make sense of things.
What had been on Jen's mind during her visits to her father
and brother the week before she disappeared? I needed to
see her last letter to Jeremy again. I retrieved my briefcase
and shuffled through the file until I found it. Once again I
read the words she'd written almost two years ago now:

> I don't see any other way out . . . it's time to move on
> . . . what this means is that you won't see me for a while.
> I don't know how long. Maybe not again in this lifetime.

I rubbed my eyes and felt a week's worth of fatigue hit
me like a tidal wave. I put the poem aside and turned out
the lights. I didn't even bother to take off my clothes before
collapsing into McGowan's bed. The last thing I remember
before checking out was the hidden message in the blood-
splattered poem:

Please help me.

I woke up the next morning hungrier than a bear and
stumbled into the kitchen in about that mood. Hoping
against hope, I opened the refrigerator. Empty, save for two
steaks of indeterminate age in the freezer section. Even if
I'd been a carnivore, I wouldn't have risked them.

The nearest grocery store was a ten-mile trek. I didn't
want to miss a call from The Bliss Project, but I had no
way of knowing how long it might be until they contacted
me again. It could be days, or even weeks. I had no intention of contacting them. This was a cat-and-mouse game
and I was playing the part of the rodent. Mice don't catch
cats.

I recorded a new greeting on the answering machine,
then punched the Playback button to be sure it was working.

"Hi, Whitney here. Leave a message."

It would do.

When I returned from the store forty minutes later, the
red light on the answering machine was glowing steadily—
no messages. I slid the groceries onto the countertop next
to my briefcase and heard some things clatter to the floor.
I bent down to pick them up.

Wedged against the baseboard was Tuesday Valentine's

Happy Massager, which I promptly threw in the trash. A cassette tape had also dropped onto the tile floor, its case cracked by the fall. I opened it and read the label, printed in italic script:

Transcending Your Darkness.

It was the tape Kami had given me on one of my first visits to the ashram. That I hung onto.

After putting the groceries away and stuffing my face with waffles and fresh fruit, I retrieved my portable tape player and popped in the cassette. For several beats, I heard nothing but a blank hiss. Softly at first, then climbing in volume, the fuzzy notes of an electronic synthesizer came through the speaker. Very New Agey. Finally, a rich baritone voice narrated over the music.

"Begin by taking a deep breath in. As you relax, imagine that you are emptying your mind of all thoughts. . . ."

I put on headphones and listened with closed eyes, curious to see where the guided visualization would lead me. The journey was innocuous enough.

"See your mind as a stormy sky. Now, as you breathe and relax, see the gray clouds beginning to break up. See the sky clearing . . . clearing . . ."

I began to float into my cloud-cleared sky. The voice guided me to relax and surrender. My breathing slowed. I felt weightless, free.

I remembered what Linda had said about how The Bliss Project had been feeding me propaganda even as I slept. Meditation tapes induce hypnosis, the optimum state for programming. An idea flashed like a bolt through the space in my brain. My eyes popped open and I picked up the phone, dialing the number from memory.

"Chatfield's Value Added Investigations."

Some people are born funny. Just the way Chatfield answered the phone made me want to bust up.

"Hey, Scott. Elizabeth Chase here."

I heard a sharp intake of breath.

"Are you transformed yet?"

"I hope not," I said, laughing.

"Aw." His voice was filled with mock disappointment.

"You'll be happy to know I did meet Malindi. You know, the woman who leaped on you."

"You don't believe it, but I swear that story is true."

"On the contrary, Mr. Chatfield, I have no doubt. Listen, I have a favor to ask. I have this tape here these people gave me. Do you know if there's anyplace I can have it analyzed?"

"Analyzed."

"You know, to see if there are any messages under the normal hearing range."

"Oh yeah, sure. I've got Tipper Gore's number right here."

"Seriously. This isn't an Ozzy Ozbourne tape. It's supposedly a guided meditation to help you 'transcend your darkness.' I have this hunch it's more about transcending your common sense."

"And this is going to help you find Ms. Shaffer?"

"I'm hanging out with these people. I want to know what I'm up against. Besides, I'm curious."

"Actually, I do know a sound engineer in town. Why don't you drop the thing by or send it to me or something. I'll have him check it out."

"Thanks. You're a dude."

Chatfield mumbled a modest denial and signed off.

I paced around the house for a while and ended up wandering into McGowan's office. The room had a deserted ambiance. Half-filled bookshelves lined two of the walls. There was an empty, dusty expanse on the desk where his computer used to be.

I abhor wasted time the way nature abhors a vacuum. I'd brought my own laptop and went about setting it up, happy to discover that the phone and modem lines remained intact. I logged onto the Internet, found the electronic archives of *The San Diego Union-Tribune*, and after keying my password, signed in.

"Let's see what we can find on you, Master."

I typed in the following search parameters: "Church of the Risen Lord, 1/1/84 to 12/31/89." I clicked the Search button and waited to see what came up.

A screen of article headlines and dates appeared. Skipping the not-quite matches, I clicked on the following item, dated 9/13/87:

Church To Host Breakfast

San Diego—The public is invited to a breakfast meeting hosted by The Church of the Risen Lord at 8:45 A.M. Saturday at The Flap Jack Shack, 956 Castro Avenue, San Diego. Rev. Malinda Vetista will be the guest speaker. For reservations, call 619-295-6061.

Malinda Vetista, speaking at a pancake house. Such humble beginnings for the Master. I printed out a copy of the item, then did a search on Malinda Vetista. No matches. I found it interesting that the transition from The Church of the Risen Lord to The Bliss Project had been a private affair, unannounced in the newspaper. As before, nothing came up when I searched under The Bliss Project.

I copied the item mentioning Malinda Vetista and e-mailed it to Joanne with a hurried cover message: "Go fish. A check is in the mail." No more favors. Before I forgot, I made out a check and put it in an envelope addressed to Joanne.

As long as I was in the archives, I decided to see if I could find the interview that Puma Man had given to the paper—The Bliss Project exposé that allegedly had cast him into a life of paranoia and secrecy. I entered "Michael Hugo" and sure enough, the article popped up.

Charges Dropped Against Former Cult Member

San Diego—Three years ago, Michael Hugo had every appearance of being a productive, well-adjusted 31-year-old with a promising career as a software developer and a house in the suburbs. Last January, he was indicted for threatening to bomb downtown's Symphony Towers—a charge later dropped by city prosecutors. Today, Hugo is an outpatient of the Sharp-Cabrillo mental health program and has accrued more than $40,000 in legal debts. He blames his current woes on a San Diego–based cult that he claims impersonated him and set him up for the bomb charges in retaliation for his leaving the group.

Hugo refuses to give the name of the organization for fear of inciting further persecution, but cautions all those curious about consciousness-raising groups to tread carefully when making commitments of time and money. "The truth about this fraud of a church," he says, "is so outrageous, so incredible, that I felt I must speak out. The organization preys on those ignorant of its nature by a barrage of outright lies, psychobabble, and promises of making you a god."

I was downloading the article in its entirety when the phone rang. Distracted by the task at hand, I picked up the receiver.

"Hello?"

I was expecting to hear one of McGowan's amusing opening lines.

"Whitney?"

It was a woman's voice. My heart went into my throat.

"Yes?"

"It's Aura. Remember me?"

With a name like that, who could forget?

"Yeah, of course," I said.

"Whoa." She drew out the word. "You sound bummed, or something."

More like wary. But I couldn't let Aura in on that. I was Whitney Brown now, a woman who was interested in psychobabble and becoming godlike.

"Do I? Guess it's just kind of dreary getting back to my old life after a week at The Bliss Project."

"You'll be out of that negative head space real soon, 'cause guess what? Remember I told you I had a room with an ocean view? Well, you're going to see it soon. You've been approved to come up to the Malibu ashram for the next level of study. Not everybody gets to do this. Master Malindi must have been really impressed with you."

There it was again: *The next level.*

I felt a quivering in my stomach, as if I were standing on the ledge of a skyscraper. Perhaps I was afraid of free-falling into the cult for good. Since my visit with Linda, I was beginning to grasp just how insidious their programming was and how much concerted effort it would take to resist it.

"Are you there?"

"Yeah. I was just letting the news sink in. That's great. When does this happen?"

"As soon as you can get here, basically. You'll be doing a special class with Abadanda. It's not really all that, uh, structured. You'll see. We're a very loose-knit group up here in many ways. You got a pen? I'll give you directions."

26
≋

I turned off the coast highway just north of the old Getty Museum, a mock first-century Roman villa that houses the priceless antiquities once owned by J.P., the oil billionaire. Interesting neighborhood for an ashram, I thought. I followed the narrow, winding road to its crest and slowed when I came to a row of tall, closely set evergreens. Aura's directions instructed me to look for carved teakwood gates marked by a pair of sandstone warrior sculptures. The warriors weren't hard to find. Rising up menacingly from either side of the entrance, each statue held a steel lance high over its head.

I rolled down my window and smiled at the scowling stone faces.

"Hi, guys."

I buzzed the intercom at the gate. A man's voice, friendly and casual, came through the speaker.

"Hello."

"My name's Whitney Brown, here to study with Abadanda."

"Come on in, Whitney."

The carved gates glided open. I tapped the accelerator and drove slowly along the narrow asphalt road, winding down through a sloping field of rye populated by live oaks and an occasional pine. After a dip at the bottom, the road began to climb. I drove up through a grove of lemon trees, their bright yellow fruit hanging heavily from deep green branches.

As I approached the summit, the grove ended and a breathtaking view began. The cliffs and beaches of the Pacific coastline stretched north and south for a good twenty miles in each direction. The road led to a small, rectangular landing. A woman was waiting for me as I got out of the car.

I recognized her raven-black Cleopatra haircut right away. It was Tiki, the woman who had demonstrated impressive psychic ability during the Initiation.

"Hey-ho," I said.

I rounded the back of my car to retrieve my luggage.

"Welcome."

Her dramatically painted eyes sparkled as she gave me an inviting smile.

I felt a moment of panic. What if she could read the real intention of my visit?

"Nervous?" she asked.

In truth, I was terrified. I remembered what Linda had said and put up a shield of white light, smiling all the while.

"More excited than nervous, I think. This is such a gorgeous place."

She walked me through a cluster of bamboo trees and over a wooden bridge. Orange and white koi fish swam languidly between lily pads in the black water below. Past the bridge, we crossed a wide lawn to the main building, a wooden structure that resembled an oriental lodge. The front doors were made of brass, embossed in a richly patterned design. Looking carefully, I saw that the scrolling arcs were actually the stylized coils of a snake.

Tiki saw me noticing.

"Do you know about kundalini?"

"Yes, I've practiced yoga for several years."

Vedic literature teaches that kundalini, the energy coiled at the bottom of the spine, rises as consciousness is raised. The powerful force is symbolized as a snake. Something about the way it was glorified here bothered me.

"Aren't these doors amazing? When the sun comes up, it hits the brass and turns them bright gold. If you're standing over there—" she pointed across the lawn "—they shine so brightly it's like seeing a star, right here on earth."

She paused to let the symbolic significance of the story sink in. A star, residing here at an ashram in Malibu.

"That must be something to see."

Inwardly, I gagged. The guru of Malibu, a star on earth? Give me a break.

We entered a large room with a cathedral ceiling. Afternoon sunlight poured through the high windows, illuminating the plush white carpet beneath our feet. There was no furniture to speak of, just a fireplace with a stone mantel along the right wall. I smelled the spicy aroma of something cooking.

"We're putting you at the end of the north wing," Tiki said.

I followed her through a pair of sliding wooden doors that opened onto a courtyard. Four wooden-planked walkways surrounded the perimeter, forming a quad. In the center, a huge expanse of pale gray sand had been raked into serene, swirling patterns around three black boulders.

Along each of the walkways, a row of black doors led into the building wings, hotel style. Our footsteps made a hollow noise as we walked over the wooden planks to the last door. There was no keyhole on the doorknob, no lock. I didn't like that.

Tiki opened the door. The first thing I saw was a single bed. I sighed with relief. At least I'd have some privacy here. A large window on the opposite side of the bed looked out onto a shady garden of shrubs and ferns. The room was simple—a night table, a desk, and a small bathroom with a shower. The plain white bedspread was made of muslin. There were no curtains on the window. A slim white telephone sat on the night table. I walked over and picked it up.

"Does this work?"

Tiki looked puzzled. "Why wouldn't it?"

"There were no phones at the Initiation."

She slid open the closet door to reveal a combination TV/VCR.

"Things are very different here. Phones, cable—we even have a video library."

"Excellent."

I put my garment bag and briefcase on the bed. I'd care-fully purged my personal belongings of any incriminating items. My briefcase contained no laptop, no address book. All I had were a notebook, pens, cell phone, tape recorder, and a few cassettes, including one labeled *Transcending Your Darkness*. I'd sent the original to Scott Chatfield for analysis. This was a dummy tape, filled with my own harm-less meditation music. Counter-programming, just as Linda had suggested.

Tiki turned to go.

"When you're settled in here, give me a call at extension two-twenty. Lord Abadanda would like to see you."

An audience with Lord Abadanda. Well, well. I was moving up in the world. After all, Malindi had been a mere Master. I smiled. If your goal is to understand an organi-zation, it never hurts to know its leader.

"I'd like to see him, too. Right away, if I can. I'll settle in later."

She looked at me approvingly, as if pleased by my ea-gerness to have an audience with Abadanda.

"Great. Come on with me."

We walked back into the main lodge and up two flights of stairs. Tiki knocked on a door at the top landing. A voice called us to come in. We entered a huge loft that was prac-tically all windows and skylights, taking full advantage of an awe-inspiring ocean view. The floor was covered with antique oriental rugs. A fragrant incense filled the air. At the side of the room, a man was sitting at a computer ter-minal, his back to us.

"Lord Abadanda? Whitney Brown is here to see you."

I heard the faint clicking of a computer mouse. The high-backed leather chair didn't move.

"The psychic one," Tiki prompted.

With that, the Lord spun around, sending the ornate clus-ter of semiprecious stones dangling from his right ear into a swinging motion. He leaned back in his chair and rocked slightly, looking me over from top to bottom.

"Ah, Whitney! I've been beckoning you on the inner planes, my dear. I'm so delighted you heard my call." His voice was rich and pleasingly modulated.

I could see on the computer screen that he'd been deep into a game of "Doom."

"I can hardly believe I'm here," I said, smiling weakly.

He blinked attentively, as if expecting me to pour out my heart or bare my soul. The silence became awkward. I reached for something to say.

"Great pants."

His lordly legs were clothed in enormous, baggy bell-bottom jeans encrusted with beads of every conceivable shape and color. He looked like he was on his way to Mardi Gras.

"Aren't these *marvelous?* One of my dear young friends made them."

His smile was boyish, charming even—but there was a touch of sleaze in those hooded eyes. They zeroed in on me now.

"I don't look like a holy man, do I?"

I had to shake my head no.

"Do you know why they call me Lord?"

Again I shook my head.

"Because I'm here to serve humanity. I'm here to assist those who wish to leave this plane of illusion. You've been peeking beyond the illusion for many years now, haven't you?"

Abadanda didn't wait for an answer. He got up from his chair and walked toward a heap of satin-covered floor pillows surrounding a low glass table near the window. He motioned for Tiki and me to come sit. When we were settled, he lowered himself across from us, the light from the window flattering his even features. He'd been a good-looking man once. Now there was a weariness in his bloodshot eyes, a slackness in his plump-lipped mouth.

"When was the first time you knew you had special abilities, Whitney?"

There it was again, the slight hesitation before saying my assumed name. Or was it in my mind? I wasn't sure and it was driving me crazy.

Tiki was watching for my answer with a frank stare. I decided to go with a true story.

"When I was seven, I dreamed that our school principal

was killed in a car accident. I told my teacher about it.
Created quite an uproar."

"Why?" Abadanda asked.

"Because the accident happened about three months
later, just where I dreamed it would."

Tiki broke in.

"But that wasn't your first memory of seeing the other
side."

Abadanda raised his eyebrows and looked at me expectantly.

"No," I said carefully, "there were earlier incidents. To
tell you the truth, I don't ever remember *not* seeing the
other side."

Tiki studied my face.

"Are you able to read minds?"

"Not really. When I was a kid, I used to be really good
at seeing the number a person was thinking, but the older
I got and the more I tried to control my ability, the less I
could rely on it. It's still that way—if I try to force it, it
doesn't work."

Abadanda and Tiki exchanged a look.

I was sitting cross-legged, my feet resting comfortably
on my thighs. Abadanda glanced at my position.

"You've studied yoga, I see."

"Yes."

"Hatha?"

"Hatha, kundalini, bhakti, dharma, plus plenty of Chris-
tianity, Islam, and Jewish mysticism. I've covered a lot of
paths on my search."

He smiled.

"Ah, yes. Many paths, one mountain. Do you know what
our path is, here at The Bliss Project?"

"Not exactly."

"This path is the rocket launch off the mountain. The
other paths are fraught with gravity, the hardships and limitations of the material world. The Bliss Project goes beyond this plane."

A path with no hardships, an easy out "beyond this
plane"? Sounded suspicious.

"You're not looking to hook up with a spaceship or a
comet or anything, are you?" I asked.

Again the two exchanged a look and smiled.

"If you're talking about all those poor souls who killed themselves, I'm afraid it's not so simple," he said. "Death doesn't guarantee a release from the illusory plane. It takes more than faith, more than death. It takes effort and an intense desire to see beyond the illusion."

He removed his earring and placed it on the low table in front of us. Next, he opened a wooden box on the table and pulled out three small oriental teacups. He placed the cups open side down on the glass and began to slide them in and out, around and around. The earring was now hidden.

"Tell me, Whitney. Which cup hides the earring?"

I frowned.

"May I touch them? Without turning them over, of course."

He nodded and sat back.

I closed my eyes and placed my fingertips on each cup, one at a time. When I was finished I opened my eyes.

"None of these cups hides the earring."

Tiki and Abadanda exchanged satisfied smiles.

Abadanda turned the cups over, demonstrating the accuracy of my answer. When I looked up at him, the earring was again swinging on his ear.

"Malindi was right to send you here," he said. "You have considerable talent. We can assist you in developing your ability. What would you like to do with your powers?"

"I'd like to find the truth," I said. No lie there.

"The truth. Of course, of course," Abadanda replied. "But this gift you have shouldn't be hoarded. You can use it to help others."

"How?" I asked.

"The best help you can give is to lead people out of the illusion. We can teach you how to use your ability to influence others. Tiki, for example, shows people what's possible when she demonstrates her psychic ability."

He gave her a knowing look.

"She's brought so many souls to our work. The more who join The Bliss Project, the more quickly the world will be transformed."

He peered deeply into my eyes.

"You're special, Whitney. You can play an important role in this great planetary event. The transformation is happening right now."

He held the intense eye contact for several seconds, then turned to Tiki and nodded.

She rose from the table.

"Thank you for your time, Lord."

With an expectant look, she prompted me to do the same.

"Yeah, thanks," I said, getting to my feet.

Abadanda stood up. Light bounced off the beads on his pants as he shook the blood back into his legs.

"A pleasure, dear ones."

He smiled and ambled back to finish his game of "Doom."

Tiki walked me out and back down the stairs.

"You passed the first test," she said.

Test. What a crock. His lordship had pulled one of the oldest sleight-of-hand moves in the book. It didn't take a psychic to see it was a parlor trick. Then again, maybe this had been a test of common sense, not of psychic ability.

At the bottom of the stairs, Tiki turned and looked up at me, her lavishly painted eyes watching for my response. I had the feeling she was looking right through me. My nervousness made me clumsy and I stumbled on the bottom step. She caught me by the arm.

"Are you all right?"

"Fine. Just a klutz, that's all."

In fact, I'd given my ankle a nasty twist and it hurt like hell.

"Are you sure? Now that you've brought your luggage in, I was going to ask you to move your car down to the lower lot. But if you're in pain, I can do it for you."

"No, I'm fine. Really. Where's the lower lot?"

"You'll see a turnoff where the lemon grove begins. Follow the road down to the right."

I did my best not to limp as I walked back out the snake-embossed brass doors and across the wooden bridge. The tranquillity of the place was enchanting and took my mind off my swelling ankle. I began to understand the appeal. With surroundings this lovely, it would be easy to become a devotee and allow someone else to make life's tough decisions for a while.

It felt wonderful to sink into the driver's seat and get my weight off my ankle. I guided the Charger back down the driveway. As Tiki had described, a narrow road appeared just before the lemon grove. I turned and followed it down a precipitous drop that leveled out into a decent-sized parking lot. I was surprised by the number of cars lined up in neat rows marked by stones. The ashram hadn't felt crowded at all, but there were at least four dozen cars parked here. I coasted along the last row, looking for a space. Then stomped on the brake.

I threw the car into reverse and backed up a few yards, not quite believing what I'd just seen. Sure enough, there it was, nestled between two compact cars:

A Dodge van sporting a brightly painted rainbow—Jen's last ride.

27
≋

Something had woken me up, but by the time my eyes opened and my brain engaged, whatever it was had slipped away. Had I heard a sound?

I lifted my head from the pillow. From the strength of the sunshine dappling the leaves of the mauna loa outside my window, I guessed the time to be at least eight o'clock. A far cry from the brutally early wake-up calls at the Initiation.

I sat all the way up. Someone had slipped into my room and placed a bamboo tray on the floor by the door. Cheery items were arranged artfully on the tray—a miniature ceramic vase filled with a single orange nasturtium, a porcelain cup and saucer, a small stainless-steel teapot, and fixings for tea. A cult with room service? Once again I could see The Bliss Project's allure.

I got out of bed and gathered up the tray. As I was preparing the tea, I noticed a photocopied sheet tucked under the saucer. I pulled it out and read today's agenda of the ashram's activities:

6:30 A.M.   Breakfast in the main lodge

I was certain that I'd missed the first scheduled event by at least an hour and a half. Fortunately, I always keep a few protein bars in my purse. Anyone who's ever done a ten-hour surveillance knows the value of protein bars. I continued studying the list of activities:

7:30 A.M.   Morning meditation in the botanical gardens
8:00 A.M.   Service work
Noon   Lunch in the main lodge
1:00 P.M.   Service work
5:00 P.M.   Afternoon meditation
6:00 P.M.   Dinner in the main lodge
7:30 P.M.   Break-out activities

There was some loopy handwriting in red ink at the bottom of the page:

> *Whitney,*
> *Meet me in the main lodge at 9:00* A.M. *for*
> *your orientation to Malibu.*
> *Tiki*

I rummaged in my garment bag and found my travel clock. I'd been close on the time—ten minutes after eight, which left me some leeway to shower, dress, and enjoy my tea. This case was suddenly feeling very civilized. If a rainbow-painted Dodge van was parked on the property, it wasn't unreasonable to think that I might bump into Jen Shaffer today. If so, it would be the easiest twenty-five grand I'd ever made.

Please help me.

I heard the poem's hidden cry for help as urgently as if it had been whispered into my ear. If that really was a message from Jen, why didn't she just take her Dodge van and drive right out of here?

I puzzled over the question while I waited for the shower water to get hot. As I stepped onto the clean white tiles, I recalled each blood-splattered verse. *Pray for the woman whose hair is red,/Love her now, she'll soon be dead. . . .* Reciting the lines took some of the glamour off the royal treatment I seemed to be getting here in Malibu.

I reached the lodge several minutes ahead of the hour, deliberately arriving early for my meeting with Tiki. The central hall was nearly empty. The few people walking through looked as if they were hurrying to be someplace else. I took the time to center myself, settle into my Whitney Brown persona and charge myself with white light. My own version of morning meditation.

Prepare as I might, my heart still thumped with fear when I saw Tiki gliding through the entryway. This wouldn't do. In my mind I reduced her to the size of a midget.

She came forward, reaching out to hug me.

"Good morning, Whitney."

I visualized myself wearing a white light suit of armor as we embraced. My techniques were working—when she pulled back, I could see a slight insecurity in her eyes. Large and beautiful, they had the disadvantage of easily giving her away. Today she wore a tiny gold ring in one nostril.

" 'Morning." I smiled sheepishly. "Guess I missed a couple of the early activities."

"Don't worry about that. Are you hungry?"

"I can always eat."

Tiki winked one of her lovely eyes.

"Follow me."

She led me into the kitchen, where a half-dozen people were busy with various tasks—rinsing enormous serving trays in industrial-sized sinks, wiping countertops, putting away the breakfast dishes, and preparing food for the midday meal. Tiki tapped the shoulder of a young man who was opening a giant oven. The heat hit us like a Santa Ana wind as he lowered the door and slid a tray of rolls inside.

"Any breakfast leftovers?" she asked.

He nodded. "Over there."

He pointed to a long countertop covered with large serving dishes. A few stray muffins and plump red strawberries remained on the trays.

"Sorry, no more eggs," the man said.

"I'll survive," I answered.

I walked over and scooped up a handful of strawberries and a banana-nut muffin, then turned to Tiki.

"Looks like they just fed an army."

"More like a platoon. We usually have anywhere from seventy-five to a hundred people here in Malibu. Of course not all of them turn up for every meal. Come on, I'll give you a tour of the grounds."

I popped strawberries into my mouth as I followed Tiki out of the lodge and across the lawn to a wooded area. We stepped onto a black asphalt path that led away from the main lodge. The narrow walkway wound in and around cypresses and pines. Lush green ferns carpeted the ground between the trees. Every so often we'd pass exotic mini-gardens within the larger garden—ponds surrounded by spongy moss and huge split-leaf philodendron; colorful impatiens blooming under the lacy canopies of Australian tree ferns. Whoever handled the landscaping at the ashram had it down to a fine science.

"Nice place," I understated.

She glanced back at me over her shoulder.

"Not a bad commute for the devotees who serve in the ashram offices. Come on, we're almost there." She picked up her pace.

The asphalt path opened onto a parking lot. Just beyond a cement entry stood a very functional-looking rectangular building. Gone was the oriental motif. This was straight-up brick and sliding-glass windows. Neither stylish nor terribly inviting.

Tiki headed for the entrance.

"In addition to your studies, you'll need to find some kind of role within our community."

It was beginning to sink in to me. I remembered an item that had appeared on the printed agenda.

"Does this have something to do with 'service work'?"

She paused at the doors.

"It's more than just work. It's how you'll channel energy into your transformation. The more energy you contribute—the more fully you give of yourself—the quicker you'll move to the next level."

The next level.

"What happens when I get to the next level?"

"Every level just gets better and better. You have more energy, more power, more bliss. It's hard to explain. You just have to experience it. Sure, you have to make a few sacrifices at the beginning, but the payoff is incredible, trust me. Are you willing to do that, Whitney, make a few sacrifices for an eternity of bliss?"

"I guess so."

"Good. What kind of role do you think you might be suited for?"

"I . . . that depends on what's available, I guess."

She opened the door and led me into a large work area. The room hummed with activity. A copy machine churned in a corner. Phones rang. Inside their cubicles, men and women spoke in businesslike tones into mouthpieces.

"Do you enjoy talking on the phone?"

"Depends on who I'm talking to."

"We have several job openings in our telemarketing department."

I stopped in my tracks, genuinely amazed.

"Do you *market* The Bliss Project?"

She laughed.

"No, nothing like that. We offer customer services to banks, telecommunication firms—companies looking to expand their markets. It's a chance for our people to connect with others."

Connect with others. Yeah, right. Perhaps some of those obnoxious phone calls I got in the evenings had originated from this very office. Cult-trained telemarketers—I should have known.

"We could use a data-entry person in our accounting department. It's not very glamorous, but you'd be doing a much-needed service."

I dreaded the thought of being chained to a desk all day, unable to roam freely in my search for Jen. I thought about my vision again—the barn, the cultivated green fields.

"Do you have any work that's more, um, outdoorsy?"

A woman carrying files walked by and waved at Tiki, who nodded in return.

"I'm not sure what you mean."

"Working with the land. You know, like picking fruit or vegetables or something."

Tiki burst out laughing.

"Heavens, no. That would be a waste of the tremendous energy, talent, and education of our community. Most of our devotees are college-educated. Aren't you, Whitney?"

For a moment I panicked, not remembering what I'd said on my entrance questionnaire. I stammered.

"Uh—"

"No need to hedge like that. Just because you didn't finish all four years doesn't take away from the education you did get."

I remembered now—Whitney was a college dropout.

"You told Abadanda and me yesterday that you were good with numbers." She arched her brows.

"I was talking about my ability to intuit them, not crunch them."

"I'm thinking of a number from one to ten. What is it? Quick, without thinking."

The number six appeared in my mind, plain as the ring in her nose.

"Twenty-five," I lied.

"Close enough. Come on, we've got a job for you."

My "service coach"—a supervisor by any other name— looked over my shoulder at the computer screen.

"Okay, repeat it back to me so I'm sure you understand."

Her name was Amber, and I didn't share her sunny outlook on office work. I tried to keep the boredom off my face.

"I take the figures here—" I pointed to a paper printout of company names and dollar amounts "—and double-check them against the figures on this screen."

"And if you find an inconsistency?"

"I go to the bankers' boxes in the archives across the hall and check the corresponding paper file to see if the previous clerk missed an entry or made a mistake."

She gave my shoulder a friendly pat.

"You're gonna do great, Whitney. I'll be on the other side of the room if you need anything. There's coffee and snacks in the break room—did Tiki show you?"

"No, she forgot to tell me about that. Thanks. She also forgot to mention how much this job pays."

Amber frowned, then smiled guardedly, as if she were catching on to a joke.

"Oh. Ha, ha, very funny."

"Seriously, I'm kind of new here. How does this all work? Do we keep track of our hours, or—"

Amber's tone was mildly scolding.

"First of all, this isn't a job. This is your *service*. As far as time cards and salaries and all that, we don't deal with paychecks and bills. Not in The Bliss Project. That's for that other world—" she waved her hand toward the window "—out there. In our world, everything's free."

I looked out the window and crunched a few numbers. If seventy-five or a hundred people lived here freely providing skilled services that would command respectable salaries "out there," the cult saved about three or four million in operating costs every year. I added that to the profits generated from the businesses themselves. (Ten million? Twenty? More?) Plus the seven or eight million in revenue from the Process in San Diego. My numbers were speculative but this much was sure: The Bliss Project was as much a corporation as a church.

I took note of Amber's outfit, a gauzy, flowered dress that suited her well.

"How do you pay for your clothes and other personal expenses, then? You know, insurance, gifts—"

Her eyes twinkled as she let me in on what she clearly considered to be a wonderful surprise.

"We don't have expenses. Food, clothes, shelter—it's all given to us freely. We're completely taken care of here."

"So if you get sick—"

"The Bliss Project has doctors, dentists, surgeons. Everything we need is here for us."

She stepped away from my desk.

"Let me know if you need any help, now."

I spent the remainder of the morning trying to keep from going cross-eyed while I checked seemingly endless columns of figures. The line items appeared to relate to the various retail outlets and services used by the ashram. The Malibu community wasn't cheap to maintain, but the costs I saw here couldn't be making much of a dent in the millions the cult was raking in.

My first two days in Malibu passed uneventfully. The ashram routine didn't vary: meditating, eating meals with the other devotees, working in my data-entry position. I kept my eye out but saw no sign of Jen. Frustrated by the way the job restricted my movements, I began to scheme a way to get out of my cloistered "service" work.

I planned to fake a case of carpel tunnel syndrome at the end of my third day on the job. But something happened that morning to change my mind. I stumbled across a pair of numbers that didn't jibe. Blue Lagoon Pool Services. Printout said $156, computer screen said $146. Nearly three days of work to find a measly $10 inconsistency.

Just as I'd been instructed, I got up to pull the file from the archives. I had to move a few bankers' boxes to get to the right files, which went back several years. Fortunately, some conscientious soul had clearly marked the outside of each box with a thick, black-felt pen. I flipped through the box labeled A–F, searching for Blue Lagoon Pool Services.

I was looking through the B files when I saw it: "Black Tower." At first I just kept flipping through the files. Then the words registered and my vision came back to me. A black tower, green fields. A woman I knew to be Jen, hurrying past a red barn.

I pulled the Black Tower folder out of the box and let it fall open on my lap. The file contained a stack of monthly statements. In the upper-left-hand corner on each page was a line drawing of a black tower, quite like the one I'd seen in my mind's eye. The logo read "Black Tower Financial Services."

Each statement showed a listing of account names. D&D Enterprises, Armstrong Motors, Seaman Lumber. A dollar figure, usually in the four-digit range, was ascribed to each account. A running total was listed at the bottom of each statement.

I shuffled through the file, hoping to find correspondence of some kind that might throw light on the nature of Black Tower's business. Was Black Tower a broker-dealer and were these stock investments? I doubted it. Amounts were listed as dollars, not as shares. The file held nothing but statements and apart from the totals, they were nearly identical.

Nearly, except for a handwritten note in the margin of the March 1995 statement:

> *M,*
> *Can't get first-quarter figures for Black Tower account to balance. I'm showing a $64,000 surplus.*
>
> *Zeus*

Zeus. Also known as David Sandberg, the guy Puma Man had accused The Bliss Project of "uncreating." How had he put it?

"There was a rumor that Sandberg committed suicide. . . ."

Something about even the rumor being destroyed.

"Whitney?"

Amber's voice was calling from the doorway.

"Hey, you'll be proud of me," I called out. "I found an error."

She poked her head into the room.

"Need any help? It's lunchtime."

"I'll be right out."

Until now, I'd honestly believed Zeus to be a figment of Puma Man's posttraumatic imagination. Yet here was a note directly relating to the vision I'd seen of a black tower. A note that might very well be written in a dead man's hand.

28

≋

"Looking for someone?"

The familiar voice startled me from my reverie. I'd been staring at the entrance to the dining hall, where residents of the ashram were gathering for the midday meal. Still holding optimistic memories of the rainbow-painted van, I'd been studying each woman who came through the door, hoping that Jen would be the next to appear.

I turned around to see who'd spoken. A woman with a streak of gray running through her long brown hair stood behind me, a plate of steaming rice and vegetables in her hands. She of the unforgettable name.

"Aura," I said.

She smiled warmly.

"Hi, Whitney. I was hoping to see you here."

I moved my chair to make room for her at the table.

"You're one of the people I've been looking for. Have a seat."

She put her plate down and settled into a chair.

"Glad you could make it. How long have you been here?"

"This is my third day," I said. "You were right. It's quite a place."

She twisted her long hair out of the way and picked up her fork. A sly smile crossed her lips.

"Have they put you to work yet?"

"You mean *service?* Yeah. But Tiki says I'll be starting my studies tomorrow."

"If you don't like what you're doing, I can get you transferred to another area. We're really not all that structured up here. You like your room?"

I thought of the hot shower and the bamboo tea tray.

"It's okay. No ocean view, though. Is that offer to visit your dream room still good?"

"Sure. I'll show it to you after we eat."

I wondered how she was doing with the death of her lover but hesitated to bring it up. Then again, mourning didn't seem to be affecting her appetite. The food on her plate was disappearing fast.

"So," I ventured, "are you still getting lots of support from your friends in dealing with Kenny's passing?"

She let out a snort.

"Yeah, the fucker." She shook her head.

It was a hell of a way to speak of the dead, but it made a certain sense.

"Ah-ha. So you're onto the anger stage of grief. Good. It's perfectly normal to be angry when someone dies. Death's the ultimate abandonment, after all."

She pulled a basket from the center of the table and ripped a hunk of bread from the loaf inside.

"Oh, it's not the abandonment that pisses me off. It's that he was lying to me." She took a bite of bread and gnawed angrily. "Jerk."

"Lying about his health?"

She let out a bitter laugh.

"His health? Yeah, you might call it that. Ken used to be a heroin addict. Supposedly, he transcended all that here in The Bliss Project. Now it turns out Mr. I've Transcended Drugs died of an overdose." She hissed. "Wonder how many years he'd been bullshitting me."

I looked at her sympathetically.

"I'm sorry."

She sat back and let out a breath. "No, I'm sorry. Kind of dumped on you there, didn't I? It's really just another lesson for me. Lets me know I'm not quite Free yet."

Aura was dealing with the double whammy of having a lover who died on her *and* lied to her. It saddened me that she was turning the facts into evidence of her own spiritual shortcomings.

"Don't be so hard on yourself. You've taken a major blow. Didn't you tell me you guys had been together for something like—"

"Nineteen years. Yeah, I did. But when it comes to the

illusion—and we're all part of the illusion, Whitney—you just never know. The only one you can trust is God."

I brought a spoonful of brown rice to my mouth, but lost interest. I set the spoon back on my plate.

"What's the matter?" Aura asked.

"Just burned out on macrobiotic meals, I guess."

Now it was her turn to look at me sympathetically.

"I'll share my chocolate stash when you come to my room later."

"Deal."

I pushed the food around on my plate. Why did I get the feeling there might be more to Kenny's death than a straightforward overdose? If he had OD'd, that meant a toxicology report existed somewhere. I spent a moment wondering how I might get my hands on it. Then reconsidered. I was here to find Mr. Shaffer's missing daughter, not to look into suspicious deaths. It was bad enough that my case was being complicated by the Black Tower Financial business and the note from Puma Man's missing friend, Zeus.

Aura opened her mouth to speak to me again, but someone on the other side of the room caught her eye.

"Bumblebee!" she called. "Come sit with us."

The middle-aged man approaching the table did not in any way resemble a bumblebee. Tall and on the skinny side, he fixed me with a pair of marine-blue eyes and smiled.

"Hi." He took a seat across the table.

I gave him a quizzical look.

"Bumblebee, is it?"

He chuckled as if he found the name funny himself.

"My nickname around here. Based on the fact that from an aerodynamic point of view, a bumblebee isn't supposed to be able to fly. But somehow it does. Well, that's me. Just gettin' higher and higher against all the odds. Right, Aura?"

She nodded. "That's right."

"Besides," he said, "my initials are B.B. So there you go. And you are?"

"Whitney."

He extended a hand.

"Nice to meet you."

"Malindi sent Whitney up here from San Diego to study with Tiki," Aura said.

He raised his eyebrows.

"Oh, really?" He sounded genuinely impressed. "A Level P initiate, are you?"

"Not yet," Aura responded. "But soon enough."

Silly nickname aside, Bumblebee seemed like a reasonable fellow. Then again, so many of these people did. I wondered what had attracted them to The Bliss Project, and especially, what kept them with the ashram.

"So how did you happen to end up here?" I asked him.

He sprinkled a few drops from a bottle of tamari onto his steamed rice.

"Long story. Basically, I came looking for one thing and found something very different. Something much better than my original goal."

Again I wasn't entirely clear on his meaning. It annoyed me the way people talked in generalities around here.

"What exactly were you looking for?"

"I thought I was looking for a woman."

What irony. I, too, was looking for a woman. I smiled coyly.

"And did you find her?"

"I found several," he answered with a roguish grin.

If this guy knew a lot of women in the cult, maybe Jen was one of them.

"Are you the resident expert on women in this ashram?" I asked.

Aura was watching our exchange with a titillated expression, as if she were mistaking my curiosity for romantic interest.

"Listen," he said, "if you'd like to discuss this some more, why don't you drop by my room later on? I'm having a little party of sorts."

Aura's knee jabbed me under the table and she cleared her throat.

"Do I dare?" I asked her.

"He doesn't sting," she answered, winking at Bumblebee.

"South wing," he said, "fourth door from the left. Any time after ten."

I planned to take him up on the offer, but not for the reason he had in mind.

Aura and Bumblebee started up a conversation about movies. I half listened while scanning the room. No sign of anyone who looked like Jen. As my eyes made one more sweep, I recognized a man with a goatee standing near the door. Kyle, whom I'd last seen in Malindi's hotel suite in San Diego. He acknowledged me with a slight nod of his head, then slipped out the door.

"This is breathtaking," I said, looking out Aura's bay windows onto the vast blue Pacific.

"Told you."

She pulled the curtains all the way back to reveal the full extent of her sweeping ocean view.

"What kind of service do you have to perform to reach this level of freedom?" I asked.

"You're so sarcastic, Whitney. What is all that tough attitude about, anyway?"

I shrugged.

"I'm just curious, really. How is it you get to have a room like this?"

She opened the door of a handsome armoire and pulled a small paper sack from inside.

"First of all, I've been with Malindi and Abadanda almost from the beginning. Kenny and I helped develop the Process, and it was our effort that really got it off the ground. When you make that kind of expansion in your heart, your physical reality also expands."

What about all the saints who've died in poverty? I wondered. I didn't want to get into it with Aura. I was sure she'd attribute their circumstances to fear, limited thinking, masochism, whatever.

I was tempted to sink into the goose-down duvet on her bed but instead, took a seat on a damask-covered chair.

"So what was your life like before The Bliss Project? Pretty limited?"

She pulled a slab of dark chocolate from the paper bag and handed it to me.

"Stifling. Politician's daughter, you know. It was a horrid life. Little Laura Linscomb, on an endless circuit of Republican party fund-raisers. Yeesh." She made a pained face.

"You're Robert Linscomb's daughter?" My mouth was full of melting, semisweet chocolate and the words came out as a mumble.

"You remember him?"

Robert Linscomb had been a fixture in California politics for most of my life, until his death a few years ago.

"I think most of us who were breathing in Southern California during the eighties remember him, Aura." This was getting interesting. "Was your dad also a member of The Bliss Project?"

She fell onto the bed laughing, her hair splayed across the pillows.

"You've got to be kidding me. He hated us. Almost cut me out of his will."

From everything I knew about the Linscomb family, cutting an heir from Robert's will would not have been an economically insignificant act.

"But he didn't?"

"No, I got my millions. *We* got our millions, I should say. More chocolate?" She held out the paper sack.

I reached in for another piece. "We?"

"The Bliss Project. God, it must have pained Dad to know that I would just pass that money on to the community."

Another potential source of revenue for the cult—member assets.

"I'll bet not every initiate is as generous as you," I baited.

She looked at me strangely.

"You still don't get it, do you, Whitney? Holding stuff back keeps you from getting Free. To the extent you resist, hang on, separate yourself—you interfere with your transformation. You've got to let go of that old way of thinking."

"Yeah, I guess it's just taking me a while to get it."

She handed me the bag of chocolate.

"Keep the rest."

"No, that's okay—"

"Go on, keep it."

"Really? Thanks."

"You have no idea how much will be available to you, Whitney, if you just stick with us."

If I weren't mistaken, I'd just been bribed with candy. Aura was a politician's daughter, all right. I wanted to ask her if a penniless initiate would ever end up with an ocean-view room, but thought better of it.

After my visit to Aura's boudoir, my own room felt more claustrophobic than cozy. The white telephone sat on the bedside table, inviting me to use it. Remembering my instincts about telephones at the cult's hotel in San Diego, I slipped my cell phone into my bag and went out for a walk. From a technical standpoint, it was possible for someone with a half-decent radio receiver to listen in as I dialed. Still, it beat creating a detailed record of my outgoing calls.

When I reached the wooded area behind the lodge, I dialed McGowan at his Quantico office, knowing the chances of catching him were slim. I got lucky.

"Agent McGowan."

As usual, just hearing his voice lifted my spirits.

"You're there."

"Hey!"

He was obviously glad to hear my voice as well.

I kept my volume low.

"Hi. Listen, I don't have much time. Do you have a piece of paper?"

"Yeah."

"Take this down. The former cult member I interviewed kept rambling about a guy named Zeus—a.k.a. David Sandberg—am I going too fast?"

"No, I got you. Keep going."

"Anyway, Puma Man insisted that this guy Sandberg had been killed by the cult and the whole thing had been covered up. Not just his murder, his whole existence. I thought it was all horseshit until I ran across a note today with the name 'Zeus' on it. I think maybe you guys should get somebody in here and check this out."

McGowan didn't sound convinced.

"Why didn't the big cat Puma Man go to the police with this Sandberg story?"

"He said he was afraid to. He claims the cult framed him for bombing Symphony Towers after he gave an interview to the *Union-Tribune*. I guess that put him off going to the authorities. Anyway, I have one more favor to ask, okay?"

"Sure."

"There was an ambulance called out to the Traveler's Inn in San Diego the first day of the Initiation. That would've been June nine. A guy named Ken Bastin died that day, supposedly of a heart attack but now apparently from an overdose. The ambulance service was California something-or-other. Do you think you can get your hands on the toxicology report and let me know the agent and cause of death?"

"Jesus. I thought you were on a missing-persons case. This is sounding more like murder."

I made a hissing sound.

"Tell me about it."

"You okay in there?"

"I'm fine. This place is gorgeous, once you get past the creepy vibes. Listen—"

"I know, you gotta go. Just so you know, I'm flying to California in a couple of days."

"To L.A.?"

"Yeah, meeting with my new boss, getting oriented with the squad, all that. Hope we'll get a chance to hook up. I'll follow up on this Sandberg situation and see what I can do about the tox report. Check your machine for updates."

"Thanks."

"No sign of Jen yet?"

No, but I'm making progress. I found her last ride—the Dodge van she was in the last time her dad saw her."

"No kidding?"

"No kidding. Which reminds me—I wanted to do a DMV search on her old VW, just in case."

"Don't bother. It expired in eighty-eight. I checked that years ago. But if you found her last ride, maybe you'll find Jen in the next couple of days. In which case, we really could get together."

"I'd love that."

"I love *you*. Take care of yourself."

"I will. Love you, too."

I dialed my home number. The machine beeped and I heard a man clearing his throat.

"Hey, it's Chatfield. I checked out your cult tape this morning with the sound guy. Turns out there *is* a subliminal message on there. It says, 'You will take down your pants and do as I command.' "

There was a snicker on the line.

"Just kidding. But there are some tracks under the main audio, about two minutes into it. Something about letting go of judgments, and concepts about right and wrong. Weird junk like that. Anyway, call me when you get a chance."

I punched the Save code and continued listening.

"Hey, Liz. Joanne here. Got your e-mail. Stop feeling so guilty about the research I do for you. Don't you realize I get a vicarious thrill playing armchair detective? Anyway, Traveler's Inn on Convoy is owned by Charles A. Lewis. The same guy, I presume, who married your friend Malinda Vetista in ninety-two. Looks like she's been something of a problem child. A bribery charge in ninety-two, a bankruptcy in ninety-three, and a drunk driving charge in ninety-six. That last case is still pending."

I folded my phone and tucked it back into my bag. Charles Lewis. I flashed on the man in the Armani suit at the party in La Jolla. As I walked through the gardens to my room, I got a clear picture of his wife, the platinum-blonde guru, submitting to a breathalyzer test.

Master indeed.

29

≈

Night fell eerily at the ashram. An unseasonable summer fog floated through the property and past the lodge, lending a surreal quality to the pagoda-shaped roof rising from the mist. I didn't see another soul as I moved along the wood-planked walkway to Bumblebee's room. I had the unsettling sense that I was the only one who wasn't quite sure what was going on around here. The sand garden in the courtyard was lit with red spotlights, giving it a Martian look. I reached the south wing and knocked on the fourth door from the left. I could hear muffled laughter inside.

The door opened a crack and a feminine voice trilled playfully.

"Who's there?"

"It's Whitney."

The voice giggled. A strange aroma hit my nostrils as the door opened. Not unpleasant, but not entirely fragrant, either. The woman standing before me was wearing nothing but a see-through, leopard-print bodysuit.

"Kami," I said with surprise. "Hi there. Do I have the wrong room?"

"Not at all. Come on in."

The only available light came from the glowing flames of a dozen or so very tall, cone-shaped candles. The room's two beds had been pushed together to form an island of sorts, populated by three castaways: Bumblebee, clad in a pair of smiley-faced boxers; Raj, the guy I'd met at the party in La Jolla, still wearing his Yankees' cap but nothing else; and a young woman I'd never seen before, whose purple-leather camisole and panties were at least not see-through. Good and wasted, they looked up at me with sloppy smiles and murmured slurred greetings. The stereo, turned down low, piped out "Magical Mystery Tour."

In my wholesome jeans and button-down shirt, I felt like a fifth wheel. Hesitantly, I stepped inside.

"You sure you want to let me in? I mean, I'm not exactly in compliance with the dress code. Or undress code, whatever."

Kami crawled back onto the bed and giggled more than the quip warranted.

"Of course we want you. Here, have a drink." She grabbed a bottle of ouzo off the floor, stretched her languid limbs and passed it to me.

I set the bottle back down and gave a little wave to the woman in the purple-leather lingerie.

"Hi, I'm Whitney."

She returned a limp wave but didn't bother to give me her name.

"Mind if I ask a question?" I asked.

The glazed eyes of the castaways didn't answer.

"I've always heard that certain substances like drugs and alcohol aren't part of the spiritual path. It seems like you don't ascribe to that notion."

Raj stared up at me through half-lidded eyes. They widened when he recognized me.

"Hey, I know you!" A puzzled look crossed his face. "Don't I?"

"I've seen you around," I said.

"To answer your question," Raj continued, "all that sanctimonious crap about drugs and alcohol is bullshit. Part of the illusion."

"Hmm." It was all I could think to say.

"Yeah," Kami added, "it doesn't matter what experience you're having as long as you go deeply into that experience, see? The only way to transcend something is to really *get* it, really experience it. Know what I mean?"

I thought back to my conversation earlier today with Aura. Apparently, Kenny had really *gotten* the drug experience. I met Kami's unsteady gaze.

"So let me get this straight. If you really 'get' the experience—no matter if it's bad or good—you'll just . . . transcend it?"

Raj attempted to clarify the point.

"Yeah. You go beyond bad and good. You get so you

understand how stupid those labels are. Bad. Good. Just labels."

"Hmm." It was my word for the night.

I leaned against the wall and slid down to the floor. The room was stuffy and I began to feel woozy. I wondered if the candles were impregnated with some form of opiate. I breathed deeply, hoping for at least some oxygen, and watched as Bumblebee reached for the bedside table. He picked up a mirrored tray filled with tiny rainbow confetti and passed it to Kami. She licked her finger, picked up a bright yellow dot and put it on her tongue, then passed the tray to me.

I hadn't seen LSD used socially for years.

"What fun. But I'm gonna pass. I've got my first class with Tiki tomorrow. Want to see how well I do unenhanced, if you know what I mean." I held the tray out to Raj, who took it with a wobbling hand.

I rested my head against the wall and tried to make the best of the situation. LSD can be a decent truth serum as long as you get your answers before the tripper's brain is fully fried. If I kept my wits about me, I could turn this into a fact-gathering session. For the next several minutes I did my best to look like I was enjoying the company and the Beatles. It helped when I closed my eyes. Soon I was humming along with the psychedelic notes of "Strawberry Fields."

"You look so peaceful right now."

I recognized Kami's voice.

"I am," I said without opening my eyes.

"Boy, have you ever come a long way."

"Yeah. Hopefully, I'm getting there."

When I opened my eyes, they met with the absurdly smiling faces on Bumblebee's trunks.

"So, Whitney," he asked, "how did you wind up here?"

"Who, me? Guess I wasn't getting anywhere out there in the world. I knew if I was going to find out the truth, I needed to be here." Every word of it true.

The woman in the purple-leather camisole spoke up.

"That's so cool, how you could just follow that inner knowing."

The conversation turned briefly on the subject of inner

knowing, then slid into a dreamy silence. I studied the four of them. From their slack postures, it was safe to assume their brains were sautéing nicely.

"So, Bumblebee," I said, "what do you do?"

His response came slowly, as if I'd woken him from a sound sleep.

"What?"

"What do you do? For work and all."

He fixed me with black eyes. His pupils had completely overtaken the blue irises.

"I'm a human *being*, sweetheart, not a human doing. Change your focus."

Kami flopped her head onto Bumblebee's lap.

"Yeah, change your focus." She pulled his face to hers and they locked mouths.

When the woman in purple began rubbing Kami's thigh and Raj looked on with interest, I realized the situation was deteriorating rapidly. If I was going to get any useful information, I had to work fast.

"Can I ask you guys a serious question?"

They turned toward my voice and gave me some, though not all, of their attention.

"People warned me not to come here. They'd heard rumors about new members getting kidnapped or something. I know that sounds stupid but I just really want to be . . . open with you, you know?"

That broke the mood. The four of them burst into snot-sniffing laughter.

"Do we look like kidnappers?" Bumblebee asked.

"Seriously. I've heard The Bliss Project keeps people against their will."

I was hoping to provoke a defense. It worked.

Raj sat up straight.

"Man, that's a lie. We've heard it before, though. Mostly from parents and friends who can't accept that someone they know has seen beyond the illusion of their world. Sometimes they even try to kidnap them back." He shook his head sadly. "It's a drag, fighting against the negative energy of people like that. That's why we change our names a lot. Sometimes you have to protect yourself against people who're still living in the world of illusion."

Kami had turned over on her stomach and was watching me with bloodshot eyes.

"You really could believe we're kidnappers?"

"Not you guys. But in the back of my mind I'm wondering if somewhere down the line, The Bliss Project might get into satanic rituals or something."

Again, they laughed.

"No way," Bumblebee said.

"But are you sure? What if—"

Bumblebee held up his hand to stop me.

"Look, I used to be just like you, okay? Distrustful. Suspicious. I was a real shrewd dude out there. A real dick, literally." He laughed at the memory of his old self. "So sure I knew how the world worked."

Kami rolled over and looked up into his eyes. He stroked her face, then looked back at me.

"And that *is* how the world works. *That* world—" he jabbed his finger toward the door "—out there. But that's not how it works in here. I'm forty-five years old. I've had enough of living with the cynicism and distrust. I finally decided that for once, just once, I'd take a chance that people could be here for me. That we could live freely, in real brotherhood. Maybe not the whole world, but here, in our world. We take care of each other—" he stroked Kami's face again "—and we love each other. That's the beginning of it and that's the end of it. I hope, for your sake, that you get it one of these days."

The leader of his world was a woman facing serious criminal charges. I felt sad for this man who had exchanged his good sense for false promises. Talk about a midlife crisis.

I struggled to my feet.

"I'd better get some sleep. Thanks for inviting me. Have fun."

They all chimed good-bye. As I closed the door behind me, I heard Bumblebee call out:

"Have a little faith!"

The fog was even thicker as I walked back through the courtyard. The black boulders in the center of the sand garden looked more like moving shadows than stone.

A real dick, literally.

What had Bumblebee meant by that?

My initials are B. B. I thought I was looking for a woman. A real dick, literally.

I was halfway to my room when I realized that I'd just been talking to Barry Bell, the investigator who'd disappeared in the middle of the case.

30

≈

My week at the Malibu ashram hadn't been futile. I'd found evidence that Puma Man's talk of Sandberg's demise hadn't been crazy. I'd found the absentee investigator. I'd found the Dodge van that Vince Shaffer had described. Now I was eager to find the woman who'd last been seen with it. Instead, I was stuck in a classroom, yearning for freedom like a frustrated schoolgirl.

The class was small, just five of us. One of whom was famous. I recognized the blond Gen-X actor immediately from his breakout film in the eighties and the stream of megahits I'd seen him in since then. I admit I felt for the guy. How confusing it must be to have your identity tangled up in that greatest of illusions: fame and fortune as defined by the popular press.

We were gathered in a separate room off the main building. The exterior retained the ashram's oriental motif, but the interior was a scaled-down replica of a modern movie theater. Rows of chairs faced a low stage. The padded burgundy seats pulled down for sitting and retracted when you got up. On the wall behind the stage was a full-size movie screen flanked by heavy velvet curtains. I wondered if the Malibu ashram once had belonged to Hollywood royalty— the palace of a producer, director, or star.

We'd all arrived pretty much at the same time and had been waiting silently for a few minutes. The woman sitting next to me broke the ice.

"This ought to be interesting, don't you think?"

The woman sitting to her left flailed her empty hands.

"I feel like I should have a notebook and pen or something."

"I don't think it's that kind of class." The movie star delivered his line with his famous toothy smile.

I remembered the story my roommate at the Initiation had told me about leaving the William Morris Agency and joining The Bliss Project after going in to rescue her famous client. I turned to the star.

"Do you know Tuesday Valentine?"

He brightened.

"Yeah, sure. We go way back. You a friend of hers?"

"She was my roommate during the Process."

"How long have you been in Malibu?"

"Just a few days."

"Well? What do you think of Nirvana-by-the-Sea?"

A few hours of data-entry drudgery aside, if The Bliss Project was playing good ashram–bad ashram, this was definitely the good one. Where the Process had been a take-no-prisoners barrage on individual freedom, here the pressure came in the form of seduction, with the posh environment doing much of the persuasion.

"It's lovely here. Very . . . exclusive."

The actor nodded slowly.

"Wait until you hear Lord Abadanda speak."

"I've already spoken with him."

His eyes widened.

"Really? Isn't he amazing? Don't you just *love* him?"

"He's quite something."

The actor ran his fingers up through his hair, a gesture I'd seen him do a dozen times on film.

"You know Abadanda's story, right? How he became a fully realized being?"

"No, tell me."

"Even when he was a kid, he knew he was destined for a great mission. His beginnings are very mysterious. His parents told him he was adopted and that his birth records were sealed. But the fact is, he has no belly button." Here the actor paused, as if he'd just divulged a state secret.

"Do you know what that means?"

I shook my head.

He leaned forward and lowered his voice.

"Abadanda wasn't born of a woman."

If ever a story sounded apocryphal, this one did. But unless he was giving the performance of his career, the actor's wonder-filled eyes told me he'd swallowed the tale hook, line, and sinker. I tried to envision it and nearly burst out laughing when I realized that I was picturing His Holiness naked. My guess was that Abadanda had achieved a state of belly-buttonlessness with the assistance of a plastic surgeon. Lord knows, there were enough of them in this corner of the country.

"Did his parents give him that name, Abadanda?" I asked.

"No. His name was Patrick Teagarten before his transformation. He reached total enlightenment in the mid-eighties. I've talked to people who were around him then— people who actually saw what was going on with him. The witnesses are always so moved, man. They watched this incredible presence, Lord Abadanda, coming through Patrick's body. He's a Great Being. Capital G, capital B. Know what I'm sayin'?"

A Great Being? The man who did tacky parlor tricks?

The actor went on before I had a chance to reply.

"You and I are so lucky to be sharing this incarnation with him. Abadanda really can take us Home."

He seemed eager to talk, so I kept up the questions.

"Is Master Malindi a Great Being also?"

"She was with Patrick during the early years, you know. Witnessed his transformation. It took a little longer for her, but with Lord Abadanda's guidance, Malindi finally transcended all her darkness. Yeah, she's a Master." He nodded with certainty.

I thought back to the litany of the master's transgressions that Joanne had recited to me in her last phone message. Malindi's sins may have been washed clean by Lord Abadanda, but the State of California had not been so forgiving.

All heads turned at the sound of the doors opening at the back of the room. Tiki walked down the center aisle and onto the stage, her black hair shining like lacquer under the stage lights.

"Good morning, everybody. Welcome."

We murmured hellos.

"Has everyone had a chance to meet? Let's take a moment to get to know each other."

One at a time, we introduced ourselves. I doubted whether most of the given names appeared on the students' birth certificates. Natori, Moonstar, Aman. The actor simply introduced himself as Angel.

Tiki thanked us and continued.

"If this were a university, I suppose we'd have to have a label for this class, something like 'Introduction to Advanced Awareness.' But around here, we just call this kind of work Level P. The P stands for perception. Now, each of you has given us some indication that you're suited for training in higher perception. We'll be teaching you to recognize advanced perception skills and be working with you to develop them fully. Today we're going to work on increasing your sensitivity to the light."

The room darkened and a slide came up on the screen. It was a precise, detailed painting of a man standing naked, arms at his sides. It almost looked like an ordinary medical illustration, something you might see in *Gray's Anatomy*. Conventional in every way, except for the thin band of white light outlining the body.

Tiki took a rubber-tipped pointer and drew our attention to the band of light.

"We'll be working today on developing sensitivity to the etheric body, which exists on the level just above the material plane."

I compared the image to the auras I'd seen. The painting on the screen was a decent likeness.

"Would one of you please come forward to assist in this next process? How about you, Aman?"

The man at the end of the row stepped onto the stage with Tiki. The screen behind them went black and they stood in the glow of an overhead light.

Tiki turned and looked at her student.

"Notice the light around Aman. Can everyone see that?"

Several hands went up, mine included. It wasn't like a miracle or anything. Light from above bounced off Aman and was highlighted against the black screen behind him. Very normal, non-etheric light.

"What I'd like you to do," Tiki said to the class, "is focus your attention in a sort of open-eyed meditative state. Continue to look at Aman, but with a soft focus. You don't want to force higher perception. It's more like you just *allow* it to come forward."

We stared at Aman for several minutes. My eyes began to water. At about the four-minute point, the light around him took on a green cast. The color appeared for just a moment. Then it was gone. After a few more seconds, the house lights went up.

Tiki put her hand on Aman's arm.

"Thank you. You can step down now."

When he was settled back in his chair, she addressed the class.

"Did anyone see color around Aman?"

The woman next to me spoke up excitedly.

"Yeah, I was getting a kind of green tint."

There'd been nothing extrasensory about the green light. I wasn't quite sure if it had to do with the stage lighting or some optical illusion. But whatever it was, I knew it had nothing to do with Aman's aura.

"Excellent," Tiki said. "Anyone else?"

I resisted the urge to raise my hand and challenge her. She showed us a few more slides, held a general discussion, and ended the class.

I was following the other students up the aisle when Tiki called out to me.

"Just a moment, Whitney."

I felt my shoulders slump. What now? And why me?

She waited for the others to leave the theater. When the door closed, she spoke.

"What did you think of your first Level P training?"

I felt trapped. To tell her the truth—that I thought it was a sham—would invite discussion. But something in Tiki's penetrating eyes told me she'd see right through a lie.

"That green around Aman didn't look like any aura I've ever seen," I said. "It looked like stage lighting to me."

"It was," she replied frankly.

"Isn't that dishonest?"

"I didn't deny or confirm that Aman's aura was green. I simply asked if anyone saw color."

I looked into her exotically painted eyes.

"But you implied—"

"The purpose of the exercise is to open the mind, to . . . *suggest* what might be seen. Lord Abadanda teaches that receptivity is the first step in the transformation. What we're trying to do is open our students to higher perception. It's like using training wheels. In time, they'll be able to do it on their own."

Sounded logical, but I didn't quite swallow it. I thought of what a golf pro had once told me—that if you practice your swing the wrong way seven days a week, fifty-two weeks a year, all you succeed in doing is perfecting a lousy swing.

"But you're teaching them to look for the wrong kind of light. It's like those silly aura cameras that produce pictures of people with garish colors around their heads. Those aren't auras. Those are dark-room distortions. How can you ever see the real thing if you're looking for something unreal?"

Tiki narrowed her eyes.

"You really have quite a gift, don't you?"

I shrugged.

"I dunno. Like I told you and Abadanda before, I've been seeing these things all my life. Can you really train people to be psychic?"

"If they have the innate talent, yes." She studied me closely. "Psychics are especially valuable to our work. As long as they're clear of emotional baggage and are willing to let go of . . ."

Her voice trailed off.

"This would be a good time to do your audition," she announced abruptly.

"My audition?"

"You unload emotional baggage during an audition. It's a big part of getting Free. Everyone gets an audition eventually, and then periodically as needed. Why don't I see if Lord Abadanda is available to assist us? Wait here. I'll be right back."

I sat in the theater feeling vaguely ridiculous. Now what

did I have to go proving myself for? Intense individual attention was not what my assignment called for. I needed to remember my role here, my primary goal. I shook my head, wondering how I'd allowed myself to get so caught up in the cult's games.

I heard the door open at the back of the room. Wearing a brilliant African-print robe and a smile just as bright, Abadanda strolled down the center aisle.

"What a promising student you're turning out to be," he said.

Tiki had found a stool and was placing it in the center of the stage.

"Come here, Whitney. Have a seat."

I walked to center stage and perched on the stool. Abby sat in one of the middle rows. Tiki stood at the side of the stage.

"What color would you like your artificial aura?"

"Simple white's fine, thanks."

The houselights went off and a spotlight blazed down on me.

"Could you dim that a bit? I didn't say I wanted the third degree. Or is that the point here?"

I was trying to be funny but wasn't quite sure I was pulling it off.

The spotlight prevented me from seeing Abadanda in the darkened theater, but I heard his voice clearly.

"The point is to free you, not intimidate you. As you know, Tiki is quite telepathic. She's going to read your emotional memory banks, see if she can find any past traumas that might be freezing you up. Once you become conscious of these frozen places, you'll melt them in a sense, and be able to move quickly toward your full transformation."

This sounded like a speeded-up version of traditional therapy. The New Age microwave approach, perhaps.

Tiki left the stage and joined Abby in the darkened theater. I sat quietly, wondering what, if any, emotional icebergs she'd find. I supposed I had a few. What concerned me more were the secrets she might discover.

I was beginning to visualize a protective shield around me when I heard her speak.

"The first thing I'm getting is that you don't really trust us. Is that true?"

Her question broke my concentration.

"I trust you to be yourselves."

"Try answering the following question: Do you trust us?"

"Well, no."

In the silence that followed, I tried to remember the other defense techniques Linda had taught me. I was having a tough time focusing. Tiki's voice was crisp and assured.

"I'm going inside now, to see where some of those issues might have originated. I'm getting some images . . . I see you with a gun in your hand. I see you raising the gun."

A chill went through my body. She could see too damn much. I thought I heard whispering. Then came her voice, very matter-of-fact.

"You've killed before, haven't you?"

It was true, and just as she'd seen it. An investigation a few years ago had turned ugly and I'd had to shoot my way out of a life-threatening situation. A round I'd fired in self-defense had hit a bottle in a meth lab, resulting in a deadly explosion. My mouth went dry and I answered her question by nodding my head.

"How do you feel about that now, about knowing that you caused someone to die?" This time it was Abadanda asking.

I looked into the darkened theater.

"It was shoot or be shot."

"And you feel—?" he prodded.

"Glad to be alive."

No comment came back from the darkness. Yet I had the sense that my response had pleased them.

"Would you do it again?" Tiki asked.

"If I had to."

I tried using logic to calm my fears. How much could Tiki really read, anyway? I'd seen enough of her ability to believe that she was accessing this information psychically. Suppose she knew everything, including my real identity? Would the worst-case scenario be all that bad? Wouldn't they simply boot me out of the ashram?

"I see a tremendous amount of conflict and insecurity in

your face," she said. "What's that all about?"

"I'm not sure I'm going to find what I'm looking for here at The Bliss Project."

"I see a lot of doors opening for you if you just stick with it. You've got what it takes as long as you don't let fear stop you."

"Stop me from what?" I asked.

"From going all the way," she answered.

"All the way where?"

"To your highest level."

Abadanda's voice boomed from the darkness.

"To your highest level, my child."

There were other questions, but I'd gotten through the worst of it. When the audition was over, the houselights came back up.

Abadanda put his arm around my shoulders as we walked from the theater.

"We're going to have to find a new name for you. Every name carries a certain vibration of course. A new name will help raise your vibration as well as remind you to keep your focus on your transformation."

To my surprise, Abadanda's arm around me almost felt comforting. In a way, he *was* a master—so skilled at faking sincerity that even his body told a convincing lie.

"I'm not very good at names," I said.

He sqeezed my shoulder.

"Don't worry. We'll pick one for you."

For the next few moments, the three of us walked quietly toward the lodge. Tiki broke the silence.

"How about Liza?"

I felt a fluttering in my stomach. Liza spelled out four letters of my real name.

31

≋

When my butterflies subsided, I confronted Tiki straight-out.

"Why Liza?" I asked.

She held her hand over her brow to shade her pale face from the sun.

"The name just came to me." Her luminous eyes looked past me and focused elsewhere. "Did you have a female relative named Mary?"

That would be my grandmother and namesake, Merry Elizabeth Chase, whose legendary sense of humor began with her name. For a split second, I almost forgot myself and blurted out the truth. I lied in the nick of time.

"Not that I know of."

Tiki frowned and started to say something, but Abadanda stopped her with his hand on her arm.

"Let it go," he said gently.

We continued walking toward the lodge. Again I debated with myself. How much could Tiki really see? Mary was a common name—possibly the most common female name in the English language. Like a lot of shady psychics, Tiki undoubtedly knew how to hedge her bets.

"Something's bothering you again," she said. "What is it?"

I leaned against an adobe-brick retaining wall and faced Abadanda.

"In class, somebody told me that Malindi is a true Master. Has she really been cleared of all her darkness?"

A breeze blew a strand of gray hair across his eyes. He didn't seem to notice.

"You're asking me to judge Master Malindi?"

"Yes, I suppose I am."

He joined me against the wall, lowering his weight onto the ledge with a sigh.

"We're all light in God's eyes. Yourself included." He smiled tenderly at me.

Apparently Abadanda, too, knew how to hedge. I wanted to know what he really thought of Malindi. Did she have him hoodwinked, or was he aware of her shortcomings?

"Is Malindi an enlightened being, then?" I pressed.

"Master Malindi has a special talent to attract the people and energy we need to continue transforming the planet. Hers is a very important role. She's the one who makes much of our work possible."

In The Bliss Project, *energy* was a code word for money. I got his drift. Abadanda had made a deal with the devil, of sorts. Or maybe just a demon.

He got to his feet.

"She's coming up tomorrow morning to help sponsor a volleyball tournament for underprivileged kids. I want you to go with her. See for yourself some of the things she's doing for this world."

Tomorrow was Sunday—not that I'd been expecting rest. Work continued seven days a week at the ashram. Still, this new development spoiled my plans. I'd been hoping to get the chance to look into the Black Tower files again.

"But what about my service work?"

Tiki started back toward the lodge. "I'll make arrangements for you to spend tomorrow with Master Malindi. As far as this afternoon goes, you can help out on the phones."

I hurried to catch up to her.

"On the phones? But—"

She looked back at me over her shoulder.

"Telemarketing. We want you to get a little taste of everything here."

I thought I saw a trace of wickedness in her smile.

"Good afternoon. How are you today? I'm calling on behalf of—"

I heard a click and the line went dead. Par for the course. I noticed I might get a few more words out—"on behalf of your Millennium Bank Visa Card" or "on behalf of your Millennium Bank Visa Card about a very special offer."

That was about the limit, though. People didn't have much patience with telemarketers these days and I'd be the last one to blame them. With almost every hello, I was tempted to say, "This is a bogus phone call, just hang up on me." But I worried that someone in the room might overhear me.

The Bliss Project's telemarketing-department goal was one successful contact for every six-minute interval, or ten hits per hour. For every taker, I'd have to endure twenty or thirty slamming phones. Every once in a while I'd stop and listen to the others manning the phones. The room was filled with the soft cacophony of their overly friendly voices pitching the overpriced "free" offer. It was the kind of work that could make you hate people, especially yourself, in no time. So I wasn't surprised when the guy at the desk to my right jumped out of his chair and wailed out loud.

"Augh! I can't take this anymore!"

He put his hands over his face and stood in the center of the room, trembling. As the others finished their calls, they got up one-by-one to gather around him. A woman wearing a koala-bear T-shirt from the San Diego Zoo put her arm around the man's shoulder.

"It's okay, Brian. Take it easy."

Brian looked up at the ceiling and started to scream.

"Why am I here? What on earth am I doing here with you people? This is insane!"

He made a motion toward the door but the others blocked him with gentle force, taking his hands and stroking his hair. Since everyone else had abandoned their stations, I got up and stood on the edge of the gathering, playing the part of the sympathetic onlooker.

"Do you need quiet time?" someone asked the man.

He was getting angry now.

"No! I don't need quiet time! I need to go home!"

"We're all trying to go Home," another one of them said.

He pulled away from the group.

"No, I want to see my family. Are you telling me you're keeping me from seeing my family?"

The woman in the panda T-shirt spoke.

"For a time, yes. But only until your old dependency on your relatives is gone. Dependency is one of the most insidious parts of the illusion. You know that."

He stood silently by himself, teeth clenched.

I remembered my conversation with Jen's brother, Jeremy. He'd told me that the cult discouraged family ties, and now I was seeing the truth of his claim in action.

"We've been over this before, Brian. Remember last time? How you saw that your resistance came up just when you were getting ready to break through to a new level?"

He glared at the woman.

"There *is* no new level, Tracy!" His voice was filled with anger and despair.

The others drew in closer.

"It always seems like that when you're on the edge of clearing some more darkness," Tracy said quietly. "Darkest before the dawn."

His voice was firm.

"I want to go home."

"Okay, we can talk about that later. But you're right on the verge of a breakthrough. Hang in there, Brian. How about a meditation leave?"

Brian looked at the floor. He didn't speak. I couldn't quite see his face, but I think he was starting to cry.

Tracy took hold of his arm.

"Come on, get your things. I'll go with you."

She led him from the building. A couple of the others followed. The rest of us resumed our places at our telephones.

Before returning to my station, I stopped at the desk in front of mine. The woman there was just slipping her headset on.

"Excuse me," I said. "What's 'meditation leave'?"

She looked up at me with a vacuous smile.

"It's wonderful. Just like a vacation. Massage therapy, herbal teas, lots of guided meditation and counseling."

I recalled what Scott Chatfield had reported about the subliminal track on The Bliss Project's meditation tape. Hidden commands to let go of judgment, discernment, common sense. I was sure the herbal teas contained hidden persuasions as well. I didn't know Brian personally, but my heart went out to him.

I sat at my desk and wondered how many numbers I'd dialed this afternoon. Well over a hundred. I sincerely doubted that anyone paid attention to each and every one of these thousands of outgoing calls. Taking a quick, calculated risk, I dialed my answering machine. When I heard my message come on, I started into my pitch.

"Good afternoon. How are you today? I'm calling on behalf of—"

I entered my code and the machine told me I had one message. Just as I'd hoped, it was from McGowan.

"I followed up on those questions you raised. As far as getting someone to look into that first matter, guess what? David Sandberg's disappearance is an open case with the Bureau. We've already got a guy on it. Agent's name is Harrison. I don't know him. I'll tell you more as soon as I know more. As for that tox report you wanted, I'm still waiting. Should have an answer by tomorrow. Meanwhile, careful in there, okay? Gotta go."

I wanted to replay the message but didn't dare linger too long on a call to my own machine. I made a mental note of the agent's name—Harrison—then dialed another number and began again.

"Good afternoon. How are you today? I'm calling . . ."

32
≈

I reached the bridge spanning the koi pond just as the white van drove up. When it pulled within view, my heart skipped a beat. A brightly painted rainbow streaked along its side, leading to a pot of gold on the back doors. It was the van I'd seen in the parking lot earlier this week, the same vehicle Vince Shaffer had last seen his daughter driving.

The passenger window opened and Malindi's blonde head appeared.

"Good morning."

In spite of a casual tank top and sporty white visor, Malindi dazzled with her trademark superficial glamour, wearing a lot more makeup than was customary for a trip to the beach.

I opened the door and climbed into the backseat.

"Good morning, Master."

The word felt horribly wrong. The rainbow-painted van had me nonplussed and my thoughts were spinning. Malindi watched me settle in.

"That's an awfully troubled face for a morning as glorious as this one."

The backseat was filled with beach gear—volleyballs, beach chairs, umbrellas, coolers. I pushed aside a stack of brightly colored towels to make a little more room for myself.

"Just not much of a morning person."

She reached back to squeeze my arm, the tattoo on her bare shoulder reminding me to *Have Faith*.

"Let go of those troubling thoughts. Open to the moment."

I forced a smile.

"I'll try."

"I hear you have a new name," she said. "Liza, is it?"

I nodded.

She patted my arm and turned back to face the front.

"Welcome to the fold, Liza."

I wondered how I'd ever been even remotely impressed with this woman. There'd been moments during the Initiation when she'd appeared to be a loving, free spirit, leaping childlike from the tower to the trampoline below. I felt my cheeks flush as I remembered the way we'd all followed her like lemmings. Looking at her now, I certainly didn't see a Master. I saw Malinda Vetista, a bankrupt drunk driver who wasn't above bribery.

Kyle was driving. He skillfully navigated the van down the winding road.

"Hey, you in the driver's seat," I said. "Hello again."

He was wearing sunglasses, so I couldn't tell whether or not he was looking at me in the rearview mirror. Not until he held up a hand in greeting.

Our ride was strangely quiet. I felt the pressure to make conversation that so often accompanies an awkward silence, but held my tongue. The less I revealed about myself, the better, and the best way to do that was to keep my mouth shut. Tiki and Abadanda had already gleaned too much about me. I tried to assume a contemplative posture, as if gazing out the windows were an exercise in appreciating the glory of God.

Which, in fact, it was. From high on the unclouded headlands we looked down on the morning fog clinging to the ocean. The warming sun was breaking up the mist. Fragments of dark blue sea pierced through miles of fluffy gray like an endless patchwork quilt. The descent was steep. In minutes we were at sea level, cruising the Pacific Coast Highway along a partly sunny shoreline.

We turned into the Malibu Beach parking lot and I got a discouraging surprise. Three vans with rainbow stripes painted along their sides were parked all in a row.

Great, I thought, a generic cult vehicle.

With sinking hopes I realized that the van didn't necessarily mean that Jen was, or ever had been, at the Malibu ashram. The back doors on one of the vans burst open, splitting the pot of gold. A pack of kids poured out and ran screaming toward the beach.

I pulled a baseball cap over my head and helped Kyle haul a cooler onto the sand. We headed toward two enormous palm trees rising near the volleyball nets. A white banner had been strung up between the palms. Giant letters announced "The Big Heart Games." The logos of several prominent corporations appeared on the banner, along with a rainbow arching over the words "Sponsored and Coordinated by The Bliss Project."

I approached Malindi to ask her some questions about the event, but she rushed past me without even seeing me. I turned and saw the source of her interest. A young man was standing in the sand with a television camera perched on his shoulder. Watching Malindi go to work was fascinating in a way, like watching a spider zero in on a freshly snagged insect.

She touched the cameraman's arm and gazed deeply into his eyes. I was too far away to hear but could see by the way his scowl melted into a smile that her words had achieved the desired effect. Without taking her hand from his arm, Malindi maneuvered her hips so that she was now standing in front of The Bliss Project logo.

Just chatting. Just making friends.

It wasn't long before the camera was rolling, taking in Malindi and the logo behind her. I stepped closer to hear.

"Of the many charities we've sponsored over the years, this event is one of our favorites. Most of these kids come from communities that don't allow them to get to the beach easily. And these beautiful beaches belong to everybody, *especially* to our children. We see this as a great opportunity for these kids to come out here, get some good exercise and fresh air and have a little fun."

Malindi's glossy pink lips smiled and her white teeth gleamed in the sunshine. A stray volleyball shot in front of her. Without missing a beat, she intercepted the ball and turned to the little girl coming after it. She made a big deal of handing it back to the child, pouring on her smile for the camera.

A woman nearby turned to me with a dreamy expression.

"Isn't Master beautiful? What a beacon of light she is in this world!"

I made an effort to smile, then helped myself to an orange soda from the cooler. I popped open the can and continued my eavesdropping on Malindi. For me, she was the real game going on here. She circulated among the spectators, quickly weeding out mere parents but giving full frontal public relations to anyone associated with the sponsoring corporations.

I took a seat on the bench of a picnic table and viewed the whole panorama: youngsters, grown-ups, volleyballs, television cameras. I noticed that Kyle never strayed far from Malindi's side. Observing him was rather painless. A lot of guys with his olive-skinned male beauty might have preened and posed. Not Kyle. His swim trunks were refreshingly unfashionable. He'd slung a bulky black fanny pack around his hips. Whatever he had in there, it was heavy.

Malindi was now talking with a couple of silver-haired men wearing tiny hoop earrings and expensive sunglasses. From the intensity of her charm, I deduced that these guys must be movers and shakers of the first water. When she settled into a beach chair between them, Kyle wandered my way and took a seat on the opposite side of the picnic table. He kept his eyes on Malindi.

"You look like you're auditioning for a starring role in a dramatic bayside TV series," I said.

He pulled his sunglasses low on his nose, peered over the top of the lenses, and uttered one disgusted word.

"Please."

"Just teasing. Take no offense."

"Bayside TV series?" His lips curled in pure derision.

"I didn't mean it as an insult, really. Although the fact that you're insulted speaks volumes for you. Do you always carry a gun?"

He did the peering-over-the-lenses thing again. After a prolonged stare-down, he answered.

"It's my job. I'm the Master's bodyguard."

"Oh."

I didn't say it, but I thought it. *Why would a guru need a bodyguard?*

"I'm surprised you stayed on," he said. "It really seemed like this wasn't your cup of tea, that first week I met you."

I took a drink from my soda. The sweet orange liquid was already getting warm. I put the can back on the picnic table, done with it.

"Like I told you then, I'm looking for something in my life. And I think I might find it here."

A fly landed on the top of my can and he shooed it away.

"You haven't found it yet?"

I shook my head and looked out to sea.

"No, still searching. And you?"

He pushed his sunglasses back up on his nose.

"I know I'm in the right place."

I watched the waves break on the sand but studied Kyle in my peripheral vision, tuning into his energy. There was something terribly familiar in his demeanor. His aura was at once easy and difficult to read. The easy part was the strong sense of responsibility, the natural authority. The hard part was his inner self. Whoever Kyle was, he didn't bare his soul.

Then suddenly I *knew*.

"Agent Harrison?" I said.

He pulled his glasses back down his nose and stared at me with hard brown eyes.

"What'd you say?"

I stared into his eyes.

"Harrison," I pronounced plainly.

He knitted his brows.

"I'm sorry, I don't get it."

But he did get it, I *knew* he did.

I smiled and looked back to the sea.

"Okay, be that way."

I chatted with dozens of people over the course of the long day at the beach, seeing what dirt I might be able to dig up about The Bliss Project. From all accounts, The Big Heart Games were what Malindi had presented them to be. I mingled for a while with a delightful woman in her sixties who wore a straw hat and bright yellow shorts. The principal of an elementary school in Compton, she had a great sense of humor, no pretenses, and even fewer illusions.

"How did you happen to get involved in this event today?" I asked her.

"Just got a call one day from these people, wanting to know if we'd like to bring the students out to the beach. Told them we didn't have buses to get them here, or food money or anything else. They said they'd arrange for transportation and provide the lunch money and sports equipment."

"Why do you think they picked your school?"

She stared at me frankly.

"What, you mean as opposed to Beverly Hills 90210?"

I felt like an idiot.

"I see your point."

"I would've preferred them to give us seed money to fund decent teacher salaries. But what can I say? The kids are having a good time."

As always, I kept my eye out for anyone who even vaguely resembled Jen. Within an hour I'd managed to mingle with every person in the group, and a few local beachgoers as well. But Jen was nowhere to be seen.

As the day wore on and the sun grew hotter, I succumbed to the lure of the water. I spent the rest of the afternoon bodysurfing. An insistent undertow was moving north, so I kept my eye on a pack of kids floating on Boogie boards. Occasionally one of them would get lucky and catch the white water into shore. I made a big hit with the gang when I called their attention to a small jellyfish heading their way. After their initial screaming, the die-hards couldn't keep away from the thing, despite my warning that a tentacle across an arm or a leg was worse than ten bee stings. Fortunately, the creature drifted away without incident.

When I saw The Big Heart Games' banner come down, I knew it was time to head back in. I don't know who was less eager to return to shore, me or the kids.

Back on the sand, the swell of summer crowds had thinned out and the tide was coming in. The offshore breeze had kicked up, bringing a chill to the air. People were packing up their towels and beach chairs and gathering around the water faucets to rinse the sand from their legs and feet. As I toweled my hair dry, I heard Malindi call to me.

"Liza! Could you help Kyle with the cooler again?"

"Sure."

Kyle was tipping the cooler on its side, letting water from the melted ice drain out.

"Give you a hand?" I offered.

He looked up at me.

"Yeah, thanks."

Without the drinks and ice, the cooler wasn't heavy at all—just bulky. We had quite a hike, though, since our van was parked by the large square trash bins all the way at the end of the lot. We set the cooler down a few feet from the bumper. Kyle opened the doors, and the pot of gold painted on the back split in two. We slid the cooler in with little effort.

He handed me the car keys.

"Go ahead and get in. I'll round up Malindi."

"Okay."

I took the keys and walked around to the passenger-side door. I was turning the key in the lock when I heard something behind me. Before I could react, my arm was twisted into a half nelson and I felt the barrel of a gun pushing hard into the small of my back.

"Who the fuck are you?" Kyle growled.

33

≈

Odd as it sounds, when I felt Kyle's gun against my spine, my first thought was that I hadn't put enough sunscreen on. The skin underneath the steel barrel was unusually tender.

"You're hurting my sunburn. Could you just—"

He pressed the metal harder into my back.

"I said, who the fuck are you?"

A little late, I realized that if this wasn't Agent Harrison, I'd picked the wrong guy to play games with. But I *knew*, with the knowledge that supersedes reason. Still, I did a little hedge-betting of my own.

"I'm a psychic. When we were sitting together at the picnic bench this morning, the name Harrison just came to me. I've been taking Level P classes with Tiki—"

"Bullshit," he said flatly.

"Not bullshit," I insisted.

A seagull flew overhead, screeching brashly. Birds were the only ones who could see us. The van and trash bins completely obscured us from public view.

My body was starting to hurt, particularly my shoulder.

"Listen, as you can probably tell, I'm not wearing any concealed weapons."

Clad only in a bikini, shorts, and sandals, I gave him a moment to let that sink in.

"I'm not a martial-arts expert. You'll have to take my word on that one. Now, could you please lay off the superhero routine?"

The pressure came off my back and he loosened his grip on my arm but didn't let go.

"I'm not buying that the name 'Agent Harrison' came to you out of thin air."

"And I'm not buying that you're Malindi's bodyguard. Why aren't you protecting her now?"

I quickly realized my mistake. He knew I was onto him as a federal agent. If he thought I was snooping around on the cult's behalf, I posed a genuine threat to him.

The gun jabbed my back again.

"I am protecting her now. If you don't start talking, we're going to take a drive and you're not going to be coming back here. Do you understand?"

I nodded.

"Yes."

"Now, let's try this again. Who in the *fuck* are you?"

That shoulder he was putting so much pressure on had once suffered a bad break. The joint was screaming at me for relief. I winced.

"I'm a friend of Tom McGowan's."

He twisted my arm harder.

"Don't know him."

"Does the name David Sandberg mean anything to you?"

Somewhere in my consciousness, I felt him react to that, but he didn't let on.

"You're supposed to be answering questions, not asking them."

His neutral reply was all the confirmation I needed. If Kyle really was working for The Bliss Project, the mention of the dead man's name would have provoked a stronger response.

"I wasn't lying to you. I am a psychic. I'm also a private investigator. McGowan's my boyfriend. He's an agent with the FBI. He's the one who told me you were here on the Sandberg case."

Again he loosened his grip but didn't let go.

"Prove it."

"Check it out."

We paused at the sound of footsteps approaching. By the time Malindi appeared, Kyle had slipped his gun back into his fanny pack and was opening the door for me.

She was carrying a volleyball in one arm and a tall blue bottle of mineral water in the other.

"Did you guys have fun today?"

Her questioning eyes darted between the two of us, as if she sensed that something heavy had just gone down.

I got into the rear of the van.

"Yeah, I had fun. Except I hurt my back." I said the last words for Kyle's benefit. I couldn't see his reaction but I knew he heard me.

Malindi climbed into the front seat, watching me with curious eyes.

"Not badly, I hope."

"No, just a sunburn."

Kyle got into the driver's seat and started up the engine. He adjusted the rearview so that his sunglasses were centered in the mirror. I stared straight at his reflection, sending him a silent message.

I'm not lying to you.

"There's a nurse's station at the ashram," Malindi said. "You should drop by when we get back. Get some Solarcaine or aloe or something."

I picked up a beach towel off the backseat and wrapped it around my shoulders.

"Thanks, I'll do that."

Kyle readjusted the mirror so that I could no longer see his eyes. We pulled onto the coast highway and headed back up the hill to the ashram. The shadows were long by the time we drove past the stone warriors at the gates. Their steel lances rose menacingly over their heads, the tips glowing red-orange as they caught the rays of the setting sun.

I declined to participate in any evening activities, begging off with my sunburn excuse. In fact, I was hoping to stay out from under the cult's scrutiny, particularly Tiki's. It was also my sincerest wish to avoid any further wrestling matches with Kyle. Weary from the physical and mental exertions of the day, I retired to my room, showered, changed into nightclothes and stretched out on the bed. I tried to think out my strategy for the next few days but ended up nodding off instead.

At first I thought it was part of my dream. I was in the ocean again, tilting with the uneven swells. The fine white spray on the breaking waves was making a rushing sound.

"Shhhh."

Something came out of the water and grabbed me. I opened my mouth to gasp but couldn't, since there was a hand clamped over the bottom half of my face. Still half asleep, I instinctively reached for the gun I kept under my mattress at home, but the intruder caught my arm with an iron grip. I looked up with wild eyes and saw the man's chin-length hair streaming forward as he leaned over me.

"Shhh. Everything's cool. I talked to McGowan. Will you be quiet if I take my hand away?"

I nodded. He let go cautiously, as if he wasn't sure I'd keep my end of the bargain.

I kept my voice at a whisper.

"You are Agent Harrison, right?"

"Yeah." He crouched next to the bed, keeping his voice low. "But to you and everybody else here, I'm Kyle. Got that?"

"Got it."

I sat all the way up, the burned skin on my back feeling crispy. I pulled the sheets against my chest, a delayed reaction to having my space invaded and feeling violated.

"This is making me nervous," I whispered.

"Don't worry. I've deactivated the system."

"What system?"

He pointed to a thermostat on the wall.

"You turned off the air?"

"Video surveillance."

I squinted my eyes at the small square box on the wall.

"A camera—in there?"

"That's right. But it's off now."

Chills started on my legs and ran the gamut of my body. My mind scrambled to remember what I'd done in this room, what I might have said that could have compromised my cover. I'd used my phone that first afternoon to pick up messages on my machine. Or had I? No, I'd checked them when I called McGowan, the day after I'd visited Aura. I remembered now—I hadn't felt safe calling from my room and had gone to the woods to use my cell phone. Another case of gut instinct paying off.

"What do they know about me?" I whispered.

"Not enough, and it's driving them crazy. They know you're not Whitney Brown, though."

I thought back to the sex-and-drugs party the other night.

"Do they have cameras in every room?"

"No, just selected locations. They like to keep an eye on the newbies. That way, they can find things out about you and act like they got the information through their amazing psychic powers."

I felt the walls closing in and had half a mind to leave the case then and there, Chatfield style.

"How dangerous are these people?"

"Not sure. I'm pretty certain they offed this guy Sandberg, but I haven't found the evidence yet."

Kyle and I had a lot to talk about, but my anxiety was rising with each passing second.

"What if they catch us here together?"

He took hold of my arm.

"Then they caught us in bed. Right?"

I nodded.

"Right."

He let me go.

"But I wouldn't worry about it. I'm expected to be on rounds, so no one's going to miss me. Malindi's locked in for the night."

"Locked in?"

A silvery glow was coming through the window and as my eyes adjusted to the darkness, I could see Kyle's face more clearly. He was smirking.

"The Master doesn't take chances."

"What's she so afraid of?"

He shrugged.

"When she hired me for this job, she said that I wasn't just protecting her, I was protecting a way of life for all the members of the church. Like she takes her position pretty seriously. Personally, I think she has enemies."

I'd get into that later.

"So you talked to McGowan?"

"Yeah. Just before he hopped a plane for L.A. You

didn't tell me your boyfriend was joining C-Three. That's heavy."

There was an enthusiasm in Kyle's hushed words that made him sound very young. I wondered if he'd ever been wounded in the line of duty. Somehow, I doubted it.

"So your boyfriend's a tactical guy, huh?"

"He's more of a hostage negotiator."

"Got news for you," he replied. "No one gets into C-Three unless they're tactical freaks. Willing to take risks."

That triggered a memory of a conversation I'd had with Kyle during the Initiation, during the exercise where we'd revealed our personal secrets. He'd told me then that he liked to take dangerous risks with his life.

"I think I'd like this McGowan guy," he whispered.

I suddenly missed Tom very much.

"To know him is to love him. Isn't there someplace else we can talk? I'm nervous in here."

"This really is the safest place."

I peered outside. "But there's no curtain on that window. Plus, I'm tired of whispering."

Kyle sat on the floor of my tiny bathroom, looking uncomfortable.

"You really think this is better?"

I nodded.

"Absolutely. There's no window for anyone to look in on us. This fan makes a wonderful background noise. We can turn on the light, and best of all, there's a lock on the door."

I'd pulled a blanket off the bed and was still busy trying to wrap myself in it comfortably.

"So the FBI sent you in here to look into the disappearance of Sandberg, right?"

"Yeah. Did I get it right from McGowan that you're in here looking for his ex?" His doubts were written all over his face.

"That's right. I think I may have something useful for you on Sandberg—or Zeus, as it were."

Kyle adjusted his position on the floor, stretching his legs out straight in front of him. His feet nearly touched the shower on the opposite wall.

"I want to know how the hell you know anything about Sandberg in the first place. And how did you know his nickname here was Zeus?"

"When I started looking for McGowan's ex, I interviewed a former cult member. He told me about Sandberg and had all kinds of alarming things to say about The Bliss Project."

"Alarming?"

"Yeah. He talked about levels of the organization and getting in too deep, and never being able to live a normal life again because the cult was after him."

Kyle was starting to laugh.

"What's so funny?"

"Puma Man. We interviewed him, you know. Guy's a loon."

"Yeah? Maybe not. He told me that David Sandberg was—here's how he put it—'uncreated' by the cult."

"He may be right about that. Doesn't mean he isn't a loon. So what do you have on Sandberg?"

"I was doing some work in data entry the other day and came across a file that had a note from Zeus in it."

"Do you remember what the note said?"

"Something about wire transfers and a Black Tower account and sixty-four thousand dollars."

"Can you remember exactly what it said?"

I opened the cabinet underneath the sink and pulled out a box of tampons.

"Not exactly," I said, dumping the tampons onto the floor, "but—"

I carefully removed the piece of paper I'd taped to the bottom of the box.

"—I did remember to make a copy." I handed the paper to Kyle.

"Goddamn." He pored over the note, shaking his head in disbelief. "How'd you find this?"

"I found it when I was working in the archive files."

"How'd you know where to look?"

"I had a vision of a black tower when I started this case. So when I ran across the Black Tower file, I checked it out. I've learned to pay attention to things like that, signals from my subconscious mind."

"What a freaky coincidence."

It wasn't a coincidence. It was the kind of skill my clients hired me for, but I didn't argue.

"The freaky part was finding a note inside from a guy who might be a murder victim. I had a feeling this piece of paper might be important."

Kyle stared at Zeus's note. "Let me put it to you this way. This is the only solid piece of evidence I know of that can link Sandberg to the money laundering."

"The money laundering?"

34
≈

Sitting as it did on some of Southern California's priciest real estate, The Bliss Project had to generate ungodly amounts of cash. That much I knew. All the income sources I'd found so far—member assets, free labor, exorbitant "education" fees—had been morally questionable but legally legitimate.

I stared at Kyle.

"Laundering money from drugs, prostitution, bookmaking—or what?"

"More like *whatever*."

He held up the note from Zeus.

"May I take this?"

"Keep it."

Zeus's note had more to do with the FBI's case than my own, and I didn't want to have to explain to anyone—for example, Tiki—what I was doing with it.

I watched Kyle fold the paper and slip it into his sock.

"Who's doing the laundering? How? When? Where?"

"As laundering schemes go, it's pretty sophisticated. Here's how we think the thing works."

He tore a length of toilet paper from the roll and ripped

off several squares, lining them up on the floor. He looked over at me with a sheepish grin.

"Lovely visual aids, aren't they?"

I smiled as he pointed to the first square.

"Okay, here's Doper Doug, who's got money from a big shipment of coke—let's say twenty-five thousand, for sake of the example. You with me?"

I nodded.

"Doper Doug wants to hide the cash out of the country, away from the prying eyes of the DEA and the IRS. So he takes it to a secret location—" here Kyle pointed to the second square "—and hands it over to Master Money Launderer. Got that?"

"You mean Malindi's laundering money?"

Kyle nodded.

"With the help of her husband, a guy named Charles Lewis, who happens to own Black Tower Financial, a U.S. money exchange. Black Tower will turn Doug's cash into pesos and stash it in his Mexican account, the IRS none the wiser. For a fee, of course."

"Wait a minute. Why doesn't Doper Doug just deal with Black Tower directly? Why the secret location? Why involve Malindi?"

"Most dope dealers don't want to be seen openly doing business with a U.S.–Mexico money exchange, know what I mean?"

"Makes sense."

"So Doper Doug passes off the cash to Malindi and it first goes into the U.S. bank account of Black Tower Financial."

Here Kyle pointed to toilet-paper square number three.

"Twenty-five grand is a lot of money, so when Black Tower deposits the cash, a CTR—currency transaction report—gets filed with the IRS. But no problemo, because Black Tower's going to wire that money right into the account of Bob's Building Supplies in San Diego."

Kyle's finger landed on the fourth square.

I grabbed his hand.

"Stop."

With my sudden motion, the paper squares fluttered like feathers.

"I don't get it. Isn't the IRS more concerned about where the money's *coming from* than in where it's going? I mean, the cult didn't hide the money, they just moved it."

He straightened out the squares and smiled.

"You're right, the IRS is more interested in where the cash came *from*. That's where Mexico comes in."

He drew an invisible line under the squares.

"Imagine this is the U.S.–Mexico border."

"Okay."

He ripped off another square and placed it under the invisible line.

"Malindi's husband also happens to own a money exchange on the *Mexican* side of the border. Millions of pesos circulate through here every week. So when the IRS comes looking for the source of the twenty-five grand in Black Tower's U.S. account, Black Tower can point to any number of legitimate Mexican businessmen who regularly exchange pesos for American goods. Like Juan here—" he ripped off another square and dropped it into Mexico"—who forked over twenty-five thousand dollars worth of pesos to purchase an equivalent amount of Bob's Building Supplies in San Diego."

I puzzled over the toilet-paper tableau.

"This is confusing."

"Of course it is. That's why they've been getting away with it."

"Okay, so Doper Doug gets his money stashed out of the country and Juan gets his building supplies. But what's in it for Master Money Launderer and Black Tower?"

"They get a hefty commission. Doper Doug probably pays fifteen or even twenty percent to get the money laundered. Plus, they get a legit five percent for converting Juan's pesos to dollars."

I thought back to the Black Tower statements. They'd been legitimate businesses—lumber companies, motor manufacturers. A twenty- or twenty-five-percent commission on all those transfers would add up. But not *that* much.

"Are you telling me the whole Bliss Project organization exists to cover up a little money laundering?"

"No. They rake in most of their money through legal channels. My theory is they got into the laundering business because they knew some people in need of . . . shall we say, financial services? It was an easy way to make extra cash without much risk of getting caught."

"What do they need all this money for?"

"You gotta understand Malindi. She'll never get enough, whether it's money, attention, power—what do you call those people?"

"Megalomaniacs."

"That's Malindi. I've been around her every day for months now, and I seriously think she wants to take over the world. I've heard her talking about setting up shop in Amsterdam, Frankfurt, even South Africa. Creating all those new ashrams requires money. And she'll take that money any way she can get it."

"Ashrams." I scowled. "More like labor-free factories."

Kyle imitated Malindi's breathy voice.

"The energy that will transform the world is increasing in power all over the planet. You are a part of this transformation. You are a part of this power."

He rolled his eyes.

"She's sick, willing to go as far as murder to *transform* the world."

"Murder?"

Kyle pulled the note from Zeus back out of his sock and held it up.

"Our friend Zeus—David Sandberg—was with The Bliss Project from nineteen ninety-one to nineteen ninety-five. A CPA before he found God. They put him to work in the accounting department, where he was supposed to write checks for ashram supplies and services. But he did his job too well and began noticing that significant amounts of money—"

I remembered the figure in the note.

"Like sixty-four grand?"

"Sixty-four grand here, eighty grand there—were mysteriously showing up in the Black Tower account."

"How do you know this?"

"He began to lose his faith and contacted the IRS. A special agent was actually scheduled to meet with Sandberg two years ago. That's when he disappeared."

Two years ago. Could the fact that Jen Shaffer and David Sandberg disappeared at the same time be a coincidence? Had Jen also been "uncreated"?

"Are you telling me Malindi had David Sandberg killed because he questioned the books?"

"Unfortunately, what he knew could bring the whole Bliss Project down, so yeah, I think she had him eliminated. 'For the greater good,' I'm sure she'd say."

"Did she actually kill him?"

Kyle shook his head as he folded the note and again slipped it into his sock.

"Not directly. You remember that guy who passed out across the aisle from us during the Initiation?"

"Yeah, Ken Bastin. And I know he didn't just pass out—he died. I called the ambulance company the next day and checked up."

Kyle looked surprised.

"Why'd you do that?"

"I knew he was dead when they dragged him out of that room. There was something funny about the whole thing."

"*Very* funny. Before he disappeared two years ago, Sandberg had given Ken Bastin's name to the IRS as one of the people involved in the money laundering. So Ken was a person I came in here hoping to get next to. He and I both loved motorcycles, so we became good friends around that. To make a long story short, Ken confided to me that back when he was using drugs, he was involved in the Sandberg killing. Said he still had the evidence to prove it. He was about to go state's evidence when he died. Which makes the timing of his death real interesting."

"Do you know Aura?"

"Ken's girlfriend? Yeah."

"She's convinced he died of a drug overdose. Is that true?"

Kyle nodded.

"The tox test turned up fatal levels of opiates in his blood. Since a used syringe was found in his pocket, that in itself didn't point to wrongful death. It was the puncture wound in his neck that did."

"Wrongful death?"

"Yep. The M.E. didn't find any fresh tracks on Ken's arm. Somebody injected the fatal dose into the back of his neck. No fingerprints on the syringe, not even Ken's. There were a hundred other people in the room that day. Let's just say the investigation continues."

I sat for a minute, taking it all in and thinking again about the fact that Jen and Sandberg had disappeared at about the same time.

"Did Ken ever mention anyone named Jen Shaffer? Does that name mean anything to you?"

"No. But I could look her up for you."

"Look her up? How?"

"Every initiate to The Bliss Project gets an audition. It's kind of like a really intense interview."

"Yeah, I know. I was just subjected to one."

"They videotape those auditions. The whole collection is locked up in storage. I could see if there's a tape on Jen Shaffer."

"How many years back do the videos go?"

"I don't know. Pretty far, I think."

"That'd be great if you could find a tape on Jen. Thanks."

"Don't mention it." The color rose in his cheeks. "It's nice having some sane company around here for once. This has been a really tough assignment. Not tough physically. Mentally, I mean. I'm glad you're here."

"You too, although I coulda done without that gun in my back yesterday." I nudged him with my shoe to let him know I was kidding. "Hey, I was wondering—did you just happen to get paired up with me that day at the Initiation?"

"No. Malindi wanted me to keep an eye on you. Standard procedure. They keep an eye on all the new recruits."

"Figured as much."

I puzzled over the squares of bathroom tissue on the floor.

"Tell me one more thing."

I put my finger on the second square in the top row, on the U.S. side of the border.

"Where's this secret location where Doper Doug takes his cash to Master Money Launderer?"

"Don't I wish I knew."

He picked up the tissue in question and placed it in my hand.

"Get any vibes off that?"

Beneath the hum of the bathroom fan, I thought I heard a noise.

"Shhh. What's that?"

Kyle cocked his head, listening. Then we both heard it. Someone was knocking on my bedroom door. When the knocking stopped, a woman's voice called out softly.

"Liza?"

35
≋

I felt panic rising inside. The bathroom had no window, which now seemed like a terrible disadvantage. Again I had that walls-closing-in-on-me feeling. I mouthed silently to Kyle.

What should I do?

He poked his finger in the direction of the bedroom and answered wordlessly.

Answer the door. He pointed the tile floor. *I'll stay here.*

I left the fan going and shut the bathroom door behind me.

"Who is it?" I called.

The voice on the other side of the door answered playfully.

"Guess."

"That must be Tiki."

No intuition required—I recognized her voice. I took a deep breath and opened the door.

"I hope I didn't wake you, but I had a feeling you were up." She arched her brows and waited for my reply.

"I was. Couldn't sleep."

I stood in the doorway, thinking that it wasn't necessarily rude not to invite her in. Not at this hour.

"My goodness, what are you doing up so early?" I

glanced at my wrist but wasn't wearing a watch. "What time is it, anyway?"

"Almost dawn. That's why I knocked. I thought maybe as long as you were up, you could come see the sun rise on the brass doors out front. Looks like it's going to be a clear morning."

She looked different, more vulnerable somehow. She was dressed down in a hiking jacket and jeans, and her face was freshly scrubbed. Without her exotic makeup, she could almost pass for a beautiful young man. In the dark morning somewhere behind her, a nightingale was singing.

I shivered, more from nervousness than from the early morning chill.

"Wait here. I'll throw on some clothes."

I let the door close and hurried to the small closet, pulling on my baggiest outfit—low-slung, wide-legged jeans and a hockey shirt. I threw on my jacket, slipped into my shoes, and was back out the door in a matter of seconds.

Tiki led our way down the wood-planked corridor.

"You look like you got some sun yesterday."

The farther away we moved from Kyle, the more I relaxed.

"Gave myself a nasty sunburn." I could sense her probing my mind, tuning into my mood. I tried to center myself, but she'd caught me off guard.

"Is something troubling you?"

"To be honest, you make me nervous," I said.

"Why?"

"I don't know. I'm a private person and it's uncomfortable knowing how well you can read me."

"You know what Abadanda tells us about our private affairs?"

"No, what?"

"He tells us to let go of them. Our secrets separate us from one another. They can make us do terrible things. It's impossible to have secrets and truly be Free."

Tell it to Malindi, I thought to myself.

"So that old expression is true, then?" I asked. " 'Confession is good for the soul'?"

"It's true."

The darkness was beginning to recede. The sky above

us lightened from black to gray as Tiki led the way across the lawn. When we reached the bridge, I paused briefly to look at the fish in the pond below. I was trying to put Kyle out of my mind, afraid she'd see that I hadn't been alone in my bedroom.

Best defense is a good offense, I heard my silent voice say.

"Tell me your secrets, Tiki. Or do you not have any more?"

She leaned against the railing and peered into the water.

"I've cleansed myself of my secrets. Of course one must be careful whom one confesses to."

I laughed.

"Oh, so I'm not worthy?"

She glanced sideways at me.

"I didn't mean it as an insult."

I didn't pry. A leaf was balanced on the railing and I brushed it into the water. It floated on the surface, where the fish ignored it. Even in the dim light, I could make out the oranges and whites of their oversized bodies swimming lazily below. I wondered how old these creatures were.

I looked over at Tiki.

"Let me ask you this. When did you first know you were psychic?"

She starting walking toward the driveway.

"I'm just like you—I don't remember ever *not* having the ability. Even as a child, I could know what was on a person's mind, see things . . ." Her voice trailed off.

"Like what?" I prodded. "Tell me your first psychic experience."

"Well, there was the day in the park, on the playground. I was very little—not more than three or four years old at the time. Some boys were playing with a small, hard ball, hitting it with sticks. It was an awful thing. I knew it was going to happen before it happened."

"Before what happened?"

"One of the boys threw the ball—flung it like a rocket from his hand." She demonstrated with her arm, throwing an invisible ball. "The other boy didn't see it coming until it was too late. He turned just as the ball hit his face. Put his eye out, I learned later."

"What a horrible thing to see."

"It's an ugly world out there. Accidents, illness, death. That's why I've devoted my life to transcending that world, helping others to transcend it."

"And how do you do that?"

"I show people the untapped power of the mind. I use my psychic gift to . . . to *persuade* people to be more open to our teaching. If you join us, Liza—permanently, I mean—I could teach you to use your ability in ways you never dreamed possible."

In some circles, persuading others with one's psychic gift is called "black magic." I shuddered at the thought, and also at the genuine passion I heard in her voice. Surely she was intuitive enough to know that Malindi was no saint. For some reason, though, her heart was completely committed to The Bliss Project. I wondered why.

She looked at the sky and picked up her pace.

"We'd better hurry if we're going to see the morning star."

I wanted to keep the conversation focused on Tiki.

"Did your parents encourage your gift?"

She laughed.

"They didn't have time to encourage anything. They were too busy fighting. I left home when I was fifteen."

"Where was home?"

"South Africa."

So I'd been right about where the lilt in her voice had originated.

"I roamed around Europe for several years. Searching for something—I didn't know what. I traveled with a band of Gypsies for a time, if you can imagine that."

I could, quite easily. Probably where she learned most of her chicanery, no offense to Gypsies.

"Then one day I met Abadanda, a man who embodied everything I'd ever hoped for in a spiritual teacher. He was an American, which surprised me. I always thought my guru would be a Hindu from India, or someone from the Far East."

We were climbing now, getting shorter of breath.

"How many years ago did you two meet?"

Her answer was vague.

"Quite a few."

We were almost to the top of the road where the stone warriors guarded the entrance. When we reached the gates, we turned around. In the distance we could see the lodge and the wooded acreage behind it.

She stared at the lodge. "Now watch."

At first nothing happened. A gray stillness surrounded the ashram like a blanket. Then a sliver of sunlight broke above the eastern horizon. It seemed to happen in a matter of seconds. One minute, the brass doors of the lodge were in shadow; the next, they were glowing with the full reflection of the rising sun, completely transformed into a pulsating ball of brilliant orange light. Contrasted against the shadowy gray landscape, the sparkling light *did* look otherworldly.

I crossed my arms over my chest and stared at the phenomenon.

"That really is something to see."

"Abadanda has the fire." Her voice was strange, sultry.

I studied her face. No longer sharp and bright, her eyes were glazed with a look I'd never seen in them before. I took the opportunity to tune in to her, to see if I could know her secrets. In my mind's eye I saw Tiki and Abadanda in a passionate sexual embrace. Now I knew why her heart was in The Bliss Project.

The sun moved higher in the sky, and the golden-orange light disappeared from the brass doors. Tiki came out of her trance and turned to me.

"Shall we head back?" she asked.

"Sure, I could use some sleep."

She glanced at her watch.

"No time for that. You're scheduled for kitchen duty this morning. Can you handle that?"

"I don't think so, Tiki. I'm so tired—"

"If you perform service work when you really don't feel like it, that speeds your transformation. Keep this up and you'll be to the next level before you know it. We start breakfast preparation at six o'clock."

She gave me a wink.

"Be there, or else."

36

Spoonful by sloppy spoonful, I scooped the batter into the muffin tins. Around me, the kitchen hummed with breakfast-making activities. Running on practically no sleep, I should have been tired but adrenaline was keeping me wide awake.

All my worst fears about the cult were bearing out to be true. Kyle—and probably others as well—had been assigned to keep an eye on me. My room had been under surveillance. My audition with Tiki and Abadanda had been videotaped.

On the hopeful side, I didn't think Tiki knew that Kyle had been hiding in my bathroom last night. If she'd picked up on his presence, she hadn't let on. Did she know he was an FBI agent? Did anyone besides me know that? The conversation with Kyle that Tiki had so abruptly interrupted had left me with a lot of unanswered questions.

"Need some help with that?"

I turned to see who'd spoken. It was Brian, the man who'd had a meltdown in the telemarketing department the other day.

"I could use a hand, sure. How're you doing? You were so upset the last time I saw you."

He washed his hands at the sink.

"Oh, that. Just the death throes of an ego that was long overdue to die." He picked up a spoon and started helping me fill muffin tins.

"Are you going to visit your family?" I asked.

He shook his head.

"Not for a while yet. My work here is much more important than being with them. My primary commitment is to the family of humankind. Once the transformation has taken place in greater society, then I can reconnect with my birth family."

He sounded like a mechanical toy, the kind that has a string you pull to activate a recorded voice. As disturbing as the scene in the telemarketing office had been, this was much worse to me.

"Sorry I threw such a tantrum." He let out an embarrassed laugh.

I wanted to tell him that his anger had been righteous and brave. That I wanted to see him scream again, in front of the whole ashram. Instead, I had to keep quiet. My heart ached for him and the family he'd left behind.

I spooned the last of the batter into the muffin tins.

"Guess that's it."

Brian pointed to some baskets near the sink.

"If you could just put some strawberries out, that would be great."

I rinsed the strawberries and poured them onto the trays. It was beautiful fruit—firm, plump, unbruised. The berries were so deeply colored that the red seemed to vibrate before my sleep-deprived eyes. The Beatles' tune I'd heard several nights ago started playing in my head. "Strawberry fields . . . nothing is real. . . ."

When I finished with the strawberries, I helped myself to breakfast and sat with the crowd of devotees who had gathered in the dining hall.

"Do we have anything decent to eat this morning?"

Aura had come up behind me and stood looking over my shoulder at my plate, eyeing the fruit, muffins, and scrambled eggs.

"Same old, same old," she sighed, reaching for a strawberry. "Citrus in winter, strawberries in summer."

"I'm surprised to see you dining here with the masses—you of the heavenly chocolate stash."

She laughed.

"A woman can't live on chocolate alone."

"I know some women who would debate you on that. Go get your breakfast. I'll save your place. I've been wanting to talk to you."

She wandered off to the buffet and was back in a matter of minutes. She took a seat across from me.

"What's on your mind?"

"I've been thinking about Kenny."

She unfurled her napkin with a flourish.

"Yeah, the bastard. What about him?"

I leaned forward and spoke quietly.

"How do you know he was lying to you? I mean, maybe it was a mistake. Maybe the hospital screwed up the charts or something. You said he'd been with The Bliss Project from almost the beginning, that he was really committed to this work. Overdosing on drugs just doesn't make sense."

Aura slathered a muffin in butter.

"You've never known an addict, have you? They don't do things in a sensible way." She bit into the muffin and closed her eyes.

"But how can you be sure?" I asked.

Her eyes popped open.

"Look." She pointed her butter knife for emphasis. "They found the syringe right there in his jacket pocket. Filled with remnants of a heroin-cocaine-God-knows-what-else cocktail. Now you tell me what you think happened." She lifted the muffin to her mouth and took another generous bite.

I thought about it while she ate. Ken had been about to confess his murder of Sandberg to the FBI. Maybe it had been suicide after all. Maybe he'd preferred to go out that way, rather than face the corruption of The Bliss Project and his role in it. Then again, an injection in the back of the neck didn't sound like suicide. I thought back to that day in the Process. Who'd been in that room? Who could have slipped the needle into Ken's veins? About a hundred people, that's all.

Aura stared at me.

"You're thinking too hard."

"Doesn't some part of you wonder if Ken had been telling you the truth? If maybe something else happened in that room?"

"Like what?" A note of irritation crept into her voice. "Talk about denial! My boyfriend died with a syringe in his pocket and a lethal dose in his veins. Pretty hard to rationalize that one." She swatted the air, as if trying to bat away any contradictory thoughts.

"Ken was using drugs again and he OD'd. End of story. Now, can you pass me the pepper, please?"

There was a crack in Aura's bravado, though. I could see it. Doubt was beginning to creep in. I wondered if she, too, subjected herself to meditation leave when life at The Bliss Project created too much cognitive dissonance.

As I reached for the pepper, I heard a voice behind me.

"Hey, this is just like old times. How're you guys doing?"

A slender man slid in next to me and put his plate on the table. I noticed that his scrambled eggs were still steaming.

"Bumblebee," I said. "Welcome to the land of the living."

"Hello again."

The last time I'd seen him, his pupils had been so dilated that his eyes were black. This morning his eyes were clear and blue.

"How'd you do in that class you were so determined to rest up for?"

I was surprised he could remember anything of our conversation that night, high as he'd been.

"I did all right, I guess."

Aura picked up her half-empty plate.

"I've got to run. See you two later."

She gave me a wink. I would have stopped her, but I'd been hoping for a chance to confirm my suspicion that Bumblebee was in fact Barry Bell. I'd be able to question him more freely without Aura around.

He proffered his plate.

"Muffin?"

"No, thanks. I'm finished."

He scooped up a forkful of eggs.

"I've always wondered what they do in those psychic-development classes. That Tiki's really something, isn't she?"

"Yes, she's very gifted. By the way, I've been wanting to ask you something. Remember you said you were looking for a woman when you came to The Bliss Project?"

"Yeah."

"When you said those words, something came to me, and I just wanted to check it out with you."

"You mean you got like a psychic flash?"

"Yeah, something just popped into my head."

"Cool. What was it?"

"Were you looking for a woman named Jennifer?"

His expression told me that he was both amazed and impressed by my insight.

"Yeah, I was."

"Did her last name start with an S?"

His eyes bugged out.

"Hey, you're really good! I can see why Tiki recruited you."

I let him lead the conversation from there, asking him lots of questions about what he referred to as his new life—his *real* life—at The Bliss Project. I found little to gain from his chatter, but was being careful not to appear too interested in this Jennifer person. People were starting to finish up their meals, so I casually slipped in my key question as I dabbed my lips with a napkin.

"By the way, what ever happened to this mysterious Jennifer you came looking for?"

He swallowed the last of his eggs and chased them down with orange juice.

"I don't know. Never did find her."

We got up from the table and said our good-byes. I put my plate on top of the dirty stack in the kitchen and headed for the exit, feeling unsettled. I'd essentially confirmed that Bumblebee was in fact Barry Bell, but that had brought me no closer to finding Jen. I walked out of the dining hall and into the morning sunlight. Kyle was standing just outside the door.

He slipped his arm around my shoulders in a friendly gesture.

"How's that sunburn?" With his free arm, he took my hand. I could feel him pressing a piece of paper into my palm and squeezing it shut.

"The sunburn hurts, and I'm exhausted. I'm turning in for a while."

He was wearing his dark sunglasses again, so I couldn't read his eyes.

"Okay. See you," he said.

"See you, Kyle."

I walked toward my room. When I reached my door, I unfolded the paper and read Kyle's note.

Jen Shaffer videotape under your mattress.

37
≈

The room looked just as I'd left it. The bed was unmade. The trash can in the bathroom still held the toilet-tissue squares Kyle had used to demonstrate the flow of funds into and out of The Bliss Project. I flopped onto the bed, exhausted, and tried not to stare at the thermostat on the wall. What if the hidden video camera had been reactivated?

I made my complaint out loud.

"Damn, it's hot in here!"

I got off the bed and went to the thermostat, staring at the unit with a puzzled expression.

"Cooler," I said. "Much cooler."

I gave the round dial a twist and when it reached its limit, kept twisting. I continued to apply pressure until the dial snapped off. I heard something fall into the space behind the plaster. There was a gaping hole where the unit used to be.

"Oops."

I went to the bed and slid my arm between the mattress and box spring. Halfway to the other side, my fingers found the hard plastic casing of the videotape. I grabbed it and hurried across the room to turn on the television and slide the tape into the VCR.

A grainy, muddy-colored image appeared on the screen, giving me the impression that this had been videotaped during the Dark Ages of camcorder technology. Like about ten years ago. The setting was a modest living room. A younger Malindi, with a poufy eighties' hairdo and garish eighties' makeup, relaxed on one side of a sofa. Sitting next to her was the woman I'd been waiting to see for a long time.

Malindi spoke to her.

"Ready?"

The woman nodded. She looked so very young. A pair of oversized glasses dominated the small features of her pale face, but even on the muddy video, the unusual shade of her red hair was as distinctive as a signature.

Off-camera, a man spoke.

"State your name, please."

Although the sound quality was poor, I recognized the voice as Abadanda's.

The woman slumped forward.

"Jennifer Janine Shaffer."

With just three words, her voice communicated a lifetime of hopelessness.

"Do you have a heavy heart today?" Abadanda asked.

Jen nodded.

Malindi sat back on the sofa.

"That negative stuff has got to come out. We need you to be open here. We each have darkness to clear. Now, what's underneath all that sadness?"

Jen looked pained.

"All I ever wanted to do was something good for the world. To make a difference."

Abadanda spoke again.

"Until you let go of your past garbage, that dream can't come true. You've got to be honest with us, Jen. We want you to be Free. We're here to help clear you of all that negative energy you're holding. Let's start with your earliest memory of the darkness. Do you have any idea of what that might be? What's the first thing that comes to you?"

Jen bowed her head.

"My mother's death."

Nobody spoke for several moments. I felt myself wanting Malindi to say something, to reach out to Jen in some way. But she sat back in a relaxed pose, a detached expression on her face.

Jen's hand went to her mouth. A few sobs escaped her lips.

"Keep going with that, Jen," Abadanda urged. "Go all the way into the pain."

Her shoulders shook and her sobs grew louder.

"Deeper. Go deeper into the pain. That's it, all the way."

Jen's face went through a series of anguished contortions. Witnessing such a personal catharsis felt like the worst kind of voyeurism. I averted my eyes, as if the images on the screen were the rankest form of pornography. In a way, they were. Moments like these were not meant for public consumption. Any jealousy I might have felt toward Tom's former fiancée completely dissolved in a growing pool of compassion for her.

She mumbled incoherently between her racking sobs. Malindi leaned close to her, listening. Jen's mumbling grew louder.

"Say it out loud, in plain English," Malindi urged. "You can't enter the kingdom until you bring this darkness into the light."

Jen removed her glasses and sobbed hysterically, burying her face in her hands.

"Out with it." Malindi's voice was commanding.

Jen spoke through her sobs.

"I did something very, very bad."

"You can be Free only if you let it go. Let go."

Jen sagged against the side of the sofa.

"You can't help me. No one can help me. God can't help me!"

After what must have seemed an eternity to Jen, Malindi finally comforted her, stroking her arm.

"The truth will set you free."

Jen looked desperately into Malindi's face. Her words were faint but clear.

"I killed somebody."

I rewound the tape to make sure I'd heard correctly.

"I killed somebody."

She'd said it, all right. This time I paused the tape, thinking. I popped it out of the VCR and read the label again. Just as I'd remembered, it said, "Jennifer J. Shaffer, 9/87." This tape had been recorded ten years ago, eight years be-

fore Sandberg had disappeared. Whoever Jen was talking
about, it wasn't David Sandberg.

I pushed the Play button again.

"It was an accident. I was making a right turn and suddenly she was just there in front of the bumper. It was really
early in the morning. There were no other cars around. I
panicked and drove off. I thought about going back. I
wanted to, but—"

I paused the tape again. So that was the image I'd been
seeing—the human form crumpling against a front fender.
Two lines from the blood-splattered poem came back to
me:

> Hit and run, an ugly end.
> Enemies are now her friends.

When I hit Play, Abadanda's voice was booming from
the background.

"Did you confess this to anyone?"

Jen's trancelike stare told me that she was reliving the
event. Her monotone flowed with a haphazard logic, as if
she were narrating a bad dream.

"I didn't sleep all night. I was out of my mind. I started
to clean the bathroom and somehow ended up at my
brother's house. That whole night didn't seem real. I told
him what'd happened. I begged him on our mother's grave
not to tell anyone. Told him I'd find my own punishment,
take myself out of society in my own way."

She lifted her head. Without her glasses, she looked
completely defenseless. Her eyelids swollen and red, she
stared at a point beyond the camera lens.

"There was damage, blood on the fender. Jeremy followed me to Mexico the next day and I left my car out in
the desert. That was just before I came to live with you."

So all these years, Jeremy had known. Exercising his
attorney-client privilege and suffering silently.

Abadanda's voice was impartial.

"Therefore when you joined us, you were running from
your own darkness more than you were drawn to our light."

Jen put her glasses back on and nodded.

"Either way leads to transformation," he assured her.

She slumped forward again.

"There's no transformation for me."

She stared at the floor, sitting still as stone.

Suddenly there was a loud clapping in the background. A single person applauding. Soon Malindi joined in. After a strange interlude of this sparse applause, Abadanda made an announcement.

"Congratulations, Jen. You've just taken your first big step in getting Free."

38
≋

Where was she now?

I popped Jen Shaffer's audition video out of the machine, realizing that what I held in my hands was the confession to a felony. Vital evidence, should the hit-and-run case ever be tried.

Jen's confession went a long way toward explaining why she'd gone into the cult, but again I was left with no insight as to *where* she'd gone once she arrived here. I sat on the bed, trying to tune in to the present-day Jen Shaffer. For several seconds, my mind was blank. When the insight came, it arrived in the form of a memory.

Please help me.

I'd nearly forgotten about the hidden message in the poem sent to Jen's father. It had to be a cry for help from Jen. In my mind, I called out to her.

How can I help you if I don't know where you are?

Having no better ideas, I reached into my purse and pulled out my pocket astrologer. It's a palm-sized monthly calendar that lists daily planetary positions. I didn't have Jen Shaffer's chart, but at least I could get a sense of where I was, what forces were surrounding me.

Uranus, the harbinger of sudden change, was transiting Aquarius now. For many astrologers, now was the true dawning of the Age of Aquarius, the long-anticipated era when the human race would wake up to the tremendous untapped potential of mind and spirit. I wasn't sure what Uranus was doing for humanity at large but at the moment, it was wreaking havoc in my own birth chart.

Uranus square Neptune: I should watch for danger and deception through the occult.

Tell me something I don't know, I thought.

Uranus square Mars: Forces beyond my control were likely to cause sudden disruptions—even sudden death to someone near me. The planets warned of danger through electricity, automobiles, or firearms.

I'm being careful, I thought. My Glock was tucked away in a hidden compartment under the front seat of the Charger. I hadn't felt safe traveling without it, but hadn't brought it to my room. A gun would more likely create problems than solve them if The Bliss Project were to find one on me.

Pluto conjunct the Ascendant: Unavoidable, fundamental change to me at the most personal level.

Uh-oh. In astrological parlance, "change" and "death" are often synonymous. And Pluto, of course, is the ruler of death.

I put the miniature ephemeris back in my bag, sorry I'd looked. Sometimes I envied those who pooh-poohed astrology. I'd cast too many charts and peered into too many futures to enjoy that kind of cynical innocence.

The sudden ringing of the telephone beside the bed caused me to jump. I gawked at the receiver as if it were an inanimate object that had suddenly started to speak. On the third ring, I picked it up.

"Hello?"

"We're waiting for you."

Tiki's voice was friendly, expectant. I had a hard time finding my own voice.

"Waiting for me?" I asked.

"Didn't you see today's agenda? We slipped one under your door during breakfast."

I looked at the floor. Sure enough, a lavender sheet of paper lay near the door. I was certain it hadn't been there when I came in earlier. I clearly remembered checking the room carefully. A chill began a slow crawl up the back of my neck.

"Hang on."

I put the phone down and crossed the room. I picked up the lavender sheet and read the line items, then glanced at my watch. It was just past eight o'clock. According to the schedule, I was supposed to be in something called "Bliss Meditation." I picked up the phone again.

"I'm sorry, Tiki, I'm really not feeling well today. As you know, I hardly slept and—"

"All the better," she interrupted. "Trust me, there'll be very little required of you. This is the most relaxing experience you'll ever have in your life. Hurry over to the ashram theater. You remember where that is, don't you?"

"I think so, yes."

"See you in five minutes or so, then?"

"You say this is relaxing?"

"Very. Better than a nap."

"All right. I'll be there as soon as I can."

I hung up the phone with no intention of keeping my word. A feeling of dread had settled into my stomach from the moment I'd seen the position of the planets. Translated to English, the astrological warning told me to proceed with extreme caution. I looked around the small bedroom and came to a quick decision.

Time to go.

I started to pack my things and then realized I'd have to leave them here. It wouldn't do to be seen with luggage. To get away without answering questions, I would need to stroll casually through the grounds and off the property. I slipped my wallet and keys into my pockets. What about the videotape? I stuffed it into the front of my baggy jeans and covered it with my oversized shirt.

Closing the door behind me, I headed for the lodge, saying hello to a few familiar faces along the way. The theater was just beyond the wooded area. I could take the walkway into the woods, then cut through the cypresses and pines toward the bridge.

I stepped onto the black asphalt path and followed it toward the theater. I was nearly to the halfway point and just about to cut through the fern-covered undergrowth when Malindi and a man I didn't recognize appeared from the opposite direction. Quickly changing plans, I kept walking. As they approached, I bowed my head in a respectful greeting.

"Good morning, Master."

"Liza."

The authority in her voice stopped me. I turned and looked at her. There was a hard edge in her pretty blue eyes.

"We were just coming to meet you." She and her companion turned around and fell in on either side of me.

"You're going to love this process." She took me by the arm. "Everyone does."

On my left, her companion towered over me. His neck looked as thick as my waist. I watched him walk and recognized the stiff gait of a bodybuilder. I doubted he'd achieved his granite mountain of a body by eating fruit and muffins. More like steroids.

"I don't think we've met," I said by way of a hello.

Malindi made introductions.

"I'm sorry. Liza, this is Wayne. Wayne, Liza."

We exchanged hellos and I noticed a familiar bulge at Wayne's waistband. Wayne was packing a handgun.

"Where's Kyle this morning?" I asked.

"He's no longer with us."

Malindi looked into my eyes. She knew she'd shocked me, I could see by the way she watched for my reaction.

"Why not?"

"Kyle wasn't actually an initiate. He was on hire, a security guard referred to us by . . . a client. He wasn't working out, so Wayne will be replacing him."

I worked hard to keep my face calm. Meanwhile, my stomach felt like the earth had just dropped out from under my feet.

"He seemed like such a nice guy."

She sighed, sounding bored.

"I'll be frank with you. We don't discourage relationships at The Bliss Project, but certain employees are not permitted to fraternize with new initiates. Kyle knew the rules and he broke them." She looked at me, woman to woman. "I'm sorry."

I shrugged.

"Oh, well."

I did my best to make it sound casual, but with Kyle's departure, I felt dangerously exposed. What had really happened to him? Did they know he was with the FBI? How much had they found out about our meeting? Should I get the hell out, now?

I looked over at Wayne and realized it would be highly foolish to try and make a run for it.

We rounded a corner and arrived at the theater.

"Here we are," Malindi said.

Wayne held the door open for us and we stepped inside.

As my eyes adjusted to the darkened theater, I made out a number of devotees filling the seats in the first few rows. I looked up at the spotlighted stage, where a long, rectangular box sat elevated on a wooden platform. It resembled nothing so much as a coffin.

I squinted to get a better look.

"What's that?"

Malindi turned to go.

"You'll soon see. Good-bye, Liza."

Her smile was generous, in the way that winners are often gracious to losers.

Tiki came forward and escorted me to the stage.

"How are you?"

"Not well." I spoke as forcibly as possible. "I'm really not up for this today. Really."

Gone was the hiking jacket and fresh-scrubbed face. Tiki wore a bright red kimono and a dramatically painted face. Her black-lined eyes looked at me and filled with pity.

"It isn't easy being psychic, is it?"

"I'm not sure what you mean."

There was more than a little malice in her smile.

"It's a bit like living without skin sometimes, isn't it? Feeling too much, knowing too much." She turned to the audience.

"This is Liza, for those of you who don't know her. She's highly receptive. But as we know, too much information coming through all six senses can be overwhelming to the ego. That's what bliss therapy is designed for. With this technique, we're able to let situations and events flow through us without upsetting us so much."

She turned back to me.

"You'll need to get ready first. But hurry. Let's not keep the others waiting much longer."

"Waiting for what?"

"They're here to observe."

"Observe what?"

She reached into a box alongside the wooden platform, pulled out a heap of heavy canvas material and handed it to me. I let the fabric unfold. It was a baggy uniform, not unlike something a fireman or an astronaut might wear.

"Put that on," she said.

"I need to know what's happening here."

I turned to the others sitting in the theater seats. Their faces were pleasant, patient, and frighteningly blank.

"We're putting you into the Bliss Box," she said with a smile.

"The Bliss Box?"

"A sensory-deprivation tank. It's marvelous, really. Here, put these on, too." She handed me a pair of translucent goggles.

I stared at them dumbly.

"Those create a Ganzfeld—a visual field that's completely blank, with no contours or depth. Inside the tank, you'll be able to see another world. You'll be suspended in dark, silent water, free from the limiting effects of gravity. It's a wonderful experience, Liza, it really is. Please trust me."

I handed the goggles back.

"I don't think so. I'm just not ready for this yet. I'm sorry."

Her voice was cheerful.

"No is not an option. Is it, you guys?" She turned to the audience for confirmation.

A few voices spoke up.

"Go ahead, Liza."

"Go for it."

"You'll love it."

I looked at the platform and noticed a generator sitting near the base of the tank.

Danger through electricity.

"I really can't do this," I said flatly. "I'm terribly claustrophobic."

I dropped the suit on the stage and started to walk off.

As if following some silent command, the people in the front rows got out of their chairs and came toward me. A woman took me gently by the arm.

"It's okay, Liza."

I recognized Raj at the edge of the crowd. He called out to me.

"There's nothing to worry about. You'll be fine."

The group dynamic had a power all its own. It was just like the crowd that had gathered around Brian in the telemarketing department. There was no overt violence, but the collective pressure of the group forced me back onto the stage.

Someone was grabbing me around the middle.

"Let us help you with this."

I was lifted from behind and the suit was being slipped over my legs.

"No!" I cried out.

I kicked and twisted with all my might but I was no match for the dozens of hands that held me gently but firmly. I was so outnumbered that I was the only one who appeared to struggle. I pleaded with the group to let me go but their faces remained calm and assured, as if they were listening to nothing more than the cries of a tired baby. The last thing I remember seeing was a sea of lips smiling and muttering encouragement.

Then someone slipped the goggles over my head and the world went white.

39

≋

Floating.

Weightless, I sailed through an endless expanse of white. There were no walls. There was no ceiling. No floor. No up, no down. No beginning, no middle, no end. No color, no darkness. There was . . . nothing.

I heard sound but that, too, was an endless expanse of white. The hollow rushing in my head was somehow emptier than pure silence.

As far as I could tell from what little sensory information was available to me, I was suspended in a tank of body-temperature water. There was enough air space above the water for me to breathe, but I couldn't stand up, or even bend into a sitting position, as the tub was fully enclosed. The suit they'd pulled over my clothes covered my hands and feet as well. My attempts to gain some kind of hold on the smooth sides of the tank proved futile and only served to make me panicky.

So I floated, mummy-like. Soon I no longer had any sense of my legs or arms. The rushing sound between my ears became hypnotic and seductive. I could feel myself being lulled into thoughtless euphoria. At the mercy of this mind-numbing hellhole, all I could do was pray.

Need some help here.

The answer to my prayer came in an unconventional fashion. At first I didn't recognize it for the godsend it was. In fact, it annoyed me. A song started playing in my head. It was a tune from my childhood, an insidious round that we kids used to sing on long bus trips and car rides:

Ninety-nine bottles of beer on the wall,
Ninety-nine bottles of beer.

You take one down, pass it around.
Ninety-eight bottles of beer on the wall.

Then I saw the beauty in it. Maybe the song that had driven a generation of parents nuts could keep me sane now. It was worth a try. I concentrated on each round, calling out changes to stay conscious and alert. Even numbers only, counting down from one hundred.

One hundred bottles, ninety-eight bottles, ninety-six bottles . . .

Multiples of five, counting up from ten.

Ten bottles, fifteen bottles, twenty bottles, twenty-five. . . .

When my mind grew bored, I increased the challenge. Prime numbers only, as high as you can go.

Two bottles, three bottles, five bottles, seven.

After the first half hour, I lost all sense of time. Colors swam before my eyes. The urge to give up was overwhelming. It would be so easy, so pleasurable, to surrender to a weightless, hallucinogenic state. But like a snowbound hiker resisting the lure of the freeze, I clung to my beer-bottle game as if my life depended on it.

If they never released me, at least I'd go out fighting.

I was singing down from three hundred in a tricky combination of two-three-five when I felt a shudder. I fell silent, waiting. The white Ganzfeld grew brighter and I felt arms lifting me from the tank. Gravity returned, and my body became heavy again.

Someone pulled the goggles from my eyes. I found myself lying on a plastic tarp on the floor of the stage, dripping water, staring up into Tiki's curious face. She was still wearing her red kimono, looking polished and poised. Behind her, the theater was empty.

"How are you?"

I was angry. I took that as a good sign that the Bliss Box hadn't worked on me. I closed my eyes so that she wouldn't read my thoughts. My voice was groggy.

"Where did everyone go?"

"The others left once you were settled in. You've only been in for forty-five minutes. We have to cut your session short because Master needs to have a talk with you. Do you need a hand getting up?"

I nodded my head.

"Yes." Best to appear as helpless as possible.

She pulled me up by my arm. I kept my body loose, made her work hard at it. She grunted slightly from the effort.

"Looks like you had a really good session."

When I was halfway to my feet, she relaxed her grip and let me stand the rest of the way on my own. I came up with both hands and shoved her as hard as I could.

The move caught her completely by surprise. My canvas-covered hands smacked her chest straight-on, knocking the wind out of her. She fell backward and tumbled off the stage. I took a flying leap down into the center aisle and hit the ground running. As I pushed through the door, I heard two voices—a man and a woman's—call from the stage in unison.

"Stop!"

I bounded down the asphalt path, then veered off toward the woods. I didn't dare look back. I pushed out my chest and tried to make my feet fly, pumping my arms for momentum. The baggy fabric of the suit snagged on a branch like something out of a B-rated movie and I lost a few seconds working myself loose. I ran harder. My footsteps made crashing sounds as I plowed through the undergrowth. I heard the same sounds behind me, gaining ground.

I cleared the trees and burst onto the lawn. Up ahead I could see the bridge leading out over the koi pond. The sight pumped me with a new burst of energy. I pictured myself crossing to safety, but then a wall of weight hit me from behind. The next thing I knew, my nose and mouth were filled with Bermuda grass and I was gulping for the air that had been knocked out of my lungs.

"You are one very resistant initiate. We've never found anyone who couldn't be . . . *calmed* by the Bliss Box."

Malindi, arms crossed over her chest, leaned against the stage. Tiki, apparently still smarting from her tumble off the stage, glared at me from her seat in the front row.

Wayne stood behind me, holding my arms behind my back. He was fast for a big man. Outweighing me by a hundred pounds, he'd easily overpowered me on the lawn and hadn't had much trouble dragging me back to the ashram theater. I couldn't see him but I could smell him. Either he didn't believe in deodorant or his product was letting him down.

My body felt miserable. Wayne's tackle had reactivated the pain of my old shoulder injury, and my chin had been cut in the fall. I could feel a trickle of blood snaking down my neck. The suit had kept most of my body dry in the tank, but my hair was still wet. Plus, the videotape of Jen I'd stuffed into my pants this morning had worked its way down my baggy pants leg. I could feel its sharp corners lodged against my ankle, trapped inside the canvas suit.

"Who sent you here?"

Malindi's eyes were piercing.

"No one."

"You just came here alone?"

"That's right. And I'd like to leave now. I'm pretty sure this isn't the right path for me."

It was worth a try. Malindi ignored the request, narrowing her eyes.

"So you're a seeker—with no attachments."

"Pretty much, yeah."

She pulled a photograph from the pocket of her jacket and stepped forward to hold it under my nose.

"This looks like an attachment to me."

It was a photograph of me and McGowan. The one of us he kept on his bedside table. I made an effort to keep my mouth closed, my face blank. Malindi put the photo away.

"We kept track of you after the Process."

I thought back to leaving the San Diego ashram that last night, stopping at Linda's. At the time, I'd thought her sage-smudging was silly, but she hadn't been far off. The cult *had* been buzzing around me like flies on a carcass.

So they knew I had a boyfriend. That wasn't the end of the world. They didn't necessarily know I was a P.I., that my boyfriend was a federal agent. McGowan's house was held in trust. He'd taken most of his personal papers with him to Virginia. I had no way of knowing what else they might have found at the house, but I wasn't about to give anything up.

Malindi walked back to the stage and hoisted herself up, letting her legs dangle over the edge.

"We've got plenty of time when you're ready to start telling us the truth."

A cold dread came over me. The photo album on McGowan's kitchen table had pictures of Jen in it. They must have seen that. If Jen was somehow mixed up in Sandberg's killing, they'd assume I was with the police.

She took something else from her pocket and tossed it my way. The small laminated card landed face-up at my feet. It was the driver's license that I'd left in the cedar box under McGowan's bed.

"Checkmate, Elizabeth Chase."

My cheeks burned with humiliation. My mistake. Might as well learn from it.

"I thought I lost your tail."

She shrugged.

"Tiki had a bad feeling about you right from the start. We put a transmitter in the trunk of that awful car you drive."

Danger through electricity, automobiles, and firearms.

"It took us until yesterday to break into your house in San Marcos. Quite a security system."

McGowan would be glad to hear it. If I ever got the chance to tell him.

"Tiki began to get a bad feeling about Kyle, too, once he started hanging around with you. Since he was my employee, it was easy to get him out of the way. All I had to do was fire him. As for you, I don't think you'll be so easy to get rid of."

Fear was beginning to make a coward of me. I wasn't a cop, looking to bring them down. I was just looking for a missing girl.

"I'm not what you think I am."

Malindi raised her chin and peered down at me from her perch on the stage.

"Frankly, I don't care what you are. I know as much about you as I need to know. Bottom line, we've got a problem here and you're not part of the solution. And if you're not part of the solution, you're part of the problem."

Had I not been so frightened, I might have laughed at the serious way she spouted the cliché. I tried politeness instead.

"Please, just let me get out of your way."

"No. I don't think that'll solve our problem."

She groped in her pocket and came out with a ring, making a big show of slipping it onto her finger. It was the diamond that had belonged to McGowan's mother, his gift to me.

I worked hard to control my rage, keep my voice level.

"Just tell me this, Malindi. How do you justify your blatant lies, taking other people's property—"

I stopped short of adding, "other people's lives."

Her smile was as confident as her retort.

"How do *you* justify it, Elizabeth?"

To the side of the stage, a telephone rang. Tiki went to pick it up. We heard her soft hello.

Malindi turn toward Tiki.

"Who is it?" she asked.

Tiki put her hand over the mouthpiece. She looked stricken.

"It's Aura. She says there's a pair of federal marshals at the lodge with an arrest warrant."

"For what? Is this another one of those illegal land-use hassles?" Malindi rolled her eyes. "Malibu," she muttered.

Tiki shook her head.

"I think you'd better talk to her. She says they have a warrant for your arrest in connection with the murders of David Sandberg and Ken Bastin."

40

≈

Malindi looked at me in silence as she let Tiki's message sink in. I could see her mind working behind her concentrated stare. I'd seen that face once before, when she was studying the chessboard. Suddenly she jumped off the stage.

"Hang up, Tiki. We're leaving. Now. Wayne, hold on to her." Malindi pointed at me. "If there's trouble, she's our bargaining tool. Got it?"

I got a good look at the gun Wayne brought to my head. A .44 Magnum, "Colt Anaconda" etched into the stainless-steel barrel. A gun that scared me even when I was on the right end of it. I wondered where Malindi had found this guy. One of those hire-a-cop outfits? I didn't think so. He had the edgy vibe of someone who'd taken the criminal career path. He put the muzzle against my cheekbone.

"You do something stupid, I'll blow your brains out. So just don't, okay?"

I didn't answer. I kept remembering what I'd seen in my horoscope earlier today.

Danger through electricity, automobiles, or firearms.

I was trying to remember everything Tom had ever told me about being in a hostage situation, but my mind was a blank terror.

Malindi barked more orders.

"You two go first. Wayne, if we run into anyone out there, make sure they see the gun to her head and let them know you'll use it. Take the bridge to the parking lot and we'll go from there. Ready?"

We started out. Once again I made my way down the asphalt path and cut across the lawn. Not at a run, but not wasting time, either.

Halfway across the grass to the bridge, one of the marshals appeared. He was about fifty feet away, walking toward us from the lodge. It looked like he was alone. The other marshal must have stayed behind. I hoped to God this guy wouldn't try to be a hero here.

Just let us go, I thought silently.

Wayne jerked me around and pushed the tip of the Magnum against the side of my head, forcing me to bend my neck at an uncomfortable angle. He called out to the marshal, his voice surprisingly high-pitched for such a big man.

"Stop there and throw us your gun or this bitch gets whacked."

My heart sank. No way would a fed give up his gun. Totally against protocol, training, instinct. The marshal didn't move.

Wayne's voice squeaked in frustration.

"Lose your gun, asshole!"

He jammed the Magnum even harder against my skull and I cried out in pain. Then heard his ugly voice behind me.

"You're dead, bitch."

My eyes locked onto the marshal's and in the split second that followed, his training went out the window. He reached into his holster and tossed out his weapon. The gun fell short, landing closer to him than to us.

I heard Malindi's voice behind me.

"Get the gun, Tiki."

Tiki ran forward, her steps shortened by the kimono. She picked up the gun by the tip of the handle and held it like she was afraid it would go off by itself.

Wayne called out to the marshal.

"Throw us your radio, too."

The marshal hesitated.

"Throw us your goddamned radio!"

Again Wayne jammed the gun against my skull. The marshal moved quickly, tossing the radio to Tiki's feet.

If anyone else in the ashram was aware of the scene being played out on the lawn, they were keeping well hidden. Wayne barked another command.

"Get on your stomach."

The marshal, looking sick with remorse now, lowered himself onto the grass.

Tiki picked up the radio and carried it with the gun back to Malindi.

Malindi took the gun and checked the chamber.

"Okay," she said. "Let's get out of here."

Once more we headed in the direction of the koi pond. Sunshine bathed the slender reeds and glassy water in golden light. A glorious day to die, I thought dryly.

We'd just stepped onto the bridge when Tiki held out her arm to stop us.

"Wait. Shh! Stop walking," she whispered.

"What?" Malindi whispered back.

Tiki's eyes grew wide.

"There's someone under the bridge. I can feel it."

I turned to see Malindi bringing the marshal's gun to her chest. She held perfectly still, listening, then nodded toward the side of the bridge.

"Wayne. Check it out."

He dragged me to the railing and leaned over to look. I saw what was happening at the same time Wayne did. Kyle was crouched under the bridge, gun pointed directly at us. Wayne turned his Magnum toward Kyle, releasing his grip on me. Shots exploded in the bright midday sun.

I dove to the other side of the bridge and hurled myself over the railing, plunging into the water below.

The pond was deep enough to break my fall and I landed with a soft thud on the silty bottom. I struggled upright and half-walked, half-swam under the bridge, instinctively going for cover. I tried to quiet my heavy breathing, to hear what was going on above me. I couldn't see and started to panic, then realized my eyes were filled with mud droplets. I thought I heard footsteps running away, but couldn't be sure.

I shrank against the underside of the bridge, more out of fear than cunning. The water, rippled and disturbed by my fall, became calm again. A bright orange koi fish swam past. The only sound was the song of a mockingbird. Cautiously, I moved to the edge of the bank. I was clearing some reeds to get a foothold when I saw Kyle.

His body had fallen backward against the bank. The bullet had caught him directly in his Adam's apple. Blood had formed a small pool in the hollow of his collarbone and completely soaked the front of his shirt. His espresso-brown eyes, fixed with a look of determination, stared up at the bridge.

41
≋

The bullet that had ended Agent Harrison's life was a nine-millimeter, undoubtedly fired from the gun that had been taken from the marshal. Which meant that Malindi was the shooter. This, I knew, would put the Master on an unofficial FBI most-wanted list. Cop shooters get special attention from law enforcement. The violence at the ashram had stirred up the L.A. FBI like a wrench tossed into a beehive. Kyle was one of their own.

I was going over the ballistics details with Agent Danford, who jotted the information on his report in tiny, precise handwriting. Clean-cut and handsome in a hawkish kind of way, he looked at me intently.

"You're sure it was Malindi and not this guy Wayne who took him down?"

"Wayne was holding a forty-four Magnum to my head. I'm clear on this point, believe me."

We were sitting in Danford's office, a small cubicle in the monolithic Federal Building on Wilshire. To protect myself against the air conditioning, I wrapped my arms around my torso. I was wearing the tan polyester slacks and matching short-sleeved shirt that Danford had scared up from the supply room. They didn't fit well but at least they were dry. I'd salvaged Jen's videotape, and I never wanted to even look at that canvas suit again.

"And you don't remember seeing the suspects at all after you dove off the bridge into the water?"

I shook my head.

Danford made another tidy notation.

"You have no idea, then, what kind of vehicle the fugitives might be driving?"

"I've known Malinda Vetista to use a white Dodge van with a rainbow painted on the sides. I can't be sure that's what they left in, though. Or whether they took one car or three. I have no idea."

An APB—replete with the "armed-and-dangerous" tag line—had already gone out with descriptions of the van, Malindi, Tiki, and Wayne. Danford was repeating questions I'd already answered for the marshals, who'd reached the bridge seconds after I'd discovered Kyle's body. Presumably, Malindi and company had driven off the property, although no one had seen their escape. Kyle had radioed for reinforcements before he was shot, and officers had arrived just moments later.

Within a half hour of the shooting, Patrick Teagarten—a.k.a. Abadanda—had been escorted from his loft above the lodge and taken in for questioning. Emergency court orders were being written to search and seize all The Bliss Project properties. The Malibu ashram devotees had been notified that no one was to leave the property until further notice.

All this, and still no Jen.

I'd explained to the officers at the scene, and was now explaining again to Agent Danford, that I was a private investigator who'd been hired by a San Diego lawyer to find a daughter who'd disappeared into The Bliss Project. Step-by-step, I'd repeated the events leading up to Agent Harrison's death. I left out the part about being a psychic. I was too tired and too fragile to explain and defend that one.

Danford finished jotting down his notes and looked up past my shoulder, a question on his face.

"Are you Agent McGowan?"

I turned around. My heart rose at the sight.

Wearing a navy-blue athletic suit—his traveling outfit—and carrying a suitcase, McGowan filled the entryway. In three long strides he reached Danford's desk and extended his hand.

"Call me Tom."

"Bill Danford."

They shook hands. Formality out of the way, McGowan put his suitcase on the floor and bent down to wrap his arms around me. My nose started to sting and I was just about to lose it when he pulled away and fixed me with twinkling eyes.

"Collaborating on the capture of dangerous fugitives wasn't what I had in mind when I said I hoped we'd be able to get together this week."

I looked over at Danford, who had actually cracked a smile.

McGowan kept it up.

"A shoot-out at a New Age ashram in Malibu? I thought they were kidding."

"Welcome to L.A.," Danford laughed. "Who briefed you—Captain Barre?"

"Yep." McGowan stroked my face.

"You okay? You look exhausted."

I nodded, swallowed, got out a few words.

"Angry about Kyle."

McGowan blew out a breath and took a seat in the empty chair beside me.

"He called me right after Malindi fired him this morning. Told me about the warrant. He was going with the marshals as backup but said he didn't expect any trouble. We even talked about the fact that this wasn't a Waco, Texas, situation. Far as Harrison knew, his handgun had been the only weapon at the ashram. I'm sure he had no idea she'd replace him that fast."

Kyle's determined eyes burned in my memory.

"Why was he under that bridge?" I was asking the universe as much as I was asking anyone in the room.

McGowan shook his head.

"He probably saw what was happening on the lawn and took cover. My guess is that he planned to follow you once you left the property. I'm sure he never intended a confrontation."

"How did the confrontation start?" Danford interjected.

"Tiki saw him under the bridge."

I used the word "saw" in the broad sense and left it at that.

Danford frowned.

"I'm wondering why Harrison was hit and not this Wayne guy. You said Harrison was already in shooting position, sights set, right?"

I nodded.

Danford shook his head in confusion or pity, I couldn't tell which.

"What a mess."

I knew why Harrison had been hit. He had hesitated to fire for fear of shooting me. Moreover, if the marshal hadn't turned over his gun to save my life, Kyle Harrison wouldn't have been killed with it. Survivor's guilt was making me sick to my stomach.

McGowan read it in my face. He squeezed my hand.

"It's okay," he said.

A phone rang in the next cubicle over.

"So what's happening now?" he asked Danford.

"We've got agents combing the interstates, checking airports and border stops. They'll turn up."

McGowan let go of my hand and got to his feet.

"I've got to meet with my new unit chief real quick and then we can find a hotel and you can get some rest. Sound okay?"

"Sounds great," I said. "I'm going on zero sleep."

Danford looked at me sympathetically, his attitude friendlier since McGowan's arrival.

"There's a lounge on the second floor where you can crash," he said.

I stood up and shook my head.

"Naw, that's okay. I'd really like to go outside and get some fresh air."

Warm, unconditioned air. I was chilled to the bone.

I leaned against the baking cement of the building like a lizard clinging to a rock. The sun felt wonderful. Cars jammed Wilshire Boulevard, jockeying for position as they approached the intersection at Sepulveda. So many cars, so many people filling this corner of the country. Millions and millions. Small wonder I was having a hard time finding one missing woman.

Where are you, Jen?

The light turned red. Through the open window of a Volvo station wagon, a radio blasted a familiar tune.

> *Let me take you down, 'cause I'm going to Straw-*
>   *berry Fields.*
> *Nothing is real and nothing to get hung about.*

This was the third time that song had come to my attention in the past week. Could've been a coincidence. Yet I've noticed over the years that messages from my subconscious often come in threes.

I felt a thrill as my brain made a connection. Hadn't somebody at the Process mentioned something about strawberries?

"We get them fresh locally—"

Again I remembered my vision of Jen near the red barn, with cultivated green fields somewhere nearby. I'd always imagined that if such a place existed, it was far from the madding crowds of Southern California.

"—from a place in Leucadia."

It was either a loopy idea or a very inspired one, but there was only one way to find out.

McGowan was standing in front of the desk when I stopped back at Agent Danford's cubicle. Two other men now occupied the chairs. All eyes turned my way as I stepped into the entry.

"I have an idea where Jen—the missing girl—might be," I said.

Danford didn't look too thrilled.

"We're a little more interested in the missing fugitives at this point."

"This could be connected," I said. "The cult might have a strawberry farm near San Diego. In Leucadia."

Danford frowned.

"Where'd you get this information?"

I looked to McGowan, not sure how much I should reveal. He seemed to guess the reason for my hesitation.

"Tell them," he said.

I addressed all three of the men, looking directly into their curious eyes.

"When I started this case, I flashed on an image of rows of green—like farmland—and a red barn. Over the past couple of weeks I keep getting something about strawberry fields."

Danford looked to McGowan.

"What in the fuck is she talking about?"

"Elizabeth's a psychic investigator."

"Oh." Danford nodded his head slowly. "I see."

You didn't have to be psychic to read his thoughts.

Yeah, sure. Riiiiight.

"Could be worthwhile to check it out," McGowan said.

Danford looked to the others. The man on the right spoke first.

"We don't have enough bodies to cover the leaks between here and Mexico. Don't you think we should take care of that first, before we get exotic?"

McGowan looked to the other man.

"Captain Barre?"

The captain steepled his fingers and looked at McGowan.

"You're due back here Monday morning. You want to go check it out on your own time, fine."

42

≋

McGowan's hand was shaking me awake.

"Hey, Sleepy, we're just about there."

I opened my eyes, realizing I'd dozed off on the roomy passenger side of the Charger. Fortunately, I'd been able to get McGowan's car—and the Glock I'd stowed under the front seat—off the ashram property, following the convoy of police cruisers that had been dispatched to the crime scene. Once he'd heard that the cult had broken into his house in San Marcos, McGowan was doubly eager to return with me to San Diego County. Leucadia happened to lie almost directly along our route home. I'd been tightly wound during my visit to the FBI field office, but exhaustion had finally triumphed.

I looked up and read the exits on the green sign above the freeway. Leucadia Boulevard. Poinsettia Lane. Leucadia is famous as "The Flower Capital of the World." Over the past decade, the encroaching development of its more populated neighbors has shrunk the agricultural area of the small coastal town. That was a shame, but today it worked in our favor. If the barn and fields I'd been seeing in my mind's eye were in Leucadia, it wouldn't take us more than a half hour to canvass the area and find them.

McGowan exited the freeway and turned south toward the Batiquitos Lagoon. The streets wound haphazardly past rainbow-colored fields of zinnias and gladiolus, dahlias and ranunculus. I didn't see any red barns but spotted plenty of greenhouses, their opaque glass walls shining in the late afternoon sun.

The sunlight hurt my eyes. My head throbbed. My body ached.

"With the exception of seeing you, this has been the longest, most fucked-up day of my life."

McGowan gently rested his hand on my thigh.

"You did everything right, you know."

I stared out the window, noticing that the world looked different to me now. Harsher, like some kind of filter had come off and I was seeing ugliness, even while riding through fields of flowers. The price, I supposed, of witnessing deadly violence. McGowan had been a law-enforcement officer for more than ten years now. I wondered what kind of world he saw.

"I got lucky," I said.

He turned his eyes from the road to me.

"Yes, you got lucky. Thank God."

He'd seen far worse than what I'd seen this morning. I recalled his most horrific war story, watching a child on a bicycle get shot by a madman outside a fast-food restaurant. Yet there was still tenderness in his magnificent brown eyes. It gave me hope.

He took his foot off the gas.

"What's this?" he asked, peering out the window.

The car slowed. On the west side of the road, low to the ground, rows of dark green plants stretched to the horizon. The leaves were dotted with tiny white flowers.

"I think these are strawberries," he said. "The fruit won't be ripe for several weeks, but yeah, these are strawberries all right."

I tried to make the scene match the one I'd seen in my vision.

"I don't see a barn."

He turned a corner onto a two-lane, black asphalt road. "What do you call that?"

Just ahead, a red barn no larger than a two-car garage sat beyond a stand of eucalyptus trees.

McGowan pulled over alongside the eucalyptus and stopped the car. He sat back and rested his arm on the open window.

"I'll be damned. As usual, I'm impressed."

I studied the lay of the land. About a hundred yards beyond the red barn, a modest white-clapboard house sat in the middle of the strawberry field. I noted the similarities—and differences—between the reality and my vision.

"To tell you the truth, I'm impressed, too. It's such a weird talent. Within my reach, yet beyond my control."

I looked at the white house, a detail I hadn't seen in my vision.

"Do you think we should get some help here?"

"What kind of help?"

"Backup, reinforcements. You know, help."

"Let's see. I call Captain Barre, tell him that we found a strawberry field like the one you saw in your psychic vision and on that basis, ask him to send out a SWAT team. I don't think so, Elizabeth."

"Then I'll call Lieutenant Gresham at the Escondido P.D. He'll send someone out."

"This isn't his jurisdiction."

"He'll do it for me."

McGowan started to say something else, then stopped himself.

"You getting bad vibes about this?"

I tried to tune in. I'd been living with bad vibes for weeks now. I was also still shaken by Kyle's death. I couldn't tell if the cold pit in my stomach was posttraumatic stress or a premonition.

"I don't know, Tom. I honestly don't know. But it wouldn't be a bad idea—"

"Someone's coming," he interrupted.

I looked out the window. A woman wearing a straw hat had stepped onto the small front porch of the house. She walked down the steps and headed in our direction, toward the barn. Halfway across the field, she spotted the Charger and stopped. Then she broke into a run.

Toward us.

Through McGowan's open window, I heard her call out. "Tom?"

McGowan opened his door and sprang from the car. I noticed he kept his hand on the .45 he had holstered around his waist.

"I can't believe you still have that car," I heard the woman say.

"Stop there." McGowan's voice was a command. "Are you alone?"

A breeze kicked up and the woman put her hand to her hat to keep it from blowing off. Looking crushed, she nodded.

"Who's in the house?" he asked flatly.

"Nobody."

"Put your hands on the car." Again his voice was emotionless.

She complied and he patted her down.

"Get in back," he said.

I turned and watched her slide into the backseat. She was ten years older than the woman I'd seen on videotape, but time hadn't harmed her fine features. The fair skin was densely freckled now, which only made her prettier. The last decade hadn't hurt her on the outside, but you didn't have to be a sensitive to see in Jen's hollow eyes that she'd taken a serious beating on the inside.

McGowan got into the driver's side and shut the door. Suddenly the atmosphere inside the car was very close.

McGowan turned around to face her.

"Hello, Jennifer," he said quietly.

Their eyes locked, and tenderness softened McGowan's

face. Jen's eyes welled up. I felt my cheeks begin to burn
and had an urge to bolt from the car. Instead, I sat stoically,
once again feeling like a reluctant voyeur in Jen's personal
life.

Her eyes brimming with tears, she placed a freckled
hand on McGowan's shoulder.

"Hi."

His recoil was slight, but it was there. Something inside
me relaxed. He looked at her sternly.

"Are you being held here against your will?"

She winced, and the dreamy look in her eyes vanished.

"After all these years, that's the first thing you think to
say?" She pulled her hand from his shoulder and glared at
him through narrowed eyes. "You really have turned into
a cop, haven't you?"

McGowan didn't waver.

"Sorry to be so harsh, but you're running with some
dangerous people these days."

"I'm not running with them." Her words came out as a
whine. "But I can't leave. I shouldn't even be talking to
you."

"Why shouldn't you be talking to us?" I asked.

She looked at me, then back to McGowan.

"Who's this?"

McGowan looked startled, as if he was just now remembering that Jen and I had never met.

"Sorry," he said. "This is my partner, Elizabeth. Anything you say to me, you can say to her."

"Your father hired me to find you," I explained. "You
did write that poem, right? With the hidden message,
'Please help me'? Well, we're helping you."

I turned to McGowan.

"Let's get out of here."

McGowan put his hands on the steering wheel and
reached for the ignition.

Jen grabbed his arm.

"Wait! I told you, I can't just leave."

McGowan sat back in his seat.

"Why not?" he asked.

Jen looked to me.

"The answers are in the poem, but they're complicated."

I figured she was alluding to the hit-and-run accident she'd confessed to Malindi and Abadanda. She was probably afraid that if she left the cult, they'd expose her secret. She might even go to jail.

"You're not free here," I said. "So what do you really have to lose?"

"I know this sounds crazy but if I leave, they'll kill me and my family."

McGowan's eyes met mine as if to say, *Let her talk.*

"Who'll kill you and your family?" he asked.

"The people who run this organization."

"What people?" I asked.

"A man named Charles Lewis and his wife. Her name's Malindi."

"I've met her," I said. "Why will they kill you?"

"Because I've seen way too much."

"Like what?" McGowan asked.

She brought her hand to her mouth.

"I can't talk to you. She'll have me killed." Her eyes pleaded with McGowan. "She'll have Dad and Jeremy killed, too."

"When was the last time you saw Malindi?" he asked.

"A couple weeks ago, in San Diego. She doesn't come here much."

"I wouldn't worry about her now," he said. "She's wanted in fifty states. She doesn't have time to do anything but save her own ass at this point."

"Really?" Hope lit her eyes.

McGowan nodded.

"What did you see that you weren't supposed to see?" I asked.

She bit her thumbnail and looked out the window. Several seconds passed before she spoke again.

"A murder."

McGowan and I waited to see what she'd offer on her own, without prompting.

"He's right over there. If you don't believe me, you can dig him up."

"Dig who up?" McGowan asked.

"David Sandberg. We used to call him Zeus. You know, like the Greek god? It was a joke—David was anything

but. He was quiet, skinny, wore glasses. A sweet guy.
Sometimes I pick flowers from the field down the road and
put them on his grave."

McGowan looked at Jen with shock, as if he didn't quite
recognize this woman anymore.

"How did Zeus die?" I asked.

She continued to stare out the window, her eyes fixed
on the field.

"I wasn't supposed to see it. At first I thought I'd walked
in on a sexual thing. This guy, Ken—who used to be a
friend of mine, actually—was on the bed and Zeus was
lying across his lap. Ken was holding a cloth over Zeus's
mouth, and then I saw he had a syringe in his other hand.
We just looked at each other. Then Ken goes, 'You didn't
see this, right?' "

"Why didn't you go to the police?" I asked.

She looked meaningfully at McGowan.

"At the time, I had my own reasons for avoiding the
police. I hated cops."

"You were running from a crime yourself," I said.

Surprise crossed her face.

"I saw your videotaped confession at the ashram," I explained. "There's a good chance you can cut a deal with
the DA if you testify against The Bliss Project. They're not
nice people. But I guess you know that already."

"Believe it or not, I was ready to own up to my hit-and-
run accident at that point. But I couldn't leave because they
threatened me. I swear to God."

"Who threatened you?" McGowan asked.

"Malindi and Ken. They tried to justify the killing, saying that Zeus wasn't one of us, that he was trying to destroy
The Bliss Project. It was all put in terms of protecting our
'family' and our 'way of life.' They told me I'd have to
stay on the farm for a while, until things settled down. They
let me have one last visit with Dad and Jeremy, but they
made it clear that if I ever breathed a word to anyone about
what happened, they'd be *forced* to kill one or both of them.
That's how they put it, they'd be forced to kill Dad and
Jeremy."

"Zeus was killed two years ago, right?" I asked.

She nodded.

"Then why'd you start sending the packages just recently?"

"Ken came by here about a month ago. He said the FBI was looking for Zeus. They'd been talking to him about it. He was getting scared. Said it wouldn't be long until someone came around here asking questions. He reminded me what would happen if I didn't keep quiet. He kept saying that I was there that day, too, so I'd better shut up about it. I almost got the feeling he was going to tell the FBI I'd killed Zeus—if he hadn't already."

She sighed.

"That's why the messages I sent to my family were so cryptic. I needed someone to help me, but I couldn't risk Malindi finding out I was going behind her back. I had to make it look like the packages were from someone else in case they ever got back to her. I made them so that if Malindi got hold of them, I could say it was Ken, trying to blackmail my dad for money."

She took off her straw hat and revealed a nearly naked scalp, the new hair growing in a fine red fuzz.

"I even had Ken shave my head, so that I could say he put my hair in the package if they ever found out about it. He had no idea. He thought shaving my head was fun. Stupid bastard."

She cursed him, but her voice was anguished and she started to cry.

"It's okay," I said.

"No it's not. I'm the reason Ken's dead now. I told Malindi that he'd talked to the FBI about Zeus. I had to, in case he tried to make it look like *I* was the one cooperating with the cops."

She'd ratted on Ken, and now he was dead. Survivor's guilt. I understood her hollow eyes.

McGowan had been listening in shocked silence. He finally spoke.

"So you've been right here in Leucadia these past two years?"

She nodded.

"What do you do here?"

"I work in the office, get the berries out to market. Sometimes I meet with the buyers."

"You alone here?" he asked.

"Except for the pickers, yeah, most of the time."

"You ever get to leave this place?"

"Sometimes. Once in a while I deliver berries to the ashram in San Diego and help out at the Process."

I thought back to the Initiation. Hadn't I glimpsed someone with a shaved head sitting near the front? I'd been several rows behind and hadn't seen the person's face. Now that I thought about it, I hadn't seen the shaved head after that first day. I'd assumed that the bald one had left with the others who bailed out after Kenny's collapse.

"You were at the Process two weeks ago, weren't you?" I asked.

"Yeah. How'd you know?"

"I was there. You were in the room when Kenny died."

"Yeah, I was."

For a minute I wondered if Jen had killed Ken. She was the only witness to his murder of Zeus. Maybe she'd been afraid Ken would kill her, too. Or finger her for a murder she hadn't committed.

"Did you kill Ken?" I asked.

"No. After I told Malindi that Ken was talking to the cops, she said, 'Watch carefully for what happens next.' The day they took Ken away in the ambulance, she pulled me aside and said, 'That's what happens when you don't keep quiet.' "

She fidgeted with the skin on her knuckles. "As if I needed to be reminded. I'd already gotten a photo in the mail—a picture of my brother's car, trashed. Someone had written 'keep quiet' on the back."

She continued to pull at the skin on her hands. I noticed her arms were bare.

"You didn't replace your Medic Alert bracelet," I said. "I understand you're allergic to bees."

She rubbed her bare wrist.

"Deadly allergic. It scared me at first. The strawberries attract thousands of them. After a while, I didn't care. There've been times I wanted them to sting me."

I looked out the windshield and thought again of my vision. Cultivated fields, a red barn, a black tower.

A black tower. The thought made me catch my breath.

That was the missing piece here—Black Tower Financial. In my mind's eye, I was back in the cramped bathroom at the Malibu ashram, pointing to one of Kyle's toilet tissues on the floor.

"Where's this secret location where Doper Doug takes his cash to Master Money Launderer?"

"Don't I wish I knew."

"Do they keep a lot of cash here, Jen?" I asked.

"Yeah, as a matter of fact. In a safe in the floor of the barn. I don't know the combination but I've fantasized about taking the money and running. 'Course then they'd really want to kill me. How'd you know?"

McGowan must have had the same thought I had, because he reached for the ignition again.

"You're coming with us whether you like it or not, Jen. This place is hot."

He turned the key. The engine made a struggling groan, then died.

"Shit."

He tried again. This time the sound was even more pathetic, slowly tapering off to a sputter. After decades of faithful service, the Charger had finally given up the ghost.

Danger through automobiles.

On the blacktop up ahead, a black Jeep Cherokee was coming toward us.

"That's Malindi's car," Jen said. Her face was going white behind her freckles.

The Jeep slowed, and for a moment I thought it would turn into the driveway leading to the clapboard house. It braked but began rolling straight again, heading directly our way.

I put my hand on my Glock and looked to McGowan.

"Are we safer in the car?"

"We're sitting ducks."

He jerked his door open.

"Out of the car, everybody!"

43

≋

I piled out of the passenger-side door and into a ditch alongside the road. I clutched the Glock at my waist, harboring an irrational fear that it might somehow fall out of its holster. The ditch was filled with dry rye grass and the soles of my shoes slipped as I scrambled up a small rise to the eucalyptus trees. I could hear McGowan's heavy footsteps in the dead leaves just behind me.

"Which way?" I called frantically.

"Run for the field," he panted.

"No!" It was Jen. "The field is fenced on this end. We'll be trapped, with nowhere to hide."

"The barn, then," McGowan shouted.

"It'll be locked," Jen panted.

Our feet were flying, and McGowan called out as we neared the red-painted structure.

"Take cover around back."

We ran around the barn and stopped behind a wall perhaps twenty feet wide. The strawberry field—and the tall cyclone fence enclosing it—stretched behind us. Apart from the barn wall, it seemed there was nothing but open space. The exposure I felt nearly paralyzed me.

McGowan grabbed my arm and guided me against the wall. "Draw your weapon," he said.

I snapped out of it and brought my gun into firing position.

His eyes were focused intently on me. They'd never looked more beautiful.

"Three possibilities. They'll come from that way—"

He pointed to the north side of the barn.

"That way—"

He pointed to the south.

"Or both. I'll cover this side, you cover that side. Jen,

you stay between us. Elizabeth, if I'm hit, don't lose your position, and don't stop shooting."

The words echoed in my ears. *If I'm hit.*

McGowan squeezed my arm. "Did you hear me? Don't lose your position, aim for body mass, don't stop shooting, and after the firing stops, make sure there's not another opponent. Do you understand?"

"I understand."

"Repeat it."

"Don't lose position, aim for body mass, don't stop shooting, make sure there's not another opponent."

"Beautiful."

We took our positions against the barn wall, backs to each other with Jen between us. The silent waiting was the cruelest form of torture. McGowan called out softly.

"Elizabeth?"

"Yeah?"

"I got you into this and I'm going to do my damnedest to get you out."

He had a point there.

"Tom?" I said.

"Yeah?"

"I love you."

I wondered what Jen thought of this exchange. Apparently she was too terrified to speak.

My hands were sweating and beginning to shake. Not good conditions for sharpshooting.

The seconds seemed to crawl.

Without any warning, the nightmare was upon us.

I heard Jen's scream and shots behind me. I was turning toward the sound when I *felt* Malindi coming around my side.

Aim for body mass.

I saw blonde hair and squeezed the trigger. I didn't see where my round hit, just watched Malindi jerk and fall backward. Her weapon went flying.

Don't stop shooting.

I spun around, ready to fire.

Jen was huddled against the barn, sobbing hysterically. Wayne had fallen into a sitting position against the barn wall. He was down for good, missing his left eye and a good part of his forehead.

McGowan was down on his back, but I couldn't see his injury.

I started to go to him, my heart in my throat.

Make sure there's not another opponent.

Where was Tiki?

My back against the barn wall, I scooted to the corner and spun around it, gun ready.

I was just in time to see the black Cherokee pull away and head north along the asphalt road.

Then I got tunnel vision—McGowan was my only reality.

I ran back to him, skinning my knee as I dove to his side. I took his hands, clammy and limp. His shirt was wet with blood—the wound was somewhere in his abdomen. His head had tilted to the right, his eyes were closed.

"Jennifer, go to the house and call nine-one-one. Tell them an officer is down. Hurry."

My voice was calm and sure. I was not.

I turned and looked at her. She was still huddled in a ball, arms around her knees. She'd lost her straw hat.

I screamed at her.

"Jennifer, *now!*"

She struggled to her feet and to my relief, took off running for the house.

When I turned back to McGowan, his eyes were half open. I bent closer to him.

"You're doing great." I wanted so much to believe it.

He licked his lips and smiled in a way that broke my heart. Then made an odd noise in his throat that frightened me. His voice came out a hoarse whisper.

"You made it."

I squeezed his hands.

"We *both* made it."

An insecurity crossed his face, a look I'd never seen from him before. This frightened me more than anything.

"Can you hold my hand?"

I glanced down at his fingers twined in mine, confused.

"But I am—"

Then I understood. He couldn't feel his hands.

Do something.

I opened his shirt to a daunting expanse of bloody skin. Panic seized me—I didn't know what to do. Knew there was nothing I could do.

In the minutes that followed, I became aware of an immovable, impervious force, like a presence, coming between us. I knew that I was powerless against this force. Still, I cursed it, fought desperately against it. I felt my eyes and nose streaming as the conflict tore me to pieces inside.

I pressed my lips to his ear.

"Ambulance is on its way. Any minute now."

A breeze lifted the hair from his forehead. His face was turning blue.

His eyes, thank God, were still open.

"Cold."

I wrapped my arms around him, my face three inches from his, my vision blurred with tears.

"That better?"

I was keening silently now, squeezing his slack body, rocking back and forth.

"Love you," he whispered, and closed his magnificent eyes.

They never opened again.

EPILOGUE

Certain places in nature have the power to heal the soul. For McGowan and me, the Sonoran Desert had always been one of those mystical spots, the place we went when our spirits were flagging. I made my pilgrimage on the fifteenth of July, the day after McGowan was honored with a hero's memorial at a formal FBI service in L.A. Today's would be a private ceremony.

July is a crazy time to venture into this particular wilderness. Temperatures often climb well above a hundred degrees during the day. Ordinarily I would travel after sunset, but for this trip, it was important that I arrive at my destination before nightfall.

I packed camping gear, food, and several gallons of water into my new Chevy pickup. The cab was spacious enough to accommodate both me and the large Rhodesian ridgeback I'd recently adopted. I stowed Nero's kibbles and the chew toy he'd never outgrown into the front seat with us. We started out at noon, driving straight east toward the Colorado River.

I crossed the San Diego County line thinking about how sudden change can be. Hundreds of lives had been radically rearranged in a matter of days, mine included.

Malindi did not die. This news came as a shock to me. She'd looked quite dead when the paramedics had loaded her onto the stretcher, her skin so white that her *Have Faith* tattoo appeared to be printed in bold. My nine-millimeter silvertip bullet had passed cleanly through her chest cavity, missing her heart and lodging near her spine. She'd regained consciousness at the hospital and would be well enough to appear in court at her preliminary trial, where she would face an obscene list of charges, including—but not limited to—possession of stolen property, wiretapping, illegal land use, tax evasion, money laundering, extortion, kidnapping, attempted murder, conspiracy to commit murder, and first-degree murder. Special circumstances would be filed and I had little doubt that she'd get the death penalty. Transformation can be painful for cop killers.

McGowan's diamond ring had been bagged as evidence, but would be returned to me after the trial.

Malindi's husband, Charles Lewis—the man behind the Level X myth that Puma Man had ranted about—was arrested in San Diego on similar charges, sans the murder raps. He's hired a team of high-profile attorneys to wage his battle. The price tag for such representation is steep, and the Traveler's Inn, the San Diego conference center, and the Malibu ashram are all up for sale. Oddly but not really, the day after Kyle's death, a fire broke out in Malibu where the financial archives were stored.

Patrick Teagarten—a.k.a. Lord Abadanda—suffered a fatal heart attack while in custody. It was to be his last disappearing trick.

The witness-protection program that had been offered to Jen in exchange for her testimony proved to be unnecessary. Once news reached the devotees that Malindi had killed an FBI agent and Abadanda was dead, The Bliss Project unraveled in a matter of days. No one rallied to the group's cause, let alone waged a holy war. They simply packed up and moved on. In that way, Kyle had been right—this wasn't Waco, Texas.

The Jeep Cherokee was found in a parking lot a mile from the San Diego airport. Tiki hasn't turned up. I have a sense of her far away, across an ocean, or maybe two. That's fine with me. Still, I can't shake the nagging feeling that I'll see her again someday.

Vince Shaffer was visibly shaken by the news about McGowan. Yet, his own life is worth living again. He was able to celebrate his fifty-fifth birthday with his daughter after all.

Nero and I rode over bumpy terrain through a sparse forest of ocotillo, their straight, slender wands rising ten feet high above the flat desert floor. Brown and stiff now, the prickly stems would turn green with the first rainstorm. Through

my rearview, I could see nothing but the cloud of dust we
raised in our wake. My new truck had no problem with the
off-road conditions—that's what it had been designed for.
It was the car I was towing that concerned me.

I glanced at the global directional device on the dashboard, feeling bolstered by its presence. I wouldn't have
dared make this trip without it. The road Nero and I traveled was not on any map.

I guided the truck along the bottom of a rocky beige
ridge, trying to stay away from the deep sand piled along
the edges of the arroyo. We passed a cluster of hardy palms,
years of dead fronds hanging like shaggy beards down their
trunks. I pulled the rig beyond the ridge and out into open
space, letting the truck roll to a stop. I turned off the ignition.

"Think we're on Mexican soil yet, Nero?"

He stood on the seat, panting, eager to get out.

I gave his head a pat.

"If not, we're damn close."

Behind us, the cloud of dust we'd raised was settling
back into the dry earth. A bead of sweat rolled between my
breasts, even in the air-conditioned cab. The worst of the
heat would be over soon. The hot, white light of midday
had mellowed into late afternoon, transforming the desert
into a gleaming copper dreamscape.

I put on my hat for the trip outside. The heat hit me like
a wall of feverish breath as I climbed out of the truck. The
dog tagged along as I went around back and unhooked the
tow gear from the Charger.

Nero was more than happy to jump in the air-
conditioned cab again when I called him. I drove the truck
back to the ravine. The Charger sat alone, surrounded by
several hundred yards of empty desert.

"I need your help to do this, boy."

Nero picked up his ears, looking puzzled.

I lifted the box from the floor of the passenger side.

"Let's go."

Nero trotted at my side as I carried the box against my
chest. My nose stung and moisture welled in my eyes, but
my tears evaporated before they could reach my cheeks. I

smiled at that, the thought that the desert wind was wiping my tears away.

When we reached the Charger, I put the box on the ground and pulled out the urn containing Tom's ashes. I kissed it one last time, then placed it on the front seat. I reached back into the box for Tom's .45, which I put in the car beside the urn. I got the lighter fluid out next, generously dousing the upholstery.

I closed my eyes and said a prayer, then lit a match and tossed it into the car. The flame died. I lit the entire matchbook and tossed that in. After its initial sizzling blaze, the matchbook burned quietly. This time the flame grew and soon spread across the front seat.

"Come on, Nero."

We moved back toward the ravine. The dog didn't have much interest in the burning car. He put his nose to the ground, picked up a scent and followed it to a scraggly desert willow. I tagged along behind him and took shelter in the tree's modest shade.

Fire filled the inside of the car. When I saw flames licking up from under the hood, I moved back several more yards, visions of Hollywood car explosions dancing in my head. There was no such drama. Just a lot of smoke at first and then the steadily burning orange flames, blending beautifully with the copper-colored desert and the blazing ball of the setting sun.

A desert hawk appeared and circled on a thermal high overhead. I was surprised at how slowly the car burned. I settled under the willow again and watched as flame and air undulated like liquid in the sky where heat rose from the fire. Soon I was hypnotized.

Does Tom know, wherever he is, how much I love him, how much I'll always love him?

To my surprise, an answer came back. The words were clear as a bell, though I doubt if anyone sitting next to me would have heard them. The familiar voice was calm, matter-of-fact, and filled with love.

Always and ever, he said.

Read on for
an excerpt from
Martha C. Lawrence's
latest book

PISCES RISING

Coming soon in hardcover
from St. Martin's Minotaur

I rolled down the driver's side window and inhaled the dry, sage-scented air. For natural Southern California scenery, few trips are more beautiful than the one to the Mystic Mesa casino, which occupies a premium spot on the Temecu Reservation. At an elevation of nine hundred feet, the combination gambling hall/hotel is nestled about halfway up the boulder studded foothills that peak at Palomar Mountain, home of the world-renowned observatory.

Driving east, I couldn't help but think about my last trip into the back-country. After McGowan's death last summer, I'd taken his ashes and his favorite car deep into the Sonoran Desert and burned them together in a final, blazing farewell. A strange thing had happened as I'd watched the brilliant orange glow of the fire. As the bereaved often do, I'd wondered if his spirit really did live on and if so, did he know how much I loved him? He'd answered as clearly as if he'd been sitting at my side.

Always and ever.

That was the last time I'd heard his voice. I'd waited to hear it again, prayed to hear it again. The silence had stretched now for nearly three months. I was beginning to wonder if it hadn't been an auditory hallucination brought on by intense grief and desert heat.

A green road marker ahead snapped me into the present. The small white lettering read "TEMECU RESERVATION, NEXT RIGHT." Just past a ramshackle place called Ed's Country Cafe I made a right onto Mystic Mesa Road. The seat vibrated as my tires rolled over the cattle crossing that marked the western entrance to the reservation. I sped under electric blue skies along smooth black asphalt, hoping I wouldn't get lost. A half mile later I could see this wasn't going to be a problem. The casino complex was impossible to miss, distinguished as it was by a gigantic fiberglass tipi rising into the sky like Disneyland's Matterhorn.

I turned at the tipi and pulled into acres of parking spaces filled with more cars than I'd been expecting on a Monday afternoon. Instead of letters or numbers, the lot was divided into sections marked by painted metal sculptures of desert wildlife: Jackrabbit, Eagle, Coyote, Lizard. I parked under a cranky-looking coyote, chuckling at the goofiness of the neo-Native American motif.

Following the footpath to the casino, I reviewed what I'd learned from David about the murder victim, Dan Aquillo. Thirty-seven-year-old male. Luiseno Indian. Black hair, brown eyes, five-eleven, one-eighty. Statistics only—I had no sense of the inner man. I was hoping Aquillo's girlfriend would remedy that for me today. The casino grounds were beautiful; I felt more like I was going to summer camp than a house of gaming. A man-made stream gurgled over some granite boulders to my right and a high desert breeze rustled the pines overhead.

The tranquil mood vanished as I neared the casino entrance. About a half-dozen men and women stood on the sidewalk, carrying placards above their heads. Each sign was an enlarged photograph of a dark-haired man under the boldface headline: **JUSTICE NOW**. The photograph of Dan Aquillo was a two-dimensional image, no more revealing than the police report statistics. A couple of the protesters gave me the evil eye as I approached the door. I gave them a sympathetic thumbs-up and they parted to let me in.

I don't know what hit me first—the flashing lights, the riotous noise, or the adrenaline rush. Swept into the crowds milling past the slot machines, I suddenly felt high, as if I'd taken something illegal. The good-time sensation baffled me, since ordinarily I loathe casinos. I hadn't been kidding when I told Dr. Hurston that gambling made me nervous.

Hurston had said that he'd lost his last hundred dollars at the blackjack table of Aquillo's girlfriend, Trish Brown. I weaved through the milling bodies and scanned shirt fronts, hoping that the dealers might wear nametags. No such luck.

I moved through the casino in a daze, my senses overloaded by lights, noise, and the discordant vibes of the gamblers. Their emotions—numbness, excitement, anxiety, ecstasy, love, loathing—clashed all around me. It was the psychic equivalent of a heavy-metal band, jazz quartet, and full symphony orchestra all tuning up at once. Shaking my head to clear the fuzz in my brain, I kept my focus straight ahead, on the blackjack tables.

I stopped at a game where one of the few female dealers presided. Standing behind the players, I watched her toss cards onto the table with motions as fluid and precise as a dancer's. I studied the action for a few rounds and when a seat opened up, I slid in.

That's when it started. I began to *know* things. It's an unpredictable gift, an ability I can't force to come about. Nor can I stop it, once it's begun.

I *knew* that the short-haired brunette at the end of the table would lose. In spite of her pretty white smile and positive attitude, I could see her defeat as clearly as if she were wearing it like a dead albatross around her neck. I picked up nothing about the oily-looking man to my left, whose nicotine-stained fingers fiddled with his chips. As for me, it was as if I'd already played my hands and seen their outcome.

Tonight I was destined to win.

The dealer flicked our cards across the green felt tabletop. I pulled two tens. When it was time to take or decline a third card, the brunette on the end smiled brightly at the dealer, eagerness shining in her eyes.

"Hit me," she said confidently.

In the split second before her top card landed on the table, I foresaw her whole night. A series of losses, just like this one. On my inner movie screen I watched her taking a long car ride with friends, back to wherever home was. She was in the backseat, looking out the rear window at the black highway retreating behind her. I could feel her disappointment.

The jack of hearts landed on her cards, wiping her out. She looked stunned. I was staring at her stricken face when I heard the dealer prompting me.

"How about it?"

I had twenty. Anything higher than an ace would wipe

me out. The smart thing to do would be to hold, but now I had a perverse desire *not* to win.

"Go," I said.

She flicked her wrist and the ace of spades flew onto my stack. Twenty-one. So much for altering destiny.

The oily man on my left drew a high card and folded. He got up and nodded to the dealer.

"See you tomorrow, Karen."

So the dealer's name was Karen, not Trish. I'd sensed this wasn't the one I'd wanted, but I had to start somewhere. An eager young man took over the vacated seat. As the new player settled in, I leaned over and spoke to Karen.

"Have you seen Trish?"

She shook her head and began tossing us our cards.

"Trish Brown? She's off tonight."

There went my primary contact. Now what? I stayed put, deciding to play until I lost a hand. My winning streak lasted for so many rounds that I lost count. By the time I drew a losing card, I'd amassed over six hundred dollars. Not bad, considering that I started with a twenty. I scooped up my winnings and made my way toward the back of the casino.

I paused at one of the slot machines, which was being fed a steady diet of coins by a hump-backed woman in an orange cardigan sweater. I *knew* she was about to win. When the moment came and the machine burst into a spasm of flashing lights and ringing bells, I shook my head. I had to admit it was a little thrilling, *seeing* this way. It wouldn't go on forever, but I was enjoying it while it lasted.

Using two hands, the woman scooped her coins into a wicker-weave satchel and walked away with a smile on her face. Almost as an afterthought, I stepped up, slipped a coin into the slot, and pulled the handle. Again the machine erupted, this time with sirens on top of the flashing lights and ringing bells. A small mountain of coins piled up in the trough. Twice in a row, the machine had relinquished a jackpot. What were the chances? People gathered around as I scooped up the coins. Added to my blackjack winnings, my take came to nearly two thousand dollars.

I found the cashier's window and read a notice mounted on the wall: *Any Winnings Over $1199 Must Be Recorded*

On A W2G Form. I approached the clerk behind the bars.

"Guess I'll need a W2G," I said.

He was smooth and dark and adorable, with eyelashes like Bambi's. He looked too young to be betting, let alone working in a gambling joint.

"Those white forms? Um, I just ran out and I'm not sure where to find more. I gotta call my manager. Can you wait a minute?"

I nodded and listened as he picked up a phone and made his call.

"Yeah, this is Mark in the cash cage. There's a lady here who needs a W2G form and I'm all out." He studied my face. "Uh-huh. I'd say so. Okay."

He hung up.

"Go upstairs," he said as he pointed past my shoulder, "to the second door on your right. Peter Waleta's office. You can get the form there."

I walked up the carpeted spiral staircase and looked out over the casino. Mystic Mesa was funky. It had the home-spun feel of a bingo hall but reached for glamour with a few glitzy Vegas trappings, like the mirrored balls hanging from the ceiling. Eyes in the sky, each containing a video camera, I was sure.

I reached the hallway at the top of the stairs. The second door on the right stood ajar and I could hear the sounds of a televised ballgame floating into the hall. I tapped gently the first time. When I got no response I gave the door a knuckle pounding.

"Come in."

The first thing I saw were the soles of two large shoes. They belonged to a man, heavy-set but not fat, sitting behind a plain steel desk with his feet propped up. He seemed mesmerized by the football game coming through the small Sony Trinitron on the corner of his desk. His thick black hair was pulled back into a neat ponytail, his Dockers were pressed, and his sage green polo shirt looked new. The game cut to a commercial and he turned to me without smiling.

"Mr. Waleta?" I said.

"Yeah. You're the one who needs the W2G?"

I nodded and he swung his feet off the desk. He opened

the top drawer, took out a stack of forms, and slid the
bundle across the desk to me.

"Would you mind taking the rest of those down to that
dipshit in the cash cage?" He caught the swear word too
late and added, "Sorry, no offense."

"It's okay. I'm not that delicate."

That cracked a smile.

"So how lucky did you get tonight?"

I shrugged.

"Eighteen, nineteen hundred. Something like that."

He lifted his dark brows.

"You got photo I.D. and a Social Security number?
We'll need to see both before you can collect."

I stepped forward and put my open wallet on Waleta's
desk. He flipped through my ID cards, nodding slightly.
When he got to my P.I. license he looked up.

"No shit?"

"No shit. Come to think of it, mind if I ask you a few
questions?"

Peter Waleta took a hard look at my P.I. license, folded my
wallet shut and handed it back to me. I could see in the
casino manager's dark eyes that he'd shut something else,
as well. An open mind, perhaps.

"Questions about what?" he asked.

"William Hurston. The man who was arrested here night
before last." I put my wallet back in my purse and spotted
a pack of sugarless gum at the bottom. I fished it out and
held it up to Waleta. "Want some?"

He shook his head. He had the air of a man who did not
trust easily. I unwrapped a piece and popped it into my
mouth, aiming for a casual, non-threatening impression.

"Who you working for?" he asked.

"I'm not working for anybody just yet. That's why I'm
asking questions. I want to get your take on the guy."

"I already made a formal statement to the police. Once
is enough." He turned back to his football game.

"Informally, can you just tell me if Hurston was a trouble maker or a problem of any kind? His attorney wants
me to investigate the case, but if Hurston has a reputation
around here, I won't do it. Simple as that."

It appeared that the Vikings were mowing down the Packers like grass in summer. When the umpire signaled second down, Waleta returned his attention to me.

"So the defense attorney sent you."

"Nobody sent me. I came on my own. To see what I could find out about Hurston before I agree to join the defense team."

The Packers' safety intercepted the Vikings' ball and began making a hell of run down the field. The noise of an angry crowd filled the room. Waleta grabbed the remote and muted the sound.

"Like I said, I've already talked to the police. I'd like to help you out, but without an attorney here I don't think it's such a wise idea. I'm sorry." He was gentle but firm, handling me the way you might turn down a girl scout hawking Thin Mints.

"Can you just tell me if Hurston's one of those guys who's rotten inside but charming on the outside? Because when I spoke with him this morning he seemed like a genuinely nice guy. Pathetic, but nice."

"I'll go with the pathetic part," Waleta said.

"You know him, then."

He watched the TV, ignoring my comment.

"I wonder," I said, "could a pathetic man do the kind of damage that was inflicted on Dan Aquillo?"

Waleta pointed the remote in my direction, his dark eyes flashing.

"Don't go there, okay?"

I held up my hands in mock surrender.

"Sorry. Please don't mute me."

A smile tugged at the corner of his mouth.

"Can you just tell me if Dan Aquillo knew Bill Hurston?"

He crossed his arms over his chest and glared at me.

"This is beginning to sound like official-type questions."

"No, not at all. I'm just trying to get a sense about Hurston. Because if Dan ever mentioned that Hurston was an asshole or a problem or something that, then I'm off the job, period. Let someone else take up the cause of the sleazeballs, that's what I say."

My eyes were drawn to the muted television set. In a

precognitive flash I *saw* the final score. I was definitely having one of those nights.

"Packers have got this one," I said, "thirty-one to twenty-eight."

"Yeah, right. Dream on. So you're one of them emotional Packers fans, huh?"

"A branch of my family lives in Wisconsin, so I follow the team. But I'm not particularly invested."

"Well, that's good, because they've got five minutes to pull off a miracle." Waleta leaned his bulky body back. His chair squeaked in complaint. "You know, I would like some of that gum, if you don't mind."

I fished the pack out of my purse and tossed it onto his desk.

"Keep it," I said.

"Thanks." He unwrapped a piece and chewed thoughtfully for a minute or so.

"You promise this is just between you and me?" he asked.

"Yeah, I promise."

"Okay. I didn't know Hurston personally, but he ran up some debt awhile back and was about to be cut off here. Dan and I were partners in the casino, so we discussed it. Like I said, I didn't know Hurston personally but I knew he was trouble. I was you, I'd turn the job down."

"Thanks for the advice. And—" I held up the stack of W2Gs"—for the tax forms."

"No problem. So how much was it you won tonight?"

"Eighteen hundred something," I said again.

He dug in his back pocket and came up with a slim black wallet. He fished out a hundred dollar bill and held it out to me.

"Sounds like you're hot. Go win some more."

I stepped forward and took the Ben Franklin from his fingers.

"Why, thank you," I said with feeling.

"Don't mention it."

It looked like an expansive gesture, but I knew that Waleta was counting on his hundred dollars to shut me up and lure me back to the game tables, where he hoped I'd play until the house recouped some of my winnings. I walked to the door and when I reached it, turned back.

"One last thing. Hurston said he made a phone call to his ex-wife from his hotel room the night of the murder. I'll trade you this hundred for a look at the phone record."

"Your attorney can subpoena those records, you know."

"I know. But time is money, Mr. Waleta."

He smiled. "Yes, time is money and the Packers have three minutes to live. All right, you got a deal. This game's over, anyway."

I handed the hundred back to Waleta as he walked past and followed him down the stairs. The game room was more crowded with night coming on, the cacophony of vibes raised to an even higher pitch. Waleta and I dodged customers drunk on alcohol and anticipation. Beneath the din of the ringing slot machines and conversational noise, I heard the PA system piping out a steady stream of moldy oldies. *If you want to know if he loves you so, it's in his kiss.*

"What kind of lousy relationship advice is that?" I shouted into Waleta's ear.

"What's that?"

"That song. Telling girls that they can tell how much a guy loves them by his kiss."

He shrugged. "Sold a lot of records, didn't it?"

True, I thought. No wonder baby boomers were so confused.

At the rear exit, Waleta held the door and I stepped outside. The sun had gone down and the air had the kind of chill that let me know summer was on its way out. We stood facing a single-story building with a row of gold-numbered doors. The Mystic Mesa Hotel.

"So this is where it happened." I glanced over at Waleta as we walked toward the main office. His profile was as stony as a Mt. Rushmore carving and he was about as talkative. "I feel sorry for whoever found Aquillo's body," I went on. "Jesus, that must have been awful."

He turned and fixed me with a heavy look. He'd seen the body, I knew by his haunted eyes. When we reached the hotel office, he held the door for me.

I heard a familiar sound as we walked in. A television set was mounted in the corner of the room near the ceiling, tuned to the Packers-Viking game. A frowning gray-haired woman sat behind the registration desk, arms crossed over her chest. She was wearing a shapeless floral-print dress that could have fit a woman twice her size.

"Hey, Rosemary," Waleta said.

"Shhh!" She glared at him, her deeply lined face full of menace. "This is an important call." On screen, the umpire signaled off-sides and the crowd booed. "Damn." She glanced at us with a scowl. "Game's gone into overtime."

Waleta walked to the counter and spoke quietly but firmly.

"This lady needs to see some records."

"Hold your horses," she said, without taking her eyes off the TV.

The Packers scored a field goal and the crowd roared. The three of us craned our necks, waiting to see the score. When thirty-one/twenty-eight flashed on the screen, Waleta did a double-take on me.

"Son of a gun. You psychic or something?"

"Sometimes," I said.

Rosemary turned away from the television and gave us her attention, a satisfied look on her face.

"Okay. What is it you need?" She peered at me with eyes that looked like they'd seen it all at least twice. I wasn't fooled by the grandmotherly flowered dress. It would be difficult, if not impossible, to get anything by this woman.

"She an investigator," Waleta said before I could introduce myself. He looked at Rosemary with an expression that left something unspoken, I wasn't sure what. "She needs the September thirteen phone record for room one-oh-nine."

Rosemary rolled her chair to a computer and tapped the keyboard with her bony fingers. She'd put her gray hair up in a bun, but some of the hairpins had fallen out and the left side was drooping in back.

"You want a copy of this?" she asked.

"If you don't mind," Waleta said.

A dot matrix printer churned out the invoice. She tore it off and handed the track-fed sheet to Waleta. He placed it on the countertop and we scanned the listings.

"This just gives the date and cost of the call," I said to Rosemary. "Do you have something that shows the actual phone number that was called?"

She looked to Waleta, a question in her ancient eyes.

"Go ahead," he said. "The attorneys are gonna get these anyway."

She made a few more keystrokes, printed out another sheet, and handed it over. Again Waleta and I scanned the page. Hurston had made two calls that night. I pointed to the number with the coastal prefix.

"This must be the ex-wife's number. But he also called extension three-oh-three. Is that a room number at the hotel?"

"No," Waleta said slowly, "that's Dan Aquillo's extension at the casino."

"So Hurston called Aquillo from his room at eleven-thirty the night of the murder. That doesn't look so great, does it?"

Waleta raised an eyebrow. "I told you I'd decline his case if I were you."

The facts were falling into a straight line that pointed directly to Hurston's guilt. But I wasn't getting a straight feeling. I folded the phone record and put it in my purse.

"Maybe you're right," I said. "Is there any chance I could take a look at the room where it happened?"

"That area's out of bounds," Waleta said firmly.

"I just want a sense of where it happened, is all."

Rosemary was surfing through the channels now, pretending not to listen.

"Tell you what," I said. "I'll give you half of the money I won at the casino tonight if you let me take a look at that room."

"Fifty percent of eighteen hundred is nine hundred bucks." Waleta's voice had climbed half an octave. "Are you crazy?"

"Sometimes," I said with a shrug.

He shook his head.

"Sorry, but the cops have got that all roped off."

"They've already taken prints and fibers," I interrupted. "Besides, I won't touch a thing, I just want a look."

"For crying out loud, Peter," Rosemary mumbled without moving her eyes from the TV. "Take the money and let her look at the damn room."

I followed Peter Waleta's linebacker-sized body past the Mystic Mesa Hotel guest rooms, their curtains shut tight. An occasional wall sconce lit the passageway, leaving dark patches of shadow in between.

"We grew a lot faster than we ever expected to, so we're adding a second story to the hotel," he said. "That's why the area up ahead is roped off."

The passageway ended sharply in an L. Sawhorses strung with yellow CAUTION tape blocked off the wing that continued to the right. A cardboard sign on the middle sawhorse apologized for the construction mess beyond:

PARDON OUR DUST!

I chuckled under my breath.

"What's so funny?" Waleta asked.

"Oh, nothing. It's just that phrase, 'pardon my dust.' Always reminds me of what Dorothy Parker wanted put on her tombstone."

"What's that?"

" 'Excuse my dust.' "

In the dim light of the hallway, Waleta's face scrunched in puzzlement.

"This Dorothy sounds weird. She a friend of yours?"

"No," I said with a smile. "She was a writer. She's dead now."

I stood behind the sawhorse and looked at the wing under construction. The half-finished framing of the second-story add-on was silhouetted in black against the evening sky.

Waleta moved the sawhorse a few inches and slipped behind it.

"Watch out for nails," he said. "They're all over the place."

I followed him down the dark hallway, weak light from the parking lot the only source of illumination. I studied Waleta from behind, trying to get a sense of him. He swayed slightly from side to side with the lumbering gait of a large man. His aura was calm, almost placid. If he had any troubles, they were buried deep inside. He stopped at the last door at the end of the wing. Room 109.

"Why was Hurston staying in this room, if this part of the hotel was off limits?" I asked.

"Looks like Dan comped him a room last weekend. I noticed there was no charge on that invoice Rosemary gave you. Dan let him bunk for free, I guess, since we're not making any profit off these rooms anyway."

"Why would he do that?"

"I dunno. Maybe he didn't want him to drive drunk. Maybe he was giving him a break." Waleta pulled a plastic key from his shirt pocket and slid it into the door lock. The tiny light on the lock flashed green.

"Was there any sign of forced entry?" I asked.

"Not that I'm aware."

"How many of those card keys do you issue for each room?"

"Two, usually."

Waleta covered the knob with his shirt tail.

"The cops finished taking their prints and pictures yesterday, but you can't be too careful," he said as he pushed the door open.

The room was pitch dark. Waleta reached for the wall switch but nothing happened.

"Shit. Just a second. Wait here."

He walked in and a few seconds later light from the bathroom cast an oblong shaft across the floor.

"Has this wall switch been dead like that for a while?" I asked.

"Don't think so. It usually turns on the wall lamp. Must be burned out or something."

Waleta walked over to a sconce on the far side of the room. He put his hand behind the frosted glass and the light came on.

"Bulb was loose, is all."

I made a mental note of it. Had someone loosened the bulb intentionally?

Light from the sconce made plain a wide blood stain at the foot of the unmade bed. The drying blood had blackened the brown carpet, crusting the pile into spiky tufts. At the rear of the room, a sliding glass door led to a tiny balcony. The small closet stood open, empty save for a few bony hangers.

I didn't need to walk in. The atmosphere was as charged as a midwestern summer afternoon before a thunderstorm. With just one glance at the bloodstains on the floor by the bed, images began pushing into my consciousness like fresh memories from an unwelcome nightmare.

A darkened form emerging from the closet, raising a hammer over a man's head. Bringing the blunt tool down with cruel force. The body crumpling into a heap. The one with the hammer striking three more furious blows. Bending down, peering at the fallen body. After a time, walking out the front door, hammer in hand.

None of this affected me emotionally. I was an impartial observer, an objective audience. That was good, that meant the channel was clear. I waited for more, but that was it.

"Thank you, Peter," I said. "That's all I need for now."

He switched off the lights, came back out and pulled the door shut with a click.

"For nine hundred dollars? The pleasure's mine."

When Sergeant Tom McGowan of the Escondido Police
Department needs help in exploring the not-so-accidental
death of an old friend, he turns to parapsychologist P.I.
Elizabeth Chase.

Instantly, Elizabeth is absorbed by the case, and searches
the stars and her sensitive psyche for answers. Janice
Freeman, the dead woman, had a lot of friends, but as
Elizabeth meets the people she knew, she begins to pick up
a few unpleasant auras that have the unmistakable color of
evil. Trying to pin down Janice's last fateful day of life,
Elizabeth charts her final moves—and follows the celestial
signs to cold-blooded murder.

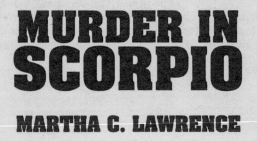

MURDER IN SCORPIO

MURDER IN SCORPIO
Martha C. Lawrence
_____95984-2 $5.50 U.S./$6.99 CAN.

A MYSTERIOUS PLAGUE
AND A VICIOUS KILLER STALK NEW ORLEANS—
NOW THE CITY'S MOST BRILLIANT FORENSIC TEAM
MUST STOP THEM BOTH DEAD IN THEIR TRACKS.

LOUISIANA FEVER

An Andy Broussard/Kit Franklyn Mystery

D.J. DONALDSON

A lethal virus similar to the deadly Ebola is bringing
body after body to the New Orleans morgue. As
Broussard and Franklyn try to uncover the source of
the virus, they come up against another killer—and this
one is human. Now they must stop a modern-day
plague and a malicious murderer before Kit and Andy
become statistics themselves.

"His writing displays flashes of brilliance...Dr.
Donaldson's talent and potential as a novelist are considerable."

—*The New York Times Book Review*

"A dazzling tour de force...sheer pulse-pounding reading excitement."

—*The Clarion Ledger*

LOUISIANA FEVER
D.J. Donaldson
0-312-96257-6___$5.99 U.S.___$7.99 Can.

In all of New York's Chinatown, there is no one like P.I. Lydia Chin, who has a nose for trouble, a disapproving Chinese mother, and a partner named Bill Smith who's been living above a bar for sixteen years.

Hired to find some precious stolen porcelain, Lydia follows a trail of clues from highbrow art dealers into a world of Chinese gangs. Suddenly, this case has become as complex as her community itself—and as deadly as a killer on the loose...

China Trade

S. J. Rozan